Book One of
A Dragon's Legacy

Dragon's Legend

By Steven R. Fischer

PublishAmerica
Baltimore

First printing

At the specific preference of the author, PublishAmerica allowed this work to remain exactly as the author intended, verbatim, without editorial input.

ISBN: 1-4241-9759-7
PUBLISHED BY PUBLISHAMERICA, LLLP
www.publishamerica.com
Baltimore

Printed in the United States of America

Thank you Brian, for inspiring me to write this novel, and to my grade 10 and 12 English teachers for that stupid bad word list, & for letting me have an open mind to eventually write this novel.

Book One of
A Dragon's Legacy

Dragon's Legend

Prologue

As the sun rose above the horizon, it lit up the surrounding land signifying that *yet* another day had come. The contingent of troops stopped to take in the view and to rest from their long journey. They saw the beautiful lush green field of long grass that had a few trees sprouting from it. The trees ranged from small and thin to tall and large, but they all had matching light green leaves and dark brown bark. There were also snow-capped mountains in the background, adding to the sceneries beauty. While the troops rested, the Commander decided to take a look around. About two minutes later, the Commander found what he was looking for.

"There it is men!" exclaimed the Commander. "The cave where that wretched beast lives. Let's hurry, before the beast wakes up and terrorizes us again."

* * *

Nine minutes later the large contingent of troops got to the cave entrance. But they were a little hesitant in entering the cave, for they did not know what was in store for them. As for the Commander, he knew exactly what they were in for. The soldiers tried to enter the cave as quietly as possible, but with their heavy armor, it was impossible. Also the darkness of the cave made it nearly impossible it see anything.

TAP, TAP, TAP. "Why is it so dark in here?"

"Shut up Jack! You'll wake the accursed beast."

"Yeah, we're already making enough noise, so be quiet."

"*Too late,*" replied a voice. "*Why have you come to disturb me?*"

Once the voice finished speaking it had left the soldiers frozen with fear. The only soldier that wasn't scared was the commander. For he wasn't scared of anything, as long as he could kill it, that is. Also with the large number of troops accompanying him, the odds were in the Commanders' favor. The Commander was a well built man, dressed in full plate mail that, unlike the troops, was so dark blue that it almost looked black. The Commander carried a broad sword that was so finally polished that the steel could be mistaken for silver. The hilt of the sword on the other hand was silver, but it was discoloured to give it the appearance of a regular brass handle. His broad sword was long, thick, and extremely sharp. The Commander also carried a large shield that was firmly attached to his right arm while his sword laid at his waist. The Commander's steel shield was dark red with a large blue Phoenix engraved on it. He was also wearing a full helm, so you could only see his dark navy blue eyes. Aside from the Phoenix on his shield, the Commander's dark blue plate mail bore a red engraving of a Phoenix on it as well.

"We have come here for two reasons," stated the Commander. "The first reason on why we have come here is simple. We simply wish to know if you are the last of your kind. The second reason is also simple. After we know the answer to the first reason, we will then kill you."

"*You can try to kill me if you so wish, but I doubt that you will succeed in your task. For I am "Drakon the Ancient", a creature more powerful then you can imagine. Not even that Sorcerer of yours can kill me,*" responded Drakon the Ancient as he let out a great burst of flame, forcing the troops into a defensive position.

"Brak!" shouted the Commander. "Is he telling the truth?"

"Unfortunately the *Dragon* is telling the truth. There is no spell in my memory or in my personal inventory that can destroy or severely injure him. I exhausted all of my spells on the last battle we had. And thanks to not being *allowed* to have the proper time to replenish my spells. Well...you're on your own for this one, Zeek, although, I think I may have a few things up my sleeves that maybe of help," replied Brak.

"Well I guess we'll have to do this the old fashion way then. Okay men.

Prepare yourselves, for this will be a difficult battle. CHARGE!" shouted Zeek.

A battle that should have lasted for minutes, or a couple of hours only lasted for seconds. As the contingent of troops, Zeek, and Brak charged towards Drakon the Ancient, their lives became worthless. For Drakon the Ancient slashed, bit, and stomped on the small, frail, armor clad, Humans that got close. It was only when the troops were swarming all over him, did Drakon the Ancient show his power. Drakon the Ancient tilted his head towards the ceiling of the cave and, let out a huge burst of flames. The flames reflected off of the ceiling and shot back at the attacking troops, and within seconds everything was engulfed in fire. When the screams of pain stopped, the fire died, and the smoke cleared, there was only one Human left standing. Brak had managed to create a flame shield around himself in time to nullify the attack from Drakon the Ancient. But sadly he had finally used up all of his offensive, and defensive spells, he would have to be very careful with his next few moves.

Brak looked around to see if there were any survivors, but all he saw was charred bones and roasted meat. Brak looked up at the dark figure of Drakon the Ancient and walked towards him creating a bright shining orb that lit up everything in the cave. Brak was dressed completely in black, save for a red insignia of a Dragon over his heart. Over his black clothes, he wore a dark blue robe with shinning gold and silver glyphs all over it. The cloaks' hood covered his head making it hard to see Brak's scarred face, but you could still see his light brown eyes and a shadow of his hair. Aside from how old Brak really was, he looked to be in his mid to late twenties. Besides a large oak staff that was covered with strange markings and symbols, Brak also carried a short sword that was hidden in a black sheath that was strapped to his left leg. He also carried a small dagger that was concealed on him somewhere. A small black pouch of miscellaneous things hung off of his black belt. When Brak thought he was close enough to Drakon the Ancient, he spoke.

"Well, are you satisfied now? You killed them all, knowing they had no chance whatsoever in defeating you. You couldn't at least let a few survivors run for their lives?" questioned Brak.

"*NO!*" stated Drakon the Ancient.

Drakon the Ancient was a behemoth of a Dragon covered in reddish blue scales from snout to tail. He had long bone white claws protruding from his two, five toed feet and two five fingered hands. Two massive dark red bat-like wings where folded and resting on his back. Drakon the Ancient also had a mane of lush silver hair, which sprouted from the top of his head and flowed down to the middle of his back to where his wings met. Drakon the Ancient's hair seemed to sparkle like diamonds when the light washed over it. His long bone white teeth were as sharp as daggers and could crush gems into powder, just as easily as a dog can break bones. Drakon the Ancient's dark golden reptilian eyes seemed to have the ability to pierce a person's soul as well. This made Brak feel uneasy and very uncomfortable when he starred up and into Drakon the Ancient's eyes.

"Alright then, now that the meager threat is gone, could you answer me a single question then?" asked Brak cautiously.

"*That depends. If it is a question not worth my time and interest, then consider yourself dinner,*" answered Drakon the Ancient as he licked his scaly lips.

"Well here goes. Seeing as my only options are don't ask and possibly get toasted, or ask and possibly get toasted. Either way, I'm cooked. Anyway, my question is this: What happened to your kind and the many other mythical beasts that used to roam this land? Before there were thousands of you: Dragons, Chimeras, Unicorns, Gryphons, and Hypogryphs, to name but a few. Even the Elves, Dwarves, and other non-Humans have dwindled in numbers to only tens, hundreds, or have become extinct. Why and how did this happen? I know that there are a few more Dragons then just you out there, but nothing else," explained Brak as he hoped that his question would interest Drakon the Ancient and not make Brak's life forfeit.

"*An interesting question, you get to live...for now. Very well, I will tell you what I know. Starting from what I can remember. I'll also include my childhood to give you a better understanding on Dragons and how they lived,*" replied Drakon the Ancient as he took a deep breath, and then blew it out. "*It all started when I was a young Whelp, and there were no Humans or Humanoid creatures around. For your kind "didn't enter the picture" as you Humans say, until my late adulthood. Anyway, like I was saying, it all started when I was young.*"

Chapter 1
My First Encounter with Life

"I broke out of my shell and saw a bright light and heard a mysterious voice coming from somewhere."

"Don't be afraid, child. For your Mother, Father, and siblings are here for you, Drakon," replied a strange obscured and yet soothing voice. "Your eyes will adjust shortly, just give it time."

"Eventually *my eyes did adjust to the wild wide world*."

"Now that you can see better how would you like to explore and play with your brothers and sisters?" questioned a huge female Dragon or Dragoness as we call the females of our species.

* * *

I could not believe my eyes, for the Dragoness standing before me was gorgeous, and she was also my Mother. My Mother was covered in scales the colour of dark rubies that sparkled when the light from the sun or the moon hit them. She had large golden wings that matched her golden hair that flowed from the top of her head, down to her hind legs. Her snow-white claws matched her light silver eyes and bone white teeth. My Mother was the most beautiful Dragoness I had ever seen in my whole life. Given my life wasn't that long at the time…but then again. I could only imagine what my Father looked like, so I asked Mother.

"Mother, where's Father?" I asked in a weak squeaky voice.

"Your Father is out hunting for food for us to eat. While we wait for him, why don't you go and play with your seven siblings. That way I can keep an eye on all of you while you play and wait, for your first meal. Also, don't worry, your voice will deepen eventually," Mother replied.

"Okay," I answered.

I ventured out from my nest and into the large wild world. When I got out of the Nest and looked around, I saw a spectacular sight. There were hundreds of Nests filled with eggs, or "Hatchlings" in Dragon terms, and other baby Dragons or "Whelps". Their parents were close by them for reassurance of the big wild world. The Nests were vast, able to hold up to hundreds of Hatchlings at a time. Of course it was the parents though, that decided on how many Hatchlings they wanted, some wanted a few others wanted many. The Nests were made up of various things, ranging from mud and twigs, to small trees and bushes. I walked around for what seemed like an eternity taking in the sights, sounds, and smells of my surroundings. I also walked around a lot to strengthen my legs, for I had seen many older Dragons with strong bodies, and I wanted to be like them. I eventually found my brothers and sisters playing with each other and other Whelps. It was hard to tell all of us apart from one another, for we were all the same colour: Black. We weren't able to show our true colours until we were older and all of our Whelp scales fell off. None of the Whelps had wings either, for they would develop as we grew. I decided to join in the fun that everyone was having, that way I could make friends and show off. We played for hours until our parents called all of us for supper.

When my siblings and myself got back to our nest I made a count and found that there were eight of us, but seeing Father and the meal drew my attention to him. Father was a huge jet black Dragon with large silver wings that were folded and resting on his back. His wings were so big that they covered the sun whenever he flared them. Father also had pure white claws that matched his bone white teeth. His cyan coloured hair matched his light green eyes. His long hair flowed down from the top of his head and ended just past his shoulders and before his wings. Father was the most handsome Dragon that I had ever seen in my life, which at the moment wasn't that long. Father and Mother were perfect together. I hoped then that one day I would find a beautiful mate that could match my Mother's beauty.

"Okay Young Ones, your food a waits. There are a couple of Gryphons, some Chimeras, and a Hypogryph. Toasted and ready to be eaten," announced Father.

So the ten of us gathered around the food and dug in. It was the best meal I ever had, so far. While we were eating, I saw a strange four legged creature with a horn on its' head in the distance of the Nesting Grounds. As I studied it, I noticed that it was white, not just white, but white. Its' hair was white, its' lush long mane of hair was white, and its' horn was white, and its' hooves were white. The only thing that wasn't white on the creature, was, its' eyes. Its' eyes were black, so black that when you looked into them you got a sense of great power and loneliness. After I looked at it for what seemed like ages trying to figure out what it was, and what it was doing, I finally looked away and turned to Father.

"Father," I asked.

"What is it Drakon?" questioned Father as he gulped down a mouthful of Gryphon.

"What is that four legged creature over there in the distance? Is it eatable?" I questioned.

"That is called a *Unicorn.* It is a very powerful and deadly creature. A Unicorn has the ability to harness mystical energies, so it can cast enchantments to attack or defend itself. They are very skilled at fighting too, for we have fought against them in the past, and they have proven to be evenly matched against us. As far as I know, no one has managed to eat one. At least not yet. As to why it is so close to the Nesting Grounds, I have no idea, but if it's smart it will leave and fast," explained Father distastefully.

"I'll be the first to catch and eat one then," I stated confidently, which made Father smile at me.

I set off on my first adventure with one big goal in my head: to eat a Unicorn. As I was heading off to accomplish my goal, my brothers and sisters couldn't resist making fun of me for what I was going to do. They also decided to follow me for a while to see if they could get under my scales with their teasing. I ignored them of course and continued on my quest of a unique tasting meal. When I was half way from my Nest to the Unicorn, my siblings stopped following me, and decided to sit back and watch my success, or failure. As I got closer I could see that the Unicorn was grazing in a nearby field. So I decided to sneak up to it and get the jump on it. As I crept towards it, I kept my eyes on the Unicorn and stopped moving whenever it turned its' head up to look around at an unfamiliar sound. Closer, closer, and closer I crept until...

"*CRACK!*"

I stepped on a dry twig that snapped into two and made a sound louder then I thought possible. I dropped to the ground in hopes that the Unicorn did not see me. I peered through the long grass and saw that the Unicorn was glowing with a white aura and was looking around. It looked like I was in the clear until we locked eyes with one another. Simply put, the battle was started. The unicorn dropped its' head and charged at me. I couldn't move a muscle, and to this day, I still don't know why I didn't move out of the way. It might have been that I was too terrified to move or that I was too intrigued by the sight and forgot to move. Either way the fight between the Unicorn and myself didn't last long. Long battle summarized, I lost.

I was lying on the ground beat up and bleeding pretty badly too. While I was lying there the strangest thing happened. The Unicorn walked up to me with a pink glow surrounding it this time. But I was terrified, when the Unicorn began to make its' way over to me. As it got closer, I started to feel better and stronger as well. My wounds were also closing up and disappearing. While I was realizing this, I noticed that the Unicorn was right in front of me. At the sight of it so close to me, I jumped back a couple of feet. While I looked at the Unicorn, I noticed that its' eyes were glowing white and its' body was glowing pink.

"*Young One, you fought well for your very first battle. Given you have yet to be trained in the ways of your kind. But I am still impressed at your skill so I have rewarded you by healing your wounds, and restoring your strength,*" exclaimed the Unicorn in a soft male voice.

"What? I won? How...how can I understand you? I don't understand," I asked.

"*It is simple. You have a special gift that can allow you to speak to other animals and creatures. Otherwise we would not be speaking to one another. Unless I use my gift of speech, but as you saw, I haven't. As for you winning this battle, you've lost this one, but you will win others. You will also prove to be very important in the far future,*" exclaimed the Unicorn. "*Now that you know this, and have experienced what it is like to fight a Unicorn. I must leave before I am discovered by others of your kind. Farewell Young One, we will never meet or see each other again.*"

I saw the Unicorn turn around and disappear into the forest. After it was long gone I stood there staring for a little while longer until Father hollered for us to come back to the Nest. Like me, my brothers and sisters were interested in exploring the wild land and its' inhabitants. But this time, my brothers and sisters took it upon themselves to see me get my tail handed to me. It was also late in the day and we were all tired, going back to the Nest sounded like a good idea. When we all got back to the nest, all of us fell asleep instantly. The next day, Mother went out to hunt for our meal while Father stayed behind to teach us something. Later we found out what he intended to teach us. Father wanted to teach us on how to defend ourselves incase we were ever attacked by one of our "Enemies", and how to make and breath fire. Learning how to defend ourselves was the easy part, all we had to do was: Roar loudly, and know where to bite and slash on our opponent. But at the time our roars sounded like obscured squeaks, and we could really bite or slash until our teeth, and claws grew stronger, and harder. How to make and breathe fire though, was a different story. Of course we wouldn't learn all of this in a single day, it would take a few dozen years or so at least.

To make fire, we had to do a lot of breathing exercises, to get ourselves ready to make smoke. After the exercises, we attempted to make smoke, for smoke equals fire and fire equals a lot of fun. After many tries all of us were eventually blowing smoke in no time flat, which got us excited and made all of us very happy. We had smoke coming out of our mouths and noses, those of us that had smoke coming out of our noses were laughed at. With the breathing exercises done and smoke coming out of our nose or mouth, we were eager to start making and blowing fire. Father told us that all it took was confidence and patience to make and blow fire, but who cares about that? We just wanted to do it, so we had something new to amuse ourselves with.

With all of us trying our hardest, and accomplishing nothing, we were starting to give up on making and breathing fire. But I had to try one last time, before I gave up, and as luck would have it, I blew fire. After I made a small flame appear out of my mouth that surprised my bothers and sisters, they started to breathe fire too. With flames coming out of our mouths and lighting anything we saw on fire, we lost track of time. When it came time for supper, we were disappointed for our fun had to come to an end. Once we got back to the nest, we feasted upon large sea creatures that were delicious. As we were eating, I was going though the things that we were taught over the past months and years. I found that something was not right. We could defend ourselves, somewhat fight, and make and blow fire, yet we could not fly. Our parents hadn't taught us how to fly. I knew that the wings on our backs were small now but they are big enough to carry our weight, or so I thought.

"Father?" I asked.

"Yes Drakon?" replied Father.

"You and Mother have taught us a lot of things over the past few years. Except, you haven't shown us how to fly. Why?" I questioned.

"The answer to your question is simple. Your wings cannot support your weight for any long or short distances. You will have to wait a few more years until your wings are fully developed. So you are grounded to your Mother or myself, think that you and your siblings are ready. You all can do some exercises, so when the time does come to fly, it won't be so difficult," Father replied as he stood up and showed us the exercises that we could do.

After watching Father jump and hop around on all fours, we fell asleep, for we were too exhausted from breathing fire and jumping around all day. The next day, and the following days, my siblings and myself were doing wing, and jumping exercises until Mother and Father told us that it was time to fly. This was when the real fun started for all of us. Before we could fly however, we had to learn how to takeoff. This was done by jumping into the air and flapping our wings: easier said then done. For every time we jumped into the air and flapped our wings, we would loose concentration and plop back down to the ground. After about a few hundred times, we finally managed to stay in the air for a while before our wings gave out and we tumbled back to the earth.

When we finally got the jumping into the air part figured out, Mother and Father showed us how to takeoff from standing still. This was a lot harder to do for we had to put more effort into making our wings move up and down to support our weight as we lifted off the ground. We didn't stay too long in the air, for once we got airborne, our wings were sore and we were tired. After we had fallen back to the ground my brothers, sisters, and I, just laid on the ground, too tired to get up. So our parents just let us rest and recuperate until we were ready to fly again. When all of us were reenergized again, we were ready to learn how to takeoff again. The next lesson Mother and Father taught us, was how to takeoff while running. When my siblings and myself tried this, we found it to be a lot easier then the first two lessons, that, and we could fly higher up into the air. Also all of us could land without crashing to the ground, although we didn't really practice on how to land just yet. Once all of the takeoffs were taught the next steps in the learning process were how to land and how to fly. It took a while to figure it all out, but once we managed to figure everything out, we were set for life, or so I thought. I didn't plan on what Mother and Father were going to teach us next.

Chapter 2

The Trial and Error Begin

"Does your childhood have *anything* to do with why there are so few of you? I don't think it does. But then again, that's just my opinion," Brak stated as he stood up to stretch his arms and legs.

"*If you are not interested about our history, then, how about I fry you on the spot?*" questioned Drakon annoyed and very insulted to the point that he had smoke rising from his closed mouth.

"I'm interested in learning about what happened, but why are you telling me something that I don't really need to know? Like your life story, is that really important?" replied Brak as he sat back down on the cold cave floor, and trying to keep his anger in check, unless he wanted a death wish.

"*The reason why I'm telling you my life story,* HUMAN, *is so that you can understand. If you don't understand, then your question is pointless, and you traveled all this way for nothing. And those poor fools that came with you died for nothing,*" growled Drakon as he stifled his own anger.

"What do *YOU* mean? I don't understand? Understand what?" snapped Brak.

"*You have to understand how we lived and thrived. Not to mention on how we survived the harsh wild world,*" explained Drakon with yet another growl. "*Once you understand this, then you see how we are so few in numbers.*"

"Alright then, continue with your story," exclaimed Brak as he finally calmed down.

"*Very well. But I will jump ahead five hundred years to my youth. So that I can tell you how my parents put my siblings and myself through a survival test that would either make us stronger or kill us*," explained Drakon.

* * *

"De'kon, Claire, Jax, Mearl, Balt, Marie, Drakon, Charlotte! Come here at once! Your Father and myself have something to tell and show you!" roared Mother.

No matter how close or how far away my siblings and myself were, all of us heard Mother, and Father calling us. Like the good little obedient children that we were, we went to see what they wanted. We all gathered in a clearing by our new home, for we had moved from the Nesting Grounds after two hundred years had passed. We searched for a while until Mother and Father found the perfect spot. It was a large clearing that could easily house all ten of us. The clearing had huge dark green trees surrounding the clearing making it only accessible by flight or by destroying the outlying forest. The long grass that covered the clearing was light green and soft like a feather to the touch. To add to it's beauty, the clearing had a vast lake beside it. The lake was clear as crystal and it was very refreshing when it was time for a wash. The only thing that looked out of place was our dens and our food traps.

We were in our early to mid teens as you Humans call it when we finally established ourselves in our new home. A Dragon in his or her early to mid teens is known as a Youth in the Dragon tongue. The Dragon is no longer a whelp for we had our true colours showing, but we were not yet old enough or knowledgeable to be considered an Adult. As we neared the clearing we saw Mother and Father standing there waiting for us. We didn't know what to think when we saw them either for they had no expression on their faces. Whether we did something right or wrong, none of us knew.

"Okay children, listen up," Mother stated. "Your Father and myself have decided that it is time for "*The Test*". This *Test* will determine whether you can survive on your own or not. We will explain what *The Test* is now, instead of when we get to your destination."

"The explanation of *The Test* is easy, it's doing *The Test* that's hard," explained Father. "You all will have to spend seventy days in a dense forested, mountainous, and dangerous area. Flying is strictly forbidden until the seventy days are up. If you even attempt to fly you will fail. Also when your Mother said "Survive", she meant it! You will get no help from us whatsoever, what you do and how you do it, is all up to you. If *you* want help, you'll have to help each other out. But that is if you can find each other. It is a guarantee that some of you will not survive *The Test*, but we have faith in all of you. None of this will probably make sense to all of you now, but when you're all older you'll understand why we did this. When you finish *The Test* you will be taken to the Council of The Elders, and they will decide your future from there."

With that said Mother and Father took to the sky and we followed shortly after. We flew for what seemed like eons, or so. As all of us were wondering how much further, Mother and Father just stopped, turned around to look at us, and hovered in the air.

"Okay children, this is the place. I want all of you to fly in separate directions, until I look small," exclaimed Mother.

So we flew away form each other until Mother and Father looked small. Or rather Mother looked small, Father was nowhere to be seen. I hovered in the air for a while until, I felt searing pain in my back. The next thing I knew, I was falling to the ground. I looked up to find Father hovering in the sky with smoke coming out of his mouth. At that moment I realized what Father did, he torched my wings so I couldn't fly, and I assumed he did the same with my siblings as well. As I was falling, I watched Father fly away, and I didn't see him or Mother ever again. The next thing I remember was, hitting the ground extremely hard and blacking out.

When I woke up, my back and head really hurt, plus I was very hungry as well, for it was late in the day. I stood up slowly to make the throbbing in my head stop, and then started making a shelter to give myself a place to sleep and think. I broke large trees and dragged them into a pile that resembled a crude hut. But in actuality, it was just a large pile of broken trees. I dug a large deep hole underneath the pile of trees so I could turn my "hut" into a Den. When I was finished I had created a crude Den it didn't look all that fancy, but it would suffice. Also, due to the injuries that I had sustained from the fall, I was in extreme pain, and was on the brink of passing out again. I silently thanked Mother for showing us how to create Dens when we moved to our new home. Next I gathered lots of branches and saplings and piled them into my Den and lit the pile on fire to keep warm. We might be warm blooded but the additional heat helps. After the fire was lit I thanked Mother again for teaching us how to make our fire last outside of our bodies. Once all of my work was done, the next thing on my agenda was food, for I had worked up a large appetite, also, the sky was now dark.

As I walked around in search of food, I tried flaring my wings and found that it hurt immensely. So I folded what remained of my burned wings and hoped that the pain would subside, and that my wings would grow back. I went back in search of food, and came across lots of berries, roots, and fruit, but no animals around. I could have eaten the plant life but a Dragon thrives off of meat. So I decided to set a trap that Father showed me how to make, to see what I could catch. I dug a large deep hole in the ground and covered it with broken branches, then used the plant food I found, and piled it all on top of the branches. Once done, I jumped into the bushes and waited for my meal to come to me. It wasn't a long wait, for as soon as I hid myself, there were a lot of creatures and animals that came out of hiding and went about their business. But none of the creatures or animals went for my nicely laid out trap. After what seemed like a very long wait I got tired of waiting and went with plan "B". I jumped out of my hiding spot and chased the closest creature to me until I caught it and ate it. I did this for a while until I was full and there was nothing around to chase anymore. I headed back to my Den, carrying branches with me to put onto the fire that was still hopefully burning. Once I got back, I tossed the branches on the fire and fell asleep. As I fell asleep I wondered what the next day would bring.

Chapter 3

Peek-a-Boo, I Found You

"So that's how your kind decreased in numbers? By sending the young Dragons to their doom," sated Brak as he smacked his fist into his palm.

"*No, that's how my Clan decreased their numbers. Other Clans had their own way of killing each other off,*" growled Drakon.

"Ah, I still don't see why your Father torched your wings. But I can see that they've grown back, but still," mused Brak.

"*It's simple, it makes it more of a challenge. Of course it made travel a little more difficult and lengthy. But it showed us that we can still function, even without our wings,*" explained Drakon.

"It makes sense in a way, I guess. I still have more questions to ask you, but then again, I'll let you continue with your story," replied Brak.

"*Very well, I'll continue,*" started Drakon.

* * *

On day two, I decided to look for my brothers and sisters to see how they were doing. But before I set off I wanted to make sure, I knew where my camp was. I climbed to the top of my Den, and let out a large stream of fire around my Den. I was burning everything until there was a large black area around my Den. Once that was done, I set off in search of my siblings. As I was walking around, the sun was starting to set, so I decided to point my nose to the sky and sniffed the air for any familiar sent. When I finally picked one up, I followed it. The sent lead me to a small clearing, and once I arrived there I saw my eldest Brother De'kon.

De'kon was fire red, with sharp white teeth and claws. His eyes were also red and sparkled like rubies, which matched his sapphire coloured mane of hair. De'kon's hair flowed from the top of his head down to where his wings met. He also had a well built body that looked like it could take a beating or two. Nothing could be said for his wings though, for they were the same colour and shape as mine: black as ash and just as burned. I realized then that what Father did to me, he did to the rest of my siblings. As I looked at my brother, I noticed thought that his red scales weren't red but brown with mud and twigs caked all over them. Looking at him made me wonder if he had a softer landing then I did.

"De'kon, I found you," I cried with joy.

"Drakon? Is that you? What are you doing here?" questioned De'kon.

"I decided to go on a search for you, Claire, Jax, Mearl, Marie, Balt, and Charlotte. I guess that I got lucky in finding you first," I explained. "I'm about a days walk from here, so I figured everyone else would be as well. Once we're all together again, we should be able to survive out here with no problems."

"But Mother and Father wanted us to survive for seventy days on our own. But then again it would be easier to hunt down food if there are more of us," speculated De'kon.

"Exactly, so lets go looking for the rest of our family," I stated.

With that said De'kon and myself set off back to my camp for a meal and some sleep. The next morning the two of us set off together in search for more of our siblings. As night was approaching, De'kon and myself were getting ready to camp out, so we could resume the search when day broke, when De'kon spotted a light in the distance. We headed towards the light, for it was now completely dark and hard to see with the dense forest all around us. When we were closer we saw that it was another camp that some creature set up. De'kon and myself decided to snoop around to see whom the camp belonged to. There was no Den, but there was a fire going, and a couple of set traps, also, there were lots of lush green bushes in the area. As we were roaming around the encampment, I noticed slight movement in the bushes.

"Who's there? I can see and smell you," I shouted.

"Fine, I'll come out. Drakon *you* just *had* to go and ruin my fun. Didn't you?" questioned a familiar voice.

"*Please* Claire, we could smell you a Kilometer away. With that rank smell of yours, it wasn't hard," replied De'kon mockingly.

"Yeah, and it's not hard to see you in that bush over there," I added. "Come on out so we can rejoice that De'kon and myself found you, and we can all eat and sleep."

"Alright, I'm coming, I'm coming," exclaimed Claire as she shook her head in mock disappointment. "There should still be something in the trap we can eat…I hope."

Claire emerged from the bushes in a quick short jump. She was a silver coloured Dragoness, with a slim body, that made her look like she could fit through any tight space. Her green eyes matched her teal coloured hair that flowed down from her head to over her shoulders and down to the ground, making her look stunningly beautiful. It was to bad she was my eldest sister and not from another Clan. As she left the bushes she did a short trot over to an area of the encampment that looked like part of the border-lining forest. But a closer look revealed that it was a pit trap like mine, only better. Looking at Claire's trap made me jealous of her.

"Is there any food?" I asked hungrily. "Where's your Den? Or are you like De'kon and like to sleep outside in the mud?"

"Yeah we're hungry…Hey! What's that supposed to mean? Some of us like to sleep in the mud…I mean—," snapped De'kon as Claire cut him off before he could speak his mind.

"To answer your first question boys: yes there is food. Plenty of it, for the three of us. The answer to your second question Drakon is simple: why build a Den, when I have shelter provided by the trees and bushes to keep me warm. Cause unlike you Den Whelp, I like sleeping under the stars and not in a Den. But unfortunately no mud, so I can't possibly look like De'kon," answered Claire while I made a face at her.

"Hey, I resent that," stated De'kon.

"No, you resemble that. And hey! Who are you calling a Den Whelp? Hatchling? I shot back with a smile.

"Very funny," grumbled De'kon.

"Always with the size jokes with you males," growled Claire.

"A Den or shelter is a lot warmer than mud, or trees, and bushes Claire. Don't you remember what Mother and Father told us?" I questioned.

"Fine, then tomorrow, we'll spend the night in *your* precious Den, or shelter, or whatever it is that you took pride in building. But tonight I hope you enjoy sleeping outside underneath the nice star filled night sky," snapped Claire.

"Fine by me, but we won't be staying long for there are the rest of our brothers and sisters that we have to find," I replied with a shrug.

That night De'kon and myself spent the night at Claire's encampment and it was cold. Even with a nice warm fire going I missed my nice warm Den. As I was thinking of my Den, I was also thinking of how I was going to make it larger. For if I was to house everyone, then there was going to have to be more room. Then again, I could just sleep inside and everyone else could sleep outside. Or I could always just add another section to my Den and make it larger that way. I mussed over my Den problem until I fell asleep on the cold earth.

The next morning, we set off for my Den and more food, seeing as with De'kon's and my arrival at Claire's encampment, we sort of…cleaned her out. Also we'd plan our next course of action when we would arrive at my Den. When we arrived at my Den though, we encountered some unwanted guests: Basilisks. The vile creatures had taken over my camp and Den that I worked so hard to create. Also they weren't like the small Basilisks at home., they were five times the size. I remembered what Father said as soon as I saw the vile creatures. He said that a Basilisk is a four legged lizard that ranges from brown coloured scales to black coloured scales. Their teeth maybe short, but they can tear a Dragon to pieces in mere seconds. They are also quite long depending on their size. Anywhere from two to thirty feet. No one knew what colour their eyes were, for if you even glanced at them you'd die. It was rumored to be a defensive trait that the Basilisk had, but no one really knew. All I knew was, that these Basilisks were about fifty feet long, really tall, and were dark blood red.

We realized that we were outnumbered two to one, and seeing as all of us had no wings, we couldn't attack from the air. On the plus side though, none of the six Basilisks had seen or smelled us, so we had the upper claw at the moment. We waited and watched the vile creatures until nightfall when they all moved into *my* Den. As we watched them go inside, I had a plan on how we could deal with the Basilisks and get a good meal out of it. I told Claire and De'kon my idea and they liked it. Once the last of the Basilisks went inside the Den, the three of us snuck out of hiding and crawled up to the entrance. We all took in a deep breath of the fresh smelling air, and blew a large stream of fire into my Den. It was a good thing I dug a really deep hole, otherwise my Den would have gone up in flames. After we finished our stream of fire, all of us took in another deep breath and smelled cooked meat. So we went inside and feasted on roasted Basilisk. After we ate, all of us fell asleep for we were tired and full.

When we woke up the next day we finished the remains of last night's supper. When there was nothing left we set out to find our siblings. We set off when the sun was a quarter of the way in the sky. After five days of searching we came to a vast forested area with huge trees. These trees weren't like the other part of the forest that the three of us were in. These trees were very thick and had a red coloured trunk and bark instead of brown. But the branches still sprouted lush green leaves. While we searched the new area, we killed more Basilisks, and feasted on them. As we continued our hike through the forest we arrived at a huge deep river. We stopped for a drink of water, for Basilisk meat is very salty for some reason. As we were getting a drink of water, we encountered another one of our siblings, Jax.

Jax was the third oldest of us, and he was covered in bronze coloured scales, with abnormally long white teeth and curved claws. He had a set of soft green eyes that mismatched with his light red hair. Jax's red hair flowed from the top of his head and ended at his shoulders. He had popped up from being underwater with a large fish in his mouth. Jax was looking the other way when he surfaced so he didn't see the three of us right away. Once he got out though he dropped his fish in amazement to see the three of standing there looking at him.

"What are you guys doing here? Aren't we supposed to be on our own for this *Test*?" questioned Jax.

"We came to see how you were doing," answered Claire.

"Yeah and we *don't* have to be alone for this *Test* either remember. Besides, we'll survive longer if we stay together," added De'kon.

"Also, how would you like to stay with the three of us? There's food, warmth, and shelter," I finished.

"Hmm, I don't know what to do. There's food and shelter here, plus all the water I want," mused Jax.

"But is your shelter warm, like a Den?" I questioned, while Claire just rolled her eyes when I mentioned my Den again.

"Well, not really, no," answered Jax.

"Ah, I see," I started. "Well my Den is nice and warm, just ask Claire and De'kon. Although, I'll have to make my Den bigger or add on to it."

"Yep," stated De'kon.

"I'll have to admit that Drakon's right," added Claire.

"All right, I guess I'll come and stay with you three, we are family after all. How far away is your camp from here?" asked Jax.

"It's a five day trek from here," I answered.

With that said the four of us set off to my encampment. On our trip back though, we encountered a heard of Unicorn, and we had no clue what to do. As we stared at them, they stared back at us with a look that could kill. We knew they weren't happy to see us and we didn't know why.

"*What are you doing here in our land?*" questioned who seemed to be the leader.

"We did not mean to intrude on your land. We got stranded here for some unknown reason. We would've flown away but as you can see, our wings are no more," I replied.

"Drakon?" Claire asked with a confused look on her face.

"Yes?" I asked.

"You can talk to, and understand those creatures? Those Unicorns?" questioned Claire.

"Yeah, can't *you*?" I asked a little annoyed at Claire's questions.

"No, neither can Jax or De'kon," answered Claire.

"*It's simple,*" stated the Leader. "*The one you call Drakon has a mystical power or what your kind call a gift. He can understand any creature, but we can choose whether we want to talk to him or not.*"

We all looked at the Leader in awe and shock now that we finally got over the overwhelming sight of all of the Unicorns. The Leader was tall, and unlike the others, it was covered in black hair. It's horn was a dark yellow colour, and it's hooves were black. The Leader had a mane of rouge hair that matched hers dark red eyes. I had forgotten about the gift I was born with, that and none of my family knew I had this gift either. I was intrigued by this newly remembered knowledge. For if I had a gift then surely my siblings had gifts as well. As I was musing over this, the snort form one of the Unicorns brought me back to the matter at claw: the Unicorns. Before I could think of something De'kon stepped forward. I guess he knew what he was doing.

"We do not wish to fight you. We were only on our way back to Drakon's camp to eat and sleep. Then we were going to continue on our search of the rest of our family," explained De'kon.

"*And let you destroy more of this forest? I don't think so, for you are all intruders in this land and shall pay for your transgressions,*" stated the Leader as she started glowing with a black aura around her.

Without thinking I blew out a great plume of smoke in front of the heads of the Unicorns and ran full out in the direction of my camp. As I ran, De'kon, Claire, and Jax followed close behind, not wanting to stick around to see what the Unicorns were planning. When I reached my camp, I leapt up onto the top of my Den and took in a deep breath and blew out a large long river of fire in the direction I came from. De'kon, Jax, and Claire just made it past in time. For within the flames we heard cries and screams of pain and anger. The Unicorns obviously weren't happy for what I had done to them. So the remaining Unicorns gathered together and started to glow with a dark blue aura. All of us were starting to feel light headed and woozy.

"There's only one way to finish them off. We must combine our fire into a flame wall," Claire started. "I just hope what Father taught us, works."

The rest of us agreed to Claire's idea, for it was a good plan. The four of us all took in a deep breathe of fresh air and let loose a blast of fire. With control over our fire, we managed to make it stop when it engulfed the Unicorns, and held the fire there. All of us held the firewall there for what felt like eons. While the wall burned, we could hear screams of pain, and anger, which were disturbing to hear. But we didn't dare stop, until we heard nothing. When the screams finally stopped, we ceased our fire breathing. When the fire died away, there was nothing but ash. Although we knew that it wasn't over for any Unicorn that survived our attack, would return in force. At this realization, we knew, we might not be so lucky the next time, but we would be ready for them when the time came.

Chapter 4

Survival in the Wild

"So that's why the Unicorns Hate and Fear you," stated Brak.

"*No. The Unicorns and Dragons have always been at war in one way or another. It has only been a few thousand years since peace began between the two races,*" corrected Drakon.

"Do you remember why your two races started fighting each other in the first place?" questioned Brak.

"*No, unfortunately I do not know why or who started the war between the two races,*" replied Drakon.

"Okay then. I guess I'll let you continue on with your tale then," responded Brak.

"*You'd better, unless you wish to become my appetizer,*" stated Drakon as he licked his lips.

* * *

As the four of us: De'kon, Claire, Jax, and myself started up the search for our siblings again after the threat of the Unicorns, the next Dragon we came across was Balt. Balt was impaled on a tree, and by the looks of it he died instantly. Balt was a sapphire scaled coloured Dragon. He was also well built but he wasn't as muscular as De'kon was. With a mane of lush black hair that that flowed down to his wings past his shoulders. Balt's silver eyes matched his short bone white teeth and claws, when we saw him, we cried out for him and grieved for a time. Balt was the middle Whelp of the family, so he was also the fire of our family. He was always getting in trouble and testing our parents' patience. With our heads hung low in mourning, we retreated back to my Den to plan and think.

A few days later when we resumed the search, we came across the still bodies of Marie and Charlotte. Both of them looked like they had suffered from deep cuts and gashes. It was also impossible to tell what they looked like for their bodies were badly damaged and covered in blood and gore. We figured that Marie and Charlotte encountered a heard of Unicorn as well, only, they weren't as lucky. After another grieving period, the four of us became filled with murderous rage. For the Unicorns were attacking us for no apparent reason, I mean yeah sure we burned some land, but it'll grow back, as for us being here. There was nothing we could do about it until our wings grew back or if our parents came for us. Until then we decided to do one thing to keep us occupied. Kill the Unicorns for what they did, but first, dinner.

On the twentieth day of our exile, the four of us were hunting for dinner when we ran into Mearl…literally. Mearl was covered in golden coloured scales with silver mixed in giving her body the look of always moving. She, unlike Claire had a muscular body, which almost made her look like a male, which we all made fun of at times. Mearl had long elegant claws and teeth that were white. Mearl's eyes were also a mix of gold and silver, depending on how you looked at them. Mearl's hair though was a strange mix of colours, ranging from light blue, green, and red. Her hair also flowed down from the top of her head to where her tail began past her hind legs. Sadly though, Mearl's wings looked like the rest f ours: burned and crippled. Mearl would have looked beautiful if it wasn't for the fact that she was covered in mud and branches. Mearl looked worse then De'kon did when I found him.

Mearl had explained to us that it was "Camouflage", for she was hiding from the Unicorns in the huge trees where no one could see or smell her. After we all got together, we did some rejoicing for Mearl was alive and well. We filled her in on what happened to the rest of our siblings, which made Mearl very upset and angry at the Unicorns. Mearl also informed us of the large Unicorn herds that were roaming this area and a few other areas surrounding the one that we ended up in. Mearl suspected that they might be looking for the five of us, seeing as we caused them some grief already. We decided to do some training, so we would be for the next attack from the Unicorns. After a long argument of deciding on where to stay with the Unicorns roaming around, we all headed back to my camp to start the training

Training was long and hard, for we made ourselves get up early, just as the sun was rising. We all did lots of hard hunting and fighting exercises that Mother and Father taught us until our muscles hurt. We did the exercises until you could just see the sun rise just above the tall trees and mountains. After the exercises, the five of us ran nonstop, straight to Jax's camp, seeing as it was the farthest camp away. Once we got there, we turned around and ran strait back to my camp. Normally it should have taken five days of walking but with no stops and running flat out at our full speed it only took us a day, that and we were pushing our already hurting muscles to their limits. Once we couldn't run anymore, we started to climb the large trees and once we were high enough we hopped from one tree to the next, until our hands and feet couldn't take it anymore. After we got to the ground, we continued our exercises with fighting each other with close combat and ranged combat. When it became very late in the night we stopped to catch our supper or to eat whatever was in the trap. When supper was done we went to sleep until the next morning when we did it all over again. We became stronger over the time we did this and we wouldn't stop either, not till the Unicorns came back for us and find us, which they did.

When the Unicorns finally came, we were ready for them. They came in a large numerous force that pretty much outnumbered us, but the battle was long. The ironic part about the battle was that it was taking place on the day that Mother and Father were suppose to come for us. But as we fought and waited into the night, our parents never came, so we kept on fighting. Even though we knew we were seriously outnumbered, we were winning, which didn't surprise us. For we had some experience in fighting Unicorn, even if it wasn't much, it still helped. The fighting lasted for what seemed like days, the Unicorn numbers were shrinking, but not fast enough. Meanwhile, we were tiring, for Youths weren't meant to go to war or fight battles, only fight amongst themselves. That was what the Drakes and the full grown Dragons and Dragonesses did.

Jax was the first to fall out of the five of us. He had underestimated the power of the leader and fell by her horn. Claire was the next to go, for the Unicorns swarmed her like flies to dung, giving Claire no chance to counter attack. But like a true Dragon, she went down in flame and glory. As Claire fell, she let loose a wide burst of flame, that torched the swarming Unicorns to ash and bone. De'kon fell shortly after Claire, but before he died, he let out a large river of flame that surrounded Mearl and myself giving us some meager protection. We were safe for the time being, so I decided to try something, for it didn't look like it would matter whether it would work or not. I flared my wings again and was expecting searing pain, like when I first flared my wings on the first day, but the pain never came. So I flapped my wings experimentally and there still wasn't any pain. I then raised myself off the ground and into the air looking down at Mearl who was preparing for a final assault.

"Mearl, follow me. I have an idea of how to loose these accursed creatures," I yelled down to her.

"Okay, I'm on my way up," hollered Mearl as she took to the sky.

We flew low to the ground, but not low enough to get hurt by the Unicorns and their mystical powers, but not high enough to be above the trees completely. We flew for what seemed like eons until we arrived at a nearby lake. The lake was vast with a large island that was covered in trees in the middle of it with a sandy beach surrounding the trees. The lake had crystal clear water, so you could see the bottom of it, even in the deepest parts. You could also see what swam in the vast lake. I gazed into the lake to see what I could see, and I couldn't see that many sea creatures in the lake. Mearl and myself flew close to the surface of the water to avoid being attacked by whatever mystical or magical things the Unicorns could throw at us.

"Why are we flying so low Drakon? We have the opportunity to fly away from here, why don't we?" asked Mearl.

"We might have the opportunity to leave this place, but where would we go? We can't exactly go home...wherever home is. Frankly I don't know or remember for I was too busy following Mother and Father, and I'm sure you don't remember where home is either. Plus, how do we know that this isn't still part of *The Test*? Mother and Father aren't here yet, but we shouldn't give up hope. At least…not yet," I reassured.

"Once this is over, I think I'm going to have a nice chat with The Elders on exiling your Young Ones and letting them get killed off by the locals," I added.

"I think I'll be joining you for that conversation, I have a few things I'd like to talk to The Elders with myself," exclaimed Mearl.

Once we landed on the large island, we started setting up traps for the Unicorn threat, for we didn't know if they could swim, for I've never seen a Unicorn by a large body of water. But if they could, the vile creatures had a surprise or two waiting for them. After we finished putting up traps and snares all over the island, we set up more traps, but the latter ones were for food not the Unicorns. After we finished, Mearl raised her head to the sky, I did the same and caught the sent of the Unicorns. Both of us took to the sky and circled the island. We spotted the Unicorns as they were advancing to the lake, some began to swim, and others began to walk on the water. We didn't bother to wonder why there were some Unicorns swimming and others walking on the water. Instead we let out a large jet of flame along the shore of the island, encircling it in a wall of flame. The wall of fire made the Unicorns think twice on what they were up against, but it didn't scare them off, instead they waited for the fire to die out. When the flame wall did die the Unicorns advanced.

Stepping on the island was the Unicorns first mistake, for a great deal of them, fell prey to our traps that we had set up. Mearl and myself also took to the trees, so it would be difficult to see us, which gave us an advantage. Any Unicorn that got close to one of us, the other would set the Unicorn on fire, and then we would jump to a new hiding spot. The screams of pain and agony would never be forgotten, but we were in a battle for our survival, and couldn't care less about our enemies. After all of the traps had been sprung there weren't that many Unicorns left, and those that were left, were tired from the long chase and the hunt in trying to find both of us. This made it easy for Mearl and myself to take down the accursed creatures. When it became late in the night, the remaining Unicorns broke off the attack, giving Mearl and myself a chance to relax and catch some much needed sleep, in our hiding spots.

When morning broke, the fighting started again, only this time Mearl and myself took to the air and set the whole island ablaze. If there were any survivors from the final attack that Mearl and myself did, we would be amazed. But the two of us knew that we were extremely lucky in winning this battle for we were only two young Dragons up against an entire herd, and more, of Unicorns. As we took to the sky, both of us searched for any sign of Mother and Father but there was no one in the sky except for some birds and the two of us. This confused and worried us, maybe Mother and Father weren't coming back for us, and if *that* was the case. Then we would have to find a way to survive and live with the threat of the Unicorns always hunting us. For if Mother and Father would not come back, then we would never go home. As this thought was going through my head, I realized that Mearl and myself would be staying here a lot longer in this foreign place then we planned.

Mearl and myself decided to find a nice secluded area, so we could live and survive without the threat of the Unicorns looming over us. We flew to an area that was covered in lush bushy, dark green trees. Among the trees flowed a dark blue river that was cold to the touch, but it contained many strange and wondrous creatures. I looked at Mearl, and she looked at me, with a single nod we both agreed that this would be a good place to stay for a while. We had built two large Dens, for we both liked to have a lot of room, and we had grown from all of the training that we did before battling the Unicorns. As we lived in isolation, we explored the area and found out that we weren't the *only* Dragons to be exiled to this unknown, Unicorn infested land.

Chapter 5

My First Love, but Not My Last

"So, your parents abandoned you, and yet you found a way to survive in hostile territory. Wow, and I thought Dragons were extremely stupid, even the ones that could talk. Except *you* of course," stated Brak sarcastically as he stood up to stretch.

As Brak stood up to stretch his arms and legs again, he had to dive out of the way of a small fireball. Before Brak could stand and regain his balance to cast a protective spell, he was blown off the ground. He landed with a hard thud on the hard cold cave floor of Drakon's lair.

"*I will not be insulted constantly by a mere Human Sorcerer who can't even stand up straight, and keep his flapping mouth closed,*" roared Drakon as he stood up, shook himself to wake his muscles and took a step towards Brak.

"*Insult me again, and you will be torn apart, and eaten very slowly,*" threatened Drakon as he brought his massive head down to stare into Brak's eyes.

"Okay, okay. I'll be on my best behavior from now on. You may continue with your tale," replied Brak as he stood up again, only to sit back down on the cold floor.

"*Very well, I'll continue with my tale. Just remember what I said,*" snarled Drakon as he laid back down on the cold cave floor as well.

* * *

Two hundred years have passed since Mother and Father have exiled us here in this strange land. We have made some allies in our war with the Unicorns. We have also made more enemies as well. On our exploration of the foreign land that Mearl and myself now called home, we've found other stranded and exiled Dragons battling the same enemy. That enemy was none other then the *vile* Unicorns that roamed throughout the lands. The two of us helped whomever we could, and in exchange, the Dragons would help in our search for others like us. Eventually there were enough of us that we found a suitable place to turn into our new home. Our new home had a lush green forest on one side, a huge crystal lake on the other, plus there were snow-capped mountains behind us. This gave us more than enough to live off of and to protect ourselves against any threats. Mearl showed the "Survivalists" as we were now called, how to make traps so we wouldn't be taken by surprise by the Unicorns. There were also others who shared their knowledge of things to help us thrive and survive. We had a system of patrols and guards in and around our large encampment, we even had guards posted in the air, so we had all angles covered. Mearl and myself were the "voted" leaders of the encampment for we had the most knowledge of our enemy. Plus we also had excellent knowledge of the surrounding area for it wasn't far from where Mearl and Myself first relocated.

With this new power of leadership I had, it got to me sometimes, so I finally decided to go and clear my head. I spread my wings and took to the air. As I was making a large circle around the encampment, I noticed something strange in the bushes to the far east of the encampment. So I folded my wings and dove down to take a closer look. As I got closer I noticed that it was a Dragoness clawing her way to the encampment. It was had to tell what she looked like, due to the mass amount of injuries she sustained so I could only guess at what she looked like. It was also hard to tell that it was a Dragoness, due to the state she was in. Behind her though, was a large contingent of Unicorns. My guess was that they would let the injured Dragoness get to the encampment, kill her when she was close enough and ambush the encampment. So I did what I thought was right, I swooped down in front of the critically injured Dragoness and let out a large river of fire in front of the Unicorns. This in turn caught the advancing herd completely off guard and made them scatter. I carefully picked up the critically injured Dragoness and flew back to the encampment with my heavy burden to raise the alarm.

Once I made it back to the encampment I hunted down our only two healers to see what they could do. Even though there were plenty of Dragons with gifts in the encampment, we only had two that had the gift to heal others. The healers were a set of Dragon twins with the exception of one being male and the other female. I learned when I was younger that Dragons who had "gifts" were very rare, but, twins were extremely rare. The twin's scales were a mix of red and white with long thin white teeth and claws. Their hair that flowed from their head to their wings, was also a mix of red and white. Also to add to their bizarre colouring, their eyes were a mix of red and white, as well as their wings. This made the twins very unique, stunning, and confusing to look at, whether they were together or apart. Both of them though were in the Healing Den, doing whatever it was they did in there.

"Maya, Zack! I have a Dragon that is in serious need of healing, fast!" I yelled.

"Okay we'll get right on it," replied the twins in unison as they appeared from the Healing Den.

Everyone thought that it was creepy the way Maya and Zack talked. They would always talk in unison, or finish each other's sentences. They were twins after all and it was said that twin Dragons were very unique to say the least. Once I gave the injured Dragoness to Maya and Zack, I went in search of our Defense Master. To let him know what I saw while I rescued the Dragoness. I was hoping that he had a plan and a reasonable force ready for what was to come.

"Hey Scythe! You around?" I hollered.

"*What is it?*" replied Scythe from a nearby tree.

Scythe was a chimera, one of our allies that we made in our fight against the Unicorns. He had dark brown fur, but he had a habit of changing his colour to dark green whenever it suited him. He had a long hard-shelled, barbed tail, like a scorpions, two fair sized wings that looked like they belonged to a bat or a Dragon, unnaturally long teeth and claws.

Scythe also had a lion's mane of black hair that flowed halfway down his back. His body also looked as thought it should belong to a lion. Scythe also had a round catlike face with catlike eyes that were the colour of dark red blood. Unlike Dragons who used their front legs, as arms and hands when they need to, Chimeras only had four muscular legs that ended with large paws. With their sharp claws they could scale trees easily, like Dragons and various other large cats.

"I need you to set up a defense along the outside of the encampment. Make sure that there is a little more on the eastern side. The reason why I ask this, is that there is a large herd of Unicorns headed this way. They should only be a short flight away now. I would also like the encampments defenses to be stronger as well if they do attack," I ordered.

"*Alright, there will be a defense set up before the sun is down to the tree level,*" replied Scythe as he disappeared into the nearby bushes.

With that said and done I set out to find Mearl and let her know what I found. I also wanted her to get the hunting party out and back early incase the Unicorns tried something underhanded and sneaky. I also didn't want to loose any more family, friends, and allies. I eventually found Mearl in the Food Den. After I found her, I explained our developing situation. Mearl was with five other Dragons who were storing various fruits, berries and cooked meats into groups that were for food, and groups that were for the food traps. After I finished explaining, Mearl agreed to send out the Hunting party early and get them to return early. Before Mearl gave the order, she wanted to take a quick survey of the area to see where would be a safe area to send the Hunting party. When she flew back, Mearl had a pale look on her face.

"The Unicorns are on their way here, and there are thousands of them. I don't think we'll be lucky enough to survive this time Drakon," exclaimed Mearl worriedly.

"We will," I reassured. "As long as the traps do their job and our sneak attacks, and ambushes do theirs, we'll have the upper claw. Don't forget about Scythe and the other Chimeras either, they are very skilled at battling the Unicorns and have a knack for the element of surprise."

Scythe appeared out of nowhere after Mearl and myself finished talking. He had a grim look on his face, and was badly limping. We looked at Scythe and guessed that he just came from a confrontation with the Unicorns.

"*My troops have engaged the enemy, and so has our outer defenses. The traps that have been laid are proving to be quite effective against the Unicorns but...*," reported Scythe.

"But what?" questioned Mearl and myself in unison.

"*There are just too many of them. No matter how many we slash, bite, and burn, they just keep coming. It's almost like every Unicorn we kill, thirty take its' place. I don't think the defenses can hold out much longer. I fear that what you two have work so hard for, might have been in vein*," finished Scythe.

"This has to end. I've seen too much suffering and death then I could ever imagine, and I'm not even a Drake yet. I've made up my mind. I'm going to put an end to this," stated Mearl.

When Mearl finished her short speech, she took to the sky and headed to the battle that was being waged not too far from our encampment. I followed close behind, for Mearl was the last of my siblings and I didn't want to loose her as well. As we got closer to the battle, we saw bodies of all three races strewn out everywhere. Also there were no plants and trees that were lush, green, and alive. There was just burned stumps and Black Death everywhere. Looking at this made my stomach churn, even though I was a Dragon, I still valued life. Once we landed, Mearl let out a very loud, harsh, and terrifying roar that seemed to stun all the fighting creatures and make them look at her.

"STOP! Why are we fighting? We have no quarrel with you Unicorns. I know you can understand me. All we want is to be left alone. Can't you see that all of the Dragons here have been exiled or abandoned here by their parents, and loved ones? So that we may fend for ourselves or die trying. The Chimeras that you see here are only trying to help us survive. They are no threat to you. We don't need anymore bloodshed! We've all lost friends and family do to our exile and to the petty fights and skirmishes between you. We don't want to loose anymore, so please, leave us in peace," Mearl shouted for all to hear.

"*Never!*" shouted the Leader of the Unicorns. "*You... Dragons are vile spawn, only bent on destroying everything you touch. Don't try to deny it, we've seen you destroying our land and desecrating innocent creatures and animals. We've dealt with you in the past, and will do then, what we will do now. KILL YOU ALL!*"

As soon as the Leader finished her ranting she started to glow black for a second, then she turned back to her white colour save for her now black horn. She turned her head towards Mearl and nodded her head releasing a huge void of black energy that flew towards Mearl. Mearl soared high into the sky in hopes of dodging the energy, but she couldn't avoid it for it was moving far too fast. Unfortunately, there was nothing either of us could do, to stop or avoid being hit by the energy.

"Mearl! Noo!" I yelled as I saw the black void hit and consume her.

As I watched the scene unfold in front of my eyes, my heart was breaking in two. Abandoned by my parents in this unknown land and forced to live on my own with danger around every tree and rock. Now, I was the last survivor out of my siblings. Mearl was destroyed right in front of my eyes, I couldn't believe it, I was now the last one. Before the smoke had a chance to clear I flew high into the air and in a psychotic rage that filled me. I swooped down to the ground, burning everything in sight, enemy or ally. Those that were smart enough, got out of my way, anything else burned in my inferno. I still had enough self-control though to turn my rage onto the Unicorns, or more specifically: the Leader. As I headed straight for the Leader, the fighting started up again, which only added to my rage.

As I sighted down the Leader, I noticed that I couldn't sense any fear or see that she was preparing for a counter attack for the impending death that awaited her. All I could see was that she had the look of acceptance across her face. The Leader knew what she had done, and would pay the price in blood. The Leader was covered in dirty, muddy hair. Her main of hair that flowed down her neck and overlapped her shoulders was also dirty. The Leader's horn was also caked in mud and dirt. Her eyes were a dark deep purple, which made them stunning to look at. I didn't care though, one way or another, this vile creature would *burn*, for what she did to me. As I got closer, I inhaled deeply ready to make and launch the biggest fireball that I will have ever created. I was on the verge of releasing it when I heard a voice.

"DRAKON! Stop!" shouted Mearl. "I'm alive thanks to *her*, please don't do what you're about to do."

I looked up to see the Dragoness that I had rescued earlier, hovering in front of Mearl. To my amazement neither of them were hurt, not even a scratch on them. I was so relieved to see Mearl alive, that I let the fireball disintegrate. I let out a plume of smoke from my nose instead of fire from my mouth. Breaking off my assault, I flew over to my sister and her savior to thank Mearl's savior and too see if Mearl was truly alright. Even though the battle still raged on down below us, I didn't care at the moment. I didn't even care about killing the Leader of the Unicorns at the moment either. I only cared that my sister was alive.

"Mearl, I thought you were dead," I breathed with a sigh of relief.

"I thought so too, but thanks to um...her gift. She nullified the energy blast, good thing too, otherwise I'd be Basilisk chow," explained Mearl.

Mearl then turned to look at the battle raging below her, with a loud voice that could be heard miles away Mearl spoke. "Unicorns! LEAVE US ALONE! You've lost this battle. Your numbers are now few, while ours are numerous. If you think you still have a chance, you are mistaken, for our reinforcements are on their way as I speak."

"All of your allies that you have waiting to try and take us off guard can go with you. For I can hear and understand what they are saying as well as what you are saying to one another. You have no chance, so give up and leave us alone," I added.

"*You can understand our allies? Without having to create a new language from scratch? Hmm, then that would explain why you can talk to the vile Chimera, interesting. Then this means...oh may the Great Oracle forgive me. Troops! Stand down! They are the wrong targets. Please forgive me for the pain and suffering that we have caused you*," shouted the Leader.

After the order for the Unicorns to stand down was given, Mearl and myself did the same, only we told our forces to wait until the enemy made a move. Mearl, the newcomer, Scythe and myself met on the ground and had a brief meeting on what to do. After we talked it over we all started walking towards the Unicorn Leader, for we had questions for her. As we walked towards the Unicorn Leader, she in turn began walking towards us. With both armies behind us, the four of us met in the middle of the battlefield, or somewhere there of. As soon as all of us were in earshot I was the first one to speak my mind to the Unicorn.

"For starters, why did you attack us when we meant you no harm whatsoever? Second, what are you going to do about all of the pain and suffering you caused us? Third, why did you continue with your attacks when we told you, pleaded with you, and ran from you? Also, if you are looking for any type of forgiveness, you can forget it. You and your *kind* don't deserve it or will ever have it," I questioned and stated.

"*I thought you were in league with the other Dragons that have battled with us on the other side of our lands. For they have been attacking and killing our kind for months, or years. It's been too long since I remember the first attack on our people. The Queen thought that you were reinforcements that were sent to reinforce the Enemy Dragons. When word got out that there were a great deal of you here, that were injured, we figured that it would be easy to finish you off. We also knew about Youngling Dragons that were appearing in our lands and thought that they were of no threat to us. That's what we thought of you all at first until you gained allies and began attacking us in return. We also didn't count on you massing together, finding allies and retaliating. My name is Elexia, I am the commander of the Unicorns in this part of our lands*," explained Elexia.

"Well, what do these "Enemy Dragons" look like?" I questioned.

"While you're asking that Drakon, how about asking these *cursed creatures* on how they are going to repair the damage and fix the death they've caused. Also, could you get them to speak so all of us can hear what they have to say? You're not going to help them are you? After all of the Dragons' Wrath these...these...*Monsters* put us through?" interrupted Mearl angrily.

"*Your wounded can easily be healed and mended by our healers. I'm guessing you have none of your own, as for being heard by others...*" Elexia raised her head and her horn glowed. "Is no problem, all we have to do is adapt to the language that we hear. It is quite easy to do. The Chimeras can do the same."

"Is that true Scythe?" I asked curiously.

"Yes," answered Scythe.

"Now onto the problem with the *Enemy* Dragons," started Elexia. "They are all pitch black in colour. They all have long curved spikes protruding from the back of their head all the way down to the tip pf their tail. Their claws and teeth are as small saplings, and their eyes are bright blood red. Do you know these Dragons? And on that topic can you help us?"

"First, you and your band of merry healers can heal our wounded and resurrect our dead. I know *you* Unicorns have that power. Then we'll see what we can do for you," growled Mearl.

"Very well, we'll heal your wounded, but unfortunately we can't resurrect your dead, for you killed all of the Unicorns that had the ability to. So neither side can bring back their fallen comrades," exclaimed Elexia.

"Follow me, and brings those healers of yours," snarled Mearl at Elexia.

"If they can't resurrect them then those damn Unicorn can bury them," growled Mearl to herself as she left.

As I watched Mearl, Elexia and a small herd of Unicorn Healers go over to our side of the battlefield, I gave the order for our troops to fall back to the encampment. While our troops headed back to the encampment, some carried the injured with them. I gave out a small sigh for Maya and Zack were already swamped with work and would be furious with the amount of wounded. I watched the last of our troops disappear into the bushes, then I watched as the Unicorns seemed to follow Elexia without any order. At this sight I told one of the passing scouts to spread the word and to keep an eye on the Unicorns that weren't healing. Once everyone was gone, I surveyed all of the death and destruction, before I turned to the Dragoness that had saved my sisters life.

"Thank you for saving my sister," I started. "I don't know what I would've done if I had lost her too…what is your name? I would have asked you earlier, but, we were sort of…busy."

"My name is Sisillia. I figured I had to repay you somehow for saving my life. So I guess I did what I thought was right. I'm still in your debt though," replied Sisillia.

Sisillia was a fare-sized Dragoness for her age. She was covered in clear crystal like scales that shimmered in the sunlight. She had short but sharp snow-white teeth and claws. Her wings though didn't match her body, instead they matched her eyes, which were silver with a hint of red. Sisillia also had a long mane of hair that flowed from the top of her head and covered a good portion of her back. Depending on how the wind blew, her hair went from gold to ruby colour. She was the most gorgeous

Dragoness that I had ever seen in my life, aside from my Mother.

"I think we're even, but if you like," I moved closer to Sisillia. "We could work something out."

"*Yeah*, we'll work something out," repeated Sisillia as she moved closer to me.

When the two of us were close enough, we passionately kissed each other. After our kiss that seemed to last forever, we headed back to the encampment. We walked with our wings touching each others backs and we didn't care who saw us. After we got back to the encampment, Mearl greeted us and made a snide remark that made me blush. Then from nowhere, Scythe showed up and the four of us stared at the encampment. Taking in what we were seeing. The Dragons, Chimeras, and Unicorns were all working together, it was a lot to take in. It was strange to see how the three races could set aside their problems and work for a common goal, even if we were forcing the Unicorns a little bit.

Elexia came trotting up to the four of us, she looked a lot better then the last time I saw her. Elexia was covered in bone white hair, like a good portion of the other Unicorns. The only difference between her and the other Unicorns, were her eyes, which were dark deep purple, instead of brown, black, green, blue, gold, or red. Also her horn wasn't bone white, or a soft yellow either, in fact it was a very light soft blue. She had a mane of soft white hair as well that ended at her shoulders. All of this made Elexia very stunning for her kind.

"Amazing isn't it," exclaimed Elexia. "Three races working together to fix a problem caused by misunderstanding and stupidity."

"You *are* referring to your own kind...right?" questioned Sisillia,

"Yeah, a problem that *you* started," added Mearl.

"MEARL! Hold your tongue," I snapped. "What's done is done, we can't change what's happened to us. For all we know we're the only two left of our family, no, our Clan. We have to be strong and not fight new allies, no matter what they did or how they did it. For they've lost friends and family by our claws too, or have you forgotten?"

"What about Sisillia? She started it," growled Mearl angrily at me.

"It's okay, I deserve it. For it was my decision to attack in the first place with the knowledge I had attained. I didn't stop to think on it, I just acted.

I couldn't see clearly, you see. I've been fighting Dragons for so long that I…we didn't stop to consider what we were becoming, and what damage we were doing. Even the land has become our enemy. I'm truly sorry for what we have caused, I know you all might never forgive me. I will also understand if you treat us poorly and unfairly. It is what we deserve after all," explained Elexia with a tear falling form one of her eyes, and falling to splash on the ground.

After Elexia finished her little speech, we all just stared at her. None of us showed any emotions, for the simple reason that, we didn't know what to think or say. True, Elexia's speech made our mouths drop. We were all pretty much expecting a few curses and an insult or two for making her and her kind heal and treat all of our wounded before her own. But not the speech she gave. As we stared at Elexia, she hung her head low and started to turn away from us and walk away.

"Elexia, wait!" I hollered to her. "I have a question for you. Why do the Unicorns and Dragons hate each other? I asked this question to my parents once but they didn't know. So I figured I'd ask a Unicorn if I ever got the chance to. Now that I have the chance I'm asking."

Elexia turned her head and looked straight at me, our eyes locking together. "I do not know why our two races fought…fight with each other. The only one who would probably know the answer to your question would be the Great Oracle himself. Unfortunately, he only makes himself known if he finds something that intrigues him or if he thinks that there is someone of great importance to him that needs help. Also, he'll find you, you can't find him…you've seen him before haven't you?"

"Yes. Once when I was a little Whelp. I thought that I could fight and win against him. I was wrong," I answered.

"I see. Now if you'll excuse me. I've got some work that I have to do," Elexia mussed as she turned her head and walked away.

As we watched Elexia leave, I sent Mearl after her to go and apologize for letting her anger get the better of her. Mearl did as I asked but not without saying something to me that I'm not going to repeat. After Mearl left, Scythe decided to go back to his duties and see what he could do for improving the defenses of the encampment. That just left Sisillia and myself alone to do whatever we wanted to do. The two of us walked around seeing who needed or wanted help. Eventually Sisillia found work in helping out in the Food Den. After I roamed around a bit more, I decided to find Scythe and see if he could find out where these Enemy Dragons were located, and how much of a threat they were.

I eventually found Scythe, he was talking to a group of Chimera scouts about keeping an eye on the Unicorn camp that was made a short flight distance away from us. As I approached, all of the scouts save for Scythe looked up at me in awe and fear. I got a little chuckle out of it, for I didn't think I looked that frightening. But then again actions do speak louder then words. I was sure the scouts didn't want to upset me or else. I chuckled again at the thought.

"Scythe!" I hollered. "I would like to speak to you."

Scythe finally turned his head towards me and with a smile on his face, said a few words to the scouts. Then said something to me that made all of the scouts go pale. "WHAT? Can't you see I'm busy here?"

I laughed at the remark and the looks of the Chimera scout's faces. Then I got serious. "I would like for you to check out these Dragons that Elexia mentioned. If they are intent on killing everything in sight and anything that moves then consider them a threat that needs to be eliminated. If they seem to be peaceful and only fight defensively, then extend an invitation to them to join us. If the Unicorns capture you, tell them that you are friends with Elexia and give them a vivid description of her. If you end up getting captured by the Dragons, then kill everything in your path and escape."

"Very well, when I return, I will tell you of my encounters with the Dragons. Wait twenty days for me, if I do not return within that time, then look for one of my scouts by the name of Shadow Claw. He and four others will assist me in this task," replied Scythe.

When we finished talking, Scythe turned around and roared. A Chimeras' roar was a lot like a Dragons, but it wasn't deep like a Dragons, either way, it was an impressive sound. As soon as he finished five scouts appeared one at a time out of nowhere. Once they were all visible, Shadow Claw introduced himself to me. He looked exactly like Scythe in everyway with the exception of his fur being light brown and a dark green mane, with three scars going across his left eye. The other four Chimeras looked identical to one another. Light brown fur covered their bodies, with a lush black mane of hair. The only difference between the four Chimeras were their eyes. From right to left, the eye colours were watery blue, forest green, fire red, and dirt brown. After the meeting, the six Chimeras disappeared into the forest to complete their task that I had assigned them.

After the last scout left I went looking for Sisillia seeing as I had had twenty days of nothing to do but wait and give people orders. So I'd figured that I'd spend those twenty days with her. As I was looking for Sisillia, I walked into Elexia, literally. She told me that Mearl came and apologized for being stubborn and that made me smile. I told Elexia about my plan for the Enemy Dragons. I would see what they were like and how they acted before doing anything towards them. Elexia was happy to hear my plan and thought it was a good course of action. I said good bye to her after we finished talking and I continued my search for Sisillia. I eventually found Sisillia in the Smoke Den, helping to prepare for tonight's meal.

When Sisillia saw me, she stopped what she was doing and walked over to me. Once she got close enough to me, we kissed again. After we kissed we touched wings and strolled around the encampment or rather, the settlement that had formed over the past few days. We eventually ended up at my Den, I let Sisillia enter first, then I followed, once we were inside, we let nature take its' course. Twenty days was a long wait, but we could manage. After the twenty days had passed, Sisillia and myself emerged from my Den, both of us looked a little exhausted and our hair was a mess around our faces and backs. As we emerged, we were a little shocked to see Scythe and Shadow Claw waiting patiently fir us. Both of them were pretty beat up and had small cuts and bruises here and there. At the sight of the two Chimeras, both of us wondered how loud we really were and the thought made us both blush. But that didn't matter at the moment. I called for Mearl and Elexia to meet us in the Great Den. Once all six of us were in the Great Den, we listened intently to what Scythe and Shadow Claw had to say.

Chapter 6

Unexpected Enemies

"So you found a Lover and had *fun* with her. It makes me wonder who's more superior: dragons or Humans. We can choose our own mates, unlike you who just decide to fall in love with the one you see. Or in this case, saved," mocked Brak.

"*Shows how much you know Human. At least we don't go through great lengths and lots of precious valuables, just to impress the favored female,*" retorted Drakon.

"Guess I'll keep my mouth shut to that comment. For I like my head on my shoulders," exclaimed Brak.

"*Good idea,*" replied Drakon.

"Did you ever get back home to your Clan?" asked Brak.

"*Be patient. I haven't even finished the part of what happened to us in the foreign land. But don't worry, I'll tell you in time,*" reassured Drakon.

"Alright, continue with your tale then. I'll wait and listen," stated Brak.

Drakon bowed his head and continued on with his tale. "*Everyone either took up a seat or laid down on the warm floor of the meeting chamber in the Great Den. We all listened intently on what Scythe and Shadow Claw had to say, from their encounter with these "Enemy Dragons" that Elexia talked about.*"

* * *

"As we set off to find the other Dragons that have been warring with the Unicorns, we had encountered many rogue Unicorns and other threats. It took us ten long days and nights to find their settlement. We fought and ran every step of the way, for the rogue Unicorns didn't believe us, and the other threats were just as annoying. Accursed Basilisks. We mostly ran and flew though, because we didn't know what to expect when we got there," started Scythe.

"Anyway," continued Shadow Claw. "During our flight and fight, we lost one of our group members. We were ambushed once we thought it was safe to stop and take a break. Obviously we all thought wrong. After Blade fell our running and fighting started again. Eventually we fought them off and lost our enemies to the sky, we then continued with our task. A while later we came across the settlement, and we were completely taken aback from what we saw."

"The settlement was vast, it made the Chimera Kingdom look small in comparison. It had dozens of Dens that made our largest Dens in this settlement look small and insignificant. The Dens were constructed out of tress and branches. Aside from the large settlement, we couldn't believe what we saw taking place inside of it," explained Scythe. "Complete and utter chaos. There were huge Dragons fighting each other in death matches. And other large Dragons mating right out in the open. There were Dragons eating each other, and other pieces of we don't know what. The Dragons also had captured Unicorns and other forest creatures. Most of them were being tortured to death, not for information, but for fun."

"That wasn't the worst of it, for the Leader of the settlement was pleased to see this. He was enjoying the pain and suffering that was taking place in his settlement. As we watched all of this, we noticed that there were a lot of Dragons preparing for a large scale invasion, or war, we couldn't tell which."

"We didn't give up when we were captured either," added Shadow Claw. "We battled the Dragons. But our fight didn't last long, another one of our group members was killed and the rest of us were thrown into a small crudely built cage. After a day in the cage, the three of us were herded in front of the Leader. The Leader's name was Slash & Burn."

"Slash & Burn? I've heard of him," interrupted Sisillia. "He's a huge black Dragon with a blood red strip of spikes going from the tip of his head to the tip of his tail. His black wings can support him, which is a mystery for there are hundreds of holes in them. He has black claws and teeth to match his scales. He also has bright blood red eyes that can pierce a creature's soul. He was known by another name, which has been long forgotten. He managed to get this name for the ruthlessness towards his enemies and his disregard for his own Clan. From what I've been told he can get whatever he wants through deceit, deception, revenge, and he can hold a grudge against someone until he ends it."

"How interesting, now that we know who he is and what he can do. Why don't we let Scythe and Shadow Claw continue with their report," replied Mearl a little annoyed that Sisillia interrupted the Chimeras.

"Thank you," Scythe and Shadow Claw replied in unison. "Like we were saying, we were brought in front of Slash & Burn. He had asked us many questions, but we refused to say anything for we didn't want our recovering settlement to fall under attack again. In our refusal to answer his questions, Slash & Burn decided to tear apart our fourth party member and eat him right in front of us. Watching this filled us with rage that we didn't even know a Chimera could posses. Not caring on how many guards there were, both of us attacked Slash & Burn. Our attacks proved to be pointless, after quickly realizing this, we took to the sky, then dove into the foliage of the trees. We heard a very angry roar in the distance, but didn't stop to look. We didn't stop for anything this time, which made getting back here a lot faster. Do not worry though, both of us made sure that we weren't followed. For a Chimera has an innate ability to move abnormally fast if it doesn't want to be seen or caught, and it knows the location of where it's headed. As we left though, we saw the large army of Dragons take to the sky and fly off."

A concerned and worried look crossed Elexia's face. "Which direction did they fly off in?" asked Elexia.

"They were headed due east, as far as we could tell. Neither of us could really get a good look, on account we were fleeing for our lives. Why do you ask?" questioned Scythe.

"The Unicorn Palace is northeast of here, well very far northeast from here. But it's visible from the dry grassy plains that are in the lands east of here. It's heavily guarded, but if it is a large enough army that you've told us about, then the Unicorn Palace won't stand a chance. We must attack them *NOW* before they strike," explained and demanded Elexia.

"Hold on Elexia. We don't want to go rushing into this or burst into the Unicorn Palace. For everyone but the Unicorns would get killed off on the spot. Plus, we don't even have the numbers needed to be of any assistance to anyone. Even if there are those of us who are stronger and more powerful then others. It doesn't take that much to have two or six times our number, overwhelm us, and *kill* us. First thing we'll have to do is see if there are any more abandoned, exiled, or stranded Dragons out *there*. Not to mention the entire rogue Unicorn parties we'll have to befriend. Unless we want another repeat performance of our "first" encounter with each other. Also there are other threats in this foreign land that we'll have to consider avoiding or attacking. Like the local Dragons that are everywhere here, who don't like us, and don't want any part of joining our settlement. On top of that, there's the Gryphon and Hypogryph threat we'll have to contend with on the plains. Not too mention the fun loving Basilisks that we'll have to deal with as well. Frankly, I don't feel like having anymore needless deaths that can be avoided," I explained.

"Then what do *you* propose we do? Sit around? Mate with one another? Wait until our Younglings are born? Then do more waiting until they're ready to attack with us? Ignore this threat? Well? What do you say to that?" snapped and raged a very angry Elexia.

"It's very simple. You and Sisillia will take a group of our explorers and map out the surrounding area, up to Slash & Burn's settlement. Scythe and Shadow Claw will take a larger group than last time to keep an eye on Slash & Burn's settlement for any changes or anything suspicious, with a runner giving a report every quarter sun and moon movement. Mearl will take a small portion of the Defense Force, all of the food gatherers, and Hunters, and start stocking up on food for our movement to assault the enemy settlement. I will send our ambassadors with another small portion of the Defense Force to see how many creatures we'll be able to ask in joining us in the assault. I will remain here to train everyone on how to take down something bigger then they are. I will also train the newcomers as well. When we do attack, we won't bring the full might of the settlement, incase our battle ends in failure. This way, *if* we do loose, we'll be able to rebuild," I explained with a serious look on my face. "If we're going to do this, I would like to do this right, with as few deaths as possible."

After I finished my plan of action towards Slash & Burn, we all set off to do our respective tasks. When Scythe and Shadow Claw got established. I had reports coming in, at precisely every quarter sun and moon. I also had a runner from Sisillia and Elexia giving our Mapping Den a run for it's' valuables. For they were reporting in once every day and night with new information for our Mappers to add to our Map of the surrounding lands. I was also kept busy with training everyone, plus every newcomer that came to stay and join the fight. There were Dragons, Unicorns, and Chimeras coming in from the Great Dragon only knows where. We also had the odd Gryphon come and join us, but they never stayed for too long. Within twenty days, we had enough creatures and food to last us a full-scale war that could give Slash & Burn something to worry about. If he was expecting us that is, but I highly doubted it. We set off for the settlement on the twenty-fifth day. But instead of going in the direction that Scythe and Shadow Claw suggested, due east, we headed northeast until we're directly south of the settlement. Once it was in sight, everyone got into their mixed battle groups and readied ourselves for a battle that would leave most of us scarred, physically and mentally.

Chapter 7
All's Not Fair in Love and War

"I don't understand a few things Drakon," questioned Brak. "First of all, how can you hate something for generations, only to make peace with them and be friends with them later. Second, why did you fight amongst your own kind? Third, I thought a Dragons' enemy was every creature that wasn't a Dragon."

"*To answer your first question, is easy. Why do you write down everything a past enemy has done to you, if you've come to an agreement to stop fighting and become…companions? Not to make the same mistakes your ancestors did when you were at war with your companions. So we changed our views and opinions according to what our past mistakes have done, and taught us. I believe you Humans call it history. I could just as easily asked you: why does your own kind fight amongst themselves only to be companions later*," explained Drakon.

"I see your point. You fight for control and power, over your Clan and other Clans. But seeing as you have or rather had a different agenda you decided to make some changes to what you were taught. This is all very interesting, if I was a history teacher that is," responded Brak.

"*If you do not wish to learn what you wanted to learn then leave now. I have no interest in killing or eating a stupid Human. I'd rather leave that up to you. Your second question was answered with the explanation of the first question*," growled Drakon as he raised one of his massive clawed hands and pointed at the clave entrance.

"Well, duh," mocked Brak as he dove out of the way of another fireball that seemed to be bigger then the other one Drakon had let loose at him earlier.

Drakon snorted before continuing. "*Stupid Human. You are right though on us hating everything, for the simple fact that everything hates us in return. It has always been that way. Ever since the first Clan War started. But there are those of us who are willing to extend companionship towards one another and to other creatures. You however are still debatable. Are you satisfied with your answers? Or are you going to ask more simple minded questions?*"

"Yes. I'm satisfied with the answers you gave me. Although I still have many more questions that need to be answered. But I'm sure I'll get my answers. There's still my main question though that needs to be answered still: What happened to your kind and the many other mythical beasts that used to roam this land?" exclaimed Brak.

"*Heh, persistent little Human aren't you? In time you will know the answer. Until then, you'll just have to listen to my tale for your answer,*" replied Drakon.

"Alright, I'll listen and wait. Continue with your story," Brak admitted.

"*Very well,*" Drakon stated.

* * *

When we attacked Slash & Burn's settlement, they were caught completely off guard. But then there weren't that many Dragons there, we came to the conclusion that the large army had left to assault the Unicorn Palace. This made taking out the settlement all the more important. For we did not want any reinforcements coming at us from behind, and catching us off guard. Before we could worry about the army though, we had to empty our claws, paws, and hooves, of the matter at claw. When we encountered the *Enemy Dragons*, we realized that this wouldn't be an easy battle. For they were unnaturally strong, even if they were fighting on the defensive. As the fighting got under way, Scythe, Shadow Claw and a few others managed to slip away to the torture area and freed the prisoners. There weren't that many left that were alive, but those that were, desired to get some much needed revenge. With the extra help from the prisoners, it gave us an edge, for the *Enemy Dragons* weren't expecting anyone to still be alive. Even with this advantage we were loosing troops, healers, and scouts to the opposing force.

As the battle became long and difficult we had to go on the defensive for the *Enemy Dragons* were proving, that even outnumbered they could easily hold their own. That and their size made it difficult to take them down. They were massive, even for adult Dragons, and unfortunately, our Dragons mostly consisted of Youths, Drakes, and the odd Adult. But we refused to give up, for these butchers had to be stopped at all costs. They caused too much pain and suffering to the inhabitants of the lands, and the lands themselves. Not to mention it would be a great burden lifted from the Unicorns' and Chimeras' shoulders. Also the Unicorn Palace was depending on our victory over the *Enemy Dragon* settlement. If we failed, then there would be nothing to stop these murderers from destroying the rest of this beautiful foreign land. We could *NOT* loose, no matter the cost.

The battle lasted for thirty-five days and nights. Neither side was tiring or relaxing for if they did, then they would be open for attack. And that was something neither side could afford. It didn't matter anyway, everyone was either brimming with energy or hyped up on adrenaline. The reason for this, was no one had ever experienced this kind of thrill and battle in a long time. It was also the first real battle for some of the fighting creatures that joined in the battle. Besides sleep wasn't the only problem that both sides were having, there was also the problem of food. Everyone had been battling nonstop and we were all very hungry. Even though we brought a large supply of food we dared not stop to eat unless we wanted to give the opposing side a chance for victory. So to sum up our predicament, being hyped up on adrenaline or energy, we were starving up to the point that we could eat anything. Unfortunately the *Enemy Dragons* had us beat in cannibalism, but that didn't really bother us, we'd eat once this was over.

On the thirty-sixth day there were signs of the battle finally clawing to an end. The *Enemy Dragons* were tiring faster then we were. This was due to the fact that we were attacking form all sides and angles. Giving them no chance to retreat, the *Enemy Dragons* were forced to fight their way to a safe area. But once they thought they were safe, our scouts ambushed them. Also our reinforcements had finally arrived giving the already fighting factions a chance to rest and eat. This proved to be a huge advantage over Slash & Burn's Dragons. Seeing as their main army had left them behind, no one would be coming to save them. As our healers worked their gifts, we were finally whittling down the *Enemy Dragons*, to only a handful. We had the remaining Dragons surrounded on all sides and had control of the air so they could not escape. I flew down from the sky and landed in front of the battle captives.

"I have a proposition for you," I stated. "If you join us, we will not kill you. Also we will consider *not* killing you, if you answer some simple questions."

"Never," stated one of the *Enemy Dragons.*

"Elexia?" I asked.

"Consider it done," Elexia replied.

Elexia walked up to the captive Dragon that refused to cooperate, staring at the Dragon while she was walking towards him. When Elexia was a few paces away. She started to glow with a pitch black aura. As she glowed, Elexia lifted her head and as she did this all the blackness that surrounded her seemed to seep into her horn, turning it black as night. Then without warning Elexia brought her head down in a half circle, with her horn pointed at the Dragon. The Dragon then exploded into a flaming ball of fire. At the sight of this, the other captives were willing to talk. Although there were some who still refused. They however met with an unfortunate end by Mearl's, Scythe's, and Shadow Claw's brutality.

"First question," I stated. "Where did Slash & Burn go? Second Question, how long ago did he leave? Third question, what direction did he go in? Answer all three questions correctly and you'll get to live. Give a wrong answer and we'll decide to have some *fun* with you, like how you had some *fun* with our allies, and mates."

The remaining captives told us what we wanted to know. Slash & Burn *was* headed to the Unicorn Palace to deal with the threat of the Unicorns. This information had startled Elexia greatly for her fear had become a reality. What made it worse was that the army left fifteen days before our attack, which meant that they deceived our visual source, which made Scythe very angry for being fooled. The only good thing was that Slash &

Burn decided to take the long route to the Palace. For he thought that going north then east, would be the fastest way to go. Unlike Slash & Burn though we had knowledge on how to get there faster, and we had excellent scouts and explorers with us. Elexia knew the fastest way to the Unicorn Palace, she was born and raised there after all. With luck, we would end up intercepting Slash & Burn along the way. This was under the assumption though that we would leave this cursed settlement right now.

Unlike Slash &Burn who headed north then east, we headed due east across the plains. With any luck we'll hit the halfway point and be able to see Slash & Burn's forces. If we couldn't then we'll head northeast to intercept him at the Unicorn Palace Gates. If only it went as easily as it sounded at the time. Our war party ran into complications and problems with the locals. For we didn't expect that there would be little settlements of Basilisks that populated the border of the forest lands and the lands of the plains. The local Dragons also decided to attack us whenever we stopped to rest, which made it hard to reenergize ourselves. Eventually we did find Slash & Burn, but there was a problem, we had lost a little more then a quarter of our forces. The strike against Slash & Burn had to be planned carefully if we were to succeed in our goal. When we did attack Slash & Burn, we were expecting an easy victory. Seeing as he had made his army go through a long strenuous path to get to the Unicorn Palace that would've given him some losses, but we were wrong, not just wrong, but painfully wrong.

When our attack hit Slash & Burn's forces we attacked hard and fast. To keep him off guard. Unfortunately for us, Slash & Burn had been expecting an attack like this. If you are going to destroy everything in front of you on your way to a Palace, you're bound to call attention to yourself. All of us experienced great losses, the Dragons, the Chimeras, and the Unicorns. This battle was turning from meaning something to pointless. Everyone was loosing friends and family. It was on this day that my heart also shattered into pieces. For I witnessed Mearl die again, only this time she really did die. Slash & Burn decided to dive bomb her from above and rip her to pieces, one limb at a time. Her scream of pain and agony still rings in my head till this day. As I watched the horrific scene, I became so full of rage, to the point that I didn't care who or what was in my way. I was going to take down Slash & Burn, even if it was going to cost me my life. It wouldn't be nice and quick either, I was going to make Slash & Burn watch, as I tore him limb from limb. I do not know what it was called, for I know I was beyond what you *Humans* call Berserk, and Psychotic.

I challenged Slash & Burn to a fight to the death. It didn't matter whether I won or lost, as far as I was concerned my parents abandoned me and all of my siblings were dead. I did have Sisillia, but we had just met, and as far as I knew she would probably leave me for a more *worthy* and *suitable* lover to mate and have Hatchlings and Whelps with. I flew high into the air, and waited until Slash & Burn wasn't looking in my direction. Next, I folded my wings and dove at Slash & Burn. As I dove, I mustered all the energy I had and let loose a white-hot jet of fire at Slash & Burn, before I slammed into him. With the amount of force I was traveling at, I tore into and through Slash & Burn's body. When I exited, I flared my wings, turned, and launched myself at Slash & Burn tearing into him at his mortal wound that I caused him. Due to my size, I was too small, to have any fatal blow dealt to me, also where I was, didn't help Slash & Burn at all. As I bit, slashed, clawed, and blew fire. I could hear Slash & Burn cry out in pain. I found his pain to be very pleasing and relaxing for Slash & Burn was getting a death that he wasn't planning for.

In the end of my battle, I won and Slash & Burn was dead and in pieces. I didn't win without a scratch though, I had plenty all over me, including burn marks, and a broken bone or two. I didn't care for my well being at the moment though, I had won, and that's what mattered. I flew down to the now scarred land, which was now marked as a permanent battlefield. As soon as I landed on the scarred earth, I started to weep. I wept for all of the friends and family that were now lost to us. I also wept for the loss of the last of my siblings, dying again by the claws of war. I had also wept for all the other Dragons that had been abandoned by their parents to live *here*. As I cried my tears reflected the scene of war going on around me, sure we were winning now that Slash & Burn was dead, but this victory seemed pointless and hollow.

"Drakon why are you crying? You should be celebrating, we won. You should be overwhelmed with joy, that the Unicorn Palace is safe," exclaimed Elexia joyfully as she jumped in the air and landed softly.

"Overwhelmed with *JOY*? Why should I be? I am now *alone.* All of my siblings are *gone. Dead.* My mother and Father all but abandoned us... me here, in this "Great Dragon" forsaken land. What we've worked so hard to gain has nearly been destroyed with over half our troops...no, our people *dead.* And *you* expect me to be overwhelmed with *JOY*?" I raged.

"We have healers Drakon. Remember, they can revive our fallen comrades, and family, from the dead and save those who are in need of healing. So there's no need to worry, they'll be fine. You aren't alone either Drakon, for you have me and I have you," pleaded and soothed Sisillia as she made her way to me and tried to kiss me.

"That still won't bring back my siblings, which have been crushed into pulp, left at the bottom of lakes, burned to ashes, and torn apart. And as for you and I, how do I know if you'll stay with me, and not going off to some other *Dragon*? Yes we saved each others life, yes we mated, but we both know that that doesn't mean anything. For we're *Dragons*, we only love one another when it suits us. Then like the *Dragons* we are, we leave each other and move on to the next opportunity," I snarled as I pulled my head away from Sisillia.

Before *anyone* could say anything, I jumped into the air beat my wings, and then took off. I didn't bother to answer or listen to the pleas that Sisillia made. I wanted to clear my head and think things through. I decided to go to the one place where I knew I could be alone with my thoughts. The only problem was, it contained painful memories, even if they were somewhat happy memories. They would still be painful. I flew to my camp that I had made when I first arrived in this foreign land. Once I landed, I walked into my Den, and laid down. My Den was a little small, but then again I wasn't *that* small anymore. I lit the awaiting pile of wood on fire to give me some light and too think for it was nightfall on whatever number of day it was. I hoped that no one had followed me for I was in no mood to talk or to Share my feelings and thoughts.

Chapter 8

It's About Time

"That must've been devastating for you. To loose all of your siblings like that, and to have your parents make you go through a suicidal *Test.* Then not even coming back for you. I envy you," Brak exclaimed while he inclined his head.

"*Actually, I liked watching my siblings die or coming across their cold dead bodies. And as for my parents abandoning me, well I was overjoyed. For the first time I was on my own...WHAT DO YOU THINK? Of course I was devastated. For all I knew I was the last of my entire Clan...an Orphan,*" roared Drakon who was on the brink of lashing out and killing Brak.

"*Okay*, I shouldn't have said anything, incase it might upset you," Brak pleaded defensively to save his skin. "My bad, I'll make sure I won't do it again."

"*Yes, you shouldn't have said anything,*" growled Drakon as he clamed himself down.

"Obviously you got off the foreign land and ended up back here I take it. I guess the next question I have is: how?" surmised Brak.

"*Be patient, and I'll tell you. In time of course,*" soothed Drakon. "*Until then, I'll continue with my tale.*"

* * *

A year or two later, I finally calmed down, from my outburst to everyone. As I calmed down, I started to feel bad for the way I acted to everyone, like a Dragon. Scythe had shown up from out of nowhere, and he looked tired. I guess he had some trouble in finding me. Seeing him though, didn't surprise me in the least, for I knew how good of a tracker he was. It also didn't surprise me that he had come alone. I was outside of my Den so he didn't have to look around for me.

"I've finally found you," breathed Scythe.

"What do you want?" I snapped, for I might have been calm, but not calm enough.

"To talk," Scythe answered.

"To talk? There's no guarantee that I'll listen to you though," I snarled.

"Your parents are here, and they want to see you. We kind of...guessed on where you might have gone when you stormed off, but we neglected to tell your parents. Just incase we were wrong. That and we wanted to give you some space to let off some smoke...anger. Although seeing as you are here, we didn't guess wrong," explained Scythe. "If you do not wish to return to the settlement, then that is understandable. But there is also someone there who claims she has a gift for you and only you."

"Who is *she*? And what is this *gift* that *she* offers me?" I asked somewhat intrigued but also annoyed.

"*She* is the Queen of the Unicorn Palace that *you*, decided to save to honor Elexia. The *gift* that the Queen offers you, is a *Phoenix*. The Phoenix is supposed to have the gift to grant wishes. The only catch is that it can only grant *one* wish every one hundred years," answered Scythe.

"Why give this wishing creature to me? The Unicorns seemed to have lost more then I have. Also, what use would a bird born of fire be to me?" I mussed.

"You'll have to ask her yourself. Also, Sisillia misses you greatly. I guess you were wrong about her finding a new *suitable* mate after you left. Heh, *and*, whatever it was the two of you did in *that* Den of yours must've left a mark on her. Anyway, Elexia also misses you for some reason. I guess she has grown attached to you and your leadership. You did make an impression on the Unicorns after all. Shadow Claw and myself also miss having you around to make things interesting, that and we miss you scaring our scouts. I guess that's what companions...no...*friends* do when one of them leaves for a period of time. In your case though, a year or two, but who's counting. Come to think of it, everyone misses you, and no, this is not a ploy to convince you to come back. Also being gone for over a year, kind of worried us a little bit. So, will you come back to the settlement? Or will I have to go back *alone*?" exclaimed Scythe.

I threw up my claws and wings in surrender. "Fine. I'll come back with you, as long as you stop getting so sentimental on me. You're a Chimera for Great Dragon fang's sake."

Scythe and myself flew back to the settlement, for we...I didn't want to worry everyone any longer. As we got closer to the border of our land that we claimed as our own, I noticed the silence. All of the animals and creatures had stopped their beautiful sounds, music, and conversations, which worried me. For there were always sounds in, by, and around our settlement. I was so concerned with the lack of sound that I flew to the ground and took a couple of long sniffs of the air. What I smelled was fear, and I sensed anger as well. I knew that something was terribly wrong, so I leapt into the air and flew as fast as I could to the settlement, with Scythe trailing not too far behind. We arrived at the settlement just in time by the looks of it. For Mother, Father, and about three hundred and sixty some-odd Adult Dragons were preparing to assault our settlement. I guess that none of the Adults liked the idea of Dragons, Unicorns, and Chimeras working together.

"*STOP!*" I roared. "I do not want to see anymore blood spilled and friends and family *DEAD*."

Scythe and myself landed by Sisillia, Elexia, Shadow Claw, and the rest of the Survivalists who were all grouped together. I turned my head from side to side to take in my surroundings. What looked like the Unicorn Queen and her very large contingent of Royal Guards were on the right side of the settlement. While Mother, Father, and the rest of the Adults were all on the left side of the settlement. Putting us *right* in the middle, *again*. Only this time I was in no mood to make this land suffer the same fate as the Plains had. It also looked like the Unicorns wanted to make a show of their status, for the Unicorn Guards were, unique. The Unicorn Royal Guards were all covered in black hair, by the looks of them, the only things that weren't black, were their eyes, and horns. All of the guards also had a diamond patch on their heads that was either, light blue, yellow, or white. All of their eyes were amber in colour, which mismatched with their dark blue horns.

Aside from the Unicorn Royal Guard, the Queen of the Unicorns was beautiful beyond Unicorn standards. Her beautiful snow-white hair sparkled when the sun shone over and on it. In the moonlight however, her hair would turn from snow-white to a lush silver colour that would also sparkle. The Queen Unicorn's mane of long soft yellow hair flowed from the back of her head, down her neck, and ended at her shoulders. Her horn was a unique colour like her Royal Guards. Only in this case, it was a light sky blue coloured that seemed to glow when you starred at it. The Queen Unicorn's deep dark blue eyes almost matched her dark brown hooves.

"Mother, Father," I started. "You both *Finally* show up after what? A few hundred days, or is it years? I've lost track, it's been so long. I was starting to wonder if you truly did abandon me or if you just didn't care about me anymore. If you are wondering, or even care, I'm the only one left of your *Test* that you decided to put us through. Also you can plainly see that I've made new allies, and created a settlement for those who were abandoned and exiled. Or shall I say, "The Survivalists". Oh, and I survived the first seventy days of a "Dragon's Wrath" without using my wings."

"Please let us explain why we're so late in coming for you...all of you," pleaded Mother.

"First, tell your war force of *Adults* to stand down. The same goes to you, *your Highness*. Survivalists, please stand down as well. I know we're stuck in the middle *again*, but at least we'll have the upper claw this time. Scythe, Elexia call your scouts out from hiding please," I ordered. "Now that that's done, lets get down to business. Mother, Father, why did you decide to try and kill my siblings and myself? Second, why are you so late? And third, *Love* the welcome home party."

"Let me explain," started Father. "We were on our way to come and get you, when we ran into a problem that couldn't be ignored."

"Squirrel Nuts," I interrupted.

"That problem was a rival Clan, that was on its' way here to reinforce their settlement that they decided to start building over here in these lands. So we intercepted them. There was a long and lengthy battle that lasted for days. Eventually, we won, but not without taking some losses. After the battle, we resumed the search for you and all of the others that were left here to fend for themselves. But The Elders had summoned us for a new task, that we weren't thrilled at," finished Father.

"So instead of coming to get us, all of us, *you* just turn around and headed home to see what "*The Elders*" wanted. Knowing the way home of course, for we would have left on our own accord if it weren't for two small reasons. The first is *you* Father, crippling our wings so we couldn't fly. The second is that both of *you* decided to leave us in unfamiliar territory. So even if we did have our wings, there'd be no way to know where "home" was," I stated.

"You know that whatever The Elders say, we must do. For they are the Leaders of our joined Clans," replied Mother.

"*So*, you chose the word of the blow hard *Old Lizards*, instead of coming to our aid and rescue. At least I can blame *you*, for the deaths of my siblings and friends," I snapped.

"Hold your tongue," roared Father. Don't speak ill of The Elders!"

"*You* may be my Parents, and The Elders *may* be in charge at home…wherever that is. But here in this land…this area…this settlement, *you* are the guests, while *we* are the hosts. Do *not* dare tell me what I can and can't do or say. If *you* even *think* of attacking us, you'll be struck down for the combined might of our settlement, the Unicorn Palace, and the Chimeras," I growled.

"You dare threaten us? we are bigger, stronger, faster, and older then you. *Pathetic Youth.* As for the Unicorns, and Chimeras, we use Chimeras for food. Taking down a Unicorn is nothing special either," snapped an Adult Dragon.

"You think we are *weak*? You are sadly mistaken," stated the Queen Unicorn. "We've beaten you in the past. What makes you think we can't do it again?"

"And if you think that we are *weak*, then you are painfully wrong. We are much smarter, faster, and stronger then our cousins in *your* lands also one of my scouts has brought the full might of the Chimera Kingdom here, just try us," added Scythe.

"Also the rogue Dragons that inhabit this land will fight against you as well. For they have witnessed the war between Slash & Burn, and the Survivalists, and have pledged allegiance with us if there is another threat that arises. Not to scare you, but they're much closer then you think," finished Sisillia with ice in her voice.

"The choice is yours, you can attack and loose, or you can leave in peace. Bear in mind, that there are also Gryphons flying close by, and they're eager for Dragon blood. Those of us who decide to go with you to see The Elders will come with you, I assume they wish to speak with us," I stated.

"The Elders will not be pleased with this," replied Mother.

"If they aren't pleased, then they can tell me in person. Until then, those are my terms. So make your choice, and the Survivalists will make theirs," I growled.

"Very well, we'll leave you in peace. But be warned. The Elders won't be happy with this, and don't blame us if they come in force and destroy your precious settlement," responded Father.

"Why would they do that?" I questioned.

"It's simple, to prove that they are more powerful than you. Also, because they can," answered Mother.

"Hmm, I guess I'll just have to talk to them about that, for I'm coming with you," I mussed.

After the exiled, and abandoned Dragons decided on whether they wanted to go, or stay we set off for home. The journey was long and boring, just like the journey to my abandonment. I smiled at the irony, for it amused me, that, and I had nothing else to think about at the moment. After we *finally* landed, The Elder's High Guards were waiting for us to escort us to The Elders. The High Guards were all massive sized Dragons that almost made Father look small. Their scales ranged in colour from black to gold, and no Dragon had the same scale colour. The High Guards all had short cut hair that ranged in colour and flowed from the back of their heads to the ends of their long necks. Their eyes were also a mix and range of colours ranging from bright red to a dull grey.

By the looks of everything, nothing changed, it was all the same boring wasteland that The Elders claimed as their own. On the plus side, we were lead to a place that none of the Survivalists had been to before, which was kind of exciting. As we entered the place I took note of the beautiful lights and colours that seemed to be everywhere. As I was looking around I noticed five very large and dark figures enter the wondrous place. But I didn't see how they could've entered, for there was only one-way in and out. Then without warning five pairs of glowing eyes stared at all of us.

"Why have you come to speak with us? Answer!" stated the eyes.

"We have brought the survivors of *The Test*," answered Father.

"There are so few of them. Why is that? Answer!" stated the eyes again.

"The reason is quite simple and obvious. A good portion of the "*Survivalists*" didn't survive the nice hard impact to the ground. Also there were the fun loving locals to deal with, good times there. Oh, and there were also those of us *Survivors*, who didn't feel like coming to speak with you," I mocked.

"Drakon!" snapped Mother.

"Let him speak *Fire Storm*. The same goes for you *Sharp Claw*," the eyes stated *again*.

"Yes Elders. We will be silent from now on, unless you request it," bowed Mother and Father in unison.

"Explain yourself Young One. Why have some survivors come back and not all of them?" demanded the eyes.

"No! I will *not* explain our reasons for coming or staying behind. Those that stayed have their own reasons, those that came have *their* own reasons. We don't have to explain why, to *you*, or anyone else." I growled.

"Bold statement Young One. We see why you have been selected to be the Leader of *your* settlement. Also we can see that you are favored among your allies as well," commented the eyes.

"If *you* think that was *Bold*, then you'll love what I have to say next," I mocked.

"You wish for these pointless *Tests* of ours to stop. For they are doing nothing but killing off our Whelps and Youths, which is doing serious harm to this Clan, and any of the other allied Clans. That are doing the same thing," answered the eyes.

"*That* is exactly what I was going to say. It must be nice to have the gift of reading other creatures thoughts. But there is also something you left out. We would like to be left in peace. Also, anyone who is willing to come back with us, can," I mocked, and stated.

"Very well. You and your Survivalists will be left in peace, and those who wish to join you in your return trip can. But be forewarned, other Clans will try to attack you, to gain control of your settlement. Also *you* will be called upon if *we* need assistance with something," declared the eyes.

"I will consider helping you, if and when the time comes. For the simple fact that, *you* considered to come and *save* us. As for the threat of the other Clans attacking us, we took down Slash & Burn. And if my sources are correct, not even *you* could accomplish *that.* The other survivalists and I will be leaving you now to go home," I stood up from where I had laid down when the Elders arrived, and started walking out.

"WAIT!" shouted the eyes.

I stopped and turned around to the five faces that were now visible, simply put, ugly.

"You may think that you are strong with your allies, but you are nothing compared to *US*! you *will* do as we say or you'll be faced with another long bloody war that we know you do not wish to have," hissed The Elders.

"I may be young, but I'm not *stupid.* Your threats do not scare me. You maybe in command of five Clans out of the many that like to battle you. But last I checked, I was allied with a Palace of Unicorns, and a Kingdom of Chimeras. As far as I know, we're equal in strength and power. You do *not* threaten me," I roared before turning my tail to The Elders and walked out.

As I walked out, I heard The Elders talking to my parents about how I could show great promise in the future. I heard lots of footsteps behind me, so I turned my head to see that the rest of the Survivalists were right behind me. I guess they didn't have anything nice to say to The Elders or the just didn't want to speak with them. We waited to see who would join us to go to our home…our new home. After about a quarter turn of the sun, the Survivalists took to the air, and headed back to our awaiting friends. They would be interested in hearing what The Elders said and what I said to them.

Chapter 9

War Between Survivalist and Clan

"I take it no one was thrilled when you told them that your allied Clans or a neighbouring Clan could attack anytime," exclaimed Brak.

"*No, they didn't like what I had to say. But The Elders gave us plenty of time to prepare for war,*" replied Drakon.

"What did you wish for with that Phoenix of yours?" pried Brak.

"*I had wished for one of my siblings to be brought back to life as she once looked before she died. To be more specific, I asked for: Claire, to be revived,*" replied Drakon as he looked away to blink back tears.

"Why did you just ask for one of your siblings to be brought back? Why not all of them? Or wish that everyone who died pointlessly and needlessly to be revived?" questioned Brak. "Also, why did you bring back Claire, instead of Mearl? I thought you *liked* her? Plus what happened to the Phoenix after you made the wish, and what happened to the Unicorns and Chimeras?"

"*So many questions, and from a Sorcerer no less. I could almost mistake you for a Historian. I thought Sorcerers were supposed to be extremely smart and knowledgeable in their studies, or was that wizards?*" mocked Drakon.

"Very funny," stated Brak sarcastically.

"*I thought it was. I will answer all of your questions with one answer. This answer should sound very familiar to you as well. The answer is: be patient and all answers will be made clear to you,*" explained Drakon.

"By the way, Sorcerers are very knowledgeable, and extremely smart. We just aren't perfect," responded Brak with a shrug.

"*Yeah right. I will skip a head to my young adulthood. I guess that would have made me twenty Human years old, in your Human timeline of "certain age groups". but in actuality I was, seven hundred Human years old. and no, that doesn't make me old. I was also a Drake now, capable of making their own choices whether they are good or bad. Of course I was already making my own choices, and mistakes. I guess I will tell you that I brought back Claire because she, like me, had a gift. Hers was to heal herself and others,*" explained Drakon.

* * *

Our settlement had grown to what you Humans call a city, I guess it could also be considered a kingdom, but there was no castle or palace. We had struck up trade with the Unicorn Palace and the Chimera Kingdom. The Survivalists also traded with the locals of the land. We traded things like food, knowledge, and other supplies that would benefit various creatures and animals. Our defenses had grown and improved with more troops, and new kinds of traps. There was also an increase of healers, hunters, and food gatherers. Plus we had teachers to teach us on how to use and harness mystical energy, and how to use our gifts properly. There were also teachers that taught the Young Ones (that were now appearing in our city) on how to hunt, fight, and how to gather food for others and themselves. But most importantly, we had teachers to instruct us in the ways of exploration, and healing. Our city was called: Salvation, for any abandoned or exiled Dragon, Chimera, Unicorn, or any other creature, could make a home with us. making a language for everyone to speak though was difficult at first, but with the Unicorns, Chimeras, and the aid of my gift, we managed to create one.

Salvation consisted of many different factions and the layout of the city was a little confusing, for those who where new to it. we had to create more Dens, besides the Great Den, the Smoke Den, the Food Den, the Healing Den, and the Mapping Den, to accommodate everyone's needs. There were also those of us who only wanted to join certain Dens and only work for them, for the tasks would suit us. the Exploration Den, the

War Den, the Dining Den, the Mystics Den, the Ambassador Den, and the Teaching Den were created for this purpose. We had to make at least three massive Dens for each faction, for the simple fact that the average Adult Dragon sized Den was just too small. We also added Living Dens, and Defense Dens. Each of the massive Dens, were about five Drags tall, or what you Humans call stories. Save for the Teaching Den, which was ten Drags tall. Defense Dens were small single creature Dens that the War Den used incase of an attack or an emergency. The creatures that looked down on Salvation, or looked from afar were amazed at its beauty, and love for the surrounding forest. Even though we had large and small Dens made from trees and other various things, the rest of the forest and land was untouched, unless you counted on where we made our paths from each Den.

All of the *Leaders* that helped with Salvation's creation, and who fought beside me in the battle with Slash & Burn were in charge of the separate factions. This also made it easy to understand each other without having to speak with the universal language. Scythe and Shadow Claw were in charge of the defenses of Salvation, for that was what they were they were unmatched when it came to combat and defending. They ran the War Den and taught simple, and complex combat skills at the Teaching Den. Maya, Zack, Elexia, and Claire, were in charge of healing, enchantment, mystic, and gift casting, for that was what they were unmatched in. Maya and Zack ran the Healing Den for no one not even the most skilled Unicorn could match their healing abilities. Elexia however ran the Mystic Den for she had a vast knowledge of the mystical energies of the lands and knew more then enough enchantments and gifts. This left Claire to teach everything, healing, mystical, and gift casting at the Teaching Den.

It might've seemed like Claire had her work clawed out for her, but she was glad to be kept busy all the time. Especially after what I told her what happened after she died, to keep her happy though I always made fun that she was the younger one now and needed all of the attention. Sisillia was in charge of all the trade, and food import and exports that went on in Salvation. This also meant she was in charge of the Smoke Den, Hunting Den, and the Food Den. With all of the work that Sisillia did, she taught at the Dens instead of at the Teaching Den. Lastly I was left in charge of the Mapping Den, the Exploration Den, the Ambassador Den, and I was also given charge of the Great Den. I might not have looked it but I was the best suited for these Dens for not only did I have the gift to understand anything that breathed. But I also had a gift to remember any and everything, which was extremely rare for Dragons. Even though Dragons can remember a great deal of things, their memories like every other creatures dulls in time, but I could remember everything up till I broke out of my shell, clearly.

All of us would gather in the Great Den once every few days unless there was something important to discuss. We would talk of recent events going on in Salvation: problems, business, findings, teachings, growth, and the usual. Everything usually went smoothly, unless there was a confrontation with some of the hostile locals, or a Clan of Dragons from overseas or across the lands come to destroy us. Sadly, every ten years or so, there would be a mass army of Adult Dragons, or a mass force of Basilisks that would try to destroy us, but we would always prevail. This meeting though, was important for The Elders were preparing to assault a "supposedly" small, weak, neighbouring Clan. The reason would be to get rid of the minor threat and to expand the Allied Clan's lands. We weren't impressed by this act of selfishness. According to our sources overseas, there was a messenger sent to ask for our help. This gave us time to talk and prepare what we had to say to the messenger, and for the upcoming war. When he did finally show up, we had made up our minds and I would be the one to tell him of our decisions.

The Messenger was a Drake like me, only he was large for his age. But the way he was built, that didn't really matter, for he was muscular to say the least. The Messenger was covered in brilliant purple scales, which made him look out of place. His jet black hair flowed from the top of his head down to where his wings met on his back. The Messenger's eyes were a soft yellow, and he had long black claws, with bone white teeth. The strange thing about the Messengers' colours, was, that they seemed to match perfectly, save for his bone white teeth.

"I bring you a message from The Elders," stated the Messenger. "The Elders request your assistance in fighting a rival Clan for territory that is rightfully ours. Will you assist us or not? Bear in mind that if you refuse, you'll all be considered an enemy of The Elders and will be destroyed."

"Let me think...no! we will *not* help The Elders, for we have no quarrel with this "rival" Clan of yours. So, why should we fight them? Tell The Elders that we're not interested," I answered.

"*YOU*! Refuse The Elders summons?" questioned the Messenger.

"Eh," I shrugged. "Call me old fashioned."

"All of you will be sorry for this. The Elders will not be pleased with your answer. Be prepared to *die* fools," remarked the Messenger.

"We'll see about that now, won't we?" I mocked.

When the Messenger left, we continued with our preparations for the upcoming war that was about to take place. New traps were being created and tried, enchantments, and gifts, both protective and deadly were being cast and recast. Also, the Unicorns made it a top priority to teach those who didn't have a gift of their own, or know how to wield mystical energy. We wanted as much of an advantage against The Elders as possible. Even the Healers were being taught deadly spells to confuse the enemy if they decided to attack the Healers. Only those of us who were experienced enough or had mastered the mystical energies were allowed to learn "the forbidden" cast. This cast was something the Chimeras had developed before they realized its' power and stopped learning enchantments and mystical energy completely. This of course was fifty thousand years ago. The enchantment is known as reanimation in the *Human* tongue, but was known to us as *Drags Curse*. This enchantment allowed the caster to bring the dead back to life, but not as a Healer could revive someone. For the dead stayed dead save for the fact that it could move and do what it was told, it was also only "alive" for a short amount of time. Unless the caster was killed, then the reanimated corpse would go back into eternal slumber or continue to walk the lands of the living. Also, the creature that was reanimated only had one impulse: to kill the thing that killed it. the enchantment was dangerous for the reanimated creature could easily turn on its caster and kill them at any given time.

Sisillia did her best to gather as much food and prepare it as well for everyone. She had enlisted the aid of the War Den to help her and her Dens out. In turn, Scythe and Shadow Claw lent half of the War Den's services to Sisillia, and her Hunters and Gatherers. Of course the War Den's occupants could only aid Sisillia for a small amount of time for they were kept extremely busy with their own things to do. We all agreed that it would be better to stock pile on all types of food now, then when there would be nothing left when the fighting started. After a months time we had enough food that could last us three large scale wars. This also meant that no one would go out hunting or gathering until the up-coming war was fought. For we had killed off almost all of the wildlife in and around Salvation. So the animals and creatures needed their time to replenish their numbers.

Another seven days later, The Elders made their move. Our sources overseas informed us that there were five large armies being deployed from the Allied Clans lands. Two of the armies were headed to the rival Clan to utterly destroy them, while the other three were headed to us. We were ready for them, with all of our preparations we did, we could be ready. I knew it would be a challenge for us, for the simple fact that my parents were with The Elders, and from what I learned they were both The Elders chosen Champions. Our sources also told us that there were at least thirty five hundred Dragons on their way here, on the plus side of things, this war would be an interesting one. If we succeeded in defeating The Elders and their armies, there would finally be peace, or so I hoped.

Roughly forty days later the Allied Clans came clawing at our borders. All five Elders were there as well. My guess was that they wanted to see the look on my face when they destroyed everything, too bad they wouldn't get their chance. When The Elders arrived at our borders, they had *demanded* to speak with the Leaders of Salvation. I had asked the Queen of the Unicorns: Queen Callista, and the Chief of the Chimeras: Slasher, if they could come to the *audience* with The Elders. We had agreed to meet The Elders in a private location of our choosing to discuss the terms of our "disobedience". In other words, they wanted to see how they could punish us for not doing their dirty work for them. The fifteen of us met in a clearing some four hundred kilometers away from Salvation. We had scouts spread out throughout the surrounding area, incase The Elders decided to call reinforcements.

"First of all," Started The Elders in unison. "Call off your scouts, for this is a *private* meeting."

"The scouts stay, where they are. For we don't want any unexpected company, do

we? Plus if we speak in our native tongue, they won't be able to understand what we are saying save for the creatures you see here that have been taught our language," I stated.

"*Also, our lands our rules. Sound familiar, doesn't it?*" Claire added.

"*Fair enough. We would like to discuss your disobedience and what we're going to do about it,*" stated The Elders in unison.

"*There is nothing to discuss. You asked for our help, or rather, you demanded it, and we said no. The reason why I declined is simple to explain. I didn't think attacking a Clan that we had no quarrel with, was a smart idea. Plus, I didn't feel like being Dragon chow, while you sat back and watched with a view of our demise,*" I explained. "*So if you're going to attack us, then do so. Otherwise I don't see the need to continue this lovely little chat.*"

"*You DARE speak to us like you are more powerful then us? You will pay for your transgressions. We have more then enough power here to incinerate you and your allies. So don't think for a moment Drakon, that you have more power than the five of us,*" roared The Elders in unison again.

"*I don't have the power to defeat you... but we do. And if you Old Lizards think that you can destroy all of what we worked so hard to achieve, you're sadly mistaken. Your armies can attack us if they wish, but you five won't be joining them,*" I stated coldly.

After I finished, my party ganged up on The Elders to take them down permanently, for they had ruled with their tyranny for long enough. Even if one or all of them had the gift to read minds, the look on all of their faces when we attacked them first, told us that they didn't expect *this* to happen. With The Elders caught with their defenses down it made it easier for us, even though their gifts made them formidable. We also proved to The Elders in our battle of teeth, claw, horn, and hoof, that the ten of us allied together as Chimera, Unicorn, and Dragon could easily outmatch and out power five Dragons. For we did not even call the scouts we had placed for aid when we battled The Elders. This was another shock to The Elders. But as our battle with The Elders stretched on we were unaware that The Elders gave the order to attack Salvation, the Unicorn Palace, and the Chimera Kingdom. Even in their last moments, The Elders played us for fools by being underhanded and cunning. We cursed their cold dead bodies after we won the fight, and ourselves for this predicament. We then raced to the battles in hopes of not encountering too much destruction, disorder, and loss.

Chapter 10

Victory Means Nothing, Except Pain

"So you killed The Elders, and that cost you the first strike, interesting," mussed Brak.

"*It was an error worth taking. For with no Leaders to control the armies, they were easier to defeat. But we still had our set backs,*" explained Drakon.

"In other words, you and your allies lost more than you thought you would," stated Brak.

"*That's true, we did loose more then we bargained for. It didn't matter, for the war that was waged, spread and changed our history bringing about our own demise. Of course we didn't know it at the time. Are you hungry? I am,*" replied Drakon

"I... What?" exclaimed a confused Brak.

Drakon stood up and stretched his stiff muscles. For he had been lying on the cold cave floor for far too long. It was mealtime anyway, so what better way to stretch the old muscles then to catch your own food. As Drakon walked to the entrance he turned his head to look at Brak.

"*What would you like to eat? I prefer cow myself, roasted of course. Bu if you're interested in something else let me know now before I leave,*" asked Drakon.

"...Say what?" exclaimed Brak who was still confused. "How are you going to get a cow while it's still light out? Never mind, I don't want to know. Yeah, cow is fine."

Brak stood up and brushed the dust off of his nice blue robe, but couldn't do anything to get the dust off of his nice black tunic, and black pants. He tried a few more times, then shrugged his shoulders and walked over to where Drakon was still waiting for him. As the two of them walked outside, both of them stopped for the moment to take in the view. The sun was setting behind the lush green grassy hills, and lighting up the few big puffy clouds in vibrant colours. These colours consisted of orange, pink, purple, yellow, and red. Both of them thought that the sky looked beautiful. After the moment passed, Drakon spread his large dark red wings that looked like a dream with the sun reflecting the colours onto them. With a few beats of his wings, Drakon was airborne, and heading to the nearest farm to catch and eat a cow, or two. Brak cast a speed spell on himself so he could keep up with Drakon, for Brak was interested on how Drakon would get away with this. Even though he wasn't particularly fond of seeing a Dragon feast, the thought still intrigued him. Although Brak had a huge amount of extra speed, he didn't seem to be fast enough to keep up with Drakon, which didn't bother Brak in the least.

When Brak finally caught up with Drakon, he found the Dragon circling a large herd of cattle. Drakon was just high enough not too be seen or smelt by the cattle on the ground. After three large circles, Drakon dove into the unsuspecting herd. He managed to grab two cows before they all went running for their lives. Drakon then flew into the air with the two cows. The next thing Drakon did, amazed Brak. Drakon threw the two helpless cows into the air, and before they started their decent, Drakon let out a huge plume of fire that roasted the cows instantly. On the humane side of things, the cows didn't suffer…much. Drakon then caught the roasted meat and flew back to his cave and waited for Brak to return. The whole episode lasted only a few minutes at the most, and the herd of cattle had settled down and resumed what they were doing. No one would ever be able to tell that two cows mysteriously disappeared, Brak was impressed.

When Brak finally got back to the cave, he saw that Drakon had a fire going to warm the cave. Brak was a little puzzled though for he didn't see any large or small pile of wood in the cave when he cast his light spell. Brak made a mental note though, that some Dragons were a lot smarter then they let on, which was to be a given of course. As Brak entered the cave, he saw a huge chunk of what was left of one of the two roasted cows lying beside the fire. The chunk of meat was neatly sliced, almost like a sharp sword cut it. Brak made another mental note that a Dragon's claws were extremely sharp. Brak smiled at himself for he already knew about the two mental notes from his previous experiences with Dragons. Brak touched the large scar on his cheek, in remembrance, as he walked up to the chunk of meat. Brak then sat down, took out his small dagger, which was hanging by his black pouch, but the folds of his pants concealed it. Brak looked over his dagger, to see if it needed to be polished or cleaned. The daggers' steel blade was about twelve inches long, and extremely sharp. Its' hilt was made out of solid gold, but it was discoloured to look like cheap brass. Brak flipped the dagger in the air, caught it, and then cut into his supper, tomorrows breakfast, and possibly tomorrow's lunch.

"Not too bad, for a completely roasted cow. I'll have to write down the recipe. Hmm, Dragon's fire, got it. Could use some spices though," commented Brak as he stuffed his mouth full of cow.

"*It will do for now*," replied Drakon with a yawn.

"Well, now that we've had something to feast on, I'm eager to get back to your tale of the rest of this *new* war of yours between the Survivalists and the Clans," Brak exclaimed.

"*Very well, I'll continue on with my tale*," started Drakon. "*Better not fall asleep on me, otherwise I might just eat you for a snack*."

"Yeah right. You just ate a whole cow, and seventy-five percent of mine. You might still be a touch hungry but I doubt you'll be able to eat me. That, and I'm not as meaty as a cow either, so I don't think I'll taste as good," mocked Brak.

"*We'll see about that*," mocked Drakon in return as he licked his lips.

* * *

The Survivalists stayed to defend their home, while Queen Callista, and Chief Slasher, went back to defend theirs. We would all try to send reinforcements to one another, to see who would need the extra help. Other then that, we were all pretty much all on our own for taking on the three armies. The only good thing was that the armies were spread out so

Salvation, the Unicorn Palace, and the Chimera Kingdom, wouldn't take the full might of the former Elders forces. Also the opposing Dragons might have fought Dragons, Unicorns, and Chimeras, but they never fought all three races working together. With this being our only advantage, the Survivalists used and abused it, to win.

Once our allies left us to fend for themselves, everyone in Salvation felt a sense of loneliness again, for we had to deal with this *new* Dragon threat on our own. This was what we get of course for depending on others for help to fight our battles, oh well, we knew we could survive. Or so we hoped, for these Dragons were tougher then Slash & Burn's lot, and we *all* remembered *that* battle. Even though our allies were gone, they left us with enchantments to wield at our enemies, which made us all feel a little better. That and these enchantments were nothing like the ones that the Survivalists were using, for they were more powerful, and made us stronger. We wouldn't be loosing anytime soon, with our new mystical abilities, but we had to use them sparingly. As the battle raged on, half of Salvation was engulfed in flames, with bodies of friends and foes littering the pathways. Elexia, Claire, the Twins, and all of their healers had their work clawed out for them. Sisillia, Scythe, and Shadow Claw went to check on the other half of Salvation and do what they could to stop the destruction. I remained in the city circle, with a contingent of troops fighting off the opposing Dragons. Once the city circle was cleared of the enemy, we moved onto the next area that needed our help.

The battle seemed to last for an endless amount of days, but it finally came to an end after the eightieth. After our battle was over, the survivors of Salvation went to survey the damage done by the battle. We headed to a nearby cliff that we had named: Lovers Look, and once we got there, we were shocked at what we saw. Salvation was in burning ruins, destroyed beyond repair. For once a beautiful settlement that Unicorns, Chimeras, and Dragons created in peace, was now a wasteland. This wasteland used to be full of lush green trees, creatures, and life, was now lifeless. Nothing remained, save for a few Destroyed Dens, and charred growth, with scorched earth. So we did the one thing we vowed never to do, abandon our home. The Survivalists split into two groups, half went to help the Chimera Kingdom, while the other half went to aid the Unicorn Palace.

Sisillia, Scythe, Shadow Claw, and Maya headed off to the Chimera Kingdom taking half of the Survivalists with them. While Zack, Claire, Elexia, and myself took the other half of the Survivalists, and headed to the Unicorn Palace. We said our good-byes to one another, and wished each other good luck in hopes that we would win this war. I also gave Sisillia a kiss that felt like it would last a life time for we didn't know if we would see each other again.

It was a good thing that we knew how to get to the Unicorn Palace, for we could fly there in half the time it took us to walk and fight. We came up with a plan for the Dragons and the Chimeras to carry the Unicorns, seeing as they couldn't fly. As we neared the Unicorn Palace, we saw great plumes of smoke rising from beyond its' walls. We heard battle cries from both sides in the distance as well. Aside from the Unicorn Palaces' present state, and for the fact that we could finally get a good look at it this time, it was beautiful. Like Dragons, Unicorns had created Dens, only they weren't like a Dragon's Den. The Unicorns also valued Nature, so they adapted their living style to suit the forest around them. Unlike the Dragons who just tore up everything and pieced it back together using mud, and other sticky substances to make crude structures.

There were a hundred huge trees that were arranged in a huge circle that marked the area of the Palace. These trees had dark green branches that sprouted from the top of the long dark brown trunk, and flowed down to the ground. The trees were hollowed out with large holes in them, giving them the appearance of a Human battle tower. There were thick vines and bushes in between the trees giving the appearance of large thick green walls. On one area of "the walls" there was a vast opening. The opening was covered with unusually thick vines that wouldn't move unless a Unicorn willed them to. Inside the circle of trees, resided the vast Unicorn settlement and Unicorn Castle. The settlement consisted of a variety of trees that were either hollowed out, or spun together to form an above ground Den. These Dens were called Shelters by the Unicorns, for the fact that they had thinner walls and less space then a Den. There was also two openings in the Shelter, instead of one. From the many shades of green, brown, and various flower colours, the settlement was a marvel to whomever looked at its' beauty. It brought tears to all of our eyes, to see it all ablaze, and in ruin. In the middle of the settlement stood the Castle of the Unicorns.

The Unicorn Castle was massive to say the least. In actuality, it was a group of five enormous trees that had dark brown bark. Their branches and leaves were a mix of gold, emerald, ruby colours. The five trees were entwined with one another giving them the appearance of one huge tree that could touch the sky. Like the main gate the gate to the castle was covered in thick vines draped over the entrance way. The inside of the five trees were all hollowed out, save for some areas in the trees to create levels for the Unicorns to do whatever it was they did. There were also levels underneath the trees, these levels were for the "dungeons". The dungeons were deep lightless pits, but deep was a relative term. For once you were in one of the pits you couldn't get back out.

We knew the settlement was vast, but when we got closer, we finally realized how big it really was. The settlement could house at least two Salvations, and still have room left over. After we landed in the settlement, we split up again to make it easier for all of us, for we felt like ants in a field. Claire would attack with her party from the west, Elexia would attack with her party from the south. This left the north to Zack and his assault party, and the east was left to me and my group. Before we split though, Elexia cast an enchantment on the Unicorns that would give them the ability of flight. With this advantage the Unicorns would be more of an opponent to deal with. Before I could ask, Elexia explained that her enchantment was timed, and it would take even longer to recast. Once Elexia finished her casting, all of the Unicorns had large snow white swan wings. We finally split into our mixed groups of Chimera, Unicorn, and Dragon, and assaulted our targeted areas. We would try to gain as many survivors as possible to help aid in the fight against the invading Dragons. After our assaults, we would all meet at the Palace Square before taking on the Unicorn Castle itself. We said our good-byes and headed off to our destinations.

The travel was time consuming and the battles in the ruined settlement were long and fierce. For the invading Dragons decided to make some of the ruined shelters temporary homes or feasting areas so we had to be weary of ambushes and sneak attacks. Eventually though we arrived at our destination. Elexia was the first to make it to the Palace Square, but she only had half of her force with her. Her party went about healing themselves while they waited for everyone else to show up. I was next to show up, in the square, my group had taken some losses as well but not as badly as Elexia had. Although, we were all in desperate need of healing, for we were all barely conscious when we arrived. As we waited for the others, our reinforcements finally showed up…better late then never. The Gryphons, and a few Hypogryphs flew by over head, and by the looks of it, they had suffered greatly in their own encounter with the invading Dragons. They were still a sight for sore eyes though. Claire was the next to show up, she was barely alive, and she was the only one left of her party. While Claire was being healed we waited on Zack, but he never showed up, we were told a while later by a scout, that he was ambushed by a large party of Dragons. There were no survivors, this news made all of us sad for we all took a liking to Zack. Maya though would be devastated, compared to how we felt.

After we were all back together and fully healed and fed with the meager food stuffs that we brought with us, we set our sights on the Dragons assaulting the Castle. The Unicorns knew how to build, for the castle was still standing in one piece…more or less. Then again, the invading Dragons could be having a hard time in trying to destroy it as well, either way the Survivalists were here to help. Before we advanced to the Castle, we heard loud thunderous noises and saw strange lights coming form inside the Castle. We figured there must be a great battle going on, the faster we got there, the better. Saving the Unicorns was one thing, but getting to the Castles gates, was another. With all of us taking deep breathes and claming ourselves, we set out again, to fight and save the Unicorns.

We all fought long and hard to reach the Castle gates. We managed to pick up a few survivors and the odd survivalist, on the way to help, which was a plus. Once we got to the Castle gates, we realized that all of our hard work in getting to the Castle was in vain. For we were seriously outnumbered and all hope was starting to fade. But we entered anyway to keep up the fighting. When we were inside all of the Dragons were amazed for all of us though that we would be too big and not be able to maneuver. But the Castle looked as though it was made to include adult Dragons as well as Unicorns. After battling through almost every area of the main level of the Castle, we finally came to a fork. One way lead to the lower levels and the dungeons. While the other way lead to the upper levels and the Great Hall where Queen Callista was residing. We split our forces again, only this time Claire, Elexia, and myself stayed in one group, for we all wanted to join the battle in the Great Hall.

The Great Hall was located on the top level of the Castle, which I chuckled at for I found it funny. This level though was different from the others, for it was completely open to the sky. Save for the odd large branches that hung in a few areas, creating little "private" areas. We burst through the already torn vines, only to find Mother with a squad of Elite Dragon Guards on one side. On the far side was Queen Callista with her Elite Royal Guard. Both sides looked like they were regrouping for a final attack. On the up side of things the Survivalists weren't directly in the middle…this time.

"Mother!" I hollered. "Why are you doing this? If you continue with your attack, we'll have to destroy you."

"*Don't make me laugh. You can't destroy me! None of you can, for I'm extremely powerful and can't be defeated. I wasn't chosen as The Elders Champion for nothing. As for why I'm doing this Drakon, is quite simple. We can't have you opposing our Elders. That would make us weak, and I hate being weak. Also, The Elders commanded that it be done, regardless of what happened to them,*" Mother roared. "*Now enough chit-chat, it's time for you all to DIE!*"

"Mother!" Claire and myself both pleaded.

"*Mother? There was a reason why I was named Fire Storm. And that is for the simple fact of what I can do and become. NOW DIE!*" roared Fire Storm again.

With that said, Fire Storm, and her guard took to the sky and attacked from the air before diving down to attack with fangs, claws, gifts, and fire. We were prepared for the surprise attack and acted quickly. The battle just got bloody from the surprise attack, for with all of the forces going at it with one another, the frenzy and blood lust was rising. With this happening it was becoming extremely hard to tell friend from foe, but the Survivalists managed to focus. While Claire and Elexia battle with the troops on the ground, I helped Queen Callista in battling Fire Storm, for that was what she had become. Fire Storm's body was encased with fire, and she was attacking with such savagery, that she looked more like a Demon from a Whelps tail then a Dragon. Eventually our reinforcements arrived to help us against the invading Dragons. But I wasn't concerned about that, I was concerned with the matter at claw: killing my Mother. As the three of us, Queen Callista, Fire Storm, and myself, battled, the hall seemed to go quiet. When I managed to sneak a look around, everyone, friend and foe, were watching the battle.

While I fought in the air Queen Callista fought on the ground, for it would be harder to attack the two of us, and Fire Storm was having trouble defending herself. While one of us would attack, the other would play as a decoy in getting Fire Storm's attention. With this tactic, Queen Callista's and my attacks would penetrate Fire Strom's defenses. After what seemed like an eon, I finally scored the final blow against Fire Storm, ending our long battle. Fire Storm fell in a burning blaze along with her stunned and shocked guards. As she fell, she fell outside of the Castle and landed hard on cold earth outside, and setting everything around her, ablaze. Claire and myself watched in horror as our Mother almost burned to nothing. I landed by the remains of Fire Storm's body and just starred at her. For even in death, she was still beautiful to look at. As I starred at her body, Claire, Elexia, and Queen Callista arrived at my side. Queen Callista, and Elexia wanted to voice their sympathies to Claire and myself, but the two of us just kept on starring at our Mother: Fire Storm.

"I know what you are going to say," I started with tear filled eyes. "I had no other choice, that there was no other way I could change her mind. It was for the best, and so on, and so forth."

"Mother, why?" asked Claire with tears streaming down her beautiful face. "Why did you force us to kill you?"

"I…I'm…I'm sorry for your loss. Forgive me, but that's all I can say. I can't imagine the pain, the anger, and the sorrow you feel," sympathized Elexia with tears forming in her eyes.

"She did it to be free," exclaimed Queen Callista as she choked back her own tears.

"*What?*" Claire and myself asked in unison.

"She did it to be *Free*," repeated Queen Callista. "It was the only way to be free from the influence of The Elders had over her. In a way, she sacrificed herself to be free and give us...you two, a fighting chance for freedom. *You* Drakon, was her savior, and what your Mother did to you, has now made you even stronger in the fight for freedom. Heh, I guess that's what this war, and all of the other wars throughout the ages all but stand for. Go figure."

"I still don't get it. we destroyed The Elders, how could they still control someone if they are dead?" questioned Elexia.

"Because of the influence The Elders had over her. Death was the only way out, otherwise Mother would've still been following The Elders orders, a slave to monsters. That's how they managed to control everyone. Power, fear, and influence, was The Elders way of life," explained Claire.

"In killing Mother, Fire Storm was freed from The Elders," I summed up. "Lets go, Claire and myself can't stand to be here any longer. There's too much pain and death. No offense Queen Callista, Elexia, but we have to take who we can and go help out Chief Slasher and the rest of the Survivalists."

"Take whatever and whomever you need and want Drakon, Claire. Elexia and myself will accompany you. For I'm sure you're going to need all of the help you can get. But we will need a few troops here to watch over the surviving Younglings," replied Queen Callista.

We had left the castle the way it was: in ruins. As I took in a quick glace of the Unicorn Palace, I realized then, what a Dragon really was: Death and Destruction. For not matter what I had tried to accomplish in trying to prove that Dragons were like their great ancestors: peaceful. It always seemed that destruction and death would prove me wrong. All of the people I knew and loved were dead do to my different way of thinking. Everyone that fought the opposing Dragons that was still alive joined us in our new task of helping the Chimeras. As we walked to the entrance of the completely destroyed Unicorn Palace, we encountered a lone Chimera scout. None of the Chimeras that were with us recognized him or didn't bother to say anything about him except for one thing. He was a very unique character, in more ways then one.

Chapter 11

Backwards, Forwards, Forwards, Backwards

"Does your story ever get cheerful? Because if it's all just depressing, loss of life, loneliness, pain, suffering and abandonment, then I don't want to listen anymore. I've had to put up with enough loss, and the such, in my own life," exclaimed Brak with a hint of distaste in his voice.

"*I do admit that my tale is a little depressing and violent. But what were you expecting? A tale of cute and cuddly little critters frolicking in a lush colourful field of flowers? I think not,*" stated Drakon.

"Fare enough, but could you not talk so much about your bloody fights and battles so much? For your tale is starting to sound like endless bloodshed," replied Brak.

"*Like your History and Fairytales are any different. I do remember some stories that-*,"mocked Drakon as he was cut off.

"Hey! Our History and fairytales aren't bloody. Defiantly *not* cute and cuddly with lots of flowers and frolicking. A little violent maybe, but not *that* bloody," defended Brak.

"*Hmm let me think on that…does Ancient Atlantis ring any bells with its' Gladiators? Or what about primitive and "civilized" Humans beating each other over the head with large sticks to swords? Oh, and my personal favorite, tales of Humans slaying Dragons for eating the "Helpless Princess". When they only want to be left alone in peace,*" listed and mocked Drakon.

"Okay, okay. I see your point," admitted Brak. "But could you at least talk a little less on the killing and more on what happened to your kind and why there are so few of you. I can pretty much assume that the wars you fought did a number on your kind, but there's got to be more."

"*Fine, no violence, no tale, no answers. I'll open my mouth so you can walk right in,*" stated Drakon as he shrugged his shoulders, laid his head on the floor, and opened his mouth wide enough for a Human to easily walk in.

"Alright, you win. Tell your tale how you want to," exclaimed Brak as he waved his arms in the air in surrender.

"*Thank you,*" smiled Drakon as he closed his mouth and raised his head. "*Now as was saying we ran into a unique Chimera Scout.*"

* * *

"Are you from the Chimera Kingdom?" I asked.

"*Am I yes.*" Replied the Chimera.

"What?" questioned Elexia.

"*Yes I am,*" repeated the Chimera.

"Why do you talk like that?" asked Claire.

"*Way this talk to like I because,*" answered the Chimera.

"WHAT?" stated Queen Callista, who was getting annoyed.

"*Because I like to talk this way,*" repeated the Chimera again.

"I guess he likes to confuse his enemies…and his allies." I exclaimed with a shrug. "What is your name? For we are allies of the Chimera Kingdom.

"Backwards Forwards, Forwards Backwards is my name. I also know you are allies with us. Otherwise you would have no Chimera troops with you," Backwards Forwards pointed out as he changed his language so we could all understand him.

Backwards Forwards was an average sized Chimera, which was about a little smaller then a Whelp. He was unlike any other Chimera though, for instead of one colour for his fur, he had a multitude of colours. These colours ranged from a dark brown to a dark green. His mane of hair was no different, with his colours it was actually hard to tell where he was, even if he was standing right in front of you. Backwards Forwards also had no wings, I guessed that not all Chimeras had wings. He did have the regular Chimera barbed tail though. That and Backwards Forards's face was pretty much the same as any other Chimera face. The only difference was that Backwards Forwards had snow white eyes. This made us all a little uneasy and uncomfortable when we looked at them.

"I see," I mused. "Are you here to take us to the Chimera Kingdom...the fast way?"

"Yes I am. Now, if you'll all follow me, we'll be there in no time," Backwards Forwards replied as he leapt into a nearby tree.

"You're speaking normally? That's a relief," Claire sighed.

"Now for," Backwards Forwards smiled.

Claire, Elexia, and Queen Callista gave Backwards Forwards a look that could kill, while I looked at the four of them and laughed. My laughter seemed to add to the meager cheerful and happiness everyone was starting to feel after our ordeal. I guessed that Backwards Forwards was trying to make everyone feel better, which in turn made me smile. With the introductions of all five of the "Leaders" out of the way, we all set off for the Chimera Kingdom. Those of us who could fly took to the sky, while the rest walked, or trotted on the ground. All in all, we resembled what you Humans call a convoy, for we had a mix of Dragons, Flying Unicorns, and Chimeras in the sky. While we had a mix of Dragons, Chimeras, and Unicorns on the ground. The Dragons on the ground were either grounded due to having damaged wings, or no wings at all. Some of the local and rogue Dragons that lived in the "New Lands" (as the Survivalists now called their new home) were born without wings. But that didn't mean that they were any less deadly.

With the force in the air flying back and forth, they were able to survey any and everything that moved. While the force on the ground scouted out the areas that the force in the air couldn't see. Also the force on the ground made it their top priority to protect Queen Callista, Elexia, and Backwards forwards. While the force in the air made it their top priority to protect Claire, Sisillia, and myself. Under normal circumstances, the Survivalists, and the Unicorns from the Unicorn Palace wouldn't be this over protective, but we were in uncharted territory. I found this amusing, for the Chimeras that were with us, were confused, and clueless as to where Backwards Forwards was leading us. Even though some of the

Chimeras that were with us came from the Chimera Kingdom, they couldn't tell where we were. This also annoyed me a little for all of our Mappers had gone to aid the Chimera Kingdom, but then again drawing up a map would be of little use to us right now.

As we made our slow trek through the dense wilderness, backwards Forwards proved himself to be more then just a guide and a scout. On more then one occasion, he would seemingly disappear into the wilds, and return a little while later. We eventually found out that he would go ahead of the whole convoy and take out *any* hostile or threat to us. We made this discovery when Backwards Forwards took us past a destroyed settlement with fresh basilisk bodies everywhere, and by the looks of them a Chimera had killed them. We had passed a few more encampments and settlements that were also completely destroyed. I made a mental note: that Backwards Forwards was abnormally fast and strong, and that it would be a *bad* idea to make him angry. We would also have to find a way to repay Backwards Forwards for he was also making sure that we would all be ready to fight when the time came.

"You fight like a fierce warrior or an *Elite* or *Royal Guard* rather, and yet you are only a scout. Why?" questioned Queen Callista.

"Simple is answer the," answered Backwards Forwards. "I was given the choice to see the world and her lands, or to stay behind walls and protect the Kingdom. Explore chose I."

"Interesting," mussed Queen Callista.

After a while of walking, we stopped by a large river to rest, and to take a Drink, swim or a quick wash in the nice cold refreshing water. The river though reminded me of the one that I found Jax in, at the memory, a tear began to form in my eye. Claire walked up beside me, and together we wept at the memory of our fallen siblings. With the vast army that we now controlled, no one, not even Elexia, or Queen Callista dared to comfort us. Both of us figured that everyone wanted to give us space for our reputation had spread like wild fire. I chuckled at myself for I didn't even think I had a reputation, but then again it could be that everyone was too afraid to think of what Claire and myself would do if we were interrupted. Once the two of us were back to our "normal" selves, Claire turned her head to talk to Backwards Forwards who was just finishing off a large fish.

"How, and why are you so strong and skilled? If I had someone with your talents in my command, I would have made you my Personal Guard," Claire questioned Backwards Forwards.

"Battle fierce, and training harsh of, years of, lot a with comes it. Stands still statement previous my but. Protection over exploration chose I," explained Backwards Forwards.

"Please, normally talk you can? I mean, can you talk normally please. It's very hard and confusing to understand you. Backwards then forwards, then Backwards, then vise versa," pleaded Elexia before she paused. "My head hurts now."

"It consider will I," replied Backwards Forwards with another smile.

"Can we continue on to the Chimera Kingdom? I think we've all rested for long enough. That and it would be in our best interest to get there within as few days as possible," I stated before I grinned. "Kingdom Chimera the from we are far how?"

"Oh great now Drakon's doing it," grumbled Claire.

"Far not are we," answered Backwards Forwards. "Another day or two of non stop trekking, and we should be there."

As we trekked on through the forest yet again, we had encountered large groups of opposing Dragons. As we battled these Dragons, we realized that they were tougher to outwit, and to defeat then the other two armies. At least we were slowly increasing our numbers as we got closer to the Chimera Kingdom with any survivors or camped out Survivalist. The opposing Dragons were still a formidable challenge, but not as hard to defeat when we first encountered them. After two days we finally reached the entrance to the Chimera Kingdom. With all of the extra help we picked up, our army was almost back up to full strength. It would be at full strength though when we met up with the other half of our allies and Survivalists, mind you. At the thought, I wondered on how the rest of the Survivalists and the Chimeras were doing. It had been many days since we parted, and the feeling of loss and loneliness was starting to get to me. I realized then that I valued company and friendship. This was also another non-Dragon attribute that I possessed and was experiencing, which made me think of how different from my race I truly was.

The Chimera Kingdom, like the Unicorn Palace, was vast, but unlike the Unicorn Palace, it wasn't *that* nature friendly. The Chimeras took after the Dragons, to an extent. For they had built crude Dens instead of Shelters. But these Dens were either too small looking or abnormally large for a Chimera. This of course was one of the defenses that the Chimeras created to confuse their enemies. The Chimeras also built Dens in the trees that populated the settlement. Like the Unicorns, the Chimeras built their Dens to mimic or match the rest of the forest. Unlike the Unicorns, though who had a Castle in the center of their settlement, the Chimeras had their "Royal Quarters" in the northern part of the settlement.

"Well everyone, it's time to take out this last threat. Hopefully once this is over, we'll be left in peace," I shouted so all could hear.

With the little speech I gave, we readied ourselves and marched and flew into the now smoking and burning, Chimera Kingdom. We were prepared for wins and losses that would occur in this final war with the Allied Clans. We just hoped that the losses wouldn't be too great. As we were splitting into our battle groups, Backwards Forwards had come to me with a concerned look on his face.

"Others the and, you speak to need I," Backwards Forwards stated.

"Okay, by the look on your face, I'd assume it's of great importance. We'll meet here in ten sun movements," I answered.

I set off to find Claire, Elexia, and Queen Callista, to inform them that Backwards Forwards wanted to talk to all of us. I found them all one at a time, they were giving each of their forces a "good luck" speech, which I couldn't understand. I informed them that Backwards Forwards had something very important that he needed to tell us and that it couldn't wait. After we were all together, Backwards Forwards to us why he was so concerned.

"What's wrong?" asked Queen Callista.

"Scythe and Shadow Claw have failed in their mission, and so have their parties. Their troops are few and scattered throughout the destroyed Kingdom, doing what they can to survive. Sisillia and her war party have managed to survive and have made a base camp in the Kingdom's center. But there is no guarantee on how long her position will last before it is overrun with the opposing Dragons. I have not heard or seen anything of

Chief Slasher's situation. But it is safe to say that he's holding his own in the Royal Quarters in the northern part of the Chimera Kingdom. I don't know though on how long he can hold out though. So our options are this: rescue our people and our allies, reinforce Sisillia and her base, or find out what happened to Chief Slasher. Do we shall what, is question the," explained and questioned Backwards Forwards.

"Hmm, we'll split up," I proposed. "We go with our original plan of splitting our forces, but this time we'll have half search for the troops and the other half, clearing the path to Sisillia. Chief Slasher will have to wait until we rebuild our strength back up. We'll then all regroup in Sisillia's base camp and assault the Royal Quarters, for that's where we'll find the leader to this opposing army, and Chief Slasher," I explained.

With that said, we split up and set off to do our tasks. I had hoped that we could get to Sisillia in time. If we couldn't, then it would be very difficult to win this war without the full might of the Survivalists and our Allies. Or what was left of the full might of the Survivalists and our Allies.

Chapter 12

The Last of the Clan

"So let me guess. *You* had to kill your father, and you experienced more loss," exclaimed Brak.

"*You have no idea,*" snapped and snarled Drakon. "*I lost more then you think HUMAN! My Father decided to give me a choice that not only broke my heart, but my spirit as well. And even though he's dead, I will never forgive him…ever.*"

"I think I'd better be quiet and let you continue. Seeing as I just made you a touch angry and all," replied Brak defensively.

"*Good plan,*" growled Drakon as he calmed down a bit.

* * *

Our searching was long and difficult, we encountered strong resistance and only found a few survivors. Eventually we all made it to Sisillia's base camp, just in time too, for the opposing Dragons had decided to assault it. They had the upper claw, for we were all tired from the search, and the fighting. Not too mention we were all starting to become very hungry from not eating from the past few days of non stop moving from the Unicorn Palace to the Chimera Kingdom. As we watched the opposing Dragons descend upon us, and shoot jets of flame and fire at our camp, setting it ablaze, we acted. We had no time to make a plan for a counter attack or a strategy, so we did what came naturally, we let our instincts take over. As our instincts began to rule over our reasoning and thoughts, all of us felt stronger, faster, and felt smarter instinctually. Some of us also began to see differently, certain colours stood out, while others dimmed. The smells around us also began to stick out more and we could detect more things in our surroundings. It was as though we were seeing the lands for the first time, I knew though that the feeling wouldn't last. Everyone had heard of the ancient times when creatures relied solemnly on their instincts, and died from them.

The battle was long and costly, our camp was destroyed and a quarter of our forces were lost. On top of that Sisillia told us that Maya had died in trying to save a group of young Chimeras. The only plus side to the grim news was that Maya succeeded in saving the Chimeras, as to the whole assault, we won. Unfortunately it was only the first "real" step in taking back the Chimera Kingdom. We regrouped, healed our wounded, then set off to the Northern part of the Chimera Kingdom to make a final stand against the Enemy Dragons…and my *Father*. While we regrouped Sisillia came over to me and we kissed passionately and made it seem like our kiss would last forever. But my mind was too focused on the battle at claw, and not on love. I was thinking of the many ways of getting to the Northern Quarters with minimal losses and how to save the Chimeras from extinction. When Sisillia and myself finished kissing Claire walked up to me and Sisillia left me. Sisillia and the others might've guessed, but Claire knew that I had been fighting my own war: sleep. Unlike everyone else, I didn't…couldn't sleep, for everything that I had seen, no matter how old, was still vivid in my mind, like it was only the day before. *This* gift filled me with intrigue and fear, for I doubted that I would ever be able to sleep soundly ever again.

"*How are you fairing Brother? You look like Dragon waste,*" questioned Claire in our native and personal Language.

A Dragons' personal language is shared between siblings and parents for it is their own language to use when the parents or siblings wish to talk to each other and not let other Dragons eavesdrop.

"*I've been better. I haven't been able to sleep properly in years and I doubt I ever will,*" I replied.

"*Brother?*" Claire asked. "*You know what this means don't you?*"

"*Yes I do*," I replied grimly.

"*I don't want to loose this battle*," continued Claire with tears forming in her eyes. "*But, I don't want to loose Father either. I know that you had no choice in killing Mother when we battled against her. But if Father dies, then we will have no one left except the two of us, and that scares me. For we will be the only two left of our Clan. True you have Sisillia and I will choose a mate in time, but we will still be the only two left of "our" Clan.*"

"*I know Claire, I don't want to loose Father either*," I reassured as I put a clawed hand on her shoulder and nuzzled her hair a bit. "*But we may be forced to do something that neither of us wants to do. I know that if we kill Father we will be the only ones left from our Family...no, our Clan. I don't' want that either, but...*"

After Claire and myself talked for a bit, we met up with Sisillia, Queen Callista, Elexia, and Backwards Forwards, to discuss our plans for our next course of action. When we were all together, we looked at Backwards Forwards for the solution.

"Simple is solution the," Backwards Forwards explained. "We split up into four divisions, two that can fly, and two that will battle on the ground. Sides four all on them assault will we. Making it difficult for the enemy to attack one group. Wings your still you do, Elexia?"

Elexia flared her wings. "Yes, we still have our wings, but I don't know how long the enchantment will last. Also, it will take time, "that we don't have" for my enchantment to recharge."

"I can make that enchantment permanent if you wish, but there is a costly price with the enchantment. You will have no horn, and no more mystical energy to wield. You will however, become stronger, faster, and have your life quadrupled," Queen Callista stated.

"Hmm, I'll have to talk to my group about this. But I'm sure, they'll say no be-, "Elexia started before she was cut off.

"*I'll do it*," replied a voice.

Everyone turned their heads to regard a young winged Unicorn that interrupted Elexia. The Unicorn was young due to her size and her voice. She was covered in snow white hair from nose to tail. The only thing that wasn't white on the Unicorn, were her dark green eyes, her pitch black hooves, and her golden coloured horn. By Unicorn standards, her beauty rivaled that of Queen Callista's.

"*You are but a Youngling,*" exclaimed Elexia. "*Why do you wish to take on such a burden? Also why and how are you here in this war force? You should be back at the Unicorn Palace, under the protection of the guards.*"

"*First off, I'm not a Youngling. Second, my reasons are my own. And third, no one can cage me,*" snapped the young Unicorn.

"She's an orphan," stated Backwards Forwards flatly. "This for time have don't we."

"I'm *not* even going to ask on how you know that," replied Elexia a little shocked and hurt by Backwards Forwards bluntness and disregard for Unicorn matters.

Before Elexia could have a few words with Backwards Forwards about etiquette, he had disappeared into the Settlement. Elexia shrugged her shoulders and focused back at the matter at hoof.

"*Touching*, my name is Pegasus," stated Pegasus as she switched to language so everyone could understand her.

"Interesting name, now where have I heard that name before? Of course! You're the wondering Unicorn that everyone has talked about. If memory serves, you lost your family and your whole herd in an ancient Clan war, and vowed never to fight again. So you disappeared from existence so-to-speak. But you returned a few millennia ago with unmatched skill but with no powers. I assume you've come to aid us," explained Claire.

"*How'd you know that?*" I whispered to Claire.

"*Long story,*" answered Claire.

"*Oh,*" I replied.

"Pegasus, you know the risks. Once I transform you, there will be no going back," Queen Callista explained.

"There is more then one way to use mystical energies, and to fight without it. I've lived my whole life, without any powers, enchantments, and energies. Why should this be any different?" questioned Pegasus.

"Very well. Prepare yourself for the transformation of your life," exclaimed Queen Callista.

Queen Callista walked up to Pegasus and started to glow. As Queen Callista preformed her transformation, Backwards Forwards reappeared from the Shadows, then disappeared again. I guessed that he went to go and do a quick reconnaissance of the area to make sure that there were no incoming enemies. Back to the transformation, Queen Callista was now surrounded in a glowing white light, and so was Pegasus. As Pegasus was glowing, her body began to change. She grew to the size of an adult female Unicorn, if not a little larger. While she grew her horn receded into her head, whether it was painful, or Pegasus didn't feel the transformation, she never showed what she felt. While her horn receded, her enchanted wings shimmered in gold light. Her wings then grew until they were at least ten feet long, three feet longer then her enchanted wings. Before the transformation was complete however, Backwards Forwards came rushing in.

"There is no more time for rest, we must attack now, and otherwise, all hope is lost. Well as plan new a have I. We charge the Northern Quarters. Explain to time no is there," Backwards Forwards hurriedly explained.

We gathered our awaiting troops and set off for another fight of our lives. The march to the Northern Quarters of the Kingdom was no easy task. We battled all the way to the outside of the Royal Gates. Each area of the Chimera Kingdom was "walled off" for protection purposes against attack to the Kingdom. All of us though who were on the ground thought that that was pointless, for the walls were proving hard to navigate by. That and like Salvation, and the Unicorn Palace the Chimera Kingdom was destroyed. The walls were put together by mud, rocks, and large branches, making them look like a beaver dam. Our army was stretched thin but we didn't give up the fight, for we had come across lots of Survivalists who wanted a piece of revenge. After the battle outside of the Gates, we burst through what remained of the destroyed gates, which were four large trees. The trees acted like the vines in the Unicorn Palace. When we emerged from the other side we saw the battle between Chief Slasher and my Father.

Chief Slasher was large for a chimera, he was about the size of Youth, and he was extremely muscular. His fur was a dark brown, with a light brown mane of hair, giving him the appearance of a large tree trunk. Chief Slasher had dark blue eyes that sparkled with life. But like Backwards Forwards, Chief Slasher had no wings, but his long claws, muscles, and barbed tail made up for anything he lacked. Chief Slasher had a small force of Chimera troops with him, and so had Father. The only difference though between this battle and the one that Queen Callista fought, was that this battle was over, and Chief Slasher lost. This meant that we were all in for a hard fight.

"*Father*!" I yelled in my native tongue. "*Claire and myself do not wish to destroy you like Mother.*"

"*So*!" boomed Father. "*YOU killed Fire Storm, my mate, my life partner, my lover. I sensed her death but I would never have dreamed it was YOU. How DARE YOU! What gave you the right and the reason to kill her?*"

"*She left me no choice,*" I pleaded. "*Mother chose to fight and die, to be free from The Elders. The Elders are dead as well, so you can stop this chaos.*"

"*Drakon, even though you are smart, you're a fool. With The Elders deaths, I now control all of the Clans, even if they are few in number. But there are more reinforcements at home, waiting to be summoned,*" stated Father.

I knew then that Father had become what The Elders had become. He was corrupted by power and greed, and there was no way we could reason with him. Claire knew this as well and began to shed a couple of tears. We knew what we had to do, and we would hate ourselves for it. if we didn't kill Father here and now, there would be *yet* another large-scale war. That war would end up destroying this beautiful land and all of its' inhabitants that were spread to all the corners of the lands. Sadly, if we did kill Father, then our worst fear would come to pass, and we would be the last of our Clan.

"*Father, please don't do this. I…we don't want to kill you,*" pleaded Claire for the last time.

Claire and myself got ready for the battle of our lives while the rest of our forces took on the opposing Dragons that were amassed behind Father. Before Claire and myself could act, Father blew out a large plume of smoke, which covered everything in darkness. Then the fighting started, as I prepared myself for an aerial assault, I felt something hard hit me in the head. This knocked me out for a sun movement or two…I think. I woke immediately to a blood curdling scream, only to see the smoke cleared and the Queen of the Unicorns: Queen Callista, fall to Father's claws. From the morbid scene, I now understood why Father was called *Sharp Claw.* That wasn't the only thing that got my attention though, for Father was holding onto Claire and Sisillia by their hair. Both of them were unconscious, and it looked as though Father was debating on who to kill first.

"*Father! Please don't do it. PLEASE!*" I yelled as hot tears stained my cheeks.

"*Drakon? Good you're awake, and alive. You're just in time to make a choice: who will die first? Your Sister, or your Lover? Or better yet,*" Sharp Claw stated as he took in a deep breath.

"*NOOO!*" I screamed as Father tossed the limp forms of Claire and Sisillia high into the air.

Father was strong but I never knew how strong until I saw how easily he threw Claire and Sisillia's dead weight high into the air. I spread my wings and leapt into the air and flew towards the still forms of Claire and Sisillia in hopes of getting to them. It was false hope though as I watched in horror as my Lover and my Sister died in the flames of my Father. At least they didn't suffer when they died…I hoped and prayed to the Great Dragon. With the images still fresh in my mind, I became beyond angry. I was enraged with hate towards my Father at what he had done, not only to me but to our Clan. I could feel myself change in colour and size as well. I remembered a tale at that moment told to me by an elderly Dragon when I was younger. It was about how hate could change you, and I guess he was right. My reddish blue scales turned blood red, while my eyes went from gold to black orbs, and my hair went from silver to pitch black. I don't know what happened next, whether it was due to the state I was in, what I had become, or the fact that I didn't want to remember. All I remember is, I was back to my "normal" self, and Father was *dead*, and I also had a massive headache, and I was lying on the ground.

As my headache cleared, I got up and took a moment to look around to survey the area. What I saw brought despair and tears to my eyes. Elexia came limping up and stood beside me with Backwards Forwards following, backwards forwards had four large gashes in his side and one of his eyes was closed. Pegasus came flying down after Backwards Forwards met up with the two of us, and she was also injured in the side. We all just stared at the site of the finished battle in silence. Corpses of Chimera, Unicorn, Dragon, and a couple of Gryphons littered the ground. Somewhere among the bodies, laid Queen Callista, Scythe, Shadow Claw, Claire, Sisillia, Slasher, and my Father. The war with The Elders was finally over but the cost was high, too high for a single young Dragon to bear. I realized then that I was alone, completely alone… no, truly alone.

"I shouldn't have stayed here. I should have listened to The Elders. I should have taken all of the surviving Dragons and just gone *home*," I whispered.

"Don't say that," replied Backwards Forwards.

"Yes, if it wasn't for you, there would be no more Unicorns, or Chimeras in this Land," added Elexia.

"But all of the death and destruction that has happened here. It's all because of *me*," I sobbed.

"It would have happened anyway, even if you hadn't have been here to help guide us, and protect us," replied Elexia.

"Yes, If you helped us out, or didn't, it wouldn't have mattered. We would have sustained heavy losses. Also, you have managed to show us that we could put aside our own differences and work together to battle an enemy," added Backwards Forwards.

"But," I started.

"It over get, words two," stated Backwards Forwards with a hint of annoyance in his voice.

"Backwards Forwards is right, quit sulking and get over it. you did what *you* thought was right. True you lost some friends and family, so what? We did too, how do you think we feel? Happy? Also, do you think you're the only *orphan*? There are more of us then you think," asked Pegasus a little angry.

"Also, you're a *Dragon*. Last time I checked, they don't get sentimental on things like this. They bottle up their sorrow, anger, and rage, then unleash it all on their enemies. If you wanted to get sentimental, you should've been born as a Unicorn," stated Backwards Forwards.

"Hey! We're not *all* sentimental. Also, last *I* checked, Chimeras were no better then us. The only difference between us is our opinions, and our races," shot Elexia.

"All of you are right," I agreed. "I shouldn't be sulking over the fact, that I'm the only one who lost friends and family. Or the fact that I'm the last of *my* Clan. I am a dragon after all."

But I doubted I could ever bring myself to admit that I was, also I knew that I would never forget this War or the many others to come. I vowed though that I would find a way to get through the turmoil and become stronger. While I was lost in thought for a moment, I searched with my eyes for my Father, when I finally saw him.

"Father, you may be free from the pain and suffering you were in, but I will *never* forgive you for what you have done to me. Also, I may be the last of our…my Clan, but I will *survive.* I will also keep up my efforts to everyone, that there is peace among Dragons, I might be a Dragon, but there's more to us then just bloodshed," I exclaimed to the winds and the lands as I looked up to the sky.

After we couldn't take the sight of the battle any longer, we joined what was left of our forces and departed the Chimera Kingdom. The Survivalists went their way while our Allies went another. As everyone went their separate ways we figured out what to do, the answer was simple: rebuild.

Chapter 13

Humans: The Other White Meat

"So what happened to Elexia, Backwards Forwards, and Pegasus?" asked Brak.

"*After the battle, Pegasus flew off in search of other creatures in need of help and assistance. I think she ended up living in what you Humans called Rome. Elexia and the other Unicorns went back to the remains of the Unicorn Palace to Take Queen Callista's place as Queen, and to help in the rebuilding of the Palace. Backwards Forwards and what was left of the Chimeras went into hiding so they could regroup, rebuild, and repopulate. For they took the most, and worst of the war,*" explained Drakon.

"That's it? I was expecting...more somehow," mussed Brak.

"*Why should I go on about their lives when you can ask them yourself? But first you will have to find them. Then convince them not too kill you, for last we met, they developed a thing for hating Humans,*" snapped Drakon.

Brak turned his head to the distant cave entrance and winced at Drakon's harshness towards former friends, allies, and Humans. But Brak's mussing was lost when he look up and out of the cave and up at the star filled sky. Brak took note on how the odd star would always tinkle, which seemed to be soothing to watch. He also looked at the large pale, white, full moon, and how it lit up the dark landscape. As Brak studied the view, he made a mental note to write down what the scenery looked like, completely away from civilization.

"It's getting late out, my guess would be that it's eleven o'clock. Hmm, what to do about sleeping arrangements. To sleep here and risk being a late night snack, or find a nice large rock to crawl under?" pondered Brak.

"*If you are worried about me eating you, you can stop. I had my fill of your kind for as long as I can remember meeting your kind. The same goes with Elves, Dwarfs, Goblins, Orcs, and any other Humanoid creature created by what you call magic,*" exclaimed Drakon.

"That reminds me, whatever happened to the races that you mentioned?" questioned Brak.

"*They're all dead for all I care. If you wish to know what happened to them, then hunt down the last remaining Elf that I know of. Her name in the Human tongue, is Serenity. She's about your height, long blood red hair that flows down to the ground, frosty blue eyes, long slender pointed ears, and a soft round face. Unlike most Elves, Serenity has pale white skin, but still, by your Human standards, she's beautiful. Now if you'll excuse me, I'm tired. We'll talk more tomorrow,*" explained Drakon sleepily with a hint of annoyance in his voice.

"So...you're *not* going to eat me then?" asked Brak cautiously.

"*Hmm, how about I eat half of you now and the other half later?*" snapped Drakon.

"Sleep sounds good," replied Brak defensively.

Drakon took in a breath of air and blew out the fire, darkness over took the cave in seconds and the silence began. Out of the many days of searching for a living Dragon, and finally finding one alive...and cooperative, made Brak feel happy. For it had been far too long of a search, with the results always turning up to be a dead Dragon...or killing one. Also Brak was sleeping with an ancestor, or so he hoped. Brak slept peacefully that night knowing he was safe, and secure...even if there *was* a Dragon the size of a small castle sleeping beside him. The next morning, Brak woke to the smell of roasting pig, and a large Dragon head right in his face.

"Holy shin—," Brak shouted as he jumped to his feet and almost fell over.

"*Heh, heh, heh, I've always wanted to do that,*" laughed Drakon as he grinned at Brak.

"Well, that was a first, and hopefully a last. Hmm, what's cooking? Smells like roast pig," wondered Brak.

"*That' what it is, and while you stuff your face with pig, I'll continue with my tale,*" answered Drakon.

"Did you ever encounter an ancient king by the name of King Arthur by any chance? Or how about a powerful wizard by the name of Merlin? And what about Queen Guinevere?" ask Brak as he stuffed his mouth full of pig.

"*Mention those names again and I will fry you on the spot,*" snarled Drakon.

"*Okay* then, I take you have or rather, had issues with them. Well, enough said, I'm eating," Brak exclaimed with a mouth full of food.

"*I'll jump a head, oh lets see, eight hundred years should do. I was nearing my late Adulthood. So I was now a full fledged Dragon. I was back living in my homeland and in charge of my own Clan. I was dealing with important Clan matters, when I had a scout come up to me,*" started Drakon.

* * *

"Drakon! I…I…I mean Drakon the Ancient. Sorry for disturbing you and the neighbouring Clan members, but I must speak with you privately," announced the Scout.

"It can't possibly be more important then what I'm trying to accomplish here," I growled. "Tell me what you've found, NOW!"

"I…I…but… Very well, it's hard to explain…or describe it, so I'll show you…all of you, Great Clan Leaders," sighed the Scout.

I didn't mean to snarl at the Scout, but I was stressed and the past five hundred years weren't a breeze. The Clan Wars in my homeland were at a ceasefire when I arrived, but they had began again. With more loss, pain, and death, I managed to form a peace between the major Clans. But it would only be time before the peace ended among the Clans. I made a mental note to apologize to the Scout when I had the chance. In the mean time the seven of us adjourned the meeting until this "urgent" matter was taken care of. When we all left the meeting room in my Great Den, we took to the sky. All of us followed the Scout with ease, for she might have been small for her age but she was still easy to see.

The Scout was covered in dark blue scales, but her wings were covered in gold. The Scouts' golden wings matched her golden hair that flowed down from the top of her head down to her wings. Her deep dark silver eyes were beautiful to look at as well. I knew the Scout, for she had become a friend during the end of The Elders War, that and she acted like a little sister sometimes. Her name was Blue wing, and in actuality, I knew she fancied me, half of the Dragonesses in my homeland did. While I was lost in thoughts, I noticed that Blue Wing didn't even bother to glide at certain times. Whatever it was that Blue Wing wanted to show us, must've been important for she was flying as fast as she could. We all flew for what seemed like eons until Blue Wing just stopped and hovered in the air.

"Down there. Look from here, *DO NOT* go any closer, otherwise you'll end up like the others, *dead. Those* creatures may look small and pathetic, but they're *not*," stated Blue Wing.

All of us looked down and couldn't believe our eyes, for what we saw was, a group of two legged creatures walking about and doing strange things. They were using strange brown, and silver objects. The creatures were also using a lot of animals, and making them do peculiar things. The creatures looked like they were covered in shiny grey scales, and a few of them were even on Horses. We all puzzled over why the Horses would want to work with these creatures. The creatures on the Horses seemed to be giving commands at the creatures that were on the land. It was too bad, for the height that we were hovering at, I couldn't hear them. We observed them for a while to see what they were doing and how they acted with one another. Occasionally the strange creatures would look up at the sky then go back to what they were doing.

"They're called: *Humans*, and they have already established settlements in our lands and throughout our territories. They kill anything insight, ranging from grass to trees, and from small harmless creatures, to us. The only good thing about these *Humans*, is that they have a habit of killing themselves and each other," explained Blue Wings.

"Oh?" questioned Zack the Quick.

Zack the Quick was a fair sized male, he was covered in dark yellow scales. His wings and hair were also a dark yellow to match his scales. The only things that weren't dark yellow on Zack the Quick, were his light green eyes, and his strangely coloured black claws. Unlike most Dragons, Zack the Quick preferred to look…unique, for he had very short hair. His hair flowed from the top of his head, and ended at the beginning of his neck. Even though Zack the Quick had hair, he preferred to look like the Dragons that didn't. Zack the Quick might've been yellow in colour, so you might think that he would be easy to see if he were hiding, but his gift of speed made up for the loss. If Zack the Quick wanted to, he could go from one place to another within a heart beat, and be back without anyone knowing it.

"Whenever a group of *Humans* creates a settlement, another group of *Humans* arrive and kill the first group to claim the settlement as their own. Or they will destroy the existing one and rebuild their own. There are also large groups of *Humans* that battle with each other until one or both sides are defeated. Also that shiny grey skin they have, is not their real skin, for they can take that skin on and off. Their real skin is pink, blue, red, green, or any colour but the shiny skin," explained Blue Wing

"How…interesting," remarked Silver the Pure.

Silver the Pure was a little bigger then the average adult female. She was covered in diamond white scales that always made me think of Sisillia. Her wings and hair were white as snow which matched her crystal coloured body. Silver the Pure's eyes were dark silver, while her claws and teeth were light silver. Silver the Pure's hair flowed from the top of her head to the tip of her tail. Even though you could see Silver the Pure easily on the ground, it was nearly impossible to see her in the sky in day or night. For her body would reflect the sun and make her look like a cloud from far away. Also if she chose, Silver the Pure had the gift of bending light, or going invisible in other words. The gift made Silver the Pure a very formidable fighter. It also amazed anyone who looked at Silver the Pure for her extremely long hair never got in her way.

"Can you show us evidence that these creatures…these *Humans* can slay our kind? I can see a Whelp, Youth, or even a careless Drake being killed by them, but not a full grown Dragon," asked Bark the Loud.

Bark the Loud was larger then the average adult male. He was covered in brown and black scales that were mixed in such a way, which gave him the appearance he was covered in dirt. His wings matched his scales for they were a mix of brown and black as well. His claws on the other claw were green for some unknown reason. It was a good thing though, for they matched his dark green hair and dark green eyes. His hair flowed from the top of his head down and over his shoulders, making it look as though Bark the Loud had a large bush on his shoulders. Bark the Loud may have had the perfect camouflage, but it was his gift that made him deadly and gave him his title. Bark the Loud could create sound waves that could shatter trees and crumbled mountains if he wished.

"Follow," stated Blue Wing.

Blue Wing flapped her wings and took off in another direction, we all followed. As we flew, Blue Wing came to an area and just stopped and hovered for a sun movement. She folded her wings close to her body, and dove gracefully to the ground. We of course followed her to the ground, after we all landed, Blue Wing started walking. She kept walking until she came to an area that was so badly burned and destroyed, that all of the beauty of the area was gone. In its' place was a dark vast, wasteland. When we all got to the rim of the wasteland, Blue Wing turned to us with an angry and saddened look on her face.

"You want your evidence? Then take a good look for yourselves," growled Blue Wing. "I'm *never* going into *that* place, ever again,"

So the seven of us walked into the dead wasteland, with caution in our steps and an open mind, for what we might see. As we walked into the darkness, I was starting to wish that Blue Wing had come with us, for we were all at a loss as to what we were looking for. Our eyes might be able to see at night but where we were, the wasteland was pitch black, and as far as I knew, Blue Wing's gift allowed her to see no matter how dark. After a while of getting nowhere in searching, as a group we decided to split up and search the wasteland. While we all searched the mysteries of this place, we came to the conclusion, that this wasteland was a massive battlefield with either the attacker or defender being a Dragon. We knew it was a massive area for all of us, for even though we were huge Dragons, we were spread out a good distance from one another.

"I found something," replied Reptillia the Cunning.

Reptillia the Cunning was smaller then the average female Dragon, but she was bigger then Blue Wing. She was covered in light and dark green scales that shimmered lightly whenever the sun hit them. Reptillia the Cunning's wings and hair were a light green, while her claws on the other claw, were bone white. Her bone white claws matched her bone white eyes. Her hair flowed down from the top of her head down to just below her shoulders. Reptillia the Cunning was one of the few Dragons born with disabilities, for she was blind, but that meant nothing when she battled. She was skilled in the art of strategy, and Reptillia the Cunning was famous for turning her enemies against one another. But her true power was her gift of future, for Reptillia the Cunning could see a few seconds movements into the future. This made Reptillia the Cunning a deadly fighter.

We all made our way over to Reptillia the Cunning to see what she found, but when we got to her, we couldn't see anything. Big surprise there, even our silhouettes were invisible to each other in this blackness.

"I know you're blind and all Reptillia, but how can you *see* anything in this blackness? We can easily see in the dark, but this is ridiculous, how can a place be so…so…black?" asked Jackal the Fierce.

Jackal the Fierce was an average sized male, he was covered completely in black scales, which ironically, matched the blackness of the wasteland. His wings and hair were also jet black as well. About the only thing that wasn't black on Jackal the Fierce, were his light red eyes. His hair flowed from the top of his head, and down to just passed his wings. His appearance alone could scare most enemies, for you wouldn't know if he killed you until Jackal the Fierce ate you. But it was Jackal the Fierce's gift that was the most devastating, to whomever he battled. His gift allowed him to heal himself and give him renewed strength so he could easily overpower his enemies.

"Use your nose Jackal, it's what it's there for when you can't see anything," stated Fiery the Wise.

Fiery the Wise was the size of an average female, she was covered in a mix of reddish orange scales with a hint of yellow mixed in as well. Her wings and hair were also a mix of red, orange, and yellow. Fiery the Wise's hair flowed from the top of her head, past and over her shoulders, down to the ground. Whenever Fiery the Wise moved, it looked as though her entire body was on fire. Her eyes though were a bright blue, which made it very interesting to look at Fiery the Wise. To top it off, Fiery the Wise had bone white teeth and claws. Her gift was somewhat like Reptillia the

Cunning's and mine, except that Fiery the Wise could hear and see what any living creature was thinking, which gave her a deadly edge. Also, like me, Fiery the Wise had a photographic memory, which allowed her to recall and remember anything to mind that she had seen. The only difference though was that my photographic memory was stronger and it allowed me to remember and experience more. With her photographic memory, Fiery the Wise was an excellent tactician.

"Now, now Whelps. We're all here to settle our differences, not to start *another* long Clan War. From what I was told, and from what I've witnessed, one was enough…at least for this millennium. Now Fiery and Jackal, kiss and mate. Also, what smells around here? is it this area or is it one of *you*? I mocked.

"I'll agree to *that*," added and laughed Zack the Quick.

"Shut up *Fiery the Wise*. That goes double to you *Drakon the Ancient*…how'd you get that title anyway? You can't be *that* old. you're only what, eight hundred years or so?" snapped Jackal the Fierce.

"Want to bet? I'm twenty-three hundred years old. I'm old enough to be *your* Elder, or *your* Father at least," I growled.

"I can take you anytime *Drakon*," snarled Jackal the Fierce in return.

"Boys! *Old Lizards*, whatever you want to be called, quit your squabbling and check this out," roared Silver the Pure.

We all gathered around Reptillia the Cunning and Silver the Pure, using our noses to find them. It wasn't that hard to find them either, for both Dragonesses smelled beautiful. Once we were all together we all used our noses and senses to try and get a picture of the battlefield. After a while of trying this, I got bored, for the fact that I couldn't picture anything. Some Dragons had the ability to get a mental picture of something when they used their senses and not their eyes, I wasn't one of these Dragons. I titled my head to where the sky should be. And let loose a large stream of fire, which caught quite a few dead trees on fire. As soon as the light appeared though, we all saw what Blue Wing had seen, and why she vowed never to return.

We were in a small nesting ground that was utterly destroyed beyond recognition. The once beautifully crafted nests, were either in ruins or completely demolished. While we were taking in the sight of the destroyed nests, we also saw something that broke all of our hearts. The once beautiful nests weren't empty, or abandoned either. For there were hundreds of Hatchlings, and Whelps spread all over the ground and in the nests, they were all motionless, and broken. There were at least ten sets of Adults that we could pick out, all of them were *dead* as well. The adults that laid on the cold dead earth were most likely the parents. By the position of some of the adults, they looked like they were protecting their kin, till their last breath. There were also a couple of hundred *Humans*, and about sixty Horses that littered the ground as well. These *Humans* were in a deserving state, some were burned, while others were cooked. All of them looked as though they suffered a long lengthy battle, with no winners.

At the sight of this, some of us began to shed tears for the young that didn't even have a chance to experience life. As some of us cried, our tears fell to the ground, as they fell, they reflected the horrors and carnage we witnessed. We were also beginning to hate these *Humans* that had infested our lands. It looked as though the *Humans* were the attackers and the Dragons were the defenders. After we took in the view, we turned to leave the cursed place when we heard a scream. All of us raced to the entrance to the wasteland to see Blue Wing fall from the sky. There were dozens of tiny, and large round smooth sticks protruding out of her body. In the distance, there were hundreds of *Humans* advancing to the wasteland. Some of them were on Horses, for some reason, the *Humans* liked to ride them. Once they saw us though, the *Humans* began shouting to one another.

"*There are more of those vile creatures. Let's kill them so they won't cause us anymore harm. Once they're dead, we'll dice them up so we can have food that'll last us for many seasons to come. Not to mention, we'll all become very rich men,*" yelled one of the *Humans* on horseback.

"What are they saying Drakon?" asked Zack the Quick.

"You *don't* want to know. Silver, does your gift only work on you? Or can you use it on others?" I questioned.

"I can use my gift on others, but you'll have to protect me. For I will be extremely weak, and focusing too hard to defend myself," answered Silver the Pure.

"Okay. Everyone, get ready to fly into the air and disappear. But first, Bark, would you be so kind as to get rid of the advancing annoyances?" I asked.

"It would be my pleasure. Everyone get ready to fly as soon as I open my mouth, and fly hard," exclaimed Bark the Loud.

After Bark the Loud finished speaking, we all took to the air, and flew as hard, fast, and high as we could. It was a good thing that we followed Bark the Loud's advice, for Bark the Loud had opened his mouth and put his gift to use. All of the Humans that were within easy earshot of the horrifying scream went down to their knees, clutching their ears. Some of the Humans stopped moving as they went down to the ground. Even though we were high in the air, all of us felt light headed from Bark the Loud's scream. He joined us shortly after he stopped screaming. When we were all together, Silver the Pure took over with her gift. Her eyes began to glow to a dark blue, before she disappeared from sight. The rest of us felt a strange mildly painful feeling while Silver the Pure's gift spread to the rest of us.

Then one by one, we disappeared from the Humans sight. Once we vanished, the Humans that weren't dead got up and looked at the sky. When they couldn't see, or hear us, some of them dropped to their knees and started making gestures with their hands. Also, they were speaking or mumbling to some great being about demons. Even though a Dragon can hear a pin drop from a great distance away, I was too high up to hear what they were saying. We decided to leave the murderous Humans, and return to my settlement to make plans, and discuss on how to deal with this *Human* threat. We would also discuss the more important matter on how to kill all of them.

It had been three months since the murder of Blue Wing and the destruction of the nesting ground. In that time we only accomplished nothing but fighting with one another, and coming up with useless plans.

"We should do to these *Humans*, what they did to us," stated Bark the Loud.

"And end up *dead* like everyone else who's fought them?" snapped Silver the Pure.

"Well, at least we'll show them who they are dealing with," shot Reptillia the Cunning.

"Not, if we go in force. We should personally show these *Humans* who they're dealing with. With our gifts, and the power we control, we have no equal. *And* no *Humans* either," growled Zack the Quick.

"Are you insane? I am not sending my whole Clan to the slaughter. Our clans are still recovering from the last Clan War. Also if you haven't noticed, those *Humans* have gifts as well. *Not* to mention "special" abilities, and mystical powers. They're worse then those damn vile Creatures, known as Unicorns," stated Fiery the Wise.

I glared at Fiery the Wise for insulting the Unicorns for I had friends who were Unicorns, and had helped, and fought beside them in the past. Also I had a few Unicorns living within my Clan, and settlement.

"Fiery's right, I'm not sending my whole Clan to the slaughter either. I'll protect my Clan, and defend my home first," agreed Jackal the Fierce.

"You're one to talk. Last Clan War we were involved in, you sent your *whole* Clan to their deaths. Save for *maybe* a handful of *female mates*," shot Bark the Loud.

"At least I got the job done, *unlike* some people I know. And what do *you* mean by *female mates*? Are you implying something?" snapped Jackal the Fierce.

"Where did they learn to wield gifts, and mystical abilities anyway? Last I checked, they were using pointy sticks made out of wood and metal, or just metal," questioned Silver the Pure.

"I don't know, and I don't care either. As long as they can burn, and taste good, that's all that matters," stated Zack the Quick.

"*You* catch your own food? Well, that's a first. I always thought you were *too* quick for such things, and only had one of your brain dead *mates* do all the work for you," shot Reptillia the Cunning.

"Well, at least he doesn't go around and mate with every-," Fiery the Wise began before I cut her off.

"EVERYONE ENOUGH!" I roared. "I know we're all stressed out and angry with this but I have a plan. Here's what we'll do with the *Human* threat—."

"*Oh*? And what does the *almighty* "Drakon the Ancient" have to say? Whatever it is, it will probably fail like everything else. Or, we'll all end up loosing more then what we want to the *Humans*. Like all the wars Drakon's "claimed" to have fought and won, and he *always* experienced loss. My favorite tale had to have been the war with "The Elders", who used to rule these lands. Where's your proof of your victories *Drakon*?" mocked Jackal the Fierce.

I got up from where I was laying and was about to go and rip Jackal the Fierce's head from his shoulders for making a mockery of me and what I had lost. When Silver the Pure got up at the same time and walked over to Jackal the Fierce. Once she was close enough to Jackal the Fierce, she gave him a loving smile before her expression turned to hate and disgust. Silver the Pure then spun so fast that it was almost like she never moved at all, but she had. For Jackal the Fierce was knocked off from where he was laying, by Silver the Pure's elegant tail, and beautiful hair. After the successful strike, and putting Jackal the Fierce in his place, Silver the Pure went back to her spot and laid back down. Leaving a very stunned Jackal the Fierce starring at her, while I smiled and laid back down. I knew Silver the Pure fancied me, but I didn't think that she would strike Jackal the Fierce.

"Hold your tongue *Fierce*. Drakon the Ancient has been through *more* then we could ever imagine, and has lost more then any of us combined. While we were all just starting our Clan Wars, Drakon was fighting to save a land that was against him. While we fought petty wars with one another, and let the *Human* menace get out of our claws, Drakon was saving lives and races. Now look, the *Humans* are out of control, and now a threat to our existence. The sad part is, we're all to blame for *this*," Silver the Pure snapped.

"Who cares? I could have done the same thing if I was in his position," shot Zack the Quick.

"But could *you*? Could any of *you* go through the hardships and sacrifices that Drakon the Ancient has? I know I wouldn't have been able to. Drakon fought three mass wars, as history tells it. The first was against the *Vile*...I mean Graceful Unicorns, which eventually became allies. Sadly when *that* war was over, Drakon suffered a personal loss. Remember the legend of Slash & Burn anyone? The only Dragon in our history to be "exiled" for being a little too bloodthirsty. Drakon fought against him, and again suffered another personal loss. The third war, was against "The Elders" as *you* put it Jackal the Farce. While we were still young, we all wanted them gone or dead, because of their tyranny. Drakon fought them *and* his own parents who allied themselves with The Elders.

In the end Drakon, his allies, and his legendary Survivalists won, but again Drakon suffered a personal loss, but this loss was the greatest. At the cost of victory, Drakon became, not only an Orphan, but also, he was…still is, the last of his Clan. But as we all know, that didn't stop Drakon from forming a new Clan, and coming back to his homeland, only to fight against all of us.

I can see anyone of us winning at least one war in far off lands, with enemies around every tree and rock. But not three of them, not in a row either, and carrying the heavy burden of loss and sadness," explained Silver the Pure with tears forming in her eyes.

I was a little shocked that my past was well known over here, but I made sure to keep my face expressionless, for Silver the Pure had touched on many touchy subjects.

"I remember that, I was told about the Great Wars in far off lands when I was a Whelp and a Youth. I always wondered if the tales were true. But what Silver the Pure said, I guess they are. I also understand now on how you got your title Drakon the Ancient. Whatever it is you have planned I will listen to it," reflected Fiery the Wise who was trying without success to hold back tears.

"I agree with you Fiery, it would make the most sense to listen to what Drakon the Ancient has to say. For he does have knowledge and the experience on fighting new and unknown enemies," agreed Bark the Loud with newfound respect for me.

"*Shut up* Zack before you say something you'll regret. The same goes to you Jackal. The *only* reason why the two of are here, *and* in charge of a Clan is the simple fact that your *poor* parents died," snarled Reptillia the Cunning.

As much as I liked having people stand up for me, I had to put an end to all of this bickering, and praising. For as soon as Reptillia the Cunning finished speaking her mind the arguments started up again of what to do about the Humans. I also didn't want any of us to start killing one another in my settlement, or to start another Clan War. I stood up, shook myself to get the feeling back in my muscles, and raised my right hand high into the air. If the thunderous sound that my hand made, when I slammed it into the ground, didn't silence everyone, then the loud curse I roared, did. Once everyone was starring at me, I laid out my plan.

"Here's what we are going to do," I explained. "From what we know and have seen the *Humans* are capable of making unwanted surprises. How and why they have and can make gifts, I don't know, and frankly, don't care. All I care about right now, is the protection of our own kind, for if we're not careful we'll become extinct, like so many others. We'll have large patrols and scouts set up along our borders to keep an eye out for any developments. Any neighbouring Clan that doesn't approve of this, can either join us, or fend for themselves. I don't feel like protecting idiots. I also want "The Best" Scouts that each of you can offer up, to keep an eye on the *Humans*. This is so we can plan counter strikes, and attacks if they try anything.

I also know that you all hate them, but we also need to enlist the aid of any Unicorn, Chimera, Gryphon, and I dare say Basilisk. I know they are few in numbers due to the *Humans*, and us, but if they hate the *Humans* as much as us, they should join in our efforts. It's too bad that the Hypogryphs have become extinct, because we could've used their help. But I'm sure the other four races will gladly join us, for like I said they hate *Humans* like us. Lastly, get large raid parties together to raze any *Human* settlement. Leave the settlements that have the large structures, for that is where the mystic wielders, and gift users like to live. Now if no one has any problems with this plan, then, get to work. If you don't do your part, then we have already lost and the *Humans* have won."

No one said or dared to speak after I finished my long speech. Everyone just starred at me, for they wouldn't have guessed that I would have a plan to deal with the *Humans* already. I looked at everyone in turn and laughed, for the look on all of their faces was quite funny. I then focused on the matter at claw, and called on of my scouts over and gave her a message for the Survivalists to ready themselves. I also wanted them to enlist all of the help they could find, for we were going into another long war, yet again. I also told the scout to seek out our Unicorn, and Chimera Survivalists that came to the new lands with us. Not all of the Survivalists stayed with me when I rebuilt my own Clan. As I was giving my Scout her orders, the other Clan Leaders left, to make their own preparations. Once they all left, I called over three Survivalists, to seek out the Gryphon Lord of these lands, the Queen of the Unicorns: Queen Elexia, and the Chief of the Chimeras: Chief Backwards Forwards. In the "Allied Lands". While I would seek out the head of the Basilisks and see if I could talk to them.

After many months, our efforts in defending ourselves against the Humans was working well. For our scouts and patrols could see any advancing army or war party, and we easily, and quickly disposed of them. Our raid efforts were also going well, for any new or small settlement that was being built in, or near our territories were destroyed. Before it could be properly reinforced with Humans and their gifts, and mystical abilities. When it came to destroying the settlements, we did to the Humans, what they did to us: destroy everything, including whole families. It might have sounded cruel and unjust, but the Humans started it, and we would finish it. No matter what the Humans did or tried, we always prevailed, for we were always a step a head of them. All of our plans on the Humans destruction were working out nicely. Our race, the Unicorn race, Gryphon race, and the Chimera race were all thriving again while the Humans were burning. As for the Basilisks, well they weren't faring so well but no one really cared about them, for they were Basilisks.

At first we thought we were winning, until we encountered a Human that equaled our methods and tactics. You know this Human as: King Arthur, who had a powerful advisor whom went by many names. Although *you* would know him best as: Merlin the Wizard.

Chapter 14

The Debate on King Arthur

"Not to press the matter, but, what happened with your encounter with the legendary King Arthur, Queen Guinevere, and their wizard: Merlin? I only ask because no one seems to have any knowledge, tales, facts, or stories about them. Also, you did mention him earlier. The only evidence I could find, were in fairytales, myths, and legends. But *you* actually saw him," asked Brak.

"*What did I tell you I'd do to you, if you mentioned those names?*" growled Drakon.

"But you said-," started Brak before he was cut off.

"*But I said, but I said. What I said was "If you mention those names I would fry you on the spot." And now I will,*" growled Drakon as he began to create a fireball.

"Okay, you win…again, I only wanted to know for *our* Histories sake. You can keep putting it off on telling me on why there are so few of you, but I need to know about King Arthur and his people. I need to know things like: what were they like? What did they do? Why is there no record of them? Please, Drakon the Ancient, I need to…no, I must know what happened to King Arthur, Queen Guinevere, and Merlin the Wizard," pleaded Brak.

"*You want to know? Fine! I'll tell you. Arthur and his people are dead, plain and simple,*" replied Drakon coldly.

"I know *that*, but why? How? I need details and facts," snapped Brak.

"*Alright, if it will shut you up, I'll tell you. Otherwise I know you won't stop bothering me about him. I also know you're smarter then you let other people think, and that you have a secret that you don't want anyone else to know about. That, and if I kill you, others will come in your place. I will never have peace and quiet ever again...or ever be left alone*," surrendered Drakon as he let his fireball that he was still holding onto, disintegrate.

"*Thank you.* You have no idea what this means to me," thanked Brak.

"*Whatever. I will warn you though, what I'm about to tell you, you won't like*," exclaimed Drakon.

"I don't care, I'll keep an open mind," stated Brak.

"*Very well, you've been warned*," stated Drakon.

* * *

Just when we thought we were winning against the Humans, they just *had* to have a "Hero" arise. It wasn't just one "Hero" as we found out, he had friends to help him. It was like there was an enchantment cast all over the Humans, for when the "Hero" came into power, all of the Humans stopped their fighting with each other. They started working together to destroy the "threat" namely, us. We fought against the newly united Humans, but we were loosing badly. The humans' tactics and strategies were proving to be very effective. We fought back of course, but we were no match, with reports coming in from all over our territories, that whole Clans were now falling to this "Hero" and his friends. We later found out this "Hero" was named Arthur, and we thought that his methods of attacking were very strange. He was assaulting Clan after Clan, but he wasn't touching our seven Allied Clans. After what seemed like an endless amount of fighting, we all regrouped to discuss the matter of Arthur and what we should do about him.

"This new "Hero" that the *Humans* are following, is eradicating all of the Dragon Clans, not only here but in other lands overseas," stated Zack.

"But the "Hero" has not dared to touch any of *our* Clans...why?" questioned Reptillia.

"That's the question at claw now isn't it. My *question* is: who is going to find out why? Anyone who gets within eyesight of the "Hero" ends up dead," asked Bark.

"I know, let's talk to *Drakon the Ancient*, he knows *everything*. He's old, fought in three wars, four if you count the ones against the *Humans*. Where's your "Survivalists" *Drakon*? I'm sure they'll help *you* out…I mean *us*," mocked Jackal.

"I have scouts spying on the *Humans*, and their "Hero" as I speak. Also I intend to see for myself on what this "Hero" can do. Unlike a Dragon Clan Leader I know, who is hiding behind his pathetic army of mates. Isn't that *right* Jackal?" I snapped.

"Arguing isn't going to get us anywhere, we need a plan," stated Fiery as she tried to set a calming mood.

"I agree with Reptillia. There's got to be a reason why the *Humans* aren't attacking us. Where's Silver? I thought she was supposed to be here at this meeting?" asked Zack.

"Silver had urgent Clan matters to deal with. Besides, she's a big Dragoness now Zack, so I'm sure she can handle herself. Besides I don't think she's into your type," replied Reptillia mockingly.

After Reptillia finished speaking, Silver entered into the Meeting Den. She was in rough shape, with dozens of small and large cuts, and bruises. Silver also had a wooden shaft or two lodged into and between her beautiful scales. Silver's long beautiful hair was also torn in half and partially singed at the tips. As soon as Silver took the first few steps inside, she collapsed on the ground from exhaustion. The six of us got up form where we were laying on the ground, and rushed over to Silver, to see if she was alright. Fiery called for healers, seeing as we were at her settlement to discuss the *Human* matters this time.

"Our allies on the Southern Lands and on the Eastern Lands have been obliterated," breathed Silver as she stood up, only to fall back down.

"What happened to you?" asked Bark.

"Merlin happened to me. *King Arthur's* gifted second in command. By the way that is the name of the "Hero"…*Arthur*. Anyway Merlin and a small band of *Humans* ambushed me on my return trip back to Fiery's territory. Even with my gift, Merlin and his *Humans* still saw me. It was strange though, for as soon as I reached Jackal's borders, Merlin and his party stopped the chase and retreated," explained Silver weakly.

"*Merlin*, I've heard of him. He alone has the power to destroy a whole Clan. But more importantly, he's one of the keys in destroying *Arthur*," exclaimed Jackal.

"What about *Arthur*'s mate? The one they call Guinevere, doesn't she pose some significance towards *Arthur*?" asked Fiery.

"Fellow Clan Leaders, we are loosing focus on our main concern. Our main concern right now, is why isn't *Arthur* attacking the seven of us? And how can we turn this into our advantage?" questioned Reptillia.

"That's simple, we expand our borders and merge our territories into one large one. Any *Humans* caught in our path will be destroyed. If my theory is correct, the *Humans* and *Arthur* won't do a thing," announced Zack.

"That's all well and good, but *Arthur* is nowhere near our lands. And he will probably see right through the plan. I mean we've been battling the *Humans* for what, eight or nine hundred years now, give or take a year. We were winning in the beginning, until *Arthur* showed up and started to copy our methods and tactics. Now the *Humans* are winning. By the time *Arthur* sees what we're doing, he'll turn it against us," explained Bark.

I was about to voice my own idea of what we should try to do when Fiery spoke up.

"Then we'll go with a plan that's so simple and complex, that it will stun *Arthur*," stated Fiery.

"Oh? And what devious plan do you have in mind *Fiery the Wise*? Hopefully it'll be a good working plan, as opposed to your usual failures," mocked Jackal.

At that insult, Fiery rose to her feet and launched herself at Jackal. It was a good thing that Fiery's Meeting Den was large, for the rest of us got out of the way of the two fighting Dragons. Silver on the other claw, decided to stay where she was, for the simple reason that Silver would feel extreme pain if she moved. I had moved a little closer to Silver and kept my gaze on her for a little while, to see if she needed help in moving or to be carried out of the Den. But the Dragon part of me was taking over, for the fight between Fiery and Jackal was proving to be far too interesting, not to watch. It was also entertaining and hard to watch Fiery put Jackal in his place. For every slash that Fiery inflicted, Jackal would retaliate with a lash of his tail, or the bite of his jaws. While every fire attack from Jackal, would result in Fiery using her ice breath. Fiery would've loved to use her own fire, but Fiery liked her Meeting Den in one piece.

As both Dragons fought, I noticed that a healer had arrived to treat Silver. I was shocked to see what the healer was as well. The healer was a Unicorn, which was interesting for I had thought that I was the only Dragon that had other races living within my Clan. I mused that some of the Other Clan Leaders, saw the benefits, in having allies who weren't Dragons, and decided to try it out.

"Alright, that's enough of your fighting. I'd like to treat Clan Leader: Silver the Pure, before she dies of her injuries. Or from you two Clan Leaders clawing it out with one another," shouted the Unicorn in Draconic.

Everyone stopped and looked at the Unicorn, for it was an unhealthy thing to shout an order to any Clan Leader. Especially when the Clan Leaders are arguing with one another or fighting with one another. Also it was a shock to hear another creature, let alone a Unicorn, speak in our native tongue. The Unicorn obviously didn't care about our rules, or had a high ranking status within Fiery's Clan. There was also the possibility that the Unicorn was very close to Fiery, for it wasn't unheard of, of two different creatures fancying one another. The Unicorn was tall, and muscular, with a lush long tail. Unlike most Unicorns, this one was black from nose to tail. The only thing not black was his, bone white horn and his dark green eyes.

The Unicorn walked over to Silver and started to glow with a pink aura. As the Unicorn walked over to Silver, she tried to back away, for every Dragon was taught as a Hatchling to hate and fear Unicorns. It was only recently, and thanks in part to myself, that Unicorns had become allies if the time arose. The Unicorn lowered his head when he was right in front of Silver, and touched the top of Silver's nose. Once the horn touched Silver, she was encased in a pink glow like the Unicorn. When the glow was gone, Silver was back to her normal, healthy self. Save for her long flowing hair, which only flowed down to her wings now, but she was still beautiful nonetheless.

"Now you can go back to your fighting," announced the Unicorn.

"Thank you *Sha'aid*," replied Fiery.

"You are welcome Fiery the Wise," stated *Sha'aid*.

Sha'aid bowed his head and walked out of the Meeting Den, while we resumed our debate on how best to deal with Arthur. The seven of us continued our meeting for another two days, debating, arguing, and fighting. We eventually came to a conclusion on how best to deal with Arthur. We would use an old technique of raiding *Human* supply lines, and destroy any small settlements, cities, and castles that were being constructed in our lands. With any luck, our efforts would draw out Arthur and we could destroy him. When our planning was done, we *finally* adjourned the meeting and went to go about our own personal planning.

Chapter 15

The Fall of a King and Queen

"Love the encounter with Arthur, all talk and no action. When I said I wanted details, and facts, I meant on King Arthur, Queen Guinevere, and Merlin. Not on your debate, and squabbles of what to do about Arthur," exclaimed and complained Brak.

"*Fine, if you do not wish to know about your precious history, then you can either: leave, or die,*" growled Drakon who was starting to become annoyed with Brak again.

"But you agreed to...arg, never mind. Just continue on with your tale of King Arthur," surrendered Brak.

Drakon smiled. "*I'd thought you'd see it my way.*"

* * *

All of the Clan Leaders set out to their territories to prepare for our attack on the Humans. Each Clan Leader, or Clan rather, was in charge of attacking a certain area of the "Human Lands". Bark, and Zack were in charge of laying siege to the nearby Castles. Fiery, and Jackal were in charge of assaulting any and all nearby settlements, and cities that bordered our lands. Reptillia, and Silver where in charge of raiding and destroying the trade routes and supply lines that the Humans used. I was in charge of supplying the other Clan Leaders with troops, ranging from

Unicorn, to Gryphon. As our battles lasted through the years, both, the Humans and the Dragons numbers, dwindled, but there was still no sight as to who would win. The only accomplishment though, was that we succeeded in destroying all of Arthur's "Knights of the Round Table". When they finally died, we set our sights on Arthur's home: Camelot

To describe Camelot, would be like describing the most beautiful *Human* structure you've ever seen, The kingdom was vast, as big as four average sized kingdoms combined. The Outer Walls, being made out of large bricks, were as tall as the biggest trees, and as white, and smooth as a pearl. The Gateway into the Kingdom was huge as well, it was made out of steel that was dyed red. The massive wooden door that blocked the entrance had many different designs on it. Most of them were of Humans with their swords drawn and pointed upwards to a portrait of a Dragon that was painted blue. Its' Observatory, and Battle Towers were also a marvel. They were stationed on the Outer Walls, spaced out two hundred feet apart from one another. The Towers were different in colour from the walls, for the Towers were blue, with the spires being red. Aside from the Outer Walls inside them, laid the massive city with the Castle: Camelot, on a large grassy hill over looking the vast city.

The city was unique in its' own way, for there were no two buildings the same size. Each building was ranging from the size of a small Chimera Den to the size of a large Dragon Den. The colours of the city were very interesting too look at as well. For even though the Outer Walls were white, the city was ranged from a dull brown to a bright red. The city also seemed to shine depending on how the sun shone on it. Starting from the east, the city sparkled in a blue light, but when the sun reached the west, the city sparkled in a green light. With all of the Humans running about, doing their day-to-day routines, they gave the impression of a giant anthill. It was too bad that we were going to stir up, then destroy, *this* anthill.

The Castle Camelot had to have been the biggest Castle that any living creature alive, could see. With twelve bone white towers and walls surrounding the buildings, it was a force to be reckoned with. The buildings in the inside of the walls were evenly spaced out, and like the towers, they were bone white. About the only thing that wasn't bone white in colour on the Castle, were the spire and triangular roofs. All of the roofs ranged from light to dark blue, with a tint of dark red. When you looked at the colours you could almost feel yourself being hypnotized by the "moving" colours. It was too bad, that we wanted to destroy it all, for it really was a marvel to look at.

Our assault on Camelot was long and fierce, but getting to the Castle itself, was the easy part. All seven of the Clan Leaders with their full might, were only an even match against the Outer Walls. The only way to destroy the Outer Walls was for every Dragon that could breathe fire, heat the walls. Once the walls were red hot, the Dragons that had the ability to breathe cold air, or ice, would freeze the walls. After the Dragons did their repetitive work on the Outer Walls, Bark used his gift, and shattered the walls, the magical, and the mystical barriers that protected the city and the castle. With the destruction of the Outer Walls, we had taken a heavy blow. Bark the Loud, and his entire Clan were killed, due to a surprise attack done by the gifted Humans, who were lying in wait for him. Bark never told anyone, but every time he used his gift, it made him extremely weak, sadly, the Humans knew this, and used it against him.

When we breached the Outer Walls and started our attack on the city, we encountered more resistance. The resistance was a large group of gifted Humans that put up a good fight. But in the end, the gifted Humans perished in our assault leaving the city open for attack. While we burned the city and created an inferno, we had our encounter with Merlin. Merlin was of average height and weight of an elderly Human male. His snow white long hair and his grey beard, made it hard to tell how old he really was. His brown eyes matched his dark dull brown robe, shoes, and gloves. Merlin also carried a tall bone white staff that had intricate markings and designs carved all over it. Merlin had a seemingly endless amount of gifts and mystical energies that he wielded. Merlin also proved what he was capable of, when he destroyed Reptillia without lifting a finger. With her destruction, Reptillia's Clan fell into dismay, and chaos, which tore itself apart. During our battle in the city, I learned that the Humans had captured Fiery. With the news of Fiery's disappearance, her Clan fell into dismay, which diminished the Clan to only a handful. After the city was burning as far as the eye could see, what remained of our forces advanced on the Castle: Camelot.

The battle with Merlin was a long and lengthy one, we already lost three Clan Leaders out of the seven of us, and two Clans were utterly destroyed. Zack, and Jackal were the next two, to fall in the final assault on the Castle, and Merlin. They had fallen to Merlin's spells, incantations, and enchantments. But I had managed to gain control of both of their Clans before more chaos could break out. The Unicorn, Chimera, and Gryphon forces weren't doing any better. Queen Elexia and Chief Backwards Forwards had brought their full might, but they were no match for *Merlin's*. During the end of the battle, Elexia, and Backwards Forwards had to pull their troops out of the fight, unless they wanted to risk extinction. Sadly, the Gryphons were completely destroyed save for maybe ten or twenty. With all of our forces depleting fast, everyone gathered for one final assault on Merlin and Camelot. While the Unicorns focused their energies, and the Chimeras were regrouping, the Dragons flew high into the sky taking in all the fresh air, our lungs could handle. Then the Dragons dove down to the ground and plummeted towards Merlin. We let loose a typhoon of fire, while the Unicorns let loose with their mystical energies. As the Dragons flew by the Castle, it was like seeing a variation of what you Humans call: Hell. In the end Merlin, and the Kingdom of Camelot were destroyed, razed, and in ruins, but Arthur and Guinevere, weren't around. They had fled further into their lands to probably try and rebuild their forces and assault us.

What remained of the assaulting forces regrouped in my old Clan territory, to plan our next move and to mourn the deaths of friends and family. As we planned, I had Chimera, and Unicorn scouts going to and fro, finding out what they could about Arthur. Among the reports there was grave news, Silver had encountered one of Arthur's groups, and disappeared. Her Clan was looking for her, but so far, nothing. Two months had passed and there was still no word from Arthur, and Guinevere, but there was news of Silver. She was found unconscious and severely injured, outside of the ruins of Salvation. Why she was there, and in that state, no one knew or dared to ask. Another six months passed with still no news on the whereabouts of Arthur, but one day a scout arrived with news of his location. With this news, we became eager in wanting to finish this long war, and to kill Arthur.

When the scout finished his report on where Arthur was, we set out in force. We eventually found Arthur, he had fled to the nearby island to the northeast of this land. Once we arrived, the battling and chaos began, while the destruction commenced. Arthur was found on the north part of the island with what seemed like a huge army that was ready for war. But there was a problem, it wasn't Arthur leading the army. His mate apparently wanted some "revenge" for what we did to her. So she decided to raise an army of her own. Queen Guinevere was clad in thin silver armor that conformed, and covered her whole body, save for her arms, lower legs, and head. Guinevere's hands were covered with thick white silk gloves that stopped before her elbows. While her feet were hidden behind thin silver boots that stopped before her kneecaps.

Guinevere had a long elegant golden bow that was shaped to look like a swan's wing. The bow was pulled back taunt with an arrow knocked and ready to fly. She glared at me with her dark brown eyes, with her long golden hair flying gently behind her and in front of her in the breeze. I returned her glare with one of my own, that could send a chill down any creature's spine, but Guinevere was unmoved. We both knew that it would be the end for one of us that day. As much as I wanted to fight her, I didn't dare fight Guinevere. That honor went to Silver, who wanted a little revenge of her own, for what Guinevere put her through. Apparently, Silver had a run-in with Guinevere on one of her travels to find allies, and to see what remained of our kind.

While our forces battled Guinevere and her army, I slipped off to hunt down Arthur. I knew that if his mate was here, he would be here as well. That and his scent was all over the area, so it was only a matter of "sniffing" him out. Due to the dense forest, I decided to take to the ground and smell him out. I would've set the whole island ablaze to make things easier, but I didn't want to destroy the land, *or* what remained of our forces and allies. It took three hundred sun movements, before I finally tracked Arthur down. Unfortunately, Arthur wasn't alone when I found him, he had an army of his own surrounding him. Unlike Guinevere's army, Arthur's army was mostly comprised of gifted Humans with some Humans carrying bows, and other assorted weapons. By the looks of the army, this was going to be harder then I thought. As I prepared myself for the possibly last battle of my life, I caught a glimpse of two familiar creatures with their own war parties. I took to the air to plan my own assault, as the battle unfolded.

Queen Elexia, and Chief Backwards Forwards burst from their hiding places with their war parties following them. Their surprise attack caught Arthur's army off guard, for they were expecting me or a group of Dragons to come. While the confusion and chaos began, I did the only thing I could think of. I folded my wings and dove down to the ground with my sights set on Arthur. It was too bad that I didn't have the element of surprise, for Arthur could see me flying at him a mile away, but there was no where for him to run. With his army protecting him from all sides, and the Chimera and Unicorn parties advancing, Arthur was trapped. It only took a sun movement but it seemed like an eon, as I swooped down and grabbed Arthur while he drew his sword. As my hand closed around his body, Arthur let go of his sword, and as I flew off, Arthur's sword spun to the ground. As the sword's blade bit deep into the cold red earth, its' reflection showed a picture of bloodshed on one side and death on the other.

I landed in a mountainous area far away from the final battle and set Arthur down on the ground. I wanted a few answers from him before he died, but once Arthur's feet touched the ground, and he was free, Arthur ran for his life. I gave chase for I didn't want my questions to go unanswered, plus, I wanted to be the one to *kill* him. I found Arthur hiding in a nearby rock pile and pulled him out. Only *this* time, I didn't put him down. As I looked at Arthur, I finally had a moment to study the *Human* that caused us so much harm. Arthur was clad in a full suit of gold plate mail, with an engraving of a ruby coloured lion head on the breast plate. His suit of armor also shimmered with mystical energies, but with the resistance I had built up over the years, I was immune to the effects. Arthur had short brown hair that ended at the base of his neck, his hair matched his dark brown eyes. On top of Arthur's head rested a golden crown that sparkled and gleamed with a variety of gems.

"*Why have you done this? We could have lived in peace with one another. But you just had to go and kill us one by one, or by the Hundreds,*" I growled.

"You...you can talk? How is that possible? Why is that possible?" questioned Arthur in return.

"*What I can do, and how I can do it, is none of your concern. Answer my question!*" I snarled.

"*I* could ask *you* the same question. Seeing as your *kind* murdered thousands of innocent people. Whole families were destroyed, whole cities, castles, and kingdoms were leveled, and razed. All we wanted was peace from you, and *you* responded with death and destruction," snapped Arthur.

"*Our reason for attacking you Human, is simple. We had to defend ourselves against your attacks on us, and your assaults on our Nesting Grounds. If you are unfamiliar with the term Nesting Grounds, then I will make it even simpler for your Human mind to comprehend. You slaughtered our Families, children, and other creatures. Your kind slaughtered a countless number of our race, before we even began to attack you. If you had not attacked us, we would have never attacked you,*" I growled. "*Your turn, answer my question, or suffer.*"

"We *never* attacked your "Nesting Grounds" or any other Mystical creatures. We cherished and valued them," started Arthur.

"*Don't you DARE lie to me, Human. For once in your miserable life, show some dignity and tell the truth,*" I roared.

"I…we…I would never have given any orders to attack your kind. We looked up to you. We practically worshiped you and the Unicorns, as gods," continued Arthur.

"*So you decided to decapitate our murdered brethren and bring their heads into your "Churches", and bow, and pray for more trophies? Don't deny it, I have seen it for myself, what you Humans can do to our fallen brethren and comrades,*" I snapped.

"We honestly meant you no harm. All we wanted was peace, if we did anything that might have hurt you, then I'm sorry," exclaimed Arthur.

"*Not good enough. We've tried to show you, what you were doing, but you turned our warning into a joke. Hunting us for sport, battling with us without a reason, or remorse. You also waged countless battles, and wars with us, and what you call "The mystical Creatures". We are now few in numbers, or what you Humans call: Endangered, and extinct. Whole races are gone forever. Now that we've taken from you, what you took from us, you rebuild and will try to kill us all again. Knowing that more blood and destruction will take place, and the slaughter of our race and countless others,*" I snarled and ranted.

"Your kind did this to me!" shouted Arthur irrationally. "If you hadn't of destroyed all of my hard work in uniting a nation…no, the world. I wouldn't have had to resort to killing your kind, and the many others.

Also I would never have had to resort to drastic measures."

"*Drastic measures?*" I spat. "*All of the Clan Leaders of this land, and the lands of the four corners, gave you plenty of options to rebuild far away from us. We also gave you plenty of options to stop your fighting with us. But you had to build, and rebuild, so you could destroy us, and now look where you are.*"

"Typical *stupid* Dragon. You're not-," Arthur started before I cut him off.

"*Listening to you? Yes, I am, and I'm not interested in having you accuse us of your misdoings, and mindless slaughtering,*" I growled.

"Fine. I screwed up. Is that what you want to hear?" snapped Arthur.

"*No,*" I stated.

Before Arthur could say another word, I tossed him into the air, and opened my mouth. Arthur screamed all the way until I caught him on his decent, chewed a couple of times, and then swallowed the former King. With Arthur now dead, I returned to the battle and called our forces back. We had won this endless war and it was time to leave the Humans in peace and show them another side of us. What allies stayed with us, went their separate ways when we reached our lands. The Unicorns, and Chimeras took to the dense forests and wild fields, which were spread throughout the Lands. While the handful of Gryphons, and what remained of the Dragons took to the far off mountains, and deep caves. With all of the destruction that was done to the once beautiful lands, no one bothered to rebuild destroyed settlements, and communities. For during the years that passed, and followed, we learned that it was better to hide then to prosper. While everyone went their separate ways, and vanished into the lands, some of us paired off, or grouped up so we wouldn't feel alone, or abandoned. In the end, no matter what the creature, we all went our own way and let the Lands be, and grow.

Chapter 16

The King of the Land

"That's it? That's what happened to King Arthur? You *ate* him? And there's *nothing* more on how you became so few in number? What about the descriptions about all of the Knights of the Round Table? I'm disappointed in you Drakon. I thought there was going to be more to King Arthur's tale and more descriptions. Not to mention on why there are so few of you. Also, I think I'll stick to the legends of the "good" King Arthur, and not *your* tale of him," complained Brak.

"*You wanted to know what happened! Well, I told you! If you wish to know more, then wait till my mate arrives. I'm sure she'll tell you more, at the cost of your life,*" exclaimed Drakon.

"Mate? I though you said Sisillia died in the war with The Elders," asked Brak who was a little curious.

"*She did, but that doesn't mean I couldn't take another. Oh, and she'll be here shortly as well,*" replied Drakon.

"Well, if you don't mind my asking, who is she?" asked Brak.

"*Silver,*" answered Drakon.

"Silver? You said she died," stated Brak.

"*No, I did not. Silver wasn't one of my...what do you Humans call it again? Ah I remember now, "friends" that died. She will be returning within a quarter sun or so,*" reflected Drakon.

"You mean high noon right? Hmm, this could work to my advantage.

Oh, and by the way, what do you mean by sun movement? You've mentioned it a couple of times now, and I'm interested in knowing what it means," mused and questioned Brak.

"*A sun movement to us is what you Humans call a minute*," replied Drakon. "*And what, prey tell is this* "*Advantage*" *of yours? If it involves Humans then count my mate and myself out.*"

"So I see. Well, I have been given a specific set of orders from my King, saying that he wishes to speak with *you* personally. I have no idea on what he wants to talk about, but I assume that it is important for he told me to look specifically for you. From what I can guess, I *know* that he doesn't want his kingdom destroyed. My King has also promised that no harm will come to you or whomever you decide to bring with you," exclaimed Brak.

"*I find this amusing, that Humans need my help…a Dragon's help. But, I don't think so. I've had too many bad experiences with dealing with Humans in the past, especially with the ones that have, and are, trying to kill me. Save for one Human but that is a Tale that I will not tell you. Every Human wants the same thing anyways: death and destruction, never peace. Don't even try to tell me otherwise*," stated Drakon.

"Why not? What *if* I told you that I have proof, that my King won't harm you," asked Brak as he reached for his pouch.

"*That's not what I'm concerned about. Also, I don't think a piece of what you Humans call paper, or parchment, or even a shiny object or gem is considered proof. For any and all of those things are useless to me. You might be able to…persuade another Dragon who values shiny things. But they mean nothing to me now, not since…other time*," exclaimed Drakon as he looked out at the beautiful blue cloudless sky.

"*Okay* then, what about a gift instead?" asked Brak as he pulled his hand away.

"*What could you possibly give me, which will* "*convince*" *me to go and see your* "*King*"? *That, and I'm pretty sure you have nothing I want, and what I do want, you don't have*," growled Drakon.

"How about a Human head? A famous Human…and I don't mean mine either," Brak started. "Hmm let me see, he's dead, he's been incinerated…"

"*Well, I'm waiting, and you do not want to see me Angry,*" growled Drakon again.

"*You*, angry? *Never.* Alright, I know who I want to summon, and I can guarantee you'll be shocked," stated Brak.

Brak stood up and reached into his small black pouch that hung at his side. He pulled out a rectangular crystal that was pointed at both ends. The crystals' colour was very unique for on each face was a different shade of green. Brak then pulled out a face of a Human skull that was a bone white in colour. Brak then threw the skull face onto the ground, in front of him. He reached into his pouch again and pulled out a handful of black sand, Brak then poured the sand onto the floor in a circle around the skull face.

"Latsyrc taolf," Brak shouted as he threw the crystal into the air.

As the crystal flew through the air, it stopped in mid flight above the skull face. The crystal then began to float five feet above the skull.

"*The Elves taught their magic well. Although, that, wasn't Elven,*" mussed Drakon.

Brak turned his head to Drakon. "The Elves taught our ancestors well, but Humans found a way to convert the Elven language into English. The only down fall is, that we have to speak it backwards to cast any sort of spell. Well the not so skilled spell casters anyway, the more skilled ones don't have to speak at all to cast long lengthy spells. Now if you don't mind, I'd like to get back to my spell, before the crystal falls and shatters into a million pieces. Literally."

Brak turned back to look at the floating crystal, and drew his sword. Brak's short sword was four feet long, and was constructed out of pure diamond. Both sides were sharp enough to cut through stone, like a hot knife through butter. The tip of the sword ended in a diamond point. The hilt of his sword was a mix of gold and silver with tiny bizarre symbols and pictures carved into it. Brak pointed the swords' tip at the floating crystal, which began to spin and turn. As the crystal spun and turned, it began to pick up speed, eventually it was moving so fast that it looked like a floating sphere. After Brak saw this change happen, he plunged his sword into the cold cave floor.

"Eeht esaeler I tirips degac," Brak shouted.

"*Interesting*," mussed Brak.

"Isn't it, be ready," stated Brak.

"*I was born read*," remarked Drakon.

"Not from what I remember you telling me in your tales," mocked Brak.

When Brak finished talking, he focused on the crystal, which by this time, turned blue. As it glowed, the crystal shot a ray of cyan coloured light at the skull face, and the circle of black sand. The sand ignited immediately, and burst into a white hot flame that shot high into the air, past the crystal. The white flames then burst into a bright yellow colour that seemed to be brighter then the sun itself. Brak was forced to look away from the harsh light, while Drakon just closed his eyes, and buried his face in his clawed hands. When it was over and the light faded, there stood Merlin, in wonder and in shock.

Merlin looked as he did, those thousands of years ago, an elderly looking Human male that had a well built body. His snow white hair and his grayed beard still glowed with a mystery as to Merlin's true age. His brown eyes still matched his dark dull brown, robe, shoes, and gloves, which he wore on *that* day so long ago. But this time, Merlin was unarmed, and possibly defenseless. Drakon wasted no time though in attacking Merlin, for he wanted the upper claw, and not want to see Merlin alive any longer. Also he didn't want the damnable wizard to cast any harmful spells, or attack. Drakon let out a jet of liquid fire with a fireball trailing the stream, towards Merlin. Before the smoke could even rise and clear, Drakon shot forward with lightning quick reflexes, and snapped up Merlin. With three blood curdling chomps, Merlin was no more, the whole episode lasted for just over a minute. When the episode was over, the flames finally died away, Brak went to collect his skull face, and his crystal, which was still in one piece. At the sight of the undamaged crystal, Brak felt happy.

"Well I don't think I'll be forgetting *that* sound anytime soon. Do you *always* eat people like *that*?" questioned Brak.

"*Only when I want to disgust my viewers*," smiled Drakon.

As soon as Drakon finished talking, Silver flew into the cave and she didn't look to happy. Drakon's description for Silver was nothing short of perfection, with only one exception. Silver was beautiful to look at whether you were a Dragon or a Human. As Silver landed on the cold cave floor, Drakon walked over to her and was about to give his mate a kiss, only to pull his head back. For Silver had snapped at Drakon, a little shocked, Drakon tried to kiss Silver again, but she wouldn't let him. Something was bothering Silver and she was in no mood for intimacy and comfort.

"*What in Dragons' Rage was that bright light, and that flash? Also, why is there the smell of roasted Humans in here, and why are there charred bodies lying all over the place? Are they food for later? Did they attack and hurt you? If they did they'll pay...also, why is there a living Human in here? Can it understand me? Why haven't you killed it yet? Or are you playing with your food? Are you going to keep it as a pet?*" growled Silver, angry, worried, and confused as she decided to make a meal out of some of the cooked Humans.

"*This Human goes by the name of Brak. He was sent by the King of the Land, or so I'm guessing due to that insignia of his on his breast, to get some "answers". I guess you could say he's an ally for he's given no real reason for me to kill him...yet. He also made a deal with me to see his King, by offering up an old enemy we thought was dead: Merlin. Those bright flashes, and light was a portal to another plane that Brak opened up to pull Merlin out of. And yes the Humans tried to kill me yet again, no I'm not hurt or injured, and feel free to snack on them. You know I don't much like the taste of Human. Also Brak can't understand us unless he casts some sort of speech spell on himself, or so I'm guessing. I've extended my gift to you if you wish to talk to the Human. But please Love, tell me what's bothering you, and what has got you so upset. You don't have to tell me if you don't wish to, but I'd like to know,*" explained Drakon soothingly.

Silver looked over at Brak and glared at him, but he bowed to her in response. But before Brak could say anything, Silver stormed over to him, and lowered her head so she was face to face with Brak. Silver then barred her teeth and fangs at Brak, which gave him an uneasy feeling. Brak also took a couple of steps back without realizing it.

"*What is it that you want little Human? It better be important, for I'm not as easy to befriend as Drakon is,*" snarled Silver.

"Drakon easy to befriend? You *must* be joking. He's tried to kill me a number of times. All I want is for the two of you to answer some questions I have, and for the both of you to accompany me to see my King," explained Brak.

"*You mean "The King of the Land" who has put out a warrant for all "Mystical" creatures to be either captured or killed? I don't think so. You can go and tell your King to-*," growled Silver before Drakon cut her off.

"*Silver, please calm down and show some respect. Even if the King is a selfish, greedy, power hungry—*," Drakon soothed before Brak cut him off.

"*Alright.* I get the picture. But this makes no sense. I would have been informed if the King changed his mind, let alone his plans. Hmm, I'd better speak with him," Brak exclaimed.

Brak reached into his pouch again, and pulled out a blue sphere, he then tossed it into the air. As the sphere flew up into the air, and started its' decent, Brak threw out his left hand and pointed at it. The sphere stopped in the air and began to float in place. Brak dropped his arm and took a few steps back. When Brak thought he was far enough back, he made a motion with his fingers. The sphere pulsed once, then doubled in size and turned from blue to crystal clear.

"How's *that* for skill?" asked Brak as he grinned.

"*Still pathetic, until you can show us, you can use magic without any helpful objects. You'll only be second to the Elves*," stated Drakon.

"It's never enough for you *Dragons* is it? Oh well, back to the task at hand," Brak mussed. "Your Highness, this is High Sorcerer Brak of the Red Dragon. I wish to speak to you about your change in plans concerning the "Mystical" creatures. I have also made contact with *Drakon the Ancient* and have found out some interesting facts about our History, but my findings are still incomplete."

"The King is not at his crystal ball right now. Please leave a message after the pulse," replied a feminine voice.

"*Very funny.* Where's your Father Sara? And *what* are you doing with his medallion? Asked Brak.

"*That's* Princess Sara to *you*! Brak," snapped Sara.

"I don't think so. *If* I remember correctly, which I do. You took up sorcery, instead of your *Royal* duties and career. Until that changes, I can call you whatever I want. Now where is your Father? It's important that I speak with him, about these "new plans" of his," Brak exclaimed.

"I don't know where he is. Father disappeared eight weeks ago. A week after you left to go on your errand for him. I fear that he has been kidnapped…or worse, for I have yet to receive a ransom for his return. I've been running things here and trying to keep up appearances at the Kingdom, but people are starting to become suspicious. As for the warrants that have been appearing everywhere, I nor my Father have had anything to do with them. I'm telling the truth about that as well Brak.

I don't want to ask this of you, seeing as you are still working on the quest that Father gave you, but, could you please find my Father? I will reward you handsomely if you do this for me," pleaded Sara.

"I'll take a large increase in my fee then," replied Brak dismissively.

"That's it? What about-," Started Sara before Brak cut her off.

"I don't feel like having my head on a golden platter, or having a child, or children at the moment. Ugh, children. Besides I'm very busy with your Fathers' orders…like you said, that, and I know you have *many* men over there that will *gladly* please you. Also, you've studied in the *arts*, so, I already know what you look like without clothing on. I'll admit that you're very appealing, but I'm not interested. So, you'll have to try and do something better then what you're planning," stated Brak a little annoyed.

"Fine!" snapped Sara who was a little hurt by Brak's remarks. "I'll just have to *appeal* to the other magic wielders, trackers, and hunters that are at my disposal."

With that said, the sphere went dark, then turned black, once it turned black it bobbed in the air, and turned back to its' normal size and blue colour. Once the sphere turned back to its' normal shape and size, it dropped like a stone. Brak dove to the ground and caught it, just before the sphere made contact with the ground. Once the sphere was safe, Brak put it back into his pouch. Brak then turned to Drakon and Silver with a look of annoyance across his face.

"*Unlike you Humans, Dragons treat each other as equals…most of the time,*" mocked Silver as she looked at Drakon.

"Funny. I guess I have to ask this now. Could both of you help me in finding my King?" asked Brak.

"*NO!*" stated Drakon and Silver in unison.

"Please help me. I know how much both of you hate Humans, for what they've done to you, and your kind. But wouldn't it be nice to have no one fear you? Wanting to be friends with you? Or better yet, have a whole Kingdom in your debt," pleaded Brak.

"*Sounds tempting*," mused Silver as she calmed down a little bit.

"*No*!" stated Drakon. "*Your kind cannot be trusted…ever.*"

"If *that* is true, then why am *I* still alive?" challenged Brak.

"*That's it, I've put up with your insults, and mockery for long enough. Now I am going to kill you*," snarled Drakon.

Drakon stood up, and shot forward towards Brak. But before Drakon's jaws could clamp around the Sorcerer, Brak disappeared. A second later he reappeared on Silver's shoulder as she reappeared a second later taking her hand off of Brak.

"*Drakon, think about it for a sun movement. This could work for us, we won't be hated or hunted anymore. And, you can get what you've always wanted: peace and quiet. And yes, I've calmed down some from my outburst*," pleaded Silver.

Drakon looked at Silver before sighing. "*Very well. I guess I don't have a choice in the matter anyway. I can't believe you ruined my fun Silver. I wasn't really going to eat him. I was just going to nibble on him for a while.*"

"*Nice try Lover, but I know you too well, and for too long*," exclaimed Silver jokingly, before she passionately kissed Drakon.

"Well, this is all well and good, seeing the two of you *lovebirds* kiss and make up, and all. I do admit, I'm interested in seeing the two of you mate, or do a courtship ritual, or whatever a pair of Dragons do to procreate. But more importantly, what have both of you decided? Will you help me or not?" questioned Brak.

"*We'll accompany you on your quest to find your King. But I warn you, if you try anything, like trying to kill us, I will kill you. And not even Silver will be able to stop me. I might not prefer eating Humans, but I will kill them if I need to*," stated Drakon as he kissed Silver.

"Very well. Our first stop will be the Castle. I have to pick up a few things before we go on our search. And, I also have to speak with someone and *put her in her place*. *Royalty*, they're all the same," replied Brak as he shook his head in disgust.

Chapter 17

The Search Begins

"*Where, and how far is this Castle of yours? And how much Kingdom do we have to fly over or avoid?*" asked Drakon.

"If we leave right now, it will take until the first light of the moon, by flight of course," answered Brak.

"*Well, you're not going to be riding on either of us, for we aren't dumb pack mules. So get off of me or I'll eat you instead...please,*" growled Silver.

"Since I can still understand you, and *you* asked *so* nicely, I will. As for the riding issue, don't worry, for I can fly...like an eagle. Also, the Kingdom and the Castle are northeast of your home. Shall we go then?" answered Brak.

Once Brak finished talking he jumped off of Silver and plummeted to the ground. As he fell, Brak pulled out a long colourful peacock feather, which he then waved in the air in a figure eight motion. While Brak waved the feather, he began to transform. His arms and hands turned into black feathered wings, while his legs and feet turned into yellowish black legs, ending with razor sharp talons. Then Brak's head and upper body sprouted black feathers, and his face grew outwards into a beak. Once the changes were complete, Brak shrunk to the size of a condor. With his transformation, finally complete and, landing softly on the ground, Brak had turned into a Raven.

"*That form suits him perfectly,*" remarked Silver.

"*Very funny. Don't look too surprised. When I transform into a creature of any kind, I can understand anything that breathes,*" explained Brak.

"*Amusing. Shall we go then?*" mused Drakon.

"*Do try to keep up with me. For I tend to fly quite fast,*" exclaimed Brak as he ruffled his feathers a bit.

"*Just go already,*" snapped Silver.

Without saying another word, Brak spread his wings, and flapped them a couple of times to get airborne. Once Brak was airborne he shot out of the cave like a crossbow bolt. Silver and Drakon saw that Brak wasn't kidding, when he said he could fly fast.

"*Show off,*" remarked Drakon. "*Shall we?*"

"*Lets,*" answered Silver as she launched herself into the air, and out of the cave.

Drakon stood up, shook his wings, and took to the sky after Silver and Brak. After Drakon caught up with Silver, both Dragons looked at each other and smiled. Then both of them straightened themselves out, flapped their wings and then shot past Brak, and high into the sky. This took Brak by surprise, but after a while Silver and Drakon took up their positions behind Brak for he knew where to fly. True both Silver and Drakon knew of hundreds and thousands of castles, kingdoms, cities, and settlements, but only Brak knew which one was the right one. Brak wasn't wrong either when he said they would reach the Castle, or Kingdom rather, by nightfall. As the trio neared the kingdom, its' Outer Walls loomed into view. Brak landed on the cold grassy earth and looked up at Silver and Drakon.

"*Land where you are. If you get spotted, you'll get killed on the spot. I haven't informed anyone of my arrival, and I intend to keep it that way,*" exclaimed Brak.

"*Very well,*" replied Silver and Drakon in unison.

While Brak turned back into a Human, Silver and Drakon landed as quietly as a snow flake, which took Brak by surprise. Once Brak finished with his transformation, he made his way over to the two awaiting Dragons. As he got nearer, Brak waved his hand in the air, which made his weapons, gear, and clothes reappear on his body. It was a good thing that Brak decided to put a retrieval spell on his things, otherwise his things would still be at Drakon's home. Brak was mumbling something about the transformation spell and having no clothes when he walked up to Silver and Drakon.

"Now, for the fun part. You have two choices, to get turned into Humans, or to get killed. Both of you know the right choice. I'll start the spell," exclaimed Brak.

"*I don't like this Drakon,*" started Silver.

"*Neither do I. But as much as I don't want to admit it, Brak may be right. That, and you know as well as I do, that we stand no chance in destroying this place,*" soothed Drakon.

Once Drakon finished speaking, Brak pointed with two fingers on his left hand, at Silver, then at Drakon. A bright white light shot out of Brak's fingers, and streaked across the air at Drakon and Silver. At the shock and the nature of the spell, both Dragons reared up on their hind legs, then began to shrink. When they finished shrinking both Dragons were still on their hind legs, but they were roughly the same height as an average Human adult. Next, both Dragons' scales melted and joined together, to become flesh, while their claws disappeared. Silver and Drakon's legs and arms then began to change and reshape into Human appendages. Their heads and faces, also shrunk and reshaped themselves, until they formed Human features, and looked like an average Human head. Lastly, Drakon and Silver's tails receded into their backs, leaving their wings to shrivel and disappear. But before their tails and wings could disappear, Drakon and Silver flared their wings to give them a demonic look. After the light faded away, Drakon and Silver where both Human.

Drakon's skin turned from his reddish blue scales colour to a light brown colour. His hair still remained long, and silver, which flowed down to his waist. Drakon still retained his golden eyes, they were changed from reptilian to Human though, but they still had the ability to pierce a persons' soul. Drakon was just as tall as Brak was, but he had a stronger build, then Brak. Silver's scales turned skin though, had turned from their diamond white colour, to a pale skin colour. The colour of her skin matched the colour of her snow white hair, which flowed down her back, and brushed the cold grass. Silver's eyes also retained their silver colour, and like Drakon, changed from reptilian, to Human. She was a head shorter then Drakon and Brak, but she had a strong body like an Amazon.

On top of the changes to both Dragons, both Dragons were completely naked, cold and starting to shiver a little. But this made Brak happy when he looked at Silver in her Human form and couldn't stop staring. Needless to say both humanized Dragons, were stunning and beautiful to look at, but they were highly annoyed and starting to become angry, as well as cold. For the lack of warm clothes and the constant stare from Brak was not appealing in the least.

"Silver you look-," started Brak before he was cut off.

"Repulsive, so does my *one* and *only* mate. I don't care what you say, you might be a fine *mate* to your own *kind*. But you *are* repulsive to me, so *don't* bother," stated Silver coldly, while she shivered a little.

"Do we get Outer skin, or clothes, or whatever it is you *Humans* call it, with this transformation? *Or* do we have to break this pitiful spell of yours?" questioned a highly annoyed Drakon, as he brought Silver close and wrapped his arms around her to share some of his warmth with her.

"Unfortunately, I've used up too much of my mystical energy. I will have to rest, before I use up anymore magic. I also don't have clothing on me to give to either of you. So I would have to say, that both of you are out of luck. Sorry you two," lied Brak as he continued to look at Silver.

"Very well. Drakon, let's have some *fun*," purred Silver, as she turned her head and kissed Drakon's cheek.

Silver got out of Drakon's light embrace, gave herself a light shake of her arms, then walked over to Drakon again, and grasp his hand. She then turned towards him and kissed him passionately, to annoy Brak. When both Humanized Dragons finished their kiss, they held onto each others' hands tightly, and closed their eyes. After Silver's and Drakon's eyes were closed, they began to glow with a bright blue light, which surrounded them completely. As they glowed, scales began to appear all over both of their bodies, while the scales sprouted from their bodies, they began to form, reshape, and resemble, light plate mail. The scales also retained both Dragons natural colours. Silver's, and Drakon's scales covered their entire bodies, save for their faces, and hands. Also, their small Human feet, turned into small versions of their clawed Dragon feet.

"Much better," remarked Drakon with a smile.

"Let's get going. I'd like to make it into the Castle before daylight," sighed Brak who was a little disappointed.

Brak, Silver, and Drakon set off to the Outer Wall Gates after the changes were complete. It took a few steps on unsteady legs, before Drakon, and Silver could walk like normal Humans, but they got the hang of walking on two legs in no time. The trio arrived at the huge wooden and steel doors a few minutes later. After they arrived, a guard seemed to appear out of nowhere, at the sight of him, Brak flashed a mysterious looking pendant in front of the guard. The guard took a moment to study the pendant to make sure that it had the right clearance. The pendant had a picture of a red Dragon breathing fire, on it. Beside the Dragon, laid a bluish green staff crossed with a crystal sword that looked like Brak's. After the inspection, the guard looked at Brak, saluted and disappeared. Due to the *poor* Human vision, Silver, and Drakon couldn't make out what the guard looked like in the dark. The only thing that both Dragons could make out was, that the guard was dressed in black. The doors opened a second later, after the guard disappeared, and the trio walked inside. Once the trio was inside, the doors closed, leaving them all with a "trapped" feeling. But Silver kept Drakon, and herself amused by scaring the local Human males away. With a growl here, and smoke from the nose and mouth there, sent the Humans running in fear.

"We *are* trying *NOT* to draw attention to ourselves. So, if *you* don't mind. *Please* stop," asked Brak silently.

"*Alright.* I'll be nice," pouted Silver like a little girl, which made Drakon hold back a chuckle.

After a long trek through the silent city, the trio finally made it to the outside of the Castle. It was only an hour or two of walking, but to Silver and Drakon, it felt like a full day of nonstop hiking. Both of them silently vowed to break Brak's curse once they were "away" from prying eyes. The Castle was huge, making Camelot, look like a small village, with more spires, rooms, and tall walls then Silver, and Drakon had seen in their entire lives. Of course both Dragons had seen many large kingdoms, and castles, but none of *this* size. The castle was a dull gray in colour, but in the pale moonlight, the castle sparkled in silver. The spires, and roofs were different, they were coloured in such a way, that made them sparkle. All in all, the Castle was impressive to look at but as Drakon reflected, Camelot was still the most beautiful Human built structure he'd ever seen.

Once the trio finally made it to the draw bridge, Drakon and Silver decided to rest on one of the large chains that held the bridge. While the two Humanized Dragons rested, another guard appeared out of nowhere, which was starting to bug Silver and Drakon. This time, Brak pulled out a different pendant, that had a picture of a golden scepter overlapping a crystal shield. The guard took a good look at the pendant, then disappeared. Again, due to the poor Human vision, and the lack of decent lighting, Drakon, and Silver couldn't get a good look at the guard. But Silver, and Drakon just shrugged their shoulders and followed Brak inside the Castle. They followed Brak into a large courtyard, that had a large pond and fountain in the middle of a grassy area with benches placed here and there. But Brak ignored the beauty and took a sharp right, around a corner, and stopped. He pulled out a blood red wand from the inside of his cloak, and waved it in a circle in the air. The trio, were then instantly teleported into Brak's large and cozy quarters.

Both Dragons took in the sight of the new "private" area, which was vast to say the least. They were in a large room that looked like the size of Drakon's cave, with doors on all four walls. The room was filled to the ceiling with bookshelves, loaded with strange books, that lined all four walls. In the center of the room, were four, large cushioned, red velvet, couches that were huddled around a fair sized fire. There was also a huge desk in the far corner cluttered with strange glowing objects scattered all over it. As soon as Drakon, and Silver realized they were away from the "public", both Humanized Dragons decided they had enough of Brak's *spell.* Silver, and Drakon grasp each others hands, and closed their eyes. A dark red glow surrounded both Humanized Dragons, then slowly seep into them and disappeared. When the glow was gone, both Dragons were their regular selves, but there was a problem. Both Dragons remained Human sized, at the realization, both Dragons became annoyed and weren't amused. Brak just looked at them and smiled.

"You might've broken my transformation spell, but I can guarantee you, that you can't break my shrink spell I also put on you. Only I can break that, besides I knew the two of you would want to return to normal soon," Brak announced.

"*Beautiful, at least we aren't weak,*" stated Silver angrily.

"*But, we looked like Whelps. Aside the fact that we still retain our normal colours,*" growled Drakon, who was also angry.

"Don't worry, when we leave the kingdom, both of you will be back to your normal sizes. I just have to grab a few things and cast a simple locator spell, then we can go," replied Brak.

Brak walked over to his desk, and started rummaging though the things on top of it, and in the drawers. Brak eventually found what he was looking for: a yellow six pointed diamond. As Brak opened his hand the diamond floated a couple of inches above his palm. While the diamond floated in the air it began to spin in a clockwise direction, and glowed green.

"Gink eht ot yaw eht em wohs," Brak spoke to the diamond.

Once Brak finished speaking, the diamond burst into a green fireball that looked like it was ready to shoot off. But before it could shoot off, Brak captured the fireball in a crystal ball that was a little larger then his fist. As the light bounced around frantically in the ball, Brak placed a hand on it and, and some how managed to calm the fireball down. As the fireball slowed, it began to reshape into a crude looking flaming arrow.

"*Now, can we go?*" questioned Drakon.

"Yes, we can. But, we're going to have to go through the Castle. For my wand needs to recharge," exclaimed Brak.

"*How long?*" asked Silver anxiously.

"A full day. And *yes*, I cast a speech spell on myself, but sadly it doesn't last forever," answered Brak.

"*Let's depart then. Lead the way Brak,*" stated Drakon as he raised one of his hands and swept it over all four doors.

The trio was off again, only this time, they had a long way to go to get out of the kingdom. Walking through the endless corridors, and doorways, was making it hard and confusing to take in the layout. Drakon, and Silver, didn't want to admit it, but they were glad to have someone, even if it was Brak, show them the way out. As the trio made their way to the entrance of the Castle, and its' large courtyard, everyone stopped to stare at the Dragons. In return, both Silver, and Drakon stared and glared back, scaring the people away. After a few hours of nonstop walking, the trio *finally* made it to the entrance, but before they could leave, they ran into Sara.

Sara like Brak, looked to be in her twenties but she was far older then that, she was tall for her age, she was tall enough to look into Brak's eyes. Sara had dark red eyes, which matched her long dark red hair, which flowed down to her waist. Her eyes were unlike any Human eyes, for she had adopted the colour from her late Elven mother. Sara had peach coloured skin, and a soft round face. Her ears were also slightly pointed, and at a slight angle, but they just added to her beauty. Sara was garbed in a light blue robe that was outlined in silver. Her robe also bore an insignia that was identical to Brak's: a red Dragon. After looking at both insignias on Brak and Sara, Silver, and Drakon finally realized why the pictures looked so familiar. The crude image was of Fiery the Wise, one of the Clan Leaders that disappeared during the "Arthur incident". Sara was carrying the Royal Staff, which was gold, studded with various small, well cut, gems, and had a clear diamond sphere on the head of the staff. A silver tiara also rested atop of Sara's head.

"Leaving *so* soon with your summoned pets? *And* as usual, you don't even bother to ask if I want to join you. I'm insulted," exclaimed Sara.

"I know you're *royalty* and all, but shut it Sara. I have pressing matters to attend to. Also, these two Dragons aren't my *summoned* pets. I highly suggest, and advise you, that *you* do *not* annoy them," Brak scolded.

"But they look so *cute*. I've never seen a baby Dragon before, or living ones for that matter. You *still* have that hood on Brak? Do you ever take it off? Or are you afraid of what people would think of you when they saw your hair?" replied and questioned Sara.

Brak pulled off his hood as he turned around to look at Sara, and let his long hair fly past his face and swing to the other side before resting on his shoulders and upper back. His hair was silver, with black in it, giving the appearance of a burning black fire.

"Happy now," stated Brak who was annoyed at Sara's questions.

"*Hmm, Sliver, how long has it been since we've had a Royal meal?*" Drakon asked.

Silver shrugged. "*Too long*,"

"What? I can understand them?" questioned Sara.

"*No, just me. Now if you don't mind...your Highness. We would like to leave this place, and return to our normal size. Also, both of us are older then you think. So please, don't insult us. Otherwise, we might decide on a late night snack*," answered Drakon coldly.

Silver, and Drakon walked past a stunned Sara, and pushed the doors to the courtyard open with their clawed hands. Their claws dug into the hardwood doors, so they could keep the doors open while they waited for Brak, and also leave their mark. With the Dragons holding open the door, they looked at Brak, who bowed to Sara, and followed the Dragons out. Once outside, Brak handed the crystal ball over to Drakon, and told both Dragons to take to the sky. After Silver and Drakon took to the sky, they began to grow back to their normal size. Once they reverted back to their normal size, Silver used her gift to make both of them invisible, and they flew off, so no one would notice them. Brak then turned back into a raven and took to the sky as well. Before Brak turned into a raven though he made sure to relocate his retrieval spell to his quarters, where he teleported his things to. As the trio left the kingdom, Sara watched them from her Balcony, hoping, that Brak knew what he was doing. She also hoped and prayed that her Father would be alright when Brak found him. When Sara could no longer see Brak, she went back inside to return to her "royal" work.

"*Drakon, please give me the crystal ball. So I can tell what way the arrow is pointing*," Brak asked.

"*It's pointing southeast. It's not that hard to figure out*," stated Drakon.

While the trio flew southeast, Silver turned her head back towards Brak. "*You like her don't you? Why didn't you ask her to join us? Sara might have been...useful.*"

"*Like her? Heh, I don't like her, I love her. I would like to marry Sara one day, but I know it will never come to pass. Also, I know that Sara would have been more trouble with us, then without us*," Brak exclaimed.

"*Why?*" pried Silver.

"*My reasons are my own. That is what Humans call a personal question. It is also a question I do not wish to answer. I have a question for you though: where are your*

Children? I would have assumed that you two alone, could've repopulated your kind and wiped out all of the Humans. Given Drakon's timeline of course," questioned Brak in return.

"*We don't have any,*" growled Drakon angrily as he looked down at the ground avoiding Silver's loving gaze.

"*Why?*" pried Brak.

"*I understand now. I now know what personal means,*" reflected Silver as she looked up at the night sky, also avoiding Brak's question.

"*Can we get back to the task at claw? The arrow is pointing north now,*" exclaimed Drakon to change the subject.

"*Well let's go then. There's no time to waste,*" stated Brak.

Chapter 18

Gargoyles Stone? Yeah, Right

After flying for what seemed like hours, through all night, and day, following the arrow, the sun was beginning to set again. As it set, the sun let loose brilliant colours that seemed to touch everything, making the surrounding scenery look like a child's dream. Brak folded his wings, and dove to the ground, then landed softly. Drakon and Silver landed a little after Brak did, to see why he landed. As the two Dragons landed, Brak transformed back into a Human, while he was transforming, he was mumbling something about lousy time spells and their regeneration times. He was also grumbling about how he could extend the timed spell, but how he lacked the resources. Silver and Drakon just looked at each other and shrugged their shoulders.

"*What's the matter? You can't stay in a transformation until you change back? Or did you just run out of time? Or did you loose track of which direction we're flying in?*" mocked Drakon.

"What kind of *stupid* questions are those? Look at me I'm *Human* again, and I'll be this way until morning," Snapped Brak.

"*Wonder why he's so grumpy all of a sudden. He seemed nicer earlier. He was almost likeable…I think your personality is starting to rub off on me Lover,*" Silver asked Drakon, as she kissed him.

"*Because*, it's late and we have been going nonstop for the past day and night, and I'm very, very tired. Now if you don't mind, I'm going to *sleep* Good *night!*" snapped Brak again.

Once Brak finished talking, he laid down on the cold wet ground, and tried to get himself comfortable. After Brak got as comfortable as he could, he waved his hand, and a blanket, and a pillow appeared, over his body, and under his head. Brak then reached into the sleeve of his robe and pulled out a white wand. There was a carving on the wand that looked like there was moving flame etched into it. Brak tossed the wand, about three feet away from himself. As soon as the wand landed on the ground, it burst into flames with a ring of rocks surrounding the flames. With the heat that the mystical fire gave off, Brak fell asleep instantly. Drakon and Silver, laid down beside one another, and fell asleep shortly after.

The next morning Drakon and Silver woke to a strange smell coming from a small cauldron that was hanging above the mystical fire. The Dragons looked at the cauldron curiously, for they had seen them before, but not so small, and didn't know what they were used for. Brak appeared from the bushes a little while later, holding two large rabbit bodies. Brak tossed the bodies into the air and spoke a strange obscured word, that even Drakon couldn't understand, or didn't want to. After Brak spoke "the word" the rabbit bodies exploded into hairless chunks of meat, and landed in the cauldron. When a few minutes pasted, Brak took out a spoon from his pouch, and stirred the contents in the cauldron. After a while of stirring Brak brought the spoon up to his lips, blew on it, then put it into his mouth. With the spoon still in his mouth Brak looked up to see if Drakon and Silver were still sleeping and was a little surprised to see both of them looking at him. While Brak looked at both Dragons, he took note: that both of them looked to be entwined with one another. Brak was about to ask why both Dragons were entwined with one another, but thought better of it. Once both Dragons realized that Brak was staring at them again, they untangled themselves from one another, stood up, stretched, then laid back down.

"What are the two of you staring at? This is my breakfast, and *yes*, I don't use magic all the time. That's what wizards do, and frankly I like to depend on more then just spells," Brak exclaimed as he took the spoon out of his mouth and put it back into the cauldron.

"*What is that?*" questioned Drakon.

"It's rabbit stew. I'd figured I'd better eat something while the two of you still slept. That way when the two of you woke up, I will have eaten and the three of us could be on our merry little way," explained Brak.

"*Nice to see that you're back to your usual annoying self. Also, nice assumption, but we need to eat as well. I assume that you can still understand me?*" exclaimed Silver.

"*Why* yes, I can," replied Brak with a smile.

Drakon decided to ignore the flash of affection between his mate and the Human, by sniffing the tainted air. "*Something's not right. I sense a great fear in the air. It's a mix of Human and animal. It's close, but I don't where it's coming from. All I can really gather is that the Humans are terrified.*"

"*I can start to smell it too…it's unnerving,*" exclaimed Silver as she let out a small shutter from unwanted memories.

"Well, let's check it out then. Chances are my King is with them. But if he isn't, then think of it as a good deed," stated Brak as he rubbed his hands together.

"*Amusing,*" mumbled Drakon.

Brak waved his hand, and as he did so, the cauldron shrunk to a smaller version of itself, while the fire extinguished itself, leaving a white wand in its' place. Brak walked over to the wand and picked it up, it felt cool to Brak's touch. Next he tried to pick up the cauldron and nearly dropped for it was still hot. Brak cursed his stupidity, and the ineffective cooling spell. With a couple of breaths to cool his hands, Brak attempted to pick up the cauldron again. Once Brak got a better grip on the cauldron, and didn't burn his hands, he put the wand and the cauldron into his pouch. Brak mumbled something about how he never got a decent breakfast, even if he was venturing on his own. The blanket and the pillow were the next to go into Brak's pouch. Silver and Drakon were amazed at what Brak could put into his small black pouch.

"*What can't you put in there?*" questioned Silver.

"A bath basin," stated Brak sarcastically, as he had to force the last of the blanket into the pouch.

"*Oh,*" replied Silver with a touch of confusion. "*What's a bath basin?*"

"It's something Humans and humanoids use to clean themselves…well what most Humans and humanoids use anyway. More importantly, it's something that Dragons and other creatures don't need or use," explained Brak.

"*Could you hurry it up. The sense of Fear is getting stronger,*" exclaimed Drakon a little annoyed at the small talk Silver and Brak were having.

"Alright…alright, according to the crystal ball, we're close. I guess it was a good idea that I landed then. Anyway, my guess would have to be that we're somewhere around seventy kilometers or so away from the source of the fear. I'm not too sure, for Human locator spells aren't that accurate. But, I am sure that my King is close. I just have to do this one small thing first before we can go," Brak replied.

Drakon and Silver both let out a loud long sigh as Brak prepared himself for another transformation. Brak pulled out a small piece of fur from his pouch that was yellow with a couple of black spots on it. Brak waved his hand over the piece of fur, as he made his motion, his gear and clothes disappeared. Then Brak began to change from Human to Beast. Brak dropped to his hands and knees, as he fell to the ground, he began to shrink in size. Brak's legs and arms began to reposition themselves as long white Claws protruded from his toes and fingers. His body then sprouted yellow fur that covered his entire body. Large black spots appeared here and there, while a tail sprouted from Brak's hindquarters. Before the change was complete, Brak's face sprouted whiskers, and molded into a cats' face, with Brak's eyes going from Human to Cat. When the transformation was complete, there was a large yellow furred, black spotted cat in Brak's place. Brak's eyes also changed from a brown to a green colour.

"*What are you?*" wondered Silver aloud.

"*I am what Humans call a cheetah. It's an exotic animal to this land, it is found in a far off land from here. It's very fast on land as well, it can match a Dragons speed on the ground. But as we all know a Dragon is unmatched in the air. Let's go, we don't want to waste anymore time by talking,*" Brak stated before he shot off in the direction of the arrow, and the sense of the fear.

Drakon shook his head at Brak showing off to *his* mate, for both Dragons knew what Brak had turned into, or at least Drakon did. Drakon then took to the air, while Silver stayed on the ground. It was a stealth technique that the Chimeras developed during the wars of Drakon's past. The technique had the ability to confuse any group of enemies that was hunting them. By making there seem like there were more Chimeras then there really were. While the trio got closer to the source of the Fear, they began to encounter hostile creatures. These creatures were comprised of all around, hated, Basilisks, and other large deadly lizards. It was strange for the way the creatures fought, it was as though they were trained or tamed to protect something or someone. After battling for a couple of hours, Brak, Silver, and Drakon finally caught a break, for they had arrived at the source of the Fear, and the creatures stopped their assaults. But what they saw, confused them and filled them with a sense of unease.

"*I thought they were only a legend. Tales from a child's story or told to children to scare them into sleeping, or decorative stone statues. I can't believe it, I won't believe it,*" exclaimed a shocked Brak.

"*I thought they were extinct, died and wiped out a thousand, or two thousand years ago. This makes no sense, I don't understand,*" added Silver with more then just a hint of confusion.

"*They're Gargoyles, what do you expect. Half Dragon, and half Human, with extremely long lives. Thankfully not as long as a Dragons. Whether byproducts of Human magic, or a Half Breed of Human and Dragon, they can still die. It'll just be a little hard to kill them,*" exclaimed Drakon with distaste in his voice.

"*What did I expect? I expected them to all be dead and wiped from this earth,*" snapped Brak.

The Gargoyles that the trio had spotted, were eight feet tall at the most. The colours of the Gargoyles' scales ranged from a dull grey to a dull brown. Some of the Gargoyles had horns protruding from the top of their heads, that ranged from long and slender to short and fat. Their faces were like that of a Dragons', with a muzzle and snout, but with cat like eyes instead of the traditional reptilian. Their eye colours ranged from a multitude of colours, from bright red, to a black. They had long bat like wings, that looked to be about ten feet from end to end. Their muscular inverted legs ended with a long yellow curled claw on each one of their ten toes. To top it off they had a long slender white claw on each one of their ten fingers. Most of the Gargoyles also had torn cloth, that draped off of their chests, and around their waists. But a few of the Gargoyles, just let their scales show off on their bodies, and a few areas that should have remained covered. All in all, the Gargoyles were a force to be dealt with, even with using extreme caution.

The trio watched the massive group of Gargoyles rush around carrying large and small trees, and stones. The Gargoyles were preparing for something, but it was still unclear as to what it was. While the preparations were underway, a large group of Gargoyles decided to start the festivities. Some of the winged Gargoyles danced in the air, while the non winged ones danced on the ground. A few of the Gargoyles were building, what looked like a huge bonfire. It looked like the Gargoyles were preparing for a feast that could feed a starving kingdom. After watching the Gargoyles, the trio finally figured out what the Gargoyles were doing. While the Gargoyles were busy with their festivities, two Gargoyles walked over to the unlit bonfire and set it ablaze with their fiery breath. Once the bonfire was lit and ablaze, a huge Gargoyle seemed to appear out of nowhere and landed on a large pile of dirt and began to shriek in a strange kind of draconic language.

"*Amusing. I can't understand a word it's saying,*" exclaimed Brak a little annoyed.

"*Well, duh,*" stated Drakon mockingly. "*They are speaking in a slight variation of our Native language. Well the Native language I grew up with, like your language ours changed over time as well. It's been a while since I've heard this language but thanks to my gift I can still understand it.*"

"*Show off, smart a-,*" Brak started before Silver cut him off.

"*What's it saying? Unlike you I'm not that old,*" asked and mocked Silver lovingly.

"*Something about a large scale sacrifice, bigger then their usual ones, with an added touch of Royalty. That, and their God will be very pleased and bestow gifts onto the worthy. In lemans terms, they have your King, and are planning on roasting, and eating him,*" explained Drakon.

"*Well let's do something before that happens,*" replied Brak as he turned back into a Human.

"*What do you suggest we do? Gargoyles, like some of us, are immune to fire, ice, and freezing winds. Also like us, they have strong resistances, and can take plenty of abuse before dying. Plus, there are at least three hundred of them, maybe more, maybe less, and only three of us. Drakon, and myself maybe very skilled, and stronger then the average Dragon. But Gargoyles are craftier then us, and can kill us easier then we can kill them,*" exclaimed Silver.

"*Please*, the answer's simple, we turn them to stone. It'll work too, how else do you think we got such life like statues of Gargoyles?" questioned Brak.

"*Let me guess, you "know" the spell and the ingredients for it,*" mused Drakon.

"Not exactly, the best I can do is turn them into living clay. You two will have to do the rest. *And* before either of you two say it. I'm a sorcerer *not* a wizard, so I'm not skilled in *every* type of spell," explained and defended Brak.

"*As long as they're crunchy on the outside, or creamy on the inside,*" stated Silver with a grin.

Drakon and Brak just looked at Silver with amusement and disgust.

"Funny... Not really, no," remarked Brak.

"*I thought it was,*" replied Drakon.

"Can we hurry up this conversation? The Gargoyles look as though they arte preparing to bring out their Human meals. I would also prefer to get my castings out of the way with before the roasting and dining," stated Brak anxiously.

"*We'll be waiting in the sky for your signal,*" exclaimed Silver as she took off into the sky, after Drakon.

As Brak watched the two Dragons disappear into the sky, he shook his head trying to figure them out, for they acted like Adults one minute then children the next. But Brak quickly got over his train of thought, and turned his attention to his spell. Brak sat down and crossed his legs. He then dug into his pouch and pulled out two rubies that were sculpted into spoons. With a spoon in each hand. Brak spoke a levitation word, which made him float a couple of inches off the ground. Once Brak was in the air, he thrust both spoons into the ground, and started to cast his lengthy clay spell. Brak hoped that he wouldn't be discovered before he was done, but with the amount of noise going on Brak doubted he would be discovered.

"Aelp ym raeh, htrae eht fo sseddog," Brak started. "Serutaerc eseht gnihsinab ni pleh ruoy eriuqer I."

Once Brak started chanting, he began to spin in a clockwise position. As he spun in a circle, the spoons bit into the cold earth and seemed to stretch a little bit as well. While the spoons bit into the earth, they began to make two clay towers. The towers grew until the spoons could no longer touch the cold earth. Brak then raised both spoons out of their trenches which also made the towers rise as well. When the top of towers were at Brak's eye level, he put away the spoons, and focused on the towers.

"Selyograg! Siemene ym uoy evig I srewot owt eseht ghuorht," Brak chanted.

The two clay towers began to glow and vibrate with energy as Brak chanted. A lush green glow seemed to pour out of them, making it look like a waterfall. Brak raised his right hand and pointed at a Gargoyle. The selected Gargoyle began to change from scales, blood, and bone, into a living breathing clay copy of itself. Before the Gargoyle could do anything, it saw more of its' kind turning as well. If only they knew who or what was causing their transformations, Brak in turn chuckled to himself at their predicament. One by one, all of the Gargoyles turned into clay replicas of themselves. This in turn made them very confused, annoyed and extremely angry, making the Gargoyles turn on one another. Brak was very pleased with the results of his spell, all of the Gargoyles, save for the Leader were changed into clay copies. Brak would have to deal with the Leader later, right now, his focus was on the nearest group of Gargoyles.

Brak conjured up a fireball that started to grow in shape in size, after it was created. Brak let the fireball grow until it was half the size of himself, before deciding to let it go. Brak then jumped out of hiding, and hurled the growing fireball at the group of unsuspecting Gargoyles. As the fireball left Brak's hand it continued to rapidly grow to a massive size before hitting and cooking the group of Gargoyles. This attack was the signal to the two airborne Dragons letting them know it was time for the slaughter as well. Brak in turn, was pleased to see that *this* race of Gargoyles weren't immune to fire even in their altered state. But the downfall to Brak's signal, was that the Gargoyles now knew who to set their anger on for their transformations. Brak wasted no time in continuing to cast spell after protective spell to ensure his safety, before attacking with his fire spells. As the Gargoyles got too close to Brak, he unsheathed his sword and charge them.

As soon as Silver, and Drakon saw Brak's signal, they dove down to the earth as fast as they could. While the Dragons were closing in on the ground, to do severe damage to the mass group of Gargoyles, they saw total chaos. Gargoyles were attacking each other with no remorse, or at least that's what the scenario was until Brak launched his attack. Before the Gargoyles could get within ten feet though of Brak, Drakon, and Silver attacked with all the ferocity that a Dragon was well known for. Both of them let loose jets of molten fire that burned and cooked anything in its' way instantly. Brak saw the attack coming and jumped into the air and landed on one of his enchanted flying carpets that immediately rose into the air above the flames and heat. Brak wiped his sleeve on his forehead for he had *just* managed to get out of the way of Silver, and Drakon's first attack. Brak surveyed the area as he rose in the air, and sent down more of his expanding fireballs, and chuckled. For the way Drakon and Silver were letting loose their different versions of fire blasts, they created a picture of a heart drawn by a child.

When Drakon and Silver finished attacking, both of them landed like stones on the smoldering earth crushing a few Gargoyles. Drakon and Silver then began to eat a few of the cooked Gargoyles to see if they were worth eating, but roasted clay would never taste as good as roasted meat. Brak came falling down to the ground next, for his carpet had burned up due to the immense heat that radiated from the ground. Brak let loose many different curses towards the makers and the enchanters of his very expensive flying carpet before landing. Brak hit the ground hard, but not hard enough to do any serious damage, save for a bruised ego. Brak got up off of the hot earth and surveyed the charred area, yet again, to see if he missed anything while he was in the air. Only the Leader remained unscathed, but he was too much in shock to do anything, not even flee. So, Brak decided to go and vent some anger out on the Gargoyle, instead of snapping on Drakon, and Silver. Brak stormed over to the Gargoyle with Silver and Drakon, tailing behind.

The Gargoyle was obviously the Leader of the massed group of cooked Gargoyles, aside the fact that he was immune to fire, and the clay spell. The Gargoyle also had unmistakable features aside from his immunities, for one it was at least nine feet tall. It's bat like wings were massive to match the Gargoyles height. When the wings were folded behind its' back the tips of the wings rose about a foot and a half above the Gargoyles' head. Its' eye weren't like the other Gargoyle cat eyes, for it's eyes were more reptilian, like a Dragons. It had inverted legs like its' former brethren, with long curled claws protruding from his toes. The brown claws on the Gargoyle, mismatched the yellow ones on his toes. The Gargoyle looked impressive, but to Silver, Drakon, and Brak, it wasn't even intimidating.

"Where are the hostages?" questioned Brak angrily.

"*Hostages? What are those? And why did you kill all of my brethren? We meant no harm to anyone*," asked the Gargoyle in crude English.

Brak walked right up to the Gargoyle, somehow grabbed it by the neck and lifted it straight into the air. At a second glance, Brak had grown to the same height of the Gargoyle, which explained how and where he could grab the Gargoyle. Drakon, and Silver briefly wondered on how many spells Brak knew but they dismissed the thought as quickly as it came. Both Dragons were impressed, intrigued, and a touch frightened, that Brak had the power to do this, and still manage to fight. Brak meanwhile ignored the stares of both Dragons, and glared at the Gargoyle.

"*Don't toy* with me, you *Half Breed*," Brak growled with a look of death in his eyes. "The Hostages...the Humans *your* "*Disease*" have captured, and were planning on feasting on. Where *are* they? Tell me, and show me where they are. *If* you do this, you will live...unless I see that *you* have harmed them. The, you *die*."

The Gargoyle put his clawed hand on Brak's arm and pushed away. As it pushed, it freed itself from Brak's choking grasp and landed on the ground. As the Gargoyle landed, Brak closed his hand and let it fall to his side. Brak then willed his size spell away, and he returned back to his normal six foot tall size. The Gargoyle then turned its' back on Brak and started to walk away from the trio. Brak, Silver, and Drakon followed the Gargoyle, but Silver and Drakon stayed a little further behind.

Chapter 19

A King's Reward

The trio followed the Gargoyle for a few kilometers, as they walked, the party came across a deserted town. The buildings of the town were created out of huge boulders, which seemed to lack any colour. What made the ghost town interesting, was the fact that the boulders were suspended in the air by huge logs. The logs were long, and slender, and when grouped together as they were, could hold up a great deal of weight. The trio figured that the Gargoyles that they had just killed, once populated the ghost town. The trio didn't marvel over the town for long, for they had a job to do. Eventually the Gargoyle led the trio to a huge deep pit, that was covered by a huge crude steel gate covering it. Brak peered into the dark pit, and saw movement in the darkness.

"Hello? Is anyone alive down there?" hollered Brak.

"Yes...we're alive, for now. There's a lot of us down here, we're cold, hungry, and very scared," replied a voice.

"Your Highness, is that you? How many of you are down there?" asked Brak.

"Yes, it's me. There are about four to five dozen of us...I think. It's hard to tell down here in the Darkness," answered the King.

"Okay, we're going to get you out of there in a second or two," hollered Bark again. "Drakon if you could do the honors with the gate."

Just as Brak turned around to face the Gargoyle Leader, Silver surprised him. She leapt into the air and came down with outstretched claws, and crushed the Gargoyle to nothing. Brak didn't have a chance to protect himself from a spray of blood that Silver had made. Drenched in blue Gargoyle blood, Brak looked at Silver who smiled loving back at him.

"*You boys can't have all the fun,*" stated Silver who winked at Brak, which sent a shiver down his spine.

"Amusing," grumbled Brak as he took off his robe and shook it.

Drakon tested the gate by grabbing it and pulling on it as hard as he could. With no movement from the gate, Drakon let go, and took a step back. Drakon couldn't believe that the crude gate was withstanding his efforts to tear it out, but Drakon had a different approach. He then took in a breath of fresh air and let loose with a breath of burning fire. At the sight of this, Brak and the prisoners let out a shocked scream. But after realizing that Drakon's fire wouldn't get near the prisoners, everyone began to slightly relax. Silver moved over to the opposite side of Drakon, and let loose a jet of ice cold air that froze the red hot metal. Both Dragons kept this up for a minute or two, before both Dragons grabbed the gate. With another hard tug, the gate ripped free of the earth, and was tossed aside.

"Don't be afraid of the white and reddish blue Dragons. Silver the Pure, and Drakon the Ancient are here to help rescue all of you and not harm you. They are *not* under my control, so please don't make them *angry*. Otherwise they might be compelled to eat you," hollered Brak again.

"*Do you always go overboard?*" questioned Drakon.

"I try," shrugged Brak.

"*Amusing,*" replied Drakon.

"*Now how do you propose we get to them? Drakon is far to big to get into that small hole. And I don't feel like getting stuck in that small hole either,*" questioned Silver.

"That's easy," stated Brak. "I'll do what I did before, and shrink both of you, so you two could fly down to the prisoners, and fly them out. And I promise you that the spell won't last long either."

"*Or,*" stated Silver as she began to dig.

Drakon followed suit in digging on the other side of the open pit, both Dragons were digging at a slight angle so the prisoners could easily walk out. It took Silver and Drakon some time to get to the prisoners, when they finally broke into the pit and got to them, the prisoners were a little hesitant. But when both Dragons backed out of their tunnels, and let the sunlight pour in, the prisoners started walking. As the prisoners walked, some began to run towards the light and the warmth that it provided. When all of them were finally free of the pit, the prisoners began to cheer and rejoice in their freedom. As the prisoners celebrated, Drakon, and Silver took to the sky to make themselves scarce and to *discuss* some *private* matters. Meanwhile Brak walked over to the King and knelt before him.

"Your Highness. It's good to see you again. It's been some time since we last talked," replied Brak as he bowed his head. "I have also spoken with *Drakon the Ancient*, and have found out some interesting things. But I believe there is more that he is not telling me. Also, I am quite curious as to how you came here."

"Interesting, as for how I ended up here, that's a long story that I can share with you when we return home," mused the King. "Brak of the Red Dragon, you may stand. You know that there is no need to kneel before me. I am forever in your debt for saving my life."

"Your Highness," exclaimed Brak as he stood. "I was just doing what was necessary. There is no need to-."

"Nonsense Brak," stated the King. "You will have any and all resources that you will require in your search for more Dragons. You also have my blessing if you choose to marry my daughter. Sara loves you, you know, she won't stop thinking or talking about you and your adventures. Also, when you get back to the Castle, you will receive five percent of the royal treasury."

"I...I... What? You want *me* to search for *more* Dragons? I thought you just wanted me to hunt down *Drakon the Ancient* and his allies for information on their, and our history," questioned a confused and bewildered Brak.

"Yes. I need to know the location of any and all remaining Dragons in my lands. Now where did those two Dragons go, that were with you? I wish to thank them for saving my life, and to "talk" to them about an important matter," explained the King.

"Not to be bold, but *why*? I mean, why do *you* wish to know the location of all of the remaining Dragons in your lands, and I'm also guessing the surrounding lands?" questioned Brak who was a little more then confused about his "new" orders.

"You *dare* question me?" growled the King.

Brak gave the King a look that could send a chill down a Basilisks spine before he spoke his mind. "While you were busy with your *Royal* duties, and gallivanting around, and getting captured, I've been out *there* risking my life. I have lost friends, comrades, and companions, following your orders to search for just *Drakon the Ancient.* When I finally found him, he killed what remained of the army of one hundred that I started out with. He showed me compassion…sort of. So forgive me if I'm a little protective of him and his Mate. Also for being annoyed at going on yet *another* search for Dragons. By the way, do *not* forget that I am related to the Dragons of these lands. So back to my question: *why*?"

"So it would seem that you are. We both know what will happen to you, if *you* don't keep your anger in check. As to your question, if you *must* know, our enemies are growing stronger by the day. We need protection, firepower, and allies, that only Dragons, and other mystical creatures, can provide. You understand don't you? We need to be the *only* ones to rule these lands, and the lands overseas. That's why I need you to find all of the surviving Dragons," explained the King.

"*That's it*? Out of all of the seven hundred years of my life, I've never heard of such a greedy excuse to enslave innocent creatures, and I've heard a lot of excuses. Not even Marafire would even consider doing what you are planning. You're insane if you think any Dragon will side with a *Human*, let alone *you*. And I highly doubt you have the magical resources to enslave a single Dragon for long. If *you* think that I will help you with this, you *are* mistaken," raged Brak.

"*You* dare insult me by using the name of my dead wife? Very well. Brak of the Red Dragon, I hear by banish you from *my* Kingdom, and renounce my blessing, and dismiss your reward," announced the King in a loud voice for all to hear.

"Is *that* really a *smart* idea? I am the only one here that can send you home. Also, you are still "missing" and possibly dead. So, I highly suggest that you *reconsider* your statement," Brak stated before sighing. "I can't wait until Sara rules, she's much smarter then you will ever be. She's also kinder and prettier."

"Hmm, I forgot about that. Very well I won't banish you...yet," replied the King.

"Comforting," mumbled Brak. "I'm going to get to work now on my portal spell, or portals rather. Can't forget the freed prisoners."

Brak looked to the sky, brought his right hand up to point at the sky, and made a gesture with his hand. Silver caught the sight of Brak's signal and motioned to Drakon, that Brak wanted to talk to them. Both Dragons folded their wings and plummeted to the ground. When Drakon, and Silver were close enough, they made a show of flaring their wings, and landed gently as a feather on the ground. Silver glared at the surprised King while Drakon glared at the celebrating prisoners, then at Brak.

"*Whatever it is you want, Brak, it better be important. For Silver and myself were discussing important matters,*" growled Drakon.

"It can talk!" exclaimed the King in surprise.

Drakon let out a loud roar that everyone within a thousand kilometers heard and feared.

"*Better?*" questioned Drakon angrily.

"Ignore his *Royal Highness* for the moment. I require a scale, two would be preferred though," requested Brak.

"*Why?*" asked Silver.

Brak just looked at Silver. "I can't understand you anymore Silver, my spell has just worn off. As I'm sure you can't understand me right now."

"*Why?*" repeated Drakon.

"I need them for a mass transit spell," explained Brak. "I would gladly use a portal spell, but that would take too long. Also, with so many people, I would become completely drained of my magic and probably fall into a coma. By using your scales and tapping into their energies, I can use a small portion of my magic, and at the same time teleport everyone home. After this is done, we can then be on our way,"

"*You mean, "You" can be on "your" way. Silver and myself are heading home. The "adventure" was nice, and it did bring back some old memories but...*" Drakon started.

"*We're very old, and very tired,*" finished Sliver knowing that Brak couldn't understand her.

"I see," stated Brak. "Both of your titles explain it all, especially yours *Drakon the Ancient.* I have some notion of why your *Kind* is nearly extinct. But I still have questions that need to be answered by you. Like the Clan Wars that you mentioned, and I would also like to know what happened to *my* ancestors. After I have the answers to these two questions, I promise that I will leave both of you in peace."

Drakon sighed. "*Very well. We'll help you out with what you want to know. Once you have the information, you can then leave us in peace.*"

Drakon, and Silver gave Brak one of their scales, once Brak possessed the scales, he began his spell. Brak dug deep into his pouch to pull out a crude pointed stick, which started to grow, until it was the same size as Brak. He then plunged the long stick into the ground, then Brak started to walk, dragging the stick behind him. As Brak seemed to walk in circles, a picture began to form. After Brak finished drawing the picture, it resembled a pair of long elegant swam wings. Brak then walked to the center of each wing and placed a scale on the ground. When Brak was finished with his artwork, and placing the scales in the right spots, he put his stick away and pulled out a crystal bottle. Brak took a few steps back, opened the clear bottle, and "emptied" its' contents. Silver, and Drakon puzzled over this, for there was nothing in the bottle. Brak put the bottle away after a moment, and spread his arms wide, pointing each hand at a wing.

"Nepo, yks eht ot yawrood," Brak started.

The ground started to shake and break apart, as two giant swan wings sprouted from the ground. The wings began to unfold, and as they did, they revealed a tall black archway. The archway slowly started to glow blue, while a golden orb materialized in the center of the archway. As everyone looked at the archway, it gave them the impression that they were looking at the "Doorway to the Great Beyond".

"If you want to go home, step into the archway, touch the orb, and think of home. You will then be instantly transported to you home, and loved ones. If you think of any other place, you won't go anywhere. Now go, I'm sure your families and loved ones miss you dearly," Brak explained.

The freed prisoners were hesitant at first, but what Brak had said, filled them with hope and happiness. One by one, the freed prisoners walked up to the archway, and disappeared into the golden orb, to home. But before they touched the orb, they stopped to thank, Brak, Drakon, and Silver for saving their lives, and freeing them. Brak received a hand shake or a hug from the freed prisoners, while Silver, and Drakon had their hands or a part of their arms hugged. This brought a strange warm feeling to both Dragons, for *Humans* had never thanked them before…save for one. It had also been far too long since a Human showed so much appreciation, or any appreciation towards Dragons. While the prisoners disappeared through the arch, the king strolled up to Brak and pulled him aside.

"I'm proud of you for saving everyone, and myself from those *beasts*. Your rewards will be given to you as promised, but you have shown your *true* colours. *And* for that, I can never trust you again. So I have decided to banish you from the kingdom as soon as my feet touch the ground of the Castle floor," whispered the King.

"So, I won't get *anything* for my troubles after all? Drakon was right, all of those deaths *were* pointless after all. Royalty…figures. Taolf," whispered Brak to himself as he pointed at the king.

As the King stepped through the archway, and arrived at his beloved Castle, his feet never touched the polished, tiled floor.

"BRAK!" yelled the King in furry, and hate.

"Well, *that* takes care of that. Now let's get you two home, so I can get what I want and be on my way," Brak exclaimed while he brushed his hands together.

Chapter 20

A Fiery Search

As daylight began to pour over the lush green grassy hills, three figures stopped to take in the view. Drakon, Silver, and Brak took in the sight of the morning sky, full of blue sky, and a couple of white clouds, with snow capped mountains in the distance. It had been a long four days flight from the Gargoyle's lands, making the *adventure* last about seventeen days. Even though both Dragons were accustomed to being away from home for long periods of time, it was still nice to return. But there was something...different about the beautiful scenery, that caught the eye of both Dragons. Where there should have been an opening at the base of one of the nearby mountains, there was only a large pile of rubble. At the sight of this, both Dragons began to feel their old hatred for Humans, surfacing. But of the two of them Drakon was the first to speak his mind, for the Humans had always hunted him, even after the Arthur incident.

"Hmm, I guess we'll have to find a new, quiet, and undisturbed area to continue," replied Brak more to himself then to the two Dragons.

"*My...our Den. What happened? What have you Humans done to it?*" demanded Drakon angrily.

"*Drakon, please, calm down. Don't forget, we have another Den...many more Dens,*" reassured Silver, as she tried to calm Drakon down by nuzzling him.

Silver had also been harassed by the Humans in the past, but it paled in comparison to what the Humans put Drakon through. Not even all of the mystical creatures in all the lands could equal up to the number of times the Humans had hunted or attempted to kill Drakon.

"*No we don't. My Den…this Den, was the last of all of our hidden Dens. The Humans have destroyed all of the others. You should know that. Also it would take time, that we now don't have, to create or to take over another,*" growled Drakon as he turned away from Silver to try to quell his anger.

"*What about the Dens and the Camps in the New Land?*" asked Silver as she tried to nuzzle Drakon again.

"*It's gone! It's all gone, grown over by vegetation and age. My old camp is also far too small to accommodate the two of us. Also, Salvation is still in ruins and from what I've seen, so is the Unicorn Palace, and the Chimera Kingdom. We are homeless now…again, and are probably being hunted…again. This is all your fault Human. If you hadn't persuaded us…no, me to leave, our Den would still be in one piece,*" roared Drakon as he decided to make an advance on Brak.

"*You're wrong, there is one place we can go, where it'll be safe…for a while anyway. On one of my hunts, I found the location to an old companion. Fiery the Wise, yes she is alive after all of these years. Also, you know as well as I do, that it is not Brak's fault. We would have lost our Den sooner or later. It was probably a good thing that he came along after all, otherwise we'd be buried in that Den,*" soothed Silver as she maneuvered in front of Drakon and kissed him.

"*So, she is alive. Hmm, I guess we can take refuge with Fiery the Wise until we plan our next move. That's "if" she'll let us stay with her. There is also the matter on whether she will treat us as allies or enemies,*" mussed Drakon as he finally calmed down.

"Have we forgotten about the clueless Human here? My speech spell is long gone and I need time to refresh the spell in my head. *So*, what have you two decided upon? Whatever you two decide, we'd better do it and fast. For whoever destroyed your Den, will be back in force. I have an idea of who did the damage and they are a group that we will do well to avoid. Also, if word has spread as far and as fast as I think it has, then our foes will have power at their disposal," Brak stated with a little concern and fear in his voice.

"*We're leaving to find your Goddess,*" exclaimed Drakon.

"Goddess? Oh you think that the Red Dragon on my tunic is my

Goddess? That's funny, she's not my *Goddess*. She's more of an ancestor," explained Brak.

"*Interesting. I'm sure we'll understand why, when we find Fiery the Wise. Well, enough chit-chat, let's go,*" stated Drakon.

Drakon looked at Silver who nodded, he then spread his wings, and took to the air. Silver followed Drakon into the air, after she was in the air, Silver took the lead. As Brak watched both Dragons disappear from sight, he sighed then began his transformation spell. While Brak started his transformation spell, he was caught by surprise when he began to fly into the air. It took a little while for Brak to register, that he was being carried by something large, but he couldn't see what it was. Then Brak finally clued in as Silver appeared, with her right clawed hand gently holding onto Brak. Brak cursed himself for taking so long to figure it out, if it was an enemy he would have been dead by now, then again it was still undetermined if Silver and Drakon were allies or enemies.

Silver eventually put Brak on her back, so he would be a little more comfortable, and she could have use of both hands. Meanwhile, Drakon decided to fall back and let Silver lead, for she knew where to go. But the sight of Silver showing him so much affection made his blood boil…literally. He would talk to Silver, later about this "flittering with Humans". As for Brak, the sooner he left the two of them alone, the longer he'd live to see another day.

"Silver? Why are you showing me so much affection? For lack of a better word. Doesn't this anger your mate? Seeing as he is starring daggers at me and all," questioned Brak, as he glanced back at Drakon.

"*Why? It's simple. I know what you truly are, and what you are capable of. Drakon knows what you are and what you can do as well. He…we might not show it, but we are somewhat…fearful of you. For Merlin was quite traumatizing at the time. But Drakon, also knows that I have my reasons for acting the way I do. I also see that you have enchanted yourself again,*" answered Silver.

"Sadly, my language spell will dissipate after I finish talking with you," replied Brak as he looked off into the distance.

After Silver, and Brak's little chat, Drakon flew up close to them. He had heard everything the two of them had said. Even though a Dragon's eyesight is far better then a bird of prey's, they can hear a pin drop from the normal height they fly at. When Drakon matched Silver's speed, she had kissed him, before diving towards the ground. Drakon smiled at the game Silver had selected, to make the search for Fiery the Wise more…interesting. Brak on the other hand, didn't like the game at all, but he only had two choices: hang on, and *try* to enjoy the ride, or let go and fall to the distant ground. There would have been a third option, but Silver had broken his concentration when he was casting his spell, so his bird transformation was wasted, until he renewed it yet again.

As Silver dove to the ground, Drakon was right behind her and gaining quickly. But before Drakon could touch her with one of his clawed hands, Silver flared her wings, folded one, and rolled to the right. Drakon shot past her, and did a quick survey of the area, before turning back, and flying after Silver. After Silver regained control of her direction and roll, she shot back up and into the sky. When Silver, looked over her should and past an unhappy Brak, to see if Drakon was still on her tail, she found that he wasn't. In fact, Drakon was nowhere to be seen, which gave Silver a chance to survey the new area they came to. Silver puzzled over the disappearance of Drakon though, for she knew that she was the only one with the gift of vanishing. Drakon surprised Silver though, by popping up right in front of her, and touched her arm with a clawed hand. Giving Silver a loving smile, Drakon folded his wings and dove to the ground as he avoided her.

Silver, and Drakon's game of cat and mouse seemed to go on for hours as both Dragons chased each other around the sky, and around many areas, until their game brought them to a specific forested area. As the game seemed to get more intense and dangerous, both Dragons just stopped in midair for no apparent reason, and started to plummet to the ground. Brak was holding back a scream of terror until he realized that both Dragons had their eyes closed, and weren't moving or breathing. Brak might've had the means to transform, but with his spell spoiled, and the time it would take to renew it, plus the rate he was falling at, Brak would be part of the scenery. Also, due to Drakon, and Silver's game, Brak had become very tangled in Silver's hair. While Brak fell, he screamed for dear life until, he remembered *what* he was. Brak cursed himself yet again for his stupidity, and his paranoia at not using his secret sooner.

Brak closed his eyes, took a deep breath of the fresh air, and concentrated. While Brak concentrated, two large bat like wings had ripped through his *priceless* sorcerer's cloak. Brak winced at the loss, but then again, he could always buy, or steal a new one. Claws began to grow, and tear apart his new boots, while his legs began to invert and shred his pants. Brak's gear and weapons disappeared into a dimensional void, so they wouldn't get lost. Brak was usually extremely careful of prying eyes when he transformed into his "other" self, but in this case, he made an exception. As Brak grew in size, he managed to free himself from Silver's hair and managed not to rip out too many hairs. Next long claws on Brak's now scaled body, began to appear and grow from his fingers and toes. Brak's neck then grew long and slender while his head grew larger and turned reptilian. With Brak's Human eyes becoming reptilian, the last of the changes were complete and Brak took to the air to watch his two companions hit the ground, but they never did. Instead Silver, and Drakon shot open their eyes, flipped over, and landed gently on the ground. Both Dragons then looked up and smiled at the small black Dragon, with long Silver hair with black in it to make it look like his hair was burning black, flowing down to his wings.

"*So this is why you were falling head over tail for the Half Breed. He's not even a full sized Dragon. For Blazes Sake, he's not even a full sized Drake. He's only a little larger then a Youth. Unless you're falling for him, due to his other talent*," growled Drakon.

"*Oh please Drakon. You know I'm yours for life. Bu can't I at least have a little fun?*" growled silver in return.

"*Alright I forgive you...for now. But what should we do with him?*" questioned Drakon as he nodded his head towards Brak.

"*Why don't you show me where Fiery the Wise is? I'm sure she'll be happy to tell me what I want to know*," shouted down Brak.

"*What do you think we are doing? Playing a game? Please, we were scouting the area to see where to go and what dangers to encounter, or avoid. Neither of us wants to approach another Dragon unprepared. For once an ally then, could be an enemy now*," explained Silver with a hint of annoyance at Brak's ignorance.

"*Also, we'll be walking from here on out. The skies have become a danger to us, and we will also have the element of surprise as well,*" added Drakon as he looked around.

"*Alright, I understand. You two are scared to fly in unfamiliar territory,*" mocked Brak, as he flapped his wings to rise higher in the sky.

Silver gave a look to Drakon who nodded in return, before she disappeared, while Drakon took in a deep breath and let loose a fireball at Brak. Brak noticed it just in time and avoided it by folding his wings and dove down to the ground and away from the threat. But he fell into Silver's trap, as she appeared in front of Brak, and tried to bite his head off. Brak barely escaped *that* as well, by flaring his wings at the last possible second, and sending a burst of air into Silver's mouth. Brak decided to loose both Dragons by flying into the nearby clouds, but that was his mistake. For the group of clouds weren't clouds at all, but a thick white coloured smoke, with Drakon hiding in it. Drakon burst out from the smoke, and let loose a jet of fire, while Silver appeared again and let loose her own fire. This time, Brak couldn't dodge the attacks, and was hit by both jets of fire, which crippled Brak's wings. Brak fell to the ground and landed with a hard thud, but not hard enough to do any serious damage, with Silver, and Drakon landing shortly after.

"Okay. I see your point. You didn't have to use your fire though, and OW! THAT HURT!" exclaimed Brak as he quickly turned back into a Human so his back could heal from the burns he sustained.

"*Let's go before we're found out. And put some clothes on, we don't like seeing you without them,*" exclaimed Drakon with some disgust.

"Yes Sir!" mocked Brak as he saluted to Drakon.

Brak dressed himself in another black tunic, black pants, and boots, with his Red Dragon insignia over his heart again. This time though, Brak had to take out a new cloak from his small black pouch. This cloak was pitch black with strange dark red symbols and markings all over it. also, whenever the cloak moved, its' markings seemed to shimmer with energy. Brak also had his sword strapped to his left side of his waist instead of his leg, with his black pouch moved to his right side. As soon as Brak dressed, retrieved his gear, and weapons, the trio set off once again. While they were walking through the dense forest, Silver would disappear, and reappear, then disappear again. Brak stopped and stood for a moment to watch her, but thinking he saw double, and triple, confused him.

"*Don't bother trying to keep up with her. It's one of her scouting tactics. It allows Silver to explore the surroundings while confusing any hidden enemies,*" Drakon explained.

"So I see," mussed Brak.

After about an hours worth of scouting the area, the trio moved slowly northward into the unknown. The further north the trio went, it seemed that the trees were starting to thin out. The trees finally thinned out into a large open grassy field, rich with all types of beautifully coloured flowers. The Dragons stopped to marvel at the scenery, and to see if it was dangerous, Brak just shook his head and blundered right into the field. Drakon, and Silver looked at each other, nodded for they thought the same thing and walked into the field as slowly, and gently as possible. As soon as Brak got to the center of the field though, a loud ear splitting, and horrify shriek seemed to sound from the field of flowers. Silver, and Drakon took to the sky immediately to try to avoid the shriek. While both Dragons took to the sky, Brak began to cast a deafening spell so he could tune out the annoying sound. But before Brak could finish his spell, and the Dragons could fly high enough, vines seemed to shoot out of nowhere and everywhere out of the ground. The vines wrapped around Silver, and Drakon's wings, legs, arms, necks, bodies, and mouths, preventing the Dragons from freeing themselves. Brak was similarly ensnared, but in his case only his head wasn't covered in vines.

"*You just had to tread carelessly into this shriekield, didn't you?*" stated Drakon sarcastically.

"How was I supposed to know that this forest, or this field rather, was enchanted? It's not like I can cast wide ranging detection spells on a whim!" snapped Brak.

"*You're a high ranking Sorcerer, and you didn't think to cast any spells to detect this before we left? I always fall for the dumb useless ones,*" sighed Silver.

"*We really need to talk after this ordeal Silver. Arg, if only these cursed vines would loosen up just enough for me to let loose some fire,*" growled Drakon.

"*Let loose some fire? Wouldn't be the first time,*" snarled Silver as she glanced at Drakon.

"Don't start fighting children, otherwise I might not free you. I know it might not look it, but I have this situation, completely under control," Brak scolded and mocked.

Both Dragons quit their arguing immediately and just glared at Brak, and thought of the many ways they wanted to kill, and torture him right then, and there. With a great deal of effort, Brak ignored their stares and concentrated on *his* "little" problem. Brak half closed his eyes and began to go into a trance. He knew he couldn't transform into anything, let alone his "Dragon" form, for risk of being crushed, suffocated, or strangled. *But* there was *one* way to free the three of them, and kill the imposing threat at the same time, the only down fall would be that it would hurt. Brak decided that there was no other choice, so he set his mind to a certain spell that he had memorized incase all else failed, and began to glow. The glow that surrounded Brak turned into a thick orange colour and it began to give off heat. Without warning, flames burst out from the glow, engulfing the vine wrapped Brak. The flames spread as fast as the wind could move, within seconds the whole shriekield was ablaze. After eight extremely long minutes, the fire died away, leaving the whole area charred, and black, with soot covered Dragons, and a soot covered Sorcerer who was in a lot of pain.

Both Dragons shook themselves vigorously to clean themselves, while Brak brushed the soot off of his clothes. As the trio cleaned themselves, Drakon stopped cold, looked at Silver, who also disappeared without a word. Once Silver vanished, Drakon was the next to disappear as well leaving Brak to wonder what was going on. Brak looked around quickly, a little confused, and a touch fearful, before he vanished as well. Brak took a moment to see what was going on, he was snatched up by Silver after she had disappeared. Brak also took note that he was in the air and wondered on how powerful Silver's gift was to also muffle sound as well as bend light. When Brak saw that both Dragons were looking back down at the shriekield he followed their gaze, and was shocked at what he saw. Gargoyles had shimmered into existence, and had surrounded the area, they also didn't look too happy. The two dozen Gargoyles were looking around, sniffing the air, and arguing with one another. What was disturbing to Brak though, was that the Gargoyles could teleport without casting, which to Brak, was unheard of.

These Gargoyles were a little different from the other ones that the trio had encountered a few weeks ago. These Gargoyles were tall, at least nine feet tall, with a much stronger build then the other Gargoyles. They all had hair that ranged in colour from red, to orange, to blue. Also, these Gargoyles were covered in reddish orange scales, with everyone one of them having from deep blue, to light blue eyes. All of the Gargoyles had bone white claws on their ten fingers and toes, with two large bat like wings either folded behind them, or wrapped around them like a cape. The only similarities that these Gargoyles had with the other ones, were the inverted legs. It took a moment or two for the trio to figure it out, but when they did, the realization hit them like a ton of bricks. The Gargoyles looked like Fiery the Wise…if she was a Gargoyle, that is. This got the trio thinking on whether Fiery the Wise was still alive after all this time, and if she was, did she rule these Gargoyles.

Drakon decided to take the chance. "*Were is your Clan Mother, or Leader. Fiery the Wise.*"

"*Where are you? Show your selves, and we'll escort you to her. As our Queen orders,*" replied one of the Gargoyles in perfect Draconic.

"*Do you take us for fools? I'd sooner trust a Human than a Gargoyle,*" stated Drakon.

"Gee, *thanks,*" grumbled Brak.

"*Quiet Human,*" growled Silver.

Brak might not have been able to understand Silver at that moment, but he clearly understood her growling at him.

"*It is your choice then, if you do not come with us, then you cannot meet with our Queen,*" replied the Gargoyle again.

"*Then bring her here so we may talk to her,*" exclaimed Drakon.

"*Do you take us for fools Assassin? How do we know you won't kill her?*" questioned the Gargoyle.

"*Then take these to your Queen. She'll know what to do then,*" stated Drakon as he tossed down two scales, one diamond white, the other reddish blue, then flew to a different spot.

The Gargoyle picked up the two scales off of the ground, then disappeared, the other Gargoyles followed suit. After the Gargoyles vanished, both Silver, and Drakon let out a sigh of relief. Both Dragons had prepared themselves for battle, incase the Gargoyles could "see" them. It was rumored throughout the lands and the ages that there *were* creatures that could "see" hidden things, and seeing what these Gargoyles could do, neither one of them wanted to take a chance. Thankfully though, the Gargoyles couldn't see or detect them, that didn't mean though that either Dragon would let down their guard. For there was Fiery the Wise to contend with, and both Dragons didn't know if she would accept their gifts of peace to her. Even if Fiery the Wise did, there was still the question as to whether she would show friendship, towards Silver, and Drakon, or hatred. Drakon had hoped for the best though, for he and Fiery the Wise did share a flame between them at one point in time, before she disappeared.

Chapter 21

Meeting with Fire and Wisdom

"*Your Highness. I bring you a message from the intruders we intercepted. They also gave me gifts to give to you,*" Bowed the Gargoyle holding the scales.

"*I know why you're here, and what you have in your possession! Do you take me for an incompetent? Or do you plainly NOT know who I am?*" questioned the Queen as she glared at the hapless Gargoyle from inside her Den.

The Queen didn't mean to snap at the Gargoyle but she was stressed out, and due to a recent disaster, was still in a foul mood.

The Gargoyle immediately bowed in fear of his Queen before speaking again. "*I know who you are my Queen. You are Fiery the Wise, or better known now as Queen Fiery. You are our Queen, our Leader, and our Mother. You have the ability to hear and see what other sentient creatures are thinking. Also...,*" the Gargoyle briefly paused when Queen Fiery narrowed her eyes to slits. "*Here you are my Queen. The intruders gave me these to give to you.*"

Queen Fiery's eyes opened wide in shock and amazement at the two scales, that the Gargoyle laid down in front of her Den. Queen Fiery got out of her Den and picked up both scales to study them. The Gargoyle immediately backed away when he saw Queen Fiery advancing, for he was as tall as a Human compared to his Queens' size. As Queen Fiery examined the scales, she noted they were light in weight, and both of them were shimmering with energy that only a Dragon can perceive. Queen Fiery's eyes widened again at the sight of the unusual shimmer, and she warmth they gave off and flowed into her clawed hands. Queen Fiery smiled for she knew then that she wasn't the last Dragon out there, and both Silver the Pure, and Drakon the Ancient meant peace.

"*So they are alive. That's comforting to know. Take me to them at once,*" commanded Queen Fiery.

"*But my Queen, they've disappeared, and have probably advanced further into our lands, and are on their way to do you harm...or worse,*" remarked the Gargoyle with concern.

"*Do not worry Young One. I've been alive a lot longer then you have. I also know who these "intruders" are. I also know they haven't made their way here, but are waiting for me. So take me to them...NOW!*" commanded Queen Fiery.

The Gargoyle gave Queen Fiery a look of concern, before he bowed and spread his wings. With a single flap of his wings, the Gargoyle was in the air and waiting for his Queen to follow. Queen Fiery sighed, for the Gargoyles were far more protective then a Dragoness protecting her Hatchlings. But to keep herself amused, Queen Fiery decided to make a show of taking off to her loyal kin. She unfolded her wings, spread them to their full length, and raised them into the air. Then, like a tree falling, Queen Fiery brought her wings down to the ground. After three beats of her wings, Queen Fiery's long hair was blowing all around her. This gave the image that Queen Fiery was on fire, but with a quick whip of her head, Queen Fiery's hair went dormant, and landed on her back. Queen Fiery was airborne in a matter of seconds after her little show, and following the Gargoyle to a destroyed shriekield. When Queen Fiery landed on the ground, she looked up to the beautiful blue sky to see if she could find Drakon, and Silver. After a minute or two of looking, Queen Fiery gave up, and decided to welcome the two Dragons.

"*You two can show yourselves now, and so can that Human Half Breed. Silver, Drakon...it's been a long time,*" exclaimed Queen Fiery.

"*Dismiss your Gargoyle, and the other ones that are hiding, then we'll talk,*" stated Silver.

"*Very well. Go! You all are no longer needed here. And take your scouts, and spies with you. Or they will suffer a terrible death,*" ordered Queen Fiery to her Gargoyle escort.

"*Very well my Queen,*" replied the Gargoyle, while he motioned to the others who were hiding, before disappearing.

After the Gargoyles vanished, the trio reappeared in the sky a little above Queen Fiery. Once visible again, Silver decided she was bored of holding onto Brak, and let go of him. This took Brak by surprise, but he transformed into his Dragon self, and landed lightly on the ground with a look of hate at Silver. Brak also decided to let out a long string of curses to Silver for making him destroy his second set of clothes. When Brak was finally out of breath and curses to come up with, Silver decided to land on the charred earth. Drakon on the other hand decided to make a full circle of the charred field before landing. As soon as Drakon touched the ground he made his way over to Queen Fiery and kissed her passionately. It had been far too long since he had seen, and been with her. But Drakon made his choice long ago to be with Silver for she seemed to share the same views he did.

At the sight of Drakon kissing Queen Fiery, Silver's blood turned to ice before it boiled. She knew that Drakon and Fiery *liked* each other at one point in time, and had been partners briefly, as well as Reptillia and a countless number of other Dragonesses. But Drakon was *hers* and hers alone, no other Dragoness would dare take him away from her. Silver agreed to Drakon's previous remark, and would defiantly have a talk with him when they had the chance to be alone. Drakon caught the sight of Silver's expression out of the corner of his eye, and smiled.

"*It's been too long since we've seen another friendly face. We also thought you were dead. Obviously, you're not,*" exclaimed Drakon as he broke their kiss.

"*After the Arthur incident, I figured I'd go into hiding until things between us and the Humans cooled down. After a time, I began to think that I was the only "true" Dragon left alive,*" started Queen Fiery.

"*Interesting. Drakon, and myself did the same. Also there are more "true" Dragons out there then you might think. But sadly, not as many as our kind hopes. Also, unlike you, we never got any peace and quiet after we went into hiding. It must be nice to have a wide range of territory, and Half Breed minions, or Slaves, to do with as you desire. While the rest have to fend for ourselves, and cower in fear from the ever increasing Human threat. I guess this really does make you Fiery the Wise: Ruler of the Gargoyles...oh I'm sorry, Queen Fiery,*" exclaimed, growled, and mocked Silver.

"*I'm sure she has her reasons Silver,*" started Brak.

"*Oh will you just-,*" Snarled Silver before she was cut off.

"*SILVER! Please, I'm sure Fiery has a "good" explanation for raising an army of Gargoyles, and needing more land than even a single Dragon could ever want,*" soothed Drakon as he walked back over to Silver, and kissed her.

"*Alright. Enough with the harassment, if you will let me explain myself, then maybe you'll understand why,*" started Fiery. "*But first, Silver, Drakon, I have a Den not too far from here. I suggest that the two of you get some rest, and I'm guessing that by the way the two of you are acting, it has been a while.*"

"*It has been too long. Is your Den private?*" asked Silver.

"*You will NOT be disturbed. I guarantee, and promise it,*" stated Fiery.

Fiery pointed in the direction of her "private" Den, Silver, and Drakon bowed their heads and made their way over to it. Fiery hoped that while Drakon, and Silver were in her Den, they would "reacquaint" with one another. As the two Dragons left the area, Fiery turned her head to look at the Dragonized Brak. After Fiery took a long moment of studying him, she smiled. It had been too long since Fiery saw someone like Brak. Fiery took a final look around to make sure no one was around, then laid down on the ground. Once Fiery got comfortable on the charred earth, she motioned to Brak to come closer to her. Brak hesitated at first, but eventually walked over to Fiery and laid down in front of her. He never took his eyes off of Fiery either, for like Silver, Fiery was more beautiful in person then in a tale. The only difference this time, was that Fiery let her hair grow down to the tip of her tail. But Brak still thought Silver looked the best with her hair *that* long.

"*You have a great deal of questions to ask me, don't you? Well let me answer one of them by saying, that what you Humans do in the privacy of your own Dens is your business. What Dragons do in the comfort of their Dens is their own business. Hmm, it still seems that you are confused, let me put it this way then. Drakon and Silver are going through their Bonding Ritual. Which is a good thing for they were about to kill each other. I guess the Humans never gave them anytime at all to have peace,*" explained fiery.

"*So it is true. You can read minds. I guess I don't have to ask you anything then. All I have to do, is think it,*" mused Brak.

"*Amusing. I'll answer your next question as well. First off-*," started Fiery, before she was cut off by two loud lustrous roars.

"*What was that?*" questioned a startled Brak.

"*Music to my ears*," answered Fiery.

"*Disturbing…and yet, intriguing. So, how did you get your "new" title, if you don't mind my asking? I'm sure Drakon and Silver would want to know the same thing*," questioned Brak.

"*Of course Drakon, and Silver would want to know why my title has changed. Even though it is still technically Fiery the Wise. They would also want to know why I have a small army of Gargoyles. So, if you shut your mouth, I'll tell you*," replied Fiery with a hint of annoyance.

"*Very well*," stated Brak.

Before Fiery could explain herself to Brak, on how she came to having so much power, she stood up and shook herself. After Fiery shook, she felt better, and a little more in the mood to tell her tale, she then laid back down. Fiery though wanted to learn a little more about Brak, and to see if her suspicions were right. So Fiery and Brak talked a little while off topic, until she thought she knew enough, and decided to start her tale. By this time Silver, and Drakon flew back to where Brak, and Fiery were, and landed. Both Dragons looked refreshed, and were brimming with newfound energy. Unfortunately, both Dragons still had *some* tension between each other. Fiery had a concerned look on her face, for she knew from experience, that Drakon, and Silver weren't finished their bonding. It usually, if not always took a full turn of the sun and the moon for the Bonding Ritual, and to complete it. But as fast as the look appeared on Fiery's face, it disappeared, for it wasn't *her* problem if Drakon, and Silver killed each other. But she, like Silver, did want to see Drakon happy, he was the only one of their race after all, that sacrificed so much, to make a difference.

"*Nothing in this life time would make us miss, what you are about to tell*," exclaimed Silver.

"*Yes, not all Dragons live to tell their tale of how they raised an army*," added Drakon.

"*Funny. I'll keep it short, for I know Brak has a couple of questions that both of you don't want to answer*," stated Fiery.

"*And what questions would we be avoiding Fiery?*" questioned Drakon with a hint of a challenge in his voice.

"*The Clan Wars for one. What happened to the rest of the Mystical Creatures, for two. But I think we'll let… Serenity tell that tale…assuming she is still alive,*" Fiery pointed out.

"*Point taken,*" replied Drakon.

"*Well now that that's been pointed out, could you get on with it?*" remarked Silver impatiently.

"*I will when you and Drakon stop thinking of what you want to do to me. I may be easily flattered, but I can be easily offended as well. That's better, now Brak, I'm assuming Drakon told you about our trials: how we learned to fly, how to breathe fire, and that some Dragons have "gifts". I will start my tale at the beginning of the Clan Wars, to now. And I hope you have a strong stomach Half Breed, for Drakon's story is a Whelps tale compared to mine,*" explained Fiery.

"*We shall see about that,*" growled Drakon.

Chapter 22
A Glimpse into the Past

"*Unlike Drakon's Clan, my Clans' Young, did not endure any hardships or trials. Instead, each one of the Whelps was assigned a task and if they couldn't fulfill it, they died. It was a hard life, but most of us survived to fulfill our tasks and roles in the Clan,*" began Fiery.

"*Interesting, please continue,*" mussed Brak.

"*Shut-up Half Breed,*" snarled Silver.

Brak was about to make a snide remark, when Drakon stood up and made his way over to Brak. He then lowered his head until he was staring Brak right in the eyes. Then Drakon took one more step so his mouth was right beside Brak's ear, or where an ear should be, and whispered to him in a voice so soft that it sounded like a gentle breeze. "*I suggest you hold your tongue. Otherwise, one of her Gargoyles will reappear and silence you.*"

"*I'd like to see them try,*" growled Brak.

Fiery gave Brak a look that could kill, before continuing her tale. '*While Drakon was busy battling his enemies in the 'Unknown Lands', we were fighting with ours. Too bad our enemies were each other. To understand this better I will start with a tale that every Dragon knows. The tale of the Great Dragon, and the beginning of our kind.*"

* * *

It is said, that in the beginning of time there were thousands of feral creatures, that unlike today were either reptiles or huge fish and sea creatures. These creatures would constantly fight with one another for various reasons. They fought for power, control, land, and most importantly: to prove that *they* were the strongest. Also, unlike today, most of the ancient creatures could command mystical energies, and powers that only a Human could dream of having. But like today the creatures could only command a few mystical abilities, and there weren't that many of them. Through all of this fighting there were two creatures who opposed this way of life. One of these creatures was a huge Lizard that had the ability to breathe fire. The Lizard was covered in grey scales, and walked on four muscular legs, that ended with long sharp white Claws. The Lizard also had dark golden eyes that were said to see everything that happened in the hostile Lands. The Lizard also had a long tail that, with a single swipe, could break or kill anything. The other creature was a massive winged Lizard that had the ability to breathe ice. It had two large bat like wings that could act like arms and hands, when it wasn't flying. The flying Lizard also had two muscular legs that ended with curved white claws. This Lizard was covered in dark brown scales, with light green eyes that could see far into the skies and the Great Beyond.

One day, both great Lizards were going about their usual routines of feeding, killing, and defending their lands. While both Lizards did their routines, a massive battle broke out among the other creatures, and poured into their lands. So both Lizards joined in the onslaught, for this battle was about land, and every creature, big and small, wants land. Even back in those ancient times, whomever had the most land had the power to rule over all of the lesser creatures. While both Lizards fought, they crossed paths with one another, when that happened they both stopped what they were doing and stared at each other. When they stopped, a strange sense of comfort, and balance seemed to overcome them and confuse them, for this feeling was foreign, new, and yet strangely familiar. At that moment, both of these creatures realized that they shared a common goal. This common goal was known as: peace, something that no creature felt or even knew about. When the battle was over, and no victor was decided, both Lizards decided to get to know each other better. Thus, they mated, so they could share their feelings and views of the lands with one another, and become joined.

After what seemed like an endless mating, and bonding that the two Lizards did, a new type of creature was produced, and raised. Due to the length of the bonding and the type of Lizards that they were, they could only produce one offspring at a time. The creature that the two Lizards created was a mix of both of them, and yet it wasn't. This creature was massive in size, bigger then its' makers when it was fully grown. It was covered in reflective scales that seemed to have no colour, and yet contain every colour in existence. It had two large bat like wings, that was unlike the winged Lizards, the wings were on it's back, in between it's front and hind legs. The creatures wings could also fold and rest along its' back, unlike the winged Lizard, who's wings folded into arms and hands. When the wings were resting, the only thing you could make out, was it's head, and long elegant tail. The creatures eyes were a mix of gold, and emerald, it's eyes, like that of the land Lizard, could see everything, and more. Also, unlike both Lizards, this creature had long, bone white hair, that flowed from the top of its' head, down to its' wings. With the birth of this creature, peace seemed to settle over the lands, as the creature went to, and fro, creating this strange peace. It made this peace by interfering with the feral battles, and managing to either subdue, or put the battling creatures into submission. This creature was known to every creature of the lands as a Dragon: a Peacemaker out of Chaos.

The Dragon was feared and revered by every creature of all of the lands due to his abilities, and powers. The Dragon could breathe fire, ice, and had something special that only a few creatures had. This was due to the lands, for unlike today, the lands in the distance ages were enveloped with mystical energies that granted creatures unique abilities and powers. This special mystical energy, or what we Dragons call: gifts, could only imbue a creature with a couple of gifts to use as they saw fit. The Dragon however, had many gifts that could heal, harm, protect, and kill. Out of the countless millennia, this was unheard of, a single creature having a multitude of gifts. In actuality, this was part of only one gift, the only known gift in all Dragon history: the gift, of gifts. This gift would also allow the Dragon to view things that were "right and wrong" with the feral lands, and the future that the lands held. Armed with this knowledge, the Dragon set out to create a balance among creatures. This balance would be later known to every living being as : the Law of Nature, or the Law of the Wild. But throughout the Dragon's quest of peace, he had become lonely, for the Dragon was only one, and what he wanted, required many of his kind.

Over the years that passed, the Dragon managed to convince *his* makers to create a partner for him, so he could have help in spreading his peace. Both Lizards agreed in the end to their creation, but sadly, after the second Dragon was birthed, the Lizards were killed by other new strange creatures. These creatures weren't like the Lizards, and other reptiles and creatures that ruled the savage lands. These creatures were covered in hair and fur, and seemed to be more dangerous, and feral when they attacked the Reptiles, Lizards, and other scaled creatures. Thus the peace was broken again, but this time, the Dragon had a helper, a friend, and most importantly, a mate to aid him. With his mate, both Dragons set out to try and convince these new feral creatures to stop what they were doing. Over the eons that followed though, the two Dragons got nowhere, and ended up turning feral in the end as well. It is said, that if you can't bring order to chaos, then become chaos and rule it. Also like the first Dragon, the second Dragon was also blessed with a multitude of gifts, which made both of them very deadly when they turned feral.

The two Dragons used and abused their gifts to carve out a foothold in the new changing hostile lands, to conquer and rule them. But after eighty millennia of slaughter and bloodshed, the two Dragons realized what they were doing, and stopped their tyranny. This had brought another new sensation to the two Dragons, shame, and with this sensation they tried to hide from the lands, out of fear at what they had become. Once in hiding, they took comfort in one another, and began to mate, creating more Dragons, for both Dragons knew that like their creators, they wouldn't be around forever. Even though both Dragons were siblings, they both knew that in time, their Hatchlings, and their Hatchlings, Hatchlings, would grow apart, and become different and diverse from one another. So it came to pass that the Dragons conceived, and then laid their Hatchlings. When their Hatchlings were born, both Dragons realized that the Whelps could only breathe fire, and or ice, or freezing breath. But that didn't stop them from teaching their Whelps the life skills, and problems that they endured. Whenever there was a fight or a battle among the developing Whelps, both Dragons would show their Whelps *pain*. The Dragons would kill both of the fighting Whelps and later explained that in the wild lands, that's how life flowed.

The Whelps feared and respected this way of life, and as they grew older and turned into Dragons themselves, and began to have Hatchlings of their own. These new generations of Whelps would learn the ways and life of peace, and harmony, otherwise, they'd suffer. Eventually though, like their makers, the first two Dragons died protecting their legacy from the hostilities of the lands. The Dragons deaths though, were a blessing, and not sorrow, for both Dragons could watch over their legacy, and their young. The other Dragons respected, honored, and feared their ancestors, who were known to all Dragon kind as: the Great Dragon, and his Mate. The reason for this, is that the Great Dragon came first above all else, he had requested help, which came in the form of a Dragoness...his Mate. But this didn't mean that the Dragons only created and worshiped the Great Dragon, for they held great respect for his Mate. Without her, the Dragons would not even exist, and be able to live, and prosper in the wild lands, which were eventually tamed and conquered. When this happened, there were Dragons in every part, of the lands, and living peacefully with the lands and each other.

Before our Great Elder Dragons were even born, there were around three hundred Clans or so. More specifically, there were two billion Dragons, give or take a thousand or so. These Clans covered the *world*, you couldn't even growl with love or hate, without another Dragon overhearing you. With the Great Dragon, and his Mate watching over all of the Dragons, there was peace, with the occasional fight. Each Clan traded various foods, stories, and knowledge with each other. This also meant, that the Dragons of *that* generation, were no longer brother and sister, but they were now slightly different from one another, and diverse creatures. This also meant that Dragons, and Dragonesses could mate freely without fear of mating with a sibling. Also, with all of the peace and harmony, the Great Dragon, and his Mate bestowed some of their knowledge onto a select few. This knowledge came in the form of a gift. No matter how many "Chosen" Dragons, there were, no two gifts were alike. Unless the gifted Dragons were a set of twins. But twins were extremely rare compared to the gifted Dragons. The Great Dragon, and his Mate also bestowed a single Dragon over each generation, with the gift to commune with them to make sure their ways were being followed. This gifted Dragon would be known to all others as: The Voice of the Great Dragon.

As the Dragons lived in harmony with one another, a new enemy rose up to challenge our might, and power. After years of fighting we learned the name to this enemy, they were known as: Unicorns. Unlike the small Unicorns you see today, or have heard of in tales, these ones were far larger. They were the size and height of a Youth, instead of a Whelp. Also, there were no multitude of different hair colours, white was the one and only colour. Their horns were also bone white, with no multitude or variety of colour, and their hoofs were black as shadow. The *only* thing that varied on the Unicorns, were their eye colours. The Unicorns were vast in numbers, and like our select few, had gifts of their own. Unfortunately each one of the cursed beasts had many gifts that they could use against us. The only thing that saved us from the years that followed were our own immunities, and resistances to their powers. No one knew how many Unicorns there were, but one thing was clear, they had the ability to easily obliterate a Clan if they so chose. So it began again, the battle of survival and dominance of, and over, the Lands. Sadly, to this day, it is still unknown who struck the first blow against each race.

While the Dragons battled the Unicorns in the never ending war that would last for millenniums to come, one Clan Leader changed our history forever. Her name was lost to the ages of time, but her beauty, gift, and knowledge made her unforgettable. The Clan Leader was huge compared to the average Dragoness. She was covered in bright ruby, and sapphire coloured scales, from her nose to tail. At the sight of her, you would think that you were looking at a huge pile of shiny gems. Her ruby coloured wings matched her long sapphire hair that flowed from the top of her head, down to her hind legs. She also had long slender crystal coloured claws on her ten fingers and toes. What made the Clan Leader beautiful though, was her eyes. The Clan Leader's eyes were the colour of emeralds, but when she turned her head or blinked, the colour would change to sapphire.

The Clan leader decided that she was tired of following the "rules" that were laid out by the Great Dragon, and his Mate. For the couple had told their kin to respect life and cherish it, but why would you do that when you are being attacked? There was only one option that the Clan Leader saw: try to convince everyone that the Great Dragon was wrong. The only way to do that was to become the new Great Dragon and rule everyone with teeth, and claw, for that was what the Great Dragon did before he passed on. The Clan Leader managed to convince her Clan, that they were the strongest of all the Clans, and there was no one that could or would stand in their way of power. Thus they should rule over all the other Clans, for their Clan was beyond equal to any other. With the promise of power, and a corrupt Clan Leader, the Clan followed their Leader without question. The fist Clan War began the same day the Clan Leader finally managed to corrupt her Clan, it might have also been our first Clan War, but it was not our *last.* The first Clan War lasted three thousand years, before the attacking Clan and their corrupt Leader was destroyed. During this war, no one knew what to do, for the Unicorns were one threat to contend with, now the Dragon Clans had to fight one of their own Clans.

While the Clan War raged throughout the millenniums, the corrupt Clan, had utterly decimated twenty Clans. The corrupt Clan used various methods to destroy these Clans, but it was the Clan Leaders' gift that did the most damage. The Clan Leaders' gift allowed her to kill anything with a touch, or a glance. It is a good thing that any and all gifted Dragons can choose to use their gift or not. Near the end of the first Clan War for power, the Clan Leader was finally killed, due to sheer numbers, ending her fifteen thousand year old life. With the death of their Clan Leader, and the promise of power gone, the corrupt Clan fell into chaos. With every Dragon in the Clan now wanting power, and command over the distraught Clan, an inner Clan War broke out. The Clan slowly tore itself apart, one Dragon at a time. After a few hundred years, the inner Clan War was over, there were no Dragons left, and the Clan was lost to memory.

With the results of the Clan War, and its' outcome burned into every Dragons mind, one thing became clear. The Great Dragon, and his Mate, were no longer watching over their Hatchlings and Whelps. Whether they disappeared, or finally passed on into the Great Beyond, no one was sure, for their voices were now gone. Ironically enough, we were the ones that silenced the Great Dragon, and his Mate, with our pointless Clan War. The reason for this, was that the Corrupt Clan Leader had acted as "the voice" of the Great Dragon, or his Mate. But now that she was dead due to the war that she created, the Clans were left deaf to their ancestors, or Gods if you will. For there was no one to pass on the gift of commune to. With every Clan on their own, to do as they pleased and no harm would, or could come to them, they decided to abuse their ways of life to their own selfish ways. In the past the Great Dragon, and his Mate, would punish those who would start or create a war among each other. All of this meant one thing: only the strongest Clan could survive and there was no one to tell them to stop fighting.

From that one War, our once peaceful history was changed forever. With no Great Dragon to say otherwise, the Clans could do as they pleased. So it came to pass, throughout the years, one Clan or another would claim supremacy over all the others. They would also claim to be the only Clan to be the strongest to rule over all of the others. When there was disagreement on the Clans' statement (which there always was), war would break out shortly after. Most of the time War would break out right after the statement was made in front of all the other Clans. When a Clan War would end, a Clan or five would be completely obliterated. This was due to either complete annihilation of a Clan, or the Clan losing its' Leader. Most Clans would have at least two Leaders: a male, and a female. This way, if war broke out, and one of the Clan Leaders died, the Clan could still survive. But if there was only *one* Clan Leader, and they died, the Clan would fall into chaos. The reason for this, was, a Clan Leader was the only Dragon capable of making tough decisions when it came to war, or protecting the Clan. The Clan Leader was also the only one to rule their Clan with deadly sharp claws, or so the saying goes. When the Clan Leader or Leaders died of old age their eldest Whelp would take their place. But if the Clan Leader, or Leaders, died of "unnatural" causes, then there would be a power struggle. A Dragons lust for power, and control over the other Dragons, can rival that of the Great Dragon's power himself.

Over the millenniums, the numbers of the Clans decreased to only a handful in numbers. Before Drakon the Ancient's parents were born, there were only forty Clans left, or more specifically, around sixty thousand Dragons. With this small of a number, the remaining Clans couldn't afford to loose anymore of their kind to petty wars. Also the Unicorn threat had grown out of control with no Dragons to quell their rising numbers. So, peace finally broke out among all of the Dragon Clans so they could focus on more important matters. Finally peace was restored, but over the following years, the lines of peace, and war, dwindled. Due to our nature of lust for power, we were always on edge, and eager to battle or fight with one another, if a war or a small battle, broke out. In the end, our urges, and lusts got the better of us, in other words: war had prevailed, and peace had lost. While the new Clan War raged on, through the next hundreds of years, Clans began to make alliances with one another, so they could defeat rival Clans, Clan Leaders, or specific individuals. During the new war, there was one Clan that seemed to be indestructible. No matter what Clan went up against this Clan, the Clan would always prevail. This Clan was one of the first Clans out of the original three hundred, that managed to survive the brutal wars. This Clan that had survived for over nine hundred thousand years, was now ruled by one of the fiercest Dragons known to our history, you would know him as Slash and Burn.

Slash & Burn might have been ruthless, savage, and a tyrant, but he managed to make his Clan survive. Ironically, he was envied by a great deal of Dragons, and Clans, for his savage ways of living. Slash & Burns's true name was Dragatheius, but from what he did, and how he did it, it was just as easy to call him Slash & Burn, his true name was also forgotten over time. As time passed a good portion of Clans, and Dragons sided with him to take on any opposing threat, Slash & Burn was invincible in the eyes of his allies. Too bad that didn't last forever, for there were five powerful Clan Leaders that destroyed Slash & Burn's allies. It might have taken several hundred years to obliterate Slash & Burn's allies, but they were destroyed nonetheless. These five, like Slash & Burn, were known by many names, but you would know them best as: The Elders. Also, like Slash & Burn, The Elders were leading Clans that were out of the original three hundred as well. The Elders had a ruthless, clawed grip on their Clans, that could put Slash & Burn to shame, and powerful gifts, that no one could come close to matching.

Each one of The Elders were stunning and beautiful to look and marvel at. But like a Dragon, their appearances could be quite deadly. They might have had many names, but the five of them, did have their favorites. The oldest of the five Elders, was huge even for an adult Dragon. He went by the name of Hyena, for he had a talent of laughing while he slaughtered his enemies. For a thirty thousand year old Dragon, Hyena looked pretty good for his age. He was covered in dark blue scales, that shimmered when the light reflected off of them. He had long flowing dark green hair that started from the top of his head, and flowed down to the middle of his back, just before his wings. His green hair was a perfect match with his dark green eyes, and dark green wings. Hyena's long curved teeth had also went perfectly with his long curled claws, which he loved when we was making a "point". Hyena's gift was a lot like Bark the Loud's only instead of a roar, it was Hyena's laughter that could topple mountains and destroy settlements.

Grim is Death was the next in line at twenty-five thousand years old. Grim is Death wasn't as big as Hyena, but he was still larger then the average Dragon. He was covered completely in jet black scales, save for his head, which was covered in bone white scales. Grim is Death's hair flowed from the top of his head, to the middle of his back, his hair was blood red like the inside of his wings. But on the outside, Grim is Death's wings were black. A dragon with two different wing colours is rare, like Dragon twins, for it is a colour mutation. Grim is Death's eyes were a mystery though, for they were orange, which didn't match his natural colours at all. Even though his eye colour didn't match with the rest of the colours on his body, they still made him look deadly. But it was his gift of Death Stare, that made him a terror among his Clan, and his enemies.

After Grim is Death, came Elementia, she was only nineteen thousand years old, and she was massive compared to the average Dragoness. Elementia was covered in light blue scales, with long elegant light green spikes protruding from them. This gave her the appearance of what Humans would call a pin cushion. The only difference between Elementia's spikes, and a pin cushion, were that her spikes contained a deadly poison. This poison could kill in a matter of sun movements, and it could also render any opponent useless by paralyzing the enemy. Her long dark blue hair, flowed from the top of her head, over her shoulders, and down to her tail. Elementia's dark green eyes matched her dark green wings, aside from her blue and green colours, Elementia had crystal white teeth and claws. But it wasn't her beauty and spikes that could slaughter, it was her gift of mind control, that could.

Foxy was fifteen thousand years old which made her fourth in line out of the five Elders. She was the average size of a Dragoness, but that didn't make her any less deadly. She was covered in rusty coloured scales from nose to tail. Foxy's silvery coloured hair flowed from the top of her head, down to her shoulders, then overflowed down to the ground. Her snow-white wings matched her silver hair, giving her the appearance of a red fox. It was Foxy's eyes though that gave her, her beauty, they were the colour of amber, and seemed to sparkle when she looked at someone. She had unique claws, for they were long and retained a golden colour to them. Also, Foxy acted more like a fox then a Dragon, she was very swift, and extremely cunning when she had to be, when dealing with her enemies. Her gift was unique, for she had the ability to duplicate herself, and become twice as viscous when she battled.

Lastly, there was Silent. Silent was only a few years shy of fifteen thousand, which made her the youngest out of all The Elders. She was smaller then the average sized Dragoness, but she was more then twice as deadly. It was hard to see her golden scales, for Silent's hair covered her whole body completely, save for her face. Her hair was dark blue, which also made it difficult to see her body. On the plus side, her dark blue hair wouldn't get in the way when Silent, unfolded, and used her wings. Her wings were golden which was a perfect match for her golden body. Silent's eyes were a rich cyan colour that made them stand out among her golden scales. To finish it off, Silent had pearl white claws and teeth. She was extremely rare among her kind, for she didn't have one gift, but two. Her first gift allowed her to see into a creature's soul, while her second gift allowed Silent to corrupt the soul and turn her victim into a mindless slave.

The battle between The Elders and Slash & Burn was long and lengthy, but he stood no chance against The Elders' combined power, and might. Slash & Burn fought anyway, for that was the only thing he knew how to do in the harsh Lands. The war between The Elders, and Slash & Burn lasted two thousand long years. During the end of the war, Slash & Burn's Clan was only down to a handful of Dragons. It dropped from four thousand down to three hundred, Slash & Burn had to make a life and death choice. Slash & Burn did the only thing that he could think of to save what remained of his Clan. He gathered what remained of his Clan and fled to the "Unknown Land". But he vowed he would return one day with a new army and allies. With this "new army", he would crush The Elders and take control of their Clans, and their Lands.

The lands that Slash & Burn fled to, was, called the Unknown Lands, due to the fact that no Dragon had yet explored the land, or might have long ago, but the knowledge was lost. That didn't matter anyway, for it was rumored that that was where the Unicorns originated from and lived. The Unicorns also had established a firm grasp on the lands, and no Dragon wanted to fight a losing battle. Sadly, this was where Drakon, and many other Dragons eventually ended up: eight thousand years later. Meanwhile, The Elders took Slash & Burn's escape as an opportunity, to spread the lie that they had banished Slash & Burn. By using their powers, and cunning, they whittled down Slash & Burn's Clan to only a handful. Then The Elders decided to show Slash & Burn mercy by allowing him to leave his homeland, but he may never return. The lie worked for a couple of thousand years, until a band of Clans formed an alliance that managed to match The Elders in firepower.

By this time, I was old enough to realize that my gift gave me a huge advantage over any opponent. Even though I was only six hundred years old, barely even a Drake, I decided to challenge my Clan Leader for leadership of the Clan. I might have been a little over eager, but due to my gift, I knew I would have the upper claw. My Clan leader looked like me in every way, the only difference was, he was my brother, and six hundred years older then me. I know it sounds strange, but we were twins, with the exception, that I was a few generations younger. I am known as a Delayed Hatchling, which is rare, but not unheard of. A Delayed Hatchling, is a Hatchling that isn't released from the Mother until she has her last clutch of Hatchlings. This could be due to any number of reasons, ranging from a wounded Mother, to a Mother who has an underdeveloped system. Anyway, I figured that my brother's rule had gone on for long enough, and with our parents long past dead, they weren't about to say otherwise. Our battle was long and fierce, lasting one hundred years. In the end, I won…barely, for my brother also shared the same gift. With my new position of power, I didn't hesitate to use and abuse it. I had formed my own alliances and made my own enemies, which I dealt with easily. As for holding my position over my Clan, it was easy enough, I can read minds, so I knew who was plotting or scheming against me, and I would "dispose" of them. Over the next two hundred years, I managed to gain complete loyalty of my Clan, and also managed to increase its' numbers ten fold. With my new Clan strength, I decided to take on The Elders.

I wasn't the only young Clan Leader either to have the fiery idea of taking down the accursed Elders. There were others who also wanted a piece of The Elders, in fact, the remaining twenty Clans didn't want just a piece, but a chunk of them. The Elders reined long enough, it was time for them to die. The twenty remaining Clans banded together to form the first mass alliance since ancient times. With our new found might, strength, and power, we took on The Elders, and their forces. Like our repetitive history goes, we started yet another long War. Only this time, the battle that we waged would last half a millennium. As time passed, it was hard to tell the blood from the soil, the burned, charred, dead lands from the living, thriving lands. The Elders were also starting to loose their firepower at last, and their control over their Clans. Also, their influence over the opposing Allied Clans was diminishing, giving back our hope and civility. We battled long and hard, and finally, we were getting somewhere.

As the war neared to an end, The Elders fled from us, taking their Elite and Royal Guards with them. This gave the Allied Clans the chance to obliterate what remained of The Elder's Clans once and for all. Unfortunately our history has a nasty habit of repeating itself, every so often. With only fifteen Clans left now, the fighting started up again, and this time, it got *ugly*. Each Clan brought forth their Hero, Champion, or Leader, to lead them from victory. While each Clan battled with one another yet again, word had finally spread of what really happened to Slash & Burn. We were so busy fighting each other, that we didn't realize the significance of this information. Eventually the realization finally bit into all of us. The Elders had deceived us, which made all of the warring Clans extremely angry. We decided to put our warring aside and hunt down The Elders, to finish them off permanently.

It was too bad though, for none of the Allied Clans got the chance to slaughter the Hated Elders. For word had arrived to the Allied Clans that a Rogue Clan of Dragons had defeated The Elders. This Rogue Clan was also rumored to have allies that would make a Dragon's stomach churn and expel its' contents. Chimeras were one of the rumored allies, this made no sense for they are our food, not our ally. Unicorns were another rumored ally of the Rogue Dragon Clan. This made our blood boil, for no Dragon in their right mind would consider joining with an ancient enemy. The only thing Unicorns were good for was either food, or plant food. The last of the rumored allies were Gryphons, this made no sense for Gryphons simply hated Dragons. It was unknown to us why the Gryphons and Hypogryphs hated us. But, we speculated that, making them our food, and decimating their numbers might have had something to do with it.

Once we learned of this information, we became very angry with the Rogue Clan, and each other. Within a hundred years the anger got the better of us and we began fighting again. It had seemed that fighting, hostility, and bloodlust, had finally become part of everyday life for we were always battling without even realizing what we were doing. We also couldn't shake the thoughts of this Rogue Clan destroying *our* enemies, and from the tales that we heard this Rogue Clan was invulnerable, which was ludicrous. We were more ruthless in our battles with each Clan, and less forgiving with one another. While we fought, another couple of Clans were destroyed, until there were only six Clans left in these Lands. As for the rest of the lands, no one knew, if our Clan War spread throughout the lands in the world or not. We found out a few years later, when the Rogue

Clan was coming to our Lands. We also learned that there were other smaller Clans that had survived in other lands. They too were flourishing and fighting each other for control, and power.

While the remaining Clans began another battle, the Rogue Clan, and its' allies made an appearance that took all of us by surprise and caught us off guard. Our first encounter with the Leader of the Rogue Clan did not go so well. We thought that the Rogue Clan was a threat to us, they did after all, kill Slash & Burn, as well as The Elders. The six Clans decided to form one last alliance so we could rid ourselves of the Rogue Clan, and its' allies. It was an interesting and spectacular war, for even though we were six Clans strong, with over thirty thousand Dragons in total. We could only equal the Rogue Clan's, or more specifically, Drakon the Ancient's force of two thousand. With the might of the Chimera, combined with the power of the Dragons, and the grace of the Unicorns, it was a war worth fighting.

Our war with Drakon the Ancient lasted for another five hundred years, and in that time, other creatures began to rise in power. Humans, Elves, Dwarves, Trolls, Goblins, and other Half Breed races rose and began their own battles and wars against each other…and us. Our war with Dragon the Ancient eventually ended with Drakon the Ancient, talking, and beating some sense into us. Of course, we didn't accept this at first, for our history showed us that violence was the only way. We began to battle with Drakon the Ancient's Clan again, but this time, he refused to retaliate. Drakon, kept to his method of trying to reason with us, as stubborn as we were, we didn't listen. Also, we had thought that the Unicorns had manipulated him, for no Dragon in their right mind would talk of peace. Eventually, with much talk, Drakon the Ancient forced us to see what we were doing to our lands, and to our kind. None of us thought to realize that we were also helping the *Humans* and their many different races prosper as well.

Drakon the Ancient showed us that we would drive each other into extinction if we kept up our senseless battles, and wars. Drakon the Ancient also talked about how Dragons could easily destroy all of the lands. This had frightened us, for the Great Dragon and his Mate, had sired all of us on these lands, that we grew to love and cherish…to an extent. But due to our long battles, and wars throughout our histories, we had forgotten this. With Drakon the Ancient's persistence, and reasoning, he helped us remember this, at the cost of half of his Clan, and his Survivalists. It had also seemed to us that the Great Dragon had been reborn in Drakon the Ancient, for he had seemed to share the same views as the Great Dragon. We were all just to dull witted to realize it over the times. Unlike the Great Dragon though, Drakon had sacrificed so many things to prove his points, and ideals.

With our differences finally behind us, we created yet another alliance, that was a little shaky, but we vowed to hold it together. The alliance held for about seven hundred years, it would have lasted for longer, but we ran into complications. We had encountered a ruthless Human by the name of King Arthur, who rose in power among the Humans. His one and only quest was to drive every mystical creature to extinction, of course he never claimed this, but actions speak louder then words. Fortunately for us, some of the Half Breeds, and other Humanoid races didn't want to take part in this, for they had other matters to attend to. In better words, the "other matters" simply meant war with one another. Like Drakon the Ancient, and Silver the Pure, I know what happened to them. But if you want to know, then hunt down *Serenity*, I'm sure she'll gladly tell you…for a price.

Chapter 23

Drakon's Humanly Love

"Wow, that was…short. A lot shorter then Drakon's tale of King Arthur, let alone his life story. Also, Drakon I thought that *you* would have told me about the beginning of your history. Not to mention, that was the Clan War, or Wars rather, not how *you* raised an army Fiery. *And*, Drakon, you didn't give me a description of The Elders, all you said about them was: "They're ugly"," exclaimed Brak as he turned back into a Human.

"*Simple minded Half Breed. I left out a great deal of information, because I know how bored you'll get. Not to mention all the annoying questions you would've asked me. So, don't you DARE mock me or you might not live to see the dawn of the next day. I have more to tell you. If you stop to think for a second, you'd know that,*" roared Fiery.

"Fine, I'll keep quiet and pay *close* attention to your every word. I'll also keep my thoughts to myself, but then again, does it matter? Also, if I'm real lucky you'll tell me what I really want to know…Your Highness," Brak mocked, as he bowed.

Drakon, and Silver looked at each other, and grinned at Brak's fate. Both of them stood up and took a few steps back, until they thought they were far enough. Fiery stood up and glared at Brak, before she charged at him. Brak barely avoided Fiery's lunge, only to dive out of the way again. Fiery used her claws, and tail to slash at the elusive Sorcerer, when that failed, Fiery resorted to other measures. As Fiery played her game of tenderize the Human before eating it, Drakon walked over to Fiery. No matter how enraged Fiery was, she could not hope to land a single blow on Brak. Drakon put a clawed hand on Fiery's shoulder when she brought her head up after another attack. Fiery was going to let loose a jet of molten fire, upon the Sorcerer until she felt Drakon's warm touch. She looked up, and saw that Drakon was right in front in her. Both Dragons gazed into one an others eyes, and Fiery began to shed tears. As Fiery's tears fell to the black earth, they reflected images of Fiery's past and painful memories and fears. Drakon turned his head and broke his gaze with Fiery to look at Silver. She gave the slightest nod when she saw the look on Drakon's face. Drakon turned back to Fiery and whispered something into her ear. Fiery nodded her head, spread her wings, and took to the sky, with Drakon close behind her. Silver knew the decision that she made might've been the worse one, but Drakon deserved to be happy, even if he was with another Dragoness.

"What'd I say? Was it something I did? Or was *Fiery the Wise* suppose to eat me?" asked Brak as he quickly cast a speech spell on himself to hear Silver.

Silver disappeared, then reappeared in the air above Brak, then landed on him. Silver brought down one of her clawed hands on top of Brak as she landed, forcing Brak to the ground. She would have liked to kill him outright, but that wouldn't have been right for some reason. With Silver's hand overtop of Brak, making him look like a caged animal that was too big for its' cage. But try as he might, Brak couldn't free himself of Silver's grasp. Also, he didn't get the chance to summon all of his weapons and gear, so he was left defenseless. Not too mention the position that he was in, Brak couldn't cast any helpful spells to free himself. Brak silently wished at that moment, that he should've paid more attention to spell casting with your mind, then with gestures. With Brak being pinned, and unable to do anything about it, Silver decided to vent some of her anger.

"*You insignificant little Half Breed. Do you have any shred of decency in you, to stifle your thoughts, and pitiful childish remarks? If it wasn't for Drakon, and his love for life and you...you...Humans. You would have been long past dead. To basilisks with Drakon, I'm going to tear you apart piece, by piece, starting with your arms,*" Silver snarled as she brought over her other hand.

"*Oh please.* Do you think that your *Mate* would approve of that. Also, that's been bugging me, why is Drakon *so* friendly towards Humans? Every other Dragon I've talked to, or tried to talk to, has tried to kill me," questioned Brak a little annoyed, and angry.

Silver just glared death at Brak before he continued. "Hmm, time to try a different approach. So, if I say yes, and that I'm *very* sorry for making an all powerful Dragon. Or Dragoness, *sorry*, cry, would you let me go?"

"*No, I won't, and I guess you might be right, Drakon probably won't speak to me for one hundred years or more. But then again, seeing you in sheer pain would be worth the wait...arg. I hate being in these predicaments. Fine. If you want to know why Drakon is so "generous" for lack of a better word, I'll tell you. But bear in mind, Drakon has told no one of what I'm about to tell you,*" cautioned Silver as she calmed down slightly.

"If Drakon has told no one, then why do you know?" questioned Brak mockingly.

"*That is none of your concern Half Breed. Now shut that mouth of yours and I might free you. Unless I decide to eat you instead of tearing you to pieces,*" snarled Silver.

"Fine," remarked Brak, as he squirmed under Silver's hand.

"*Guess I'm the only one who hasn't told the impulsive Half Breed a tale yet. I better make it good. I just hope Drakon will forgive me for telling Brak...unless,*" sighed Silver to herself.

"*This was before Drakon, and myself became Mates. But it was after the long battle with Arthur. Drakon was alone and hunted by every Human in the land, and he was also being haunted by his memories, and his dreams. I tried to sway him countless times to be my Mate for the fact that I fancied him, and so did Fiery...plus every other Dragoness to say the least. As you can probably guess, there is fierce competition when it comes to finding the right Mate. I fancied Drakon, for the reason that I didn't want to see him living alone anymore. But he felt that he didn't want to endanger me or any other Dragoness, so he refused any Dragoness that tried to make an advance on him, go figure, a Dragon with morals and concern for its' own kind, and not itself,*" started Silver.

* * *

Unlike most Dragons, Drakon refused to stay in one place for very long, he was always on the move, exploring any and all of the Great

Dragon's lands. Seeing as Drakon was never in one place for far too long, he never established a main Den, or territory for that matter. He only had temporary Dens. It didn't matter whether he was being hunted by *Humans* or just out exploring. Drakon would be gone from a temporary Den for eons, or years as you Humans would call them, at a time. But that didn't matter, for he would always build another Den on his travels. As Drakon explored the vast lands, he took note in where the Humans lived and thrived. Also, Drakon made mental notes of where the Mystical Creatures lived, and hid from the Humans. Drakon did this mostly to keep himself busy, and to keep his mind off of his painful memories, of the past, and to kept the manifestations away.

Eventually, Drakon tired of seeing the lands, he had lived a Dragons life: he fought, loved, and experienced loss…too much loss for one any creature, let alone a Dragon to bare. Being twenty thousand years old, Drakon decided to retire to a cave far away from any Human civilization. The cave was huge, dark, and extremely deep, even for the size of Drakon. It was naturally formed, high up, and in the side of a massive snow capped mountain. The base of the mountain was surrounded by lush, long, dark green grass, with a couple of dark green trees sprouting out of the ground. It was a good isolated Den, too bad the Humans eventually discovered it, then destroyed it. the Humans decided to burn down the cave with strange mystical fire that could burn stone. I guess the Humans chose fire, for it can be more destructive in more ways then one. During the destruction of Drakon's cave, with him inside it, Drakon barely managed to escape. With the Humans and fire at one end, and the smoke from the fire slowly filling up the cave and suffocating Drakon, his options were limited. So Drakon opted for the less painful option, and that was to dig his way out through the other side. After long grueling sun movements, Drakon broke out, he had sustained cuts, bruises and thanks to the smoke he almost ran out of air to breathe. But Drakon was healthy enough to *repay* the Humans for making Drakon make a second entrance to his cave.

It was about an eight day flight, but by nightfall, on the eight day Drakon finally caught up to the Humans, when he did, he was shocked at what he saw. The large band of Humans that had assaulted him were cloaked in black shiny skin. Some of them were on horses, while others were in strange wooden squares that were strapped to the horses. Aside from the black shiny skin, some Humans had a long black thick hair, or cloth as Humans call it that went from their shoulders to their legs. It was hard to tell what the Humans faces looked like for there was a black object covering them. The Humans that had destroyed Drakon's Den, were razing a nearby town. Drakon wanted to help the helpless Humans from their fiery demise, but he knew that if he were seen, everyone would blame him for the destruction. Once the blame was shifted to him, the Humans would start attacking him more fiercely, and would never listen to reason. Drakon landed a small distance away and watched from the shadows for hours as the town burned down to the ground. The band of black shiny skin Humans killed, pillaged, and did unspeakable things to the townsfolk. When the townsfolk were all dead, and the town was burned to the ground and was nothing but ash, Drakon made his move.

Drakon burst from his hiding spot, and attacked the unsuspecting Humans, he wasn't going to let them escape *this* time. His ambush caught the Humans unaware, and off guard., this of course was their downfall. Within sun movements, the attacking Humans lay on the ground motionless. While Drakon finished off the Humans, that destroyed the town and his home, he heard a rustle in the nearby bushes. He dropped the lifeless Human that was still dangling from his mouth, and went to investigate. Since the battle and the destruction of the town, there were no animals around, so what could be making noise besides himself? As Drakon neared the bushes, he caught sight of movement out of the corner of his golden eyes. Without hesitation, or warning, his instincts took over and the hunt was on. As big as he was, Drakon could move like the wind when he wanted to. Drakon darted around the brush, and came face to face with a Human Female Whelp.

The Human Female Whelp was tiny, by Human years she was about five years old. Her outer red skin started from her peach coloured neck and ended down at her peach coloured legs. Her outer skin was also torn down by her legs, and was completely torn away from her arms, with various tears on her chest. She had long dark red hair, that flowed down from her head to the small of her back. The Human Whelp's soft red lips matched her beautiful, long hair. The Human Whelp also had deep dark blue eyes that matched what was left of her dark blue hoofs, that showed more peach coloured skin underneath. As Drakon studied the Human whelp, he laid down in front of her, and shed a few tears. The tears reflected the horrific scene around both, Dragon, and Human Whelp, they also reflected Drakon's memories of his parents, and what had happened to Drakon. Also, he realized that he wasn't the only creature to be the only one left of a Clan. While the Human Whelp just crouched there, starring back at the sight before her. She had never seen a *real* Dragon before, and the Dragon in front of her looked...sad.

The Human Whelp stood up and walked over to Drakon, while she walked towards him, she was badly limping, bleeding, and had various cuts and bruises all over her. When the Human Whelp got close enough to Drakon, she collapsed on top of his long muzzle. The Human Whelp laid there, feeling Drakon's breath, as he breathed through his nostrils, Drakon closed his eyes, and went into deep thought. As Drakon's thoughts soared through his head, the Human Whelp fell asleep. With the many thoughts, and solutions of what to do clouding Drakon's mind, he finally settled on one. When Drakon opened his eyes, and saw the Human Whelp asleep, he contemplated on ending the Human's life. But to do so would seem...wrong in many ways, even if he was a Dragon. True, he had killed many innocent Humans, and creatures in his past, which made him ashamed of himself. But back then, it was either kill, or be killed, him or the Humans, Drakon followed his instincts instead of reasoning, for the Humans wouldn't listen to reason. He had also fought long and hard to prove that a Dragon is much more then a ruthless, mindless, killing machine, that only wanted power. Drakon had sacrificed too much in his life, to let it all get destroyed by selfishness. To *end* the Human Whelps' life, would only show the Humans, and any other creatures, they were right. It would also show Drakon, that what he had been through, and done, was in vein.

Drakon carefully lifted his head with the sleeping Human Whelp straight up into the air. Then he turned his head and looked down at his back, and nodded his head a little. The Human Whelp fell from his muzzle, and landed softly in Drakon's long hair. As soon as the Human Whelp landed, Drakon shook his hair vigorously around his body, so the

Human Whelp could get tangled in it. After the Human Whelp was safely tangled in Drakon's hair, he spread his wings, and took to the sky. As much as Drakon hated it, he knew what he had to do: return the Human Whelp. This would be difficult of course, for he was always being hunted by the Humans, whether it be day, or night. Also, if any village, kingdom, town, or city saw him, they would either flee, or attack. So, Drakon decided that the safest thing to do, was to let the Human Whelp go to the Humans on her own. This way, he would be safe, and no one would suspect that a Dragon was keeping her...a Human Whelp. Then again, she, like him, was an orphan, and where her village was located, chances were she had no other Clan, or Elders in any other settlements.

Drakon flew back to one of his many "hidden" Dens so he could get some peace and quiet. Drakon chose a "hidden" Den that was located by a huge lake, and it was only a night's flight away. The lake was crystal clear, even in the deepest parts, you could see the bottom, and its' inhabitants. Long lush brown reeds surrounded a portion of the lake, with sand covering the other portion. Long dark green, grass spread out from the reeds and sand, among the grass, rose the odd tree. The trees were tall, taller then a Dragon even, when it stood up on all fours., the trees were also very bushy and covered in dark green leaves. The scenery looked perfect, unless you saw the large hole that resided by the Crystal Lake. Fortunately, you needed a hawks', or a Dragons' keen eyesight to see the huge hole, for the long grass concealed the hole. Drakon knew where the hole was without having too look, he folded his wings, and dove into the hole. Drakon flared his wings, and landed as softly as a feather, he didn't want to wake the Human Whelp after all. After Drakon settled down, he shook his hair to untangle the Human Whelp, and give her what Humans called a blanket, at the same time. Sadly, his tough scaly hide, didn't provide much of what Humans call a pillow.

After morning broke, the Human Whelp woke up, and almost fell completely off Drakon's back. As the Human Whelp fell off, she grabbed onto Drakon's soft hair, and pulled hard, which caught Drakon's attention and brought him a painful awakening. Due to the strange pain Drakon was feeling, he lifted his head, and shook his head, and hair. While Drakon, shook his head to make the pain go away, the Human Whelp finally fell off, and landed on the muddy dirty ground. It was a good thing Drakon was close to the ground, otherwise the Human Whelp would have severely injured herself further. The Human Whelp was about to start to cry for she had just hurt herself from the fall, and what had just happened to her home, until she looked at Drakon. After a couple of seconds of staring at Drakon, the Human Whelp forgot what she was about to do. Instead, she got up off the ground, and went running to the sunlit entrance. Drakon watched her go out of curiosity, for she didn't seem to be scared of him, so why was she running away.

"*Where are you off to so early in the morning...Young One*?" questioned Drakon.

At the sound of Drakon's voice, the Human Whelp stopped dead in her tracks, and spun around, and seemed to ignore the pain that was coursing through her body. She had the look of hope, and happiness, that gleamed in her eyes, that wasn't there before. The Human Whelp went running back to Drakon with open arms, she might have been in pain, and had a bad limp, but the Human Whelp didn't care. She raced up to Drakon, and hugged his massive clawed hand. Drakon was a little confused at this, for he was expecting the Human Whelp to either freeze in terror, or run away in fear. For once in Drakon's life, he didn't know what to do. So, Drakon did the only thing that he *could* think of, he just stared at the Human Whelp, and wondered what she was doing. As Drakon looked at the Human Whelp, she returned his look, and gazed into his eyes.

"You're the one the Elders talked about. The *nice* Dragon that can talk to things. You can also talk to people when you want to. You were the one that freed all those people from that bad black Dragon," replied the Human Whelp.

"*What are you talking about Young One? I haven't freed any Human from a black Dragon. Now that I think about it, I haven't freed any Human from any Danger...save for you*," Drakon questioned.

"But you did, you did. The Elders said that a Dragon "that looks a lot like you" saved our town and many others from a huge black, mean, Dragon that was t...terr...terrorizing, the land. I know it's you, I just know it. The Elders wouldn't lie, they would *never* do *that*," exclaimed the Human Whelp.

Drakon took a moment to think before he spoke. Drakon thought of all the battles that he had fought throughout his life. Drakon shook his head in disgust at the thoughts that came flooding into his head, for he had been in far too many battles to count. *But* due to his "enhanced" memory that Drakon was born with, he could remember everything, down to every grim detail and grain of dust. The only battles that he could think of that involved a Black Dragon were the Battles with Slash & Burn, and the War with The Elders. Also, from what Drakon remembered, there weren't *even* Humans around, even in the "New Land". Those were a few memories that Drakon didn't cherish, even if they did supply some information. As Drakon took a moment to think about his memories, realization finally struck him. He remembered battling a ruthless dark purple Dragon, during his search for a quiet place to live. He also recalled the battle took place at night, and it could have possibly been near or over top of a Human populated area.

"*Young One*," started Drakon. "*This Dragon, was he huge? So big, that he could block out the sun or moon?*"

"Yes…yes he was," clapped the Human Whelp with excitement and pain.

"*Young One, I don't wish to tell you this, but I must. I didn't save your people. I fought the Dragon for his Land. The fact that your people where in his land was merely a fluke, or they were his food.*"

The Human Whelp just ignored Drakon, and continued to hold onto one of his clawed fingers for that was all she could really hold onto. As she clung to Drakon, the Human Whelp just kept repeating "Good Dragon, nice Dragon,".

Drakon knew then that the Human Whelp wouldn't want to go back to the Humans on her own, or at least…not yet. From watching the Humans over the years, Drakon had somewhat of an idea of what to teach the Human Whelp. With a large lake, lots of wild creatures, and no Humans to know where he lived, Drakon was set. The first thing on Drakon's list though, was too see if he could heal the Human Whelp. Once that was done, he would begin teaching the Human Whelp. Healing the Human Whelp was no problem, for Drakon, like any other Dragon, knew of a vast array of Healing plants. This was one of the few things that all Dragons shared to ensure their survival. But teaching a child was one thing, having a Dragon as a teacher…was another. Drakon tried his best to teach the Human Whelp what he knew about Human activities.

Drakon had collected many books over the years as well, to give him an idea of Humans, Elves, and other races. But Drakon, being a Dragon, couldn't read, even with his gift to aid him, so he could only understand so much from the books. Also, due to the fact that a book is like the size of an ant, they were extremely hard to hold onto, even if you used the very tips of your claws to hold onto the book, it was still a challenge. Not to mention, it was pain staking work to turn a page without damaging or destroying the book. So, during Drakon's teachings, he got too confused, for he didn't realize that male, and female Humans did things differently, and there were things that only males or females could do. Drakon tried to teach the Human Whelp skills that Elves, Dwarves, Orcs, and many other Humanoid creates learned and used to survive. All of these in turn made things very confusing, for both the Human Whelp, and Drakon. Drakon's size was also a problem when it came to showing the Human Whelp how to use, or create various things. Aside from these "minor setbacks", Drakon turned out to be a fine teacher…for a Dragon.

Each lesson would last a full day, so at the end of the day, Drakon would stretch his wings, and go for a flight, to clear his mind and plan for tomorrow. What the Human Whelp liked most though, out of Drakon's teachings, was at the end of every lesson, Drakon would take to the air, with her firmly tangled in Drakon's hair. On one flight though, Drakon did a roll like he always did, but the Human Whelp slipped free and started to fall to the ground far below. Even though, the Human Whelp was near weightlessness to Drakon, he still felt her fall off. As soon as Drakon readjusted, and dove down to catch the Human Whelp, he saw a strange look on her face. The Human Whelp, wasn't scared, for she had her arms outstretched, and a look of happiness and excitement on her face. When she saw the concerned look on Drakon's face, the Human Whelp, smiled and laughed, for she was flying, like her…Father. Drakon knew that the ground was vastly approaching, so he pumped his wings to get underneath the Human Whelp, caught her in his hair, then flared his wings and landed softly on the ground. From then on, Drakon would fly as high as he could before the Human Whelp passed out due to the thin air, then Drakon would turn upside down and let the Human Whelp fall off. After a few dozen sun movements, Drakon would then catch the Human Whelp, and go about their evening meal plans.

Over the years that followed, the Human Whelp matured into a stunning Youth, then into a beautiful Drake. Due to the daily exercises, and lessons, the Human Drake was skilled in practically everything that a male or female could do of any Race. This ranged from the many forms of combat, all the way to cooking, and making clothes for herself. She also became skilled in many other things that would make *any* Race envy her. The Human Drake, also went by the name that Drakon liked to call her: *Raven*. He called her this all the time when she was a little Whelp, for *Raven* was smart, beautiful, fast, and cunning, the name also seemed to suit the Human Whelp as well. This of course wasn't her real name, for she had forgotten it, with a few other memories, but *Raven* liked the name that Drakon called her anyway. *Raven* grew to about six feet in height, her long dark red hair flowed down to her legs instead of her back, and brushed against them every now and then. *Raven's* hair covered her long slender form, that could make any creature look at her with wonder, and awe. *Raven* was usually garbed in what you Humans call a tunic, which was dark green in colour, for green was her favorite colour. Her tunic stretched down to past her waist and covered her "private" area, and ended a claw before her kneecaps, for she didn't wear any outer skin on her legs. *Raven* also had a leather belt around her waist that had a couple of pouches hanging off of it, that also kept the tunic closed. She also wore long slender black hooves that went up to just below her kneecaps. *Raven* also had a gold armband with rubies embedded in it, on her left arm, and a golden locket that rested around her neck. *Raven's* hands and fingers were covered with dark red outer skin that was also studded with various gems that were found in, and around the lake.

Raven carried a long slender bow that was in the shape of a Dragon's wing, with two quivers of arrows slung in an "X" position behind her back. She also had a long slender sword, which was made out of one of Drakon's long fangs. The fang was turned from round to flat, and reshaped to look like a long blade with a slight curve in it, it might have also looked odd, but it could slice through anything. The hilt of the sword was also made out of a part of Drakon, in this case, it was one of his scales. The scale was molded and crafted into a fine handle that could be comfortable to hold in one or both hands. All in all, the sword looked…unique, but it could do whatever job *Raven* chose for it. Her sword also rested in a homemade sheath, on her right leg, instead of attached to her leather belt. *Raven* also carried one of Drakon's small fangs that she used as a dagger, this fang wasn't altered in anyway. Even though *Raven* was skilled in many different weapons, she was the deadliest with her Dragon wing bow. With Drakon's teaching *Raven's* eyes weren't like any Humans, for she could see and perceive things that were very far away. *Raven* also obtained many other abilities that could make any Royal Human envy her. *Raven* also shared Drakon's gift of understanding any creature that could breathe, this in turn made hunting hard sometimes, but every creature obeyed the laws of Nature. Drakon suspected that *Raven* wasn't actually Human, but whether she actually was or wasn't, he still respected and loved her. Drakon guessed that the village that *Raven* came from was very unique, and he would investigate the ruins. He would do this of course on one of his hunts when he hunted for food on his own.

Raven had made all of her clothes, which consisted of three different coloured tunics: green, red, and blue, and she of course made her weapons, with Drakon's help of course. The only things she didn't make were her armband, the outer skin covering her hands, and her locket which were given to her on her sixteen year of survival. Drakon had found the armband, the same night that he had found *Raven*, but he didn't tell her, for some things are better left…untold. Drakon also learned a great deal of things about *Raven* over the years as well. One of these things that Drakon found out about *Raven*, he has kept secret, and still hasn't and refuses to tell anyone what he had discovered about *Raven*. Even though *Raven* was scarcely clad, she didn't much care for the way she looked, which to any Humanoid male, was beautiful beyond measure. *If* she had it her way, *Raven* would wear nothing at all, save for her weapons, armband, locket, and outer skin that covered her hands, so she could look more like Drakon, who wore nothing. But any time *Raven* would suggest it to Drakon, he would reject the idea, saying that she was just as beautiful wearing her outer skin. He would also warn her, that if a band of Humans found her, they would do unspeakable things to her if she wore nothing. *Raven* would then voice her mind, saying that the Humans wouldn't lay a hand on her, but Drakon would always tell her "no". Of course Drakon couldn't say anything if *Raven* decided to go for a swim, or a wash, for it was easier to swim and wash without any weight holding her down. That, and the clothes that *Raven* wore were pretty much the only things she had, so she had to be careful not too get them too dirty.

"*Raven, where are you? I have found something that might interest you,*" stated Drakon as he looked around the Crystal Lake for her.

"I'm right here Father. What would you like? Are we out of food supplies *again*?" replied *Raven* as she broke the surface of the lake.

Raven was very stunning to look and marvel at when she wore nothing, but Drakon knew better. He was a Dragon after all, and he was also, very old, not to mention that would be wrong if Drakon thought such *Human* thoughts about *Raven*. She was his Daughter after all, and he would protect her till the end if he had to. Besides, if Drakon started to treat *Raven* as a mate, she would never let him hear the end of it. Plus, he would end up agreeing with her that, they were mates instead of Father and Daughter.

"*How many times do I have to tell you not to call me that anymore? My name is Drakon, Dra...Kon...Drakon. Also, I am a Dragon, not a Human,*" sighed Drakon. "*Anyway, I have found a suitable Human settlement that you can join. It's not far from here either, only a quarter sun or so. It must be fairly new and due to the reason that it's so close.*"

"*Father*, how many times do I have to tell *you*? I don't want to go and live in a settlement, or with any *Humans*. I want to live with *you*. I might not remember what my village looked like, or my actual parents for that matter, but I do remember who destroyed my village. Also you were the one that healed me back to health, raised me over the years, and taught me everything I know. So, by the Great Dragons' rule, you *are* my Father, and we should be together," remarked *Raven*.

Drakon let out a long sigh before continuing. "*Raven, we go through this discussion every four seasons. You are twenty Human years old, old enough to fend for yourself and do not need to depend on me. Besides you are only one year away from being a full fledge Dragoness, which means, that you will have to go and live on your own. Also, don't you feel lonely, not being around other Humans or other Humanoid Races? Plus, I am well over twenty thousand Human years old. I do believe that makes me capable of living on my own.*"

"That may be true, but, I know you still *need* me. From the stories that you told me...are still telling me, you take comfort in being around others. Also, as long as I'm with you, neither of us will be alone. Not to mention, I do *not* wish to go back to any *Human* settlement. We may be different ages, and different types of creatures, but does that really matter when we love each other?" stated *Raven.*

Drakon sighed again. "*Raven, you don't understand. I am destined to be alone. For you will die of old age, while I still grow old. A Dragon's life span is usually twenty to thirty thousand Human years old, give or take a few hundred years. Also, Humans are always hunting me, and it will only be a matter of time before they find this beautiful land...and destroy it. Not to mention when they find me, they will find you, and we both know what will happen. I can't take that chance. I also don't want to loose another...friend to a needless battle. If you go to the Humans now, you can live a better life, and find a suitable Mate. Forget about me, for that would be the best for both of us.*"

Drakon took much effort in holding back tears, for he knew what he said would greatly upset, and hurt *Raven*, but it was the truth, and both of them knew it. *Raven's* smooth beautiful face filled with anger and hate, at what Drakon was saying to her. She had known Drakon since she was little...a Hatchling or a Whelp as Drakon called her a few times, long ago. He *always* looked out for her, and protected her from any danger, even if she could handle herself. But then again she did remember a few times that Drakon had saved her life. Anyway, that didn't matter, for what Drakon was suggesting was uncalled for. He was saying that he couldn't watch over her anymore, which was ridiculous. Plus, the way Drakon looked after her, he was like the Father she...no, Drakon was the Father she never had.

"So that's what I am to *you*? A...a...a *friend*? So the truth comes out, you only wanted to raise me until I was ready to mate with my own kind. Then you try and get rid of me, by sending me off to a settlement full of *Humans*. I *hate you* Drakon the *old*...I mean *Ancient*. I wish you had just *killed* me when you had the chance!" raged *Raven.*

Where she lived now, was a safe place for *Raven* and Drakon to live, be happy, and no people have discovered them as far as she knew. As for finding a "suitable Mate" as Drakon put it, *Raven* had Drakon, of course they were different, but did that matter? Not to mention, if she went to a nearby settlement, she'll most likely be questioned, and Drakon would be hunted yet again. Drakon *could* look after himself of course, but what if the Humans managed to severely hurt him, he wouldn't have anyone to help protect him. *Raven* did the only thing she could think of at that moment. She turned her back to Drakon, and ran away from him. With hot tears running down her soft cheeks, *Raven* ran into the long grass and disappeared. Drakon could have easily gone after her, and caught her, but he let her go. It was now her choice on whether to return, or not. Drakon hoped that *Raven* would come back, and he knew that she was upset, and didn't mean the things she said, but then again, Drakon could only hope that *Raven* would forgive him for what he said.

Chapter 24

The Depths of Terror Mound

"Then what happened? *Don't* tell me you *don't know*. *Or*, are you waiting for Drakon to finish the tale? Also, what happened to *Raven*?" questioned Brak as he squirmed under Silver's hand.

"*The Humans found out where Drakon resided a few days later. So he took to the sky, and never returned. I assume Raven figured this out, and went her own way, but then again, Humans are very strange creatures*," explained Silver as she looked up to the sky.

"*And* this coming from a Dragon no less. So, now that I know this "vital" information, can you release me? I'm getting cramped. *Plus*, I don't think your Mate will appreciate you eating me. Also, I'm sure Fiery will be disappointed if she has no Human to tell her story to. *And* another thing, you're just as bad as Fiery, when it comes to storytelling," exclaimed, and complained Brak, as he went overboard with his whining again.

"*Arg. You Humans are all the same, annoying, stupid, and plentiful. If you kill one annoying Human, another will decide to take the formers' place. Fine, I'll let you go, and let you live. But first...*," Silver exclaimed as she brought her other hand over and slashed Brak's face with her claw tips. "*That should teach you to hold your tongue.*"

Brak just glared hatred at Silver as she took her clawed hand off of him. He slowly stood up, stretched, and brushed himself off. Brak's opposite cheek, and right side of his face also stopped bleeding after a few seconds, but it still stung. Even though Brak knew a lot of healing spells, and had plenty of healing potions, a cut made by a Dragon, and turned into a scar, could never be fully healed. Otherwise, the other scars that Brak had, on his body, and face would've been long gone by now. After Brak finished brushing himself off, he decided, he had enough of being toyed with. He was going to get his answers one way, or the other, and Brak decided on the "other". Brak half closed his eyes and began to chant in an old ancient Elven tongue. He might've told Drakon that he could cast spells via backwards English, and could do a few spells with just using the mind, but he neglected to mention that he knew Elven spells as well. But as Brak was chanting, a streak of fire cut him off, and nearly roasted him on the spot. Drakon, who seemed to have appeared out of nowhere, was the one who sent the streak of fire. Drakon landed beside Silver, kissed her passionately, and stared at Brak with murder in his eyes.

"*You want to know why we have been withholding information? Fine I'll tell you why, and if you still want to know why there are so few of us, I'll explain that too. Even though, I'm pretty sure I've done that already. But be fore warned, Brak of the Red Dragon, your life will be forever changed,*" snarled Drakon.

"That's funny, for I've heard that, oh, three times now, and still have learned *nothing.* Oh sure, I might now know that a legendary king was eaten by a big mean old Dragon, which, is highly unlikely. I also now know of the petty wars your *kind* waged with one another over the millenniums. *And,* I know the reason why you *love* Humans. But that still tells me *nothing* of what I want to know. *Also,* I am *not* a Half Breed, but a Human that can transform into a Dragon. If you *must* call me something, then call me a *Hybrid,*" raged Brak.

"*Whatever you say Half Breed. But for the time being, shut your mouth and listen to what we have to tell you,*" growled Silver.

"*And if you ever start, speak, or cast a Death Spell on my mate again. I WILL KILL YOU,*" roared Drakon.

"Fine, now tell me what I want to know," snapped Brak.

Fiery flew back after Brak finished ranting. She was still a little shaken up about something, but Fiery looked a lot better. Whatever Drakon whispered to her, and did with her, seemed to have helped. For she had a rekindled flame in her eyes, and she also wanted to see Brak cower in fear. At the sight of seeing Fiery a hint of fear washed over Brak, but the moment passed. Brak had to cast yet another speech spell on himself, to hear what the other Dragons were saying, for he wasn't in the mood for being a Dragon.

"*During one of our many battles with, and before Arthur, the Humans devised a plan that could wipe out a whole Clan of Dragons*," started Fiery.

* * *

The battles against the Humans were long and annoying, for when one group of Humans died, and two would take its' place. Drakon, Jackal, Silver, Zack, and their forces were in charge of assaulting all of the Kingdoms, and Castles. Reptillia, Bark, Myself, and our forces were in charge of assaulting any and all small settlements. Our tactics were working until the Humans found a way to defeat us. Their plan was to capture us, and harness our gifts, our fire, and our ice, using anything that would work. After many failed attempts, of harnessing these "powers" the Humans finally found a way. What they found was an energy that they could use, manipulate, and control. They called it *arcane power*, or, *magic*. With this *magic* the Humans were extremely powerful and could easily kill a Dragon without the need of sacrificing their own kind. Also with the Humans newfound powers, it was now more important then ever, that we defeat them.

During the war on Camelot, I was doing an assault run with a party of Dragons from my Clan. We had planned to take the Castle by doing many surprise attacks, but the Humans were ready for us and ambushed my party, and myself. Instead of killing us, like we hoped, the Humans decided to have some "fun" with us. They had cast freezing "spells", and motionless "spells", so we couldn't move, but we could still breathe, see, and think. While we were "stuck" the Humans tied chains and ropes around us, and cast levitation "spells" on all of us, so we would be easier to transport. The Humans ferried us to a huge mountain filled with liquid fire at its' base. The Humans knew the mountain by another name, but everyone called it "Terror Mound". For the screams, and cries that echoed from it, chilled even a Dragons' bones. It was hard to tell what scream came from what type of "Mystical creature". But we knew that there were many different kinds of creatures that were trapped, and enslaved. We also knew from reports from our scouts, and the escapees, that it was a place that you should stay away from, or assault it with a large war party. We all chose the first option, seeing as our numbers were small, and growing smaller. But my party, and myself knew, that we wouldn't be one of the lucky ones. Even *if* we could escape the Humans, there is no telling what they would do to us.

Fiery began to weep, due to all of the horrible memories flooding back to her, but she managed to continue. For she would make B[illegible]ak understand why everyone Hated Humans.

The Humans took our party into the mountain, where we saw sights that were too horrible to explain in detail. Once inside, our party saw many creatures, that were disfigured, and looked like someone was tearing apart two creatures, and piecing them together as one. All of us wished we could close our eyes, or look away, but we were stuck in place, and didn't have the strength, or energy to break the "spells". We knew that the Humans had planned this while we planned our assault on Camelot. It made perfect sense, for we would spend all of our energy on battling and making ourselves weak, which made it easy to capture or kill us. The Humans brought us to an area, where they chained our necks, heads, wings, tails, feet, waist, and arms to the floor. Then once our *muzzles* were firmly strapped, the Humans unfroze, and unstuck us. After that, they began their experimentations on us. Some of us they kept as Dragons, the rest of us, they turned into various creatures, one of them being Human. Those of us that stayed as Dragons stayed in the "torture area", while the transformed Dragons were moved to another area. When the transformed Dragons were brought to the "other area", we were split up again. I was one of the transformed Dragons, so I was "escorted" to another area of Terror Mound, *there*, I was experimented on and tortured.

The Humans knew of my status, and rank among our kind, so they decided to make me have "special" treatment. Normally Dragons are immune to most enchantments, and "spells" unless...they have been transformed, then they are as vulnerable as what they have been turned into. From the way the Humans looked at me, while I was in Human form, I think they were "in love" with me. My eyes, and hair stayed the same colour, but I had peach coloured skin, and was about six feet tall, with a beautiful Human female body. I was also left naked with no outer skin to cover myself from the Humans' eyes. So, one of the Humans decided to have some "fun" with me, what Humans consider "fun" and what we consider "fun" are two *very* different things. I was brought to a Human Sleep Chamber, and tossed inside. The Sleep Chamber was vast, but very plain. The only thing in it, was a large square object. The square object was surrounded by wood, and was very soft when you sat on it. As soon as I sat down, then laid down on the soft surface, I fell asleep.

When I awoke, I found myself bound, in yet, more chains, and strapped down to the soft square object. I also noticed that I still wasn't covered in the outer skin that the other Humans liked to wear. There was also another Human in the room, that was just putting *his* outer skin back on. I was confused at the sight of the Human, and what he was doing, or what he had done. But I eventually found out, that where I was, the Humans "fun" involved a torture that they called *pleasure*, or *rape*. When the Humans were done with me, the Humans would unchain me, and cast me aside until later. I would always be too weak, or too terrified to fight back, for each Human that entered my prison, seemed to do different things to me. These things would consist of different types of painful tortures, ranging from beatings, to rape. Every once and a while though, there would be a Human, either, male, or female, that was covered with torn dirty brown outer skin, that would bring me food. Over the weeks, and years that followed, beaten, scarred, scared, and very angry, I managed to finally focus all of my Dragon energy that I had left, and used it to transform my insides until they were that of my normal Dragon self. But I kept my feeble Human form, so no one would know.

The next time the Humans came for me, I would be ready for them, and I was going to let them know why I was feared by my enemies. Over more years, I managed to gain the Humans trust, and became *cooperative* with their *needs*. I let them do whatever they wanted to do to me, for Humans can be very manipulative. I also realized that my gift could come in handy, even though the Humans had developed a way to block my gift. One day though, after a Human finished with me…yet again, I made my move against the Humans. I opened my mouth and made a face that the Human Males enjoyed to see, but I had let loose a jet of fire, instead of saying anything. After my attack was done, I brutally killed any survivors. Seeing as I became so *cooperative* over the years, I stayed in the Sleep Chamber, the Humans decided to keep me unbound, and unchained. This made it all the more easier to get up off the square object, grab one of the Humans' "cloaks", put it on, and break the door down.

After I broke out of my prison, I went in search of any other Dragons, and creatures who wanted some serious revenge. Along my search I encountered many Humans that stopped to stare at me. In return, I either stared back, and kept on walking, or brought them aside and simply killed them using their *pleasure* against them. It turns out that a Human can't survive a fireball down its' throat. The search was long and tiring, but I eventually found out where the "Humanized" Dragons, and Mystical creatures were being held. After finding and freeing a few more "Humanized" creatures, I mustered what was left of my strength, and finally broke the transformation. The other prisoners did the same thing, once we were normal again, we set about destroying the mountain from the inside. As we were freeing more, and more captives, we came across the "abominations". They wanted to help in the destruction, but due to the way they looked, moved, and the pain they felt with each and every movement. We had to do the only "helpful" thing for them: we killed them.

When the mountain formerly known as Terror Mound was finally destroyed, and in ruins, with all of the Humans dead and buried, we all went our separate ways. After what remained of my party, we regrouped, we came to the decision to spread the word that Terror Mound was no more. But as I was flying back to the Allied Clans' borders, and the settlements that were setup, I felt a strange feeling inside me. I didn't think much of it at first, but as the strange feeling grew stronger, it began to hurt. I landed in a wooded area that we are in now, and went to seek out a cave so I could rest, and see if I could make this pain go away. Tired, weak, and feeling dizzy, I found a cave deep in the woods and passed out. When I awoke, I was laying on top of a pile of medium sized Hatchlings. This puzzled me, for I had not mated with a Dragon in over one thousand years, let alone laid any Hatchlings, or mothered any Whelps. Regardless,

I looked after the Hatchlings, and cared for them, seeing as they were *mine*, and *no one* was going to take them away.

Two years later the Hatchlings hatched, which was surprising to me, for a Dragonesses Hatchlings takes ten Human years to grow and develop, before they hatch. The reason for this, is so the Whelp inside, can develop, and adapt too its' outside surroundings, before it can actually encounter them. Also inside the egg the Hatching, receives memories from its parents, Elders, and Great Grand Elders. These memories are mainly for the Hatchlings amusement, instead of knowledge, but usually when the Hatchling becomes a Whelp, the Whelp will retain some of these passed on memories. The Hatchlings were also a light brown colour, which was strange, for a Dragon Hatchling is a dull white colour. One by one, the Hatchlings hatched, as they hatched I was shocked. I realized then, what the Humans did to me, and what I had protected for two long years. The Whelps were a mix of Human and Dragon, a Dragman...a Hybrid, or as you know them, a Gargoyle. I learned later that there were other Dragonesses, that had had the same "experiments" done to them. They also had the same results as myself, but there was a difference between them and me. My brood, didn't kill me, or anything in sight, they were in fact, very loyal to me. I had heard that other Dragonesses that had neglected, abandoned, or just ignored their Gargoyle Hatchlings were killed by them. There were also Rogue Gargoyles that the Humans had produced, or created, these Gargoyles were extremely vicious. The Rogue Gargoyles were a nuisance to every living thing, but the Rogue Gargoyles did make themselves useful, by attacking, and killing the Humans.

After one hundred years, my Whelp Gargoyles blossomed into fierce, highly skilled Youths. From the reports that my Whelps brought me, we won in the never ending war with the Humans in the war against Camelot. But even though we won, our race, the Unicorn race, and the Chimera race, sustained massive losses. So, I decided to do the smart thing, and stay dead to the lands. I knew though that the Human threat would never go away. I decided to take matters into my own claws. I showed my Whelps...my Gargoyles, how to fight, fly, and how to defend against any unknown threat. Two hundred years later, I had created my own settlement with my new Clan, that didn't look to me as an equal or a superior, but looked at me as a Queen, or Goddess. In turn, I let the power go to my head, but I still treated my Gargoyles, as my children.

It was about half a century later, that I saw a large band of captured Humans, being marched through my territory. The captured Humans outer skin was in shreds, and was only being held together by various threads and ropes. The captured Humans were also shackled in thick heavy chains that rattle with every step. While the other Humans were clad in shinny silver skin, and were carrying an assortment of weapons. My Gargoyles were going to slaughter every one of the Humans, for like me, they despised them. Also, my stories of what the Humans did to me, added to their hatred. But with a motion of my hand, and a stern look, I stopped them from attacking the large band.

For a wise Dragon once told me "If you put aside your differences and hatred against an enemy, and help them survive in a time of need, they will in turn aid you in your time of need." That, and, "The most ruthless enemy can be the best of allies."

I also remembered what I saw in Terror Mound, and realized *that* not all Humans and their other races were completely evil. I told my Gargoyles to use their gifts, and follow the large band, and if I smelled any blood on their claws, or teeth, I would have their heads. I had later found out, that the Humans had setup another "experimentation" area.

This new area was covered in a vast forest, filled with dark green, bushy trees. Within the forest laid a huge lake that was crystal clear at one point in time. But due to the Humans, experimentations, it was a dark red. The Humans had built many structures, ranging from small and squat squares, to tall and thin squares. The structures were a mix of colours, ranging from a dull brown, to a dull grey. The Humans also had the area secure, with a group of six guards posted at every entrance. There were also patrols that walked around the perimeter, and throughout the area. With all of the construction going on, it seemed that the Humans were in a hurry to get the "experimentation" area up, and running. After hearing the reports from my Gargoyles, I decided to start making plans for the Human overrun area. I also came to the conclusion, that the chained Humans were slaves, and were going to be forced to do things that they would never agree to.

The "experimentation" area was being built not to far from the borders of my lands. I knew that I had to stop the construction before there was another threat to our kind and the thought of another Terror Mound was...unsettling. Also, it felt like the *right* thing to do, which filled me with intrigue, but I would muse over the emotion I was feeling, *later*. I sent my Gargoyles out to destroy any Human structures that were being built, and to kill any creature that was in a near death state, or wore shinny skin. I also told my Gargoyles not to touch the Humans in chains, I would deal with them personally. While my Gargoyles set out to do their tasks, which they enjoyed a little, too much. I went after the large band of prisoners, and decided to make some *unique* allies of my own. I flew over to the band, and made my presence known by giving out a loud roar, that turned the organized band of guards and prisoners, into chaos. I landed in front of the band of shinny skinned Humans, who immediately began to attack me and try to kill me. It was too bad, for I kind of liked the way the shiny skinned Humans looked, but they still tasted just as good. In the end, the battle only lasted a minute or two, and I was victorious.

After the short battle, I walked up to the chained Humans who were terrified, and I gave them the best gentle loving smile that a Dragoness could muster. Which ended up looking more like a savage bloodthirsty grin, then a smile. I then laid down in front of them, and beckoned the closest Human to come forward. The Humans hesitated at first, but they eventually, slowly made their way towards me. Seeing as they knew that if I wanted to kill them I would have already. When the Humans were right in front of me, I took the time to really study them, I could have studied them from a short distance away, but what I wanted to do, I, needed to be very close to them. All of the Humans had heavy thick chains and collars around their necks, wrists, waists, and ankles. I raised one of my clawed hands and blew fire on one of my claws, until it was red hot. I brought my hand down and with extreme precision, made three quick slices, and freed the first of the Humans. It took all the way till nightfall, but all of the Humans were free in the end, and they were all very grateful. The Humans, like the Gargoyles treated me as a Goddess, or a Queen rather. Thus, my title was changed from Fiery the Wise, to Queen Fiery.

Chapter 25

Humans and Creatures, Finally at Peace

Brak just starred at Fiery, while her grim tale sunk in. He knew that Drakon's tales were Dark, depressing, and sad, but he didn't think of hearing another tale, that was a touch worse. Brak figured that Silver must have her own grim tales, but he would ask her about them some other time. Brak, also felt nauseated, and sick at what the Humans had done throughout the thousands of years, and he knew that they haven't changed. He was also starting to become ashamed of his human self, for all of the cruel, and evil things the Human race had done. Silver saw Brak's blank expression and turned her head to look at Fiery.

"*Quick Fiery, while the Half Breed is quiet for the moment. Continue with your tale,*" stated Silver in thought to Fiery.

"*Yes, please continue with your tale. It might actually get interesting,*" thought Drakon, mockingly.

"*Funny. I'll ignore that remark for now Drakon. But don't think, that I don't know what you are thinking,*" growled Fiery in thought.

"*Like you know what I am thinking. Like the insolent Humans, I have managed to find a way to block your gift,*" snarled Drakon in return.

"*Drakon. Please be nice to the Liz—I mean...Fiery. She is telling us her own tale after all, with some interesting information. And, if that doesn't change your mind, then I know what you're not getting later,*" soothed Silver as she passionately kissed Drakon.

"*That's if we are left alone after this... Amusing, very well. Fiery, please continue while the Half Breed is still speechless,*" exclaimed Drakon in thought.

"*Thank you,*" replied Fiery.

* * *

With the captured Humans now free, and the "experimentation area" in ruins, my Gargoyles, and myself decided to leave. But as we were taking our leave to the sky, a small Human Whelp came walking up to me. By my guess, the Whelp was around the age of six in Human years. The whelp was covered in badly torn brown outer skin that only covered a portion of his waist and legs, and chest. He had short black hair that ended just before his neck. Aside from his short hair, he had wondrous, and marvelous eyes, that were unique and very rare among Humans. His eyes were like nothing I had ever seen before, his left eye was a dark blue, while his right eye was a dark green, and both eyes also sparkled with energy. The Whelp looked up, and gazed into my eyes, and from the look on his face, he knew who I was and what I could do, which surprised me.

"*Miss Dragon, where are you going? Can I come with you, and bring my...my...friends? I promise you, that we'll be good. And we'll work hard as well. Just, please, don't eat us,*" thought the Whelp.

"*What is your name Young Whelp? Why do you wish to come with me...us? Do you also realize what I am, and what creatures I control? Also, how do you know of my gift, and who I am?*" I asked.

"*My name is Leon. We wish to go with you, because there is nowhere else for all of us to go. Our homes were destroyed, and most of us who had families, were orphaned or widowed. I also think that you and your animals are nice and friendly. If you weren't we wouldn't be here, we'd all be dead. As for knowing your gift,. And who you are, we all heard about your tales about you, your kind, and the other gifted Dragons. We have also heard the tales and know of the Great Dragon...Drakon the Ancient,*" answered Leon.

At the mention of Drakon's name, and the title that the Whelp had used, brought tears to my eyes. Drakon was the only one out of all Dragon kind, that showed us, and taught us compassion towards other creatures, and that there were other peaceful ways to live. I had been in isolation for far too long though, for I didn't know whether Drakon was still alive, or dead, that thought brought more tears to my eyes. But, I sighed them away, as I looked at all of the freed Humans, there were at least two hundred and fifty of them in total. There were just as many Humans as there were Gargoyles, which was going to make things…interesting, if I was going to let these Humans live with me. This would also mean that I would have to make sure that *my* Whelps would behave themselves, and *not* eat the Humans. There was also the fact that the Humans would have to behave as well, for I didn't want to have to kill them all for killing one of my Whelps. As these thoughts ran through my mind, I found it all very interesting, for I would have to find a way for everyone to live together in peace. Also, there was the matter of finding a suitable area for the Humans to live, seeing as this land was now contaminated.

"*Those of you who know who I am, know that I am using my gift to talk to all of you. Now, down to the matter at claw: how many of you are homeless, and seek a place to live? Second: how many of you wish to live with my Whelps, and myself? Bear in mind, that there is to be no fighting, battling, arguing, or disagreements between both of you,*" I asked.

I took a deep breath before I continued, "*Those of you who wish to come with us, please step forward.*"

Every Human too a step forward, it had seemed that the Humans entrusted their lives to me. Then again, I did just save them all from a horrible life, and death, so I guess it was only fair. As I studied each Human, I counted them, and made a mental note, that there were more Humans then there were Gargoyles. There were approximately two hundred and sixty three of them., I smiled at myself, for I was lucky to be a huge Dragon. The Humans also varied in height, weight, and they were all different ages, and genders. While I studied the Humans, and made mental notes about each one of them, I found that by doing this, it would make it easier, incase one of them went missing. When I finished studying each Human, I motioned for each one of my Whelps, to stand behind them.

"*Very well, I hope you all have strong stomachs, for this might feel a little unpleasant at first. But I'm sure the view will change all of that,*" once I finished I motioned to my children.

One by one, my Whelps grabbed one Human, but some of my children had to take two. In the end, all of them had to take two. After I made sure that everyone was paired up, I told my Gargoyles, to fly back home, and show them around. My Whelps flared their wings, and with a few beats, each Gargoyle with their Human load, became airborne. The Humans were stricken with terror, and fear, as they soared straight up and into the air. After a few sun movements in the air, all the Humans realized that the Gargoyles weren't going to drop them. The Humans relaxed a little, and decided to take in the spectacular view, that they were now seeing for the first time. As I prepared myself to leap into the air, I noticed that Leon, and a handful of Humans, weren't paired up with a Gargoyle. After this realization, I cursed myself for the miscount. I broke out of my takeoff, and laid down on the ground, with my wings spread out, so the Humans could climb up and onto my back. All of the Humans managed to fit on my back, save for one: Leon. I was puzzled, for it seemed like Leon wanted to go out of his way to make me notice him.

I stood up while I starred at Leon, and with lightning fast speed, I grabbed him, and tossed Leon into the air. As he flew up into the air, I took off and caught him before Leon, started his decent. He landed softly on my head, and got tangled in my hair, once Leon was safe, I gave my wings a couple of beats, and I was off. It didn't take long for me to catch up to my Whelps, then take the lead of them. When we arrived at my Den, I told my Whelps to put the Humans down *gently, or else.* After my Whelps were free of their loads, I told them to go and seek out a habitable area in our vast territory, for the Humans to live. Of course the Gargoyles voiced their opinions, distastes, and concerns, but I told them otherwise. I also told them, that what I had taught them was of the ways of a Dragon, and it was only half of what they needed to learn. If they helped out the Humans, then they would be able to learn the ways of Humans, and learn the other half. This would also allow them to be more open minded, and it would give them a new look on the world, for I knew that in time my Whelps…my Gargoyles would be hunted.

As time passed, the Humans had built a vast settlement that was very unique, to say the least. Half of the settlement was built on a huge lake, while the other half was on land. Also, the settlement was suspended in the air by large trees that were trimmed, and carved with pictures in them. These pictures depicted the lives of everyone in the settlement, and of my life, and of the lives of my Whelps. As I looked at the pictures every now and then, they always brought tears to my eyes. As I looked at them, I found that, I wasn't the only one that suffered at the hands of the Humans. Back to the settlement, each building was connected by large wooden walkways, that lead from building, to building with little areas where you could stop, and look at the beautiful scenery. There were also stairwells, and ladders, that lead down to the grassy, forested ground, and to the crystal, clear, light green lake. The buildings, aside the fact that they were in the air, were covered in elegant designs of different Dragons. Some of the Dragons were recognizable to me, while others weren't. What was breath taking about the images though, was the fact that they looked so life like, and seemed to move and shine when you looked at them. The buildings were also big, big enough, that a Gargoyle could fit inside them, and also live in them, if they chose. The settlement was a marvel to look at, but it was a shame that I couldn't actually fit inside it.

Besides the marvelous works of craftsmanship, the Humans proved, that they possessed many other talents as well. This of course brought the curiosity out in the Gargoyles, and myself. For we had hated the Humans for so long, and didn't care for their methods, and we only tolerated these Humans, because they were in debt to us. But the Humans that we had rescued, had showed us compassion, and acceptance towards us, which made us feel strange…peaceful in a sense. We did not appear to them as monsters, and what the Humans call: Demons, but as a different kind of marvelous creatures. The Humans were skilled in crafting many things, ranging from outer skin, and hooves, or what Humans called clothes, and shoes, as my Whelps, and myself learned. To crafting beautiful designed wearable shinny objects, to weapons, that were sharper then any Dragons' teeth, or claws. The Humans tried to get my Whelps to wear various clothing, but seeing a Gargoyle in a piece of hand made cloth wasn't really appealing to them. With all of my Whelps learning new and different skills throughout the days and years that followed, it was only a matter of time before my fear became a reality. That fear was: *magic*, for it was the only thing that terrified me, and filled my Whelps with wonder on how to create, and us it.

Magic was the one thing that the Humans created, that broke me, for I would never forget that time that I was captured, and with my special memory, I never will. Every time I hear the word...*magic*, it fills me with sorrow, dread, loneliness, and anger. *Magic* was the thing that transformed me, and allowed the Humans to torture me. At the first sight of it, all of my dormant rage, and hatred towards Humans began to resurface. This frightened me, for I didn't want to destroy my Whelps, or the new Human allies, that we had saved. With all of the new achievements, and advancements over the years, both Human, and Gargoyle were seeing past each other. Old hatreds towards the Humans was finally disappearing, and strangely enough relationships were forming between the two. I did the only thing I could think of, with my mind slowly breaking apart. I fled to a private area that I had established when my Whelps were still Hatchlings. I made this area, if my Whelps decided to turn on me, I would be able to hide, and never be found. I tried to make myself disappear as quietly as I could, but the way I was acting, everyone knew something was wrong with me. But everyone decided to do the smart thing, and let me be with my thoughts, except for one Human.

Leon managed to find me after a forty-five day search that finally led him to my "private" Den. But I was in no mood to see anyone, for my head felt like it could explode into a great inferno. As Leon neared my Den, he lit a torch with his, *magic*, then ventured into my Den. Once he finally saw me, out eyes locked, and he put out his torch. Leon had grown into a fine looking Human Dragon, or as the Humans prefer: Adult. He had a stronger build then the other males in the settlement which made most people wonder why he took up *magic*. Leon's hair also flowed down, past his shoulders, and stopped at the middle of his back. He had a clean shaven face, but his soft dark blue, and green eyes, had become hard and sharp, making him look more appealing. He was dressed in a thin red shirt, while his legs and feet were covered in brown pants, and black boots. He would have made a fine mate to any of the settlements females, but strangely enough, Leon would reject them, claiming they weren't "right" for them.

"*Why have you come here? Why did you seek me out? Do you have a death wish? Do you think it was wise to come HERE?*" I questioned angrily and upset, that my privacy was now compromised.

"I have come here out of concern for you Fiery the Wise. Everyone is worried about you, and are wondering if you have fallen ill. If you have, then please let us treat you. As to this being suicidal, well, that is up to you. But, before you decide my fate, I have something I would like to tell you. I *love* you Fiery the Wise, ever since we first met. And I have found a way that we can be together with the use of Magic," explained Leon, carefully.

"*Treat me? With Magic? I will* NEVER *let magic touch me...ever again,*" I roared with hate and pain in my voice.

As if I didn't have enough to think about, what Leon suggested, had broken the last scale. I felt the surge of my uncontrollable anger rising within me. Leon could see it as well, and a concerned look appeared on his face. He had heard of the tales told by storytellers of Dragons, transforming, and or destroying themselves with rage when it became too much to bear on their minds. Leon, and the other Humans had also learned of my experience with *magic*, from my Whelps. But I looked inside myself and told myself that I wasn't like the other Dragons of my kind, I was different, like Drakon is...was. I decided to do the one thing that Dragons rarely did, I turned my rage and hatred into sorrow, and wept. As I wept, I could feel my hatred of Humans, and *magic* melt away, I also felt Leon's warm touch as he walked over to me. I looked at him, and understood what he meant, when he said we could be together, he had transformed into a Dragon. Unfortunately, he wasn't' a full sized Dragon, only the size of a Drake just before its' prime, but that didn't matter at the moment.

As I gazed upon the transformed Leon, I felt a feeling that I hadn't felt in such a long time: passion. It had been a millennium or more since I had been with another Dragon, but at the sight of Leon, I felt...scared. But as I studied Leon, my fear began to melt away as other emotions flooded through me. Leon was covered in dark blue scales, with matching dark blue wings. He had bone white teeth, and claws that seemed to sparkle with his body. He had kept his black hair, only this time it flowed down to his wings. Leon also kept his unique eyes, that were so full of life, they looked like gems. Leon walked closer to me, and took me in a Dragons' embrace, and held onto me, as I still shed a few tears. We had cuddled, and nuzzled with each other, and while we did this, I felt my misery disappear, and eventually, I let my passion, and my instincts take over. With the feeling of these new emotions, I felt like a true Dragoness once again. I finally experienced a true Bonding Ritual, that seemed to last forever.

Sadly, Leon, like all of the other Humans, had extremely short lives of only sixty to early eighties. But the Humans were famous for procreating, and breeding, making their numbers rise. That was also the same with my Gargoyles, the only difference was, that my Gargoyles had a quarter of a Dragons life span. It didn't matter though, for there were no small number of either race. But both races did have something to look after, new brothers, and sisters, and their own Hatchlings, and Whelps. Leon and I had created another race, and so did the coupled Humans and Gargoyles. This new race was better know as Half Breeds, for they were either born as a Dragon, Gargoyle or a Human, but they could change or transform into either one without the use of *magic*. For that was their gift along with a few other gifts they were born with. Also, as the years went on, the new generations ventured out into the lands, to see the new life, and live in it. But there would always be people of all three races here to live, thrive, and survive with a guardian to watch over them and protect them.

Chapter 26

Departure into the Wild

When Fiery finished her tale, Brak was left completely speechless, which Drakon, and Silver thought, was very funny. Fiery also smiled at the *silent* Human Half Breed, as he took in the information. Also, seeing Brak speechless and thoughtless for the moment, made Fiery feel a lot better. There was also, the added bonus of Brak's thoughts being in a complete mess, which filled Fiery with some joy. It wasn't every day that Fiery got to mess with a Sorcerers mind. After starring at Brak, or giving him mocking glances, Drakon turned to look at Fiery. Silver in turn looked at Drakon, to see if she could tell what he was thinking.

"*Cheerful tale Fiery. I do admit that your tale was a little more violent, then mine, but we both know that I am unmatched in tale telling. Heh, I do believe Brak has nothing to joke about for once, which is quite amusing,*" stated Drakon in thought.

"*Thank you Drakon the Ancient. I figured my tale would make him think…unlike yours…no offense of course. As violent as your tale might have been, it was most likely too cheerful in some regards,*" remarked Fiery back in thought.

Drakon was about to say something when Silver stopped him. "*Don't say it Drakon. Otherwise, you'll regret it. besides every creature in the land respects, and honors you…including those with egos as high as the sky.*"

"*Very well, I'll be nice. Brak, we've held up our end of the agreement, you now have the information that you sought from us. Now the question remains, will you hold up your end?*" questioned Drakon.

"Yes I will, I know I'm...difficult at times, but I do honor my word," replied Brak as he regained control of his thoughts, and frowned. "Like you, and Silver, I now have no home to return to, and am being hunted by the *Humans* and their allies. *Only* in my case, these Humans and allies will be far more *deadly.*"

"*So, you finally admit to what you are?*" questioned Fiery.

"No. I am Human, as Human as I can be. But I am not like *them*, for I am Dragon as well, and I am one of the few who respects the creatures of these lands, and will fight to protect them. Unlike the other Humans who wish to rule over these beautiful lands, and conquer all the others. *Not* to mention, the enslavement of everything that can wield magic...or has a gift." Remarked, and stated Brak.

"*Drakon the Ancient, Silver the Pure, I know what has happened to your home. I am deeply saddened for what the Humans have put you two through, over the millennia. My land, is your land, if you wish to stay here with me,*" announced Fiery.

"*Thank you for your kindness and your hospitality. We will be forever grateful of this,*" replied Silver, and Drakon in unison.

Brak stood up and brushed himself off, turned, took a few steps, then bowed to all three Dragons. "Well, Drakon the Ancient, Silver the Pure, and Fiery the Wise, I have enjoyed your company, and you *not* killing me. I have learned many things from all of your tales, and have seen your hardships. I would love to hear more of your tales, especially yours Silver, and Fiery. Drakon, I would also like to hear more of your daughter, the beautiful *Raven*...but, I must be going. The longer I stay here, the longer I will be endangering all of your lives. While we talked, and listened to Fiery's tale, my *former* King has most likely put out a reward on my head. Also, the people who are hunting me, the same ones that destroyed your Home, Drakon, and Silver, most likely know where I am. Whether the reward is *dead* or *alive*, I don't intend to find out, or to meet the people who are hunting me either. So with *that* all said, I bid you all farewell."

After Brak's thanks, all three Dragons bowed their heads to Brak, as he transformed back into his Dragon self. Brak smiled to himself as he turned away from the three Dragons to takeoff. He was terrified of himself at times, and the other times, felt ashamed as to what he was, for his whole life. No one would come near him or show him any kindness or gratitude to him whenever he helped out others, saved lives, or protected those in need, for no one liked, or loved a Half Breed. But being by possible ancestors…no, *his* ancestors, and listening to their…no, *his* history, made him feel proud, and honored to be what he was. Once the changes were done, and Brak spread his wings to fly into the sky, Fiery got up from where she laid, and walked over to Brak. She placed a clawed hand on his shoulder, bowed her head low, as Brak turned his towards her, and kissed Brak's head. Brak in turn, kissed her clawed hand, instead of kissing her forehead, then with his wings outstretched still, flapped them, and too to the sky. As Brak soared into the air, he felt a sensation of warmth, and acceptance, fill his body.

"*Brak! Before you go, I am going to entrust one of my Whelps to you, as help, for when you need it. The Gargoyle goes by the name of Stealth, and for now, that's all you need to know. I hope your search for the last of the Elves goes well, and that you are successful in talking to her. Also, if you ever want to come back, the Humans, and Gargoyles will gladly make a home for you in the settlement,*" hollered Fiery.

"*Thank you for your hospitality, and for your concern Fiery the Wise. But, I probably don't need his help. Although, it might come in handy,*" thanked Brak.

"*I'm a Female by the way,*" stated Stealth, as she materialized out of nowhere, by Brak.

"*Charmed,*" replied Brak a little surprised.

Stealth looked like the rest of Fiery's Gargoyles, she was covered from head to toe in reddish, yellow scales, and her wings, inverted legs, and her claws looked like her siblings as well. Other then that, that was it for the similarities between her, and her siblings. Stealth had long, wild, dark blue hair, that flowed down to her waist, and her reptilian eyes, were a soft blue instead of a crimson red. Stealth also seemed to retain a few more Human features then her siblings as well, for most of her facial features were Human. Her, mouth was that of a normal Human mouth, as well, as her nose, and her round face, which came from her Father. But she had long sharp teeth, and a long tongue, and reptilian eyes to top it off from her Mother. She also had a slim muscular body, instead of large and bulky. Stealth was also scarcely clad in dull brown clothes that covered her waist, and her chest. She was a marvel to look at, and Brak felt a little drawn to her in his Dragon state.

As Brak, and Stealth flew out of sight of the three Dragons, Silver, and Drakon looked at each other, smiled, kissed, and then nodded at each other. Drakon, and Silver bowed their heads to Fiery, and thanked her for her offer, but sadly, both Dragons had to decline Fiery's offer. Even though the thought of a new home with a friend, and ally, was inviting they both still had unfinished business to attend to. Silver, and Drakon stretched, spread their wings, then took to the sky to catch up to Brak, and Stealth. Fiery spread her wings as well, and took to the sky, but she didn't follow, instead, she flared her wings and let out a loud roar. Fiery's roar was terrifying, but it held a hint of farewell, and sadness in it. when Silver, and Drakon reached Brak, and Stealth, the four of them heard the Roar loud and clear. Brak, Silver, and Drakon, turned around and roared back in return, while Stealth let loose a large bright fireball from her mouth into the sky, that exploded. In the distance, a volley of other exploding fireballs answered Stealth's unusual fireball. Stealth smiled as she watched, her siblings answer her request.

"*When the time comes, my army and forces will be with you. So will the Unicorns, and the "supposedly extinct" Chimeras in this area. Drakon, Silver, watch over my Daughter, and Brak. He might not show it, but Brak might show some great promise in the future, which I'm sure both of you already know. Also, I am not completely sure, but I think he is a great, great, grand Whelp. I also wish you luck in finding out what happened to Queen Elexia, and Chief Backwards Forwards, and the other answers you two both seek,*" Fiery exclaimed in Drakon's, and Silver's thoughts.

"*We will Fiery. And thank you, for everything,*" replied Drakon, and Silver in thought.

The party of four, stopped their roaring, and went back to flying into the unknown, to find where *Serenity* was hiding. Everyone in the party knew it would take time, for the world, and its' lands were vast, and they were only a small group. Not to mention, finding a single Elf was going to be as hard as finding a living flower in a badly charred land. Also, the four of them knew that they were most likely being hunted. In fact, the four of them *knew* that they were being hunted, they just didn't know who was hunting them…*yet.* But that wasn't going to stop the four of them from making allies, and finding out what happened to the other extinct Humanoid races. It was going to be a long journey, but it would also be a fun journey. While Brak was thinking of all this, flying through the warm air, he reflected on the past months of his adventure. He finally got what he wanted, what he longed for, and searched for his whole life. He was now part of a Dragon's Legend.

Epilogue

"Sara! Have you found a cure yet for this damnable curse that the *Traitor* Brak put on me?" demanded the King angrily.

The King was chained to a pillar in the Great Hall of his Castle. The Great Hall was massive, able to hold one thousand people, at a time. Beautifully sculpted pillars that depicted pictures of the past decorated the hall. The floor and the ceiling were also decorated in beautiful artwork. The floor was painted with a map of the kingdom with its' lands surrounding it the floor was also enchanted so it could update its' map whenever something new was built, conquered, or destroyed. While the ceiling was covered with beautifully enchanted pictures as well, on it had the image of the sky over head. In the daylight, the ceiling showed the clouds, and their positions, any birds that flew by, and of course, the sun. While at night, the ceiling showed the stars and their constellations, and the moon and its' many appearances of full, half, quarter, and crescent.

In the far end of the Great Hall was a small flight of ten stairs dressed with royal red velvet carpet. On the top of the stairs stood a single throne on the top of the large landing, which was also decorated with various beautiful flowers, and vegetation. The throne itself was crafted out of solid gold, with fine velvet cushions and backing, and studded everywhere with various gems. At one point in time there were two identical thrones side by side on the landing, but due to an unfortunate accident, one was removed. The Grand Hall used to be decorated in different types of vegetation, small birds, and animals that were everywhere, but it was now devoid of life save for what was on the landing. The emptiness didn't bother the King, for the Great Hall was his favorite room, and place to be in the whole Kingdom. Even though the King was in his favorite room, he wasn't too happy about being chained up. The chain was the only thing keeping him from flying out through the opening in the high point in the domed ceiling. On top of *that*, none of his "best" magic wielders could seem to break Brak's damnable spell. The King cursed himself, and Brak for allowing the damn Sorcerer to study in the unknown. But maybe his daughter had found something, she'd been studying for long enough to at least know *something*.

In his younger years, the King decided to have his whole Kingdom enchanted with a spell that would allow sound to travel anywhere within its' walls. Of course, only the high ranking people and the Royalty could use this enchantment to call for servants, soldiers, or each other. Even though his late wife didn't approve of this at the time, the King thought it would be important incase of an "emergency". The enchantment would carry a persons' voice at the same volume as a person spoke. In other words, a person could whisper, and it would travel, and sound like a whisper. Needles to say, Sara wasn't thrilled when she heard her Father shouting for her while she studied, and searched for a counter spell, or cure. Sara wished she could have learned more on Brak's spell, and his own studies, but with her Father shouting for her, she wouldn't dare disobey his summons. So Sara let out a sigh of frustration, and dropped the spell book she was reading, on the mass piles of all the other spell books in the huge Library, and made her way to her Father.

"I have found a way to break the spell Father, but you won't like it. If you give me more time, I can find a better and safer solution," answered Sara as she entered the Great Hall.

"It's about time…what do you mean I won't like it? If it involves a sacrifice, of an animal or Human, or *any* other creature, then *do it!* I want to be *free* of this damn curse, and have my feet on the ground again. Also, I would like to rule as a proper King again. As to your question about more time, it is denied. Seeing as you found a solution, there is no need for another one," snapped the King.

"But Father-," begged Sara before she was cut off.

"DO IT! *And* never question me ever again. You *may* be my one and *only* child, but you are not *royalty*. Ever since *your* Mother died, you wanted to follow her as a magic user. So I granted you your wish, but, did I not warn you of what you'd give up?" snapped the King again.

"But-," stuttered Sara as she held back tears from her Fathers disapproval of her.

"SARA! DO IT!" shouted the King, as he grew furious with his stubborn, naive, daughter.

Sara turned her head away to silently weep, and pointed a finger at her Father and shouted. "EID!"

The King went wide eyed as a sharp pain shot through his entire body. While the pain coursed through him, the King's body went into convulsions, and spasms. The pain only last five seconds at the most, but it felt like an eternity of torture. During the lapse of pain, the King had many flashes of his life, and he was able to see *all* of his mistakes. He finally realized that it was also *his* fault that his Elven wife was now dead and buried…somewhere. Once the pain was gone, the light in the Kings' eyes began to fade, as he floated down to the ground *motionless*. Sara walked up to her Father then, and undid the chain that was clasp around his ankle, stood up, and looked at him. As Sara looked at her Father, she only had time to shed a single tear before her grieving was interrupted.

"Your Majesty…. What has happened to the King?" replied a servant in a concerned tone as he entered the Hall.

The servant was the height of an average male. He had dark green eyes, and long blond hair, that was tied into a ponytail. The servant was garbed in the normal servant wear. Long black boots that rose half way up his lower legs, and firm white pants, that were being supported by a dark red belt. He wore a dark green shirt that covered his hairy muscular chest. With a dull dark brown jacket that covered the shirt and ended in two long tails. The servant also had a pair of wire frame spectacles that rested on his face. This gave the servant the appearance that he was much older then he appeared. But the only thing that mattered was the insignia of a Black Dragon on his jacket that showed his status among the Kingdom.

"I…killed my Father, so he could be free of the spell that the *Traitor* Brak put on him," explained Sara.

"It wasn't your fault, your Majesty. It was the Traitors fault, not yours, for if he never cast his curse on the King then you wouldn't have had to do, what you did," soothed the servant.

As the tear hit the kings' cheek, Sara looked up at him. "I suppose you're right, assemble what trackers you can. I also want my Fathers' plans to go through, so capture what creatures you can, charm them, mind control them, do whatever it takes to make them our Slaves. If that fails, then kill them all. I don't feel like having to deal with any more rebellions. I've heard what happened to the "mountain experiment."

"Very well your Majesty. Shall I also have your proper clothes put out for you?" asked the servant.

As Sara, and the servant walked to the doors, the tear on the Kings' cheek fell to the ground. While the tear slowly fell, it mirrored Sara, and the servant leaving the cold, dead, greedy king on the cold floor. Sara didn't bother to look back at her dead Father, for there was nothing more she, or anyone else could do for a corpse. The King could be revived of course, but that took time and effort, and if it was one thing that Sara's Father drilled into her head, was that time and effort shouldn't be wasted on the ungrateful dead. Sara smiled, she had become like her Father…no, her Mother…no she had become something greater then both of them, and she would prove it. As Sara left the chamber she closed the door behind her, and made her way to her quarters to change from her dreary wizard clothes to her royal clothes that she had kept aside for when the time came. Sara stopped two servants who were passing by and ordered them to get rid of the Kings' body. It was only fitting that his body disappear like her Mothers, who's was never found.

When Sara finally got to her quarters, which consisted of four huge rooms, one for her studies, one for sleeping in, one was for bathing, and washroom, and a leisure room for lounging in. When Sara walked into her bedroom she saw three different royal dresses laid out for her on her large queen sized bed. One dress was a dark rose colour with gold outlines. It had cut off arms, and went from the neck to the floor. The second dress was a dark green colour, with a bright turquoise outline. Its' sleeves went down to the elbow, and it stretched from the neck to the knees. The last dress was black with a ruby lined colour running through and around the dress. Its' sleeves just covered the shoulders, while the dress went from the neck to just above the knees. Sara decided to go with the third dress for she loved its' colour, and thought that the dark ruby colour matched her eyes. While Sara stripped down to nothing she glanced at her bare self in her huge silver, and crystal mirror. She was beautiful, and yet it seemed that she could do nothing to attract Brak enough to love her, well, if he wouldn't return her love then it would make it all the easier to hunt him down, and kill him.

After Sara got changed, she made her way over to the Royal Chamber where her late Mothers' crown, swords, wand, scepter and cape resided. It was a bit of a walk but when Sara reached the Royal Chambers, she encountered the "Two Guards". These guards were part of her late Fathers' Elite Guard, and would only listen to him, until the changes were made for either Sara or her Husband to rule the Kingdom. Even with the King already dead, they wouldn't listen to Sara's reasoning, until *after* the ceremonies were done. Both Guards were covered in crimson black plate mail, that shimmered with a mystical red glow. Their faces were also obscured by a black helm that covered everything save for their dark golden eyes. The helms were designed to look like a demonic Human skull, while their plate mail was designed to look like a Gargoyles scaly body. Both Guards also carried obsidian swords that were shaped to resemble a flame from a fire. It took some convincing, and a show of her "Royal Jewels", but Sara got into the Chamber, and dawned on her Mothers' things. Once done, Sara made her way to the balcony that over looked the entire Kingdom. The balcony was enchanted so everyone and anyone who looked up at it could here any royalty speak to the public.

"People of our Great Kingdom, I beg you all to listen to me. A *Traitor* has murdered the King of our fare Kingdom…no…our land. The *Traitors'* name is Brak of the Red Dragon. At one point he was a high ranking Sorcerer and a friend to most of us, and my Late Father. He was also my Lover, but that changed when he found our missing King and returned him, as a broken man. The only way to save my Father was for me to put him at peace. So I ask you, people of the Kingdom, to forgive me for what I have done to save our King. If you wish to go after Brak of the Red Dragon, then join our forces so we may hunt him down, and put an end to his evil ways, and to kill his allies," exclaimed Sara to the gathering crowd.

The ever growing crowd that had gathered, was enchanted by Sara's speech. They were also chanting Queen Sara, and disgracing, and insulting the "Traitor Brak". Sara smiled at the result of her speech, she was about to continue, when another one of her servants walked up behind her, leaned over and whispered something in her ear. Sara turned back to her crowd and continued on with her speech.

"I have just received word of where the *Traitor* was last seen. But alas, he is not alone. Two Dragons that are well known to all of us are accompanying him. They are Drakon the Ancient, and Silver the Pure, two very powerful Dragons, that are wanted in more lands then many of you can count. So, like the other Kings, and Queens of our neighbouring lands, I will offer a great reward for their capture, or execution. But there will be a greater reward for whomever captures, or kills the Gargoyle that is accompanying them. Also, like you, I will be riding out into the wilds, to hunt down Brak, and his allies, for I personally want to thank him for what he has made me do. Then I will kill him, now, let the hunt begin," finished Sara as she raised a clenched fist into the air.

Sara told one of her servants to go and fetch her white lion. The servant bowed, then went about his business, as Sara walked away from the balcony, and the cheering crowd, she made her way to the armory. But before she made her way to the armory, she put her Mothers things back in the Royal Chamber. When Sara made it to the armory, she picked up her long elegant hunting bow, that resembled a swan wing, and she also stocked up on armor piercing arrows. It was highly unlikely that Sara would need, or be able to use them against Brak, but then again, you never know. After Sara slung her bow, and set it aside, she dawned on sleek white silver metal shoulder pads, and gauntlets. Next, Sara dawned on a red diamond breast plate that looked like it weighed a couple of tons, but it was as light as a feather, but as strong as a Dragons' hide. Sara liked her freedom of movement, so she left her legs bare but did put on some protection for her waist seeing as the breast plate ended at her waist. After the waist protection, Sara dawned on black chrome boots that rose to her kneecaps, leaving a good portion of her legs exposed. Lastly, Sara dawned on a white silver, dove winged, helm that covered her who head and face, save for two eye holes for her dark red eyes. When Sara was finished, she looked herself over and marveled at the mixture of colours. It made her think that she looked like a beautiful, and deadly assassin. Sara mussed to herself that she should have gone into the assassination trade when she had the chance, but power is always better.

Sara picked up her bow and walked over to her two prized swords. She might have taken her mothers swords, but they were of Elven make, and one had to be skilled in the ways of Elven combat to use them properly. But her own two swords would do just as well. Sara's swords and scabbards were both in a glass case, for protection against dust, and theft, for only Sara could open up the glass case without having any traps set off. Her swords were long, diamond white, elegant blades, with a dark silver hilts. The scabbards for both swords were a dark blue with a hint of red mixed into the blue. When Sara took out the scabbards, she strapped them firmly behind her, on her lower back, then sheathed her swords. When Sara was finally finished with the armory, she made her way down to the stables where her prized pet lion waited for her.

During her walk, a portion Sara's own Elite Guards, who were clad in the same style of armor that she was in, joined her. When Sara reached the stables, she had a group of twenty Elite Guards, that she had silently called for using her Fathers sound spell. These Elite Guards would do anything for Sara without question, or hesitation. Also, aside from the armor, these Elites were like Sara, for they too, carried Elf blood in them, with mild Elf features, like the eyes, and pointed ears, with soft round faces. Sara also smiled to herself, for her Elites would tell no one if she decided to have some "fun" with them. But the "fun" would have to wait, for she heard her lion calling to her, wanting to be freed, and to taste the blood of Brak. It took about ten minutes to get saddled up on the huge lions, and to get ready for the long journey, and the hunt for Brak, and his allies. But when everyone was ready, the group of twenty-one marched down to the gates of the Kingdom, and waited for the doors to open.

"Well Brak, you threw me aside for some oversized winged Lizards. You forced me to kill my own Father, and *now* you run and hide from me with no explanation of why you did what you did," Sara mumbled to herself as the doors swung open.

After the doors swung open, Sara reared her lion, and shot out of the Kingdom's Gates, and into the wild. The other mounted Elites did the same with their own lions, for they didn't want to get left too far behind. Sara's pet lion was like the other Giant Lions that the Kingdoms royal, and Elite Guards used for traveling throughout the lands. Only Sara's was an albino lion, and was at least two times larger then the average male Giant Lion that roamed in the grass lands in the far south across the seas. Her lion was also more agile, and faster, and was a lot more deadlier then the Giant Lion. But what made the Albino Giant Lion interesting aside from it's snow white main and fur, was it's sharp pink eyes, and there was no enchantments, or spells cast on it for enhancements.

"Brak of the Red Dragon, your time has come! I *will* be the one to *kill* you, and take my vengeance for my Father, and my ruined life. Be fore warned, I am coming for *you*," shouted Sara to the winds, as her party, and herself rode into the dawning sun.

As the sun slipped into the shadows, it left behind a beautiful scene. With the few clouds in the sky changing from a light white to a multitude of colours ranging from a soft pink to gold, and orange. The grass was also lit up with a bit of colour, as its' shadows, grew long, and dark. The trees though, turned from their lush bright cheerful colours, to dark moody colours. Sara and her Elites marveled at this sight as they rode into it, for it was beautiful, stunning, and also deadly. For the real threats, and nightmares came out at night, but that didn't both Sara in the least, for all she could think of, was Brak. As Sara's eyes wondered she looked into the sky to see the first of the stars appearing with the fading sun. Soon complete darkness would envelope them, and it would feel comforting.

"Never again Brak, never again," whispered Sara as she peeled her gaze away from the sky and looked into the distance, and what the future might hold for her now.